"THE CHEMISTRY STILL WORKS, DOESN'T IT, SAM?"

Jon's voice was a seductive murmur.

Samantha's heart was beating so quickly she couldn't breathe. His lips played with hers, firm then pliant, and her own mouth opened wantonly to the touch of his tongue. His lovemaking was so familiar, so wonderfully familiar! She thrilled when his hands began to explore her body, to caress her possessively.

"I should apologize," he whispered a long time later. "I was . . . curious to find out how you felt about me now."

Samantha's stomach lurched. He'd merely been experimenting with her! "I hate to tell you this," she said shakily, "but as far as I'm concerned the *chemistry,* as you call it, is gone."

He looked at her mockingly. "Then why did you come back?"

Books by Rosalind Carson

SUPERROMANCES

16—THIS DARK ENCHANTMENT
40—SONG OF DESIRE
91—SUCH SWEET MAGIC

These books may be available at your local bookseller.

For a free catalog listing all titles currently available,
send your name and address to:

Harlequin Reader Service
P.O. Box 52040, Phoenix, AZ 85072-9988
Canadian address: Stratford, Ontario N5A 6W2

Rosalind Carson

SUCH SWEET MAGIC

A SUPERROMANCE FROM
W RLDWIDE

TORONTO · NEW YORK · LONDON · PARIS
AMSTERDAM · STOCKHOLM · HAMBURG
ATHENS · MILAN · TOKYO · SYDNEY

For Joe and Colleen
and Duane and John,
who were there.

———————————————◆———————————————

Published December 1983

First printing October 1983

ISBN 0-373-70091-1

Printed in Canada

CHAPTER ONE

THE MOMENT she set foot on Collins Island and looked around at the tall cool evergreens and the familiar view of water and distant mountains, Samantha knew she shouldn't have returned. A rush of sensation—nostalgia, anticipation, remembered grief—almost overwhelmed her, and for a few minutes she hesitated beside the small airplane, letting the other passengers go ahead. Should she ask the pilot to fly her back to Seattle so that she could catch the first available flight home to Los Angeles, she wondered.

Almost immediately, reason asserted itself. Her decision to come back to this island in Puget Sound had been made coolly and logically, without emotion. She was no longer brash little Samantha Austin, with the tangled red curls, ungainly body and coltish legs of an awkward adolescent. She hadn't come to spend another summer vacation on Collins Island, scared to death under her bold exterior that Jonathan Blake, idol of her childhood, wouldn't want to bother with her this time. Nor was she the disillusioned eighteen-year-old who had left here in tears seven years ago, her heart broken by that same Jonathan Blake. She was a grown woman now—twenty-five years old, creamy skinned and Titian haired, her hazel eyes flecked with gold. She was independent and confident, slender and well-groomed;

considered attractive by many, stunning by some. "The dazzling personification of autumn," Adrian Westcott had called her in a burst of rhetoric eighteen months ago when he'd proposed to her.

She smiled wryly to herself. Knowing Adrian as she did now, she wasn't sure that had been a compliment—possibly it had been intended more as criticism. Dear Adrian. She really did love him—he was so sure of himself and his place in the world. If their relationship lacked passion, well, that wasn't so important. Passion wasn't all it was cracked up to be.

As for Jonathan Blake. . . . Her chin lifted in the attitude her father called "Samantha defying the world." She didn't even know if Jon was still living on Collins Island. If he *was* here, she had no need to worry about his reaction to her return. That adolescent love had died years ago—murdered soon after its birth.

Straightening her spine and adjusting the weight of her tote bag on her shoulder, she moved confidently out of the shadow of the airplane into the noon sunshine, heading toward the two cars that waited beyond the airstrip—a chauffeured limousine and a white station wagon with The Retreat stenciled in blue Gothic letters on its side.

A distinguished-looking gray-haired man in a beautifully cut blue pin-striped suit stood beside the limousine. Dr. Jakob Birmann had come to meet the plane himself, as he'd promised on the telephone yesterday. He was courteously greeting the two women who had arrived with Samantha, bowing over their hands and introducing them to the slender girl at his side, who was wearing a short-sleeved blouse and full blue skirt. She must be the daughter he had mentioned—Anne Marie.

The Swiss-born doctor had described her as "only eighteen" and "rather shy." "An old-fashioned girl," he'd added with a trace of satisfaction in his voice.

Almost abreast of the group, Samantha hesitated again. The two women were to be guests at Dr. Birmann's health and beauty spa—she had guessed that fact the moment they boarded the small plane in Seattle. Their clothing, though casual, had shrieked "designer," and their luggage was immediately recognizable as Vuitton and Gucci. As guests they should naturally be welcomed by Dr. Birmann ahead of her. She was merely a new employee, hired for six months while Monique, Dr. Birmann's usual personal assistant, visited her ailing parents in France.

Stepping into the shade of the Douglas firs that fringed the airstrip, Samantha set down her tote bag and resigned herself to waiting until the doctor noticed her. At the edge of the woods wild roses flourished in hot-pink splendor. She'd forgotten how profusely and colorfully they bloomed in this part of the Pacific Northwest. Rosa rubiginosa—orginally a native of Europe. She could hear Jon's voice in her memory lecturing her on the flora and fauna of the island.

Jonathan Blake. He was suddenly so clear in her mind...tall, lean, always tanned, with strands of his blond hair bleached almost white by the sun. So strong. So *clean*. She'd teased him often that he looked so clean because he spent two-thirds of his life underwater, exploring the marine world that fascinated him. He had taught her so much. He had always known everything about the island—had always *loved* everything about it. And so had she. Just as she had loved everything about Jon.

Sighing, she glanced back at the group beside the limousine, then winced as one of the women laughed shrilly, self-consciously. Judging by the flirtatious manner in which the two women were responding to the handsome doctor, she might have to wait here quite a while. She smiled inwardly, remembering how the women had looked her over with their sharp, almost calculating eyes as they boarded the Piper Lancer, assessing the cut and probable cost of her tweed hacking jacket, cashmere turtleneck and narrow-legged designer pants. Evidently she had passed inspection. They had been cautiously friendly—until she informed them she was Dr. Birmann's new assistant. Nothing obvious had changed in their manner then—they were too well-bred for that—but a slight chill had asserted itself, as though an invisible space had opened up between Samantha and them. How mortified her father would have been, Samantha had thought in amusement, if he'd witnessed the phenomenon of Dwight Austin's daughter being put tactfully but firmly in her place.

Samantha had recognized both women. One was a news anchorwoman who had recently gone through a sensational divorce, the other an actress known for her "other woman" role in a popular soap opera. Both were slightly overweight, which probably explained their presence here.

Dr. Birmann was still talking intently with the women. His daughter stood to one side, looking as though she wasn't sure what to do with her hands. Finally she folded her arms across her chest, tucking her hands into her armpits. She was a pretty girl, in spite of her awkwardness. . . petite and slim, with an oval olive-skinned face and long light brown hair tied at the nape with a narrow blue ribbon.

The two women had thawed totally under the doctor's effortless charm. She couldn't fault them for that. She remembered how *she'd* responded when Dr. Birmann interviewed her at his spa in San Diego. He had made her feel like a princess who had deigned to grant him an audience, rather than a working girl anxious for a job. And his charm had not been assumed for the occasion—it was an integral part of the man. He had not even asked why an engaged girl would isolate herself on an island far away from her fiancé for six months, and he must have wondered.

The new arrivals were obviously as impressed by his vigorous good looks as she had been. He was in his midfifties, Samantha guessed, of average height but with such excellent posture that he seemed taller. His blunt features were tanned just enough to contrast with his thick waving gray hair, now ruffled attractively by the breeze.

The breeze was lifting her own hair, stirring it into tumbled disorder around her shoulders—a remembered blustery wind blowing across Puget Sound, with a slight bite to it here at the exposed southern tip of the island. Over the water gulls dived and swooped, calling to each other with strident voices. The air was clear; to the west, beyond the roughened blue gray water and the bluffs of the Olympic Peninsula, the snowy tops of Washington's craggy Olympic Mountains were visible. From this low elevation the Cascade Mountains, to the east, were out of sight. Only the upper portion of Mount Rainier showed like a giant scoop of ice cream beyond the trees of the mainland. Samantha had seen more of Rainier from the plane and had felt a familiar awestruck catch in her throat as she stared at its towering glacier-scoured majesty. She would have to wait until she was on higher ground to see it clearly again. Her favorite view of the Cascades, she remembered now, was from Jonathan's beach.

Jonathan. He and the island had always been inseparable in her thoughts. *Had* she made a mistake. . . coming back here?

Before her earlier panic had a chance to return, a slight movement caught her eye. A man was standing a short distance away, between Samantha and the plane, smoking a cigarette. His gaze was fixed, apparently, on the doctor and his guests. He was a short, extremely thin man, wearing worn blue jeans and a navy sweater. A soiled white cap pulled low over his forehead revealed only a strip of graying brown hair at the back of his neck. His eyes were hidden behind mirrored sunglasses. There was something odd about the man—an arrogance to his gestures and stance that didn't quite match up with his scruffy clothing.

For a few seconds Samantha watched him curiously, glad of the distraction he offered. Patience was not one of her virtues and she didn't enjoy waiting around. The man was smoking his cigarette with quick nervous puffs and shifting from foot to foot, staring at the women as though he wished they'd move on. His mouth was tightly compressed. Obviously he too was waiting to greet Jakob Birmann and was even less patient than she about the doctor's protracted welcome of his guests.

She'd noticed him on the plane, of course. He'd been sitting up front next to the young pilot when she boarded, staring fixedly ahead. She'd taken it for granted that he was part of the crew. But if so, surely he'd be doing something around the airplane right now. She could see the pilot, Steve Cory, pulling suitcases from the baggage compartment and piling them on the tarmac. The thin man was making no move to assist him. His sweater was worn in spots, she noticed, almost threadbare around the sleeve edges. He didn't seem a likely spa guest. In any case, The Retreat was restricted to women. She supposed he, too, could be a new employee.

She shrugged and turned back to watch the others. To her surprise, Dr. Birmann's daughter was staring fixedly at the man she herself had just been watching. And from the look on the girl's face, he was not someone she was pleased to see. There was a stiffness to the angle of her head, a stillness to her body that seemed to indicate shock. As Samantha watched curiously, she said something close to her father's ear and the doctor, still smiling at a remark one of the women had made, followed her fixed gaze—and froze. His reaction probably lasted only a second, but it was long enough for Samantha to wonder what there was about the man that could bring an expression of fear to the doctor's face. For Jakob Birmann looked like he had seen a most unwelcome ghost.

Almost immediately he recovered his composure and turned back to the women, ushering them into the first of the two cars so smoothly, with such a charming smile, that Samantha wondered if she'd imagined his odd reaction. As the car sped away, driven by a uniformed chauffeur, he stepped back to his daughter's side. At the same time the thin man walked past Samantha as though she wasn't there, flinging the remains of his cigarette almost at her feet.

The doctor watched him approach with a closed expression on his handsome face, one that gave away none of his thoughts. However, he glanced behind him once, as though he was considering a way to escape. His daughter put her hand on his arm, but whether the gesture was intended to reassure him or herself, Samantha wasn't sure. She felt distinctly uncomfortable. The doctor's eyes had flicked toward her momentarily as the man passed her, and she was sure he'd recognized her. But she didn't feel she could approach him now, especially as he began arguing with the other man, who, from his gestures, seemed to want to get into the remaining car.

Samantha was still standing there when the young pilot approached her, loaded down with luggage. "I guess your bags go in the station wagon with the others?" he asked, smiling.

She smiled back at him, relieved that someone was concerned about her. "Thank you, yes," she said gratefully. "And thank you for a comfortable flight. That's the first time I've flown in a small plane. I wasn't sure how I'd like it."

"A lot of people feel safer with more plane around them," he answered with a laugh. "I guess they figure a bigger plane stands less chance of falling out of the sky."

"I'm inclined to believe that myself," Samantha admitted.

"No way I'd let *you* fall."

Samantha sighed. She'd known from the moment she met Steve Cory that he was more than a little interested in her. He was an attractive young man, brown haired and even featured and looked like an athlete in his close-fitting gray jump suit. His father had started their charter business with one old plane that he'd restored himself, he'd told his passengers over his shoulder during the short flight from Seattle–Tacoma Airport. Now they had four planes serving the islands in Puget Sound, with plans for more. "I expect your charters keep you busy," she said evasively now.

He nodded. "That doesn't mean I can't take time off to help visitors check out Seattle's nightlife." The invitation was unmistakable.

Deliberately Samantha moved her left hand so that the sun struck a rainbow of color from the diamond solitaire on her ring finger. She saw Steve note the ring's presence and shrug.

Hoping she'd dispelled his interest, she gestured toward the station wagon. "Do you know that man?" she asked.

"Nope," he answered, shrugging again. "I had space, he had money." A frown marred his smooth young forehead. "No luggage," he commented. "I guess he might live on the island. I never saw him before, though. He's not much of a talker. Why do you ask?"

"No particular reason. I just . . . wondered."

"Mmm." He glanced at her sideways, brown eyes gleaming. "I suppose you'll be pretty busy yourself for a while—new job and all?" Evidently he hadn't given up on her yet despite her engagement ring.

"I expect I'll have a lot to do," she said, softening the rejection with a smile.

Steve sighed audibly, then grinned at her. "Give me a call if you get to feeling isolated. I'll be happy to shuttle *you* into Seattle anytime."

"I don't think I can afford you," she said lightly. "I'll have to take the ferry with the rest of the islanders."

He raised dark eyebrows and glanced meaningfully at her expensive luggage before striding off toward the car. Probably he'd decided she was making excuses. He had no way of knowing that she was determined to manage on her own for a while, without recourse to her father's money.

"Miss Austin," Dr. Birmann called to her, and Samantha realized with relief that it was finally her turn to be welcomed. The thin man had got into the front seat of the station wagon on the passenger side.

Dr. Birmann apologized profusely for keeping her waiting, then introduced her to his daughter, Anne Marie, who acknowledged the introduction with a sweet, rather vague smile. Finally he handed her into the back seat as though the station wagon were a Rolls Royce and she a visiting dignitary. Anne Marie joined her a moment later. As soon as Steve finished loading the suitcases into the back of the wagon, the doctor seated himself behind the steering wheel and started the car. He made no attempt to introduce Samantha to the man beside him.

As they pulled away Samantha waved to Steve, who waved back enthusiastically until they were out of sight. Settling back in her seat, she caught Anne Marie's eye and laughed.

"He's very good-looking, isn't he?" the girl said shyly.

"And knows it," Samantha agreed.

Anne Marie nodded. Her expression was demure, but her gray gaze had lingered on Steve while he loaded the luggage. Shy she might be, Samantha thought, but she obviously had a healthy interest in attractive young men.

The heavy car glided smoothly over the winding road, which had been resurfaced since Samantha's last visit. She could remember how Jon's old Jeep had bounced over the potholes. Of course, that was long before Dr. Birmann had built his luxury spa. He must have had the road redone at the same time—which made good business sense. The Retreat, opened just a year ago, was rapidly becoming as popular in certain moneyed circles as were The Greenhouse in Texas and The Golden Door in California, as well as his own original Retreat in San Diego.

"For a prodigious amount of money, fifteen to twenty of the rich and famous at a time can take advantage of two or more weeks of privacy and stress-free atmosphere," the doctor had explained to her with an attractive wry smile. "The Retreat's speciality is *thalassotherapy*—underwater massage in heated saltwater baths—which is designed to relax body and mind. Also, women who wish to lose weight, or perhaps to postpone the ravages of age, can receive treatments that include the latest rejuvenation techniques...."

Naturally, one couldn't expect such people to travel on bumpy roads. Samantha hoped, though, that Dr. Birmann's spa had not spoiled the loveliness of "her" island in any way.

Their journey was shorter than she'd expected. She knew that the spa had been built in Madrona Bay but hadn't known about the new stretch of road leading directly to it.

She felt a rush of pleasure as the car emerged from the woods. Below, the rocky arms of the bay embraced water that mirrored tall firs, alders and madronas, and that sparkled with dancing sunlight. In the curve of the

hillside the long three-storied building and the small
bungalows that comprised the spa jutted out from the
forest as though they had grown there. The buildings
were all of weathered wood. Wide expanses of glass, including long sloping skylights in the stepped roofs, took
advantage of solar heat and probably gave maximum
natural light to the interiors. In the cedar decks that
fronted the main building, large holes had been cut to
accommodate the vivid red brown trunks and showy
foliage of several madronas. Whoever had landscaped
the grounds—a series of terraced lawns—had made
lavish use in the wide rock-strewed borders of native
salal and ferns, interspersed with hybrid rhododendrons
and azaleas that were in full colorful bloom.

At each side of the spa, trails led into the woods. Dr.
Birmann had told her that his guests' regime included
early-morning walks, Samantha remembered. It would
be good to explore the woods again. How green everything was! And how fresh and surprisingly sweet the air
smelled through the open window of the car. Already
she could feel the island atmosphere casting its old spell
on her, making her wonder again if her return had been
a mistake.

She looked around with interest as the doctor parked
the car at the side of the main building. Several women,
some wearing caftans, some in sweat suits, were sitting
on slatted benches that surrounded the trees on the
decks. A white-jacketed attendant was serving bever-
ages in dainty china cups. The scene had a decidedly
continental air.

Dr. Birmann turned and smiled in a rather strained
manner over his shoulder. "We serve a variety of herbal
teas that are very good for the health," he told Saman-

tha. "You will enjoy them, I'm sure." His precise voice held only a slight trace of his native Swiss accent.

As a confirmed coffee drinker, Samantha wasn't sure she agreed, but she smiled dutifully. Since leaving the airstrip, neither he nor the thin man had addressed a single word to her or to Anne Marie—or even to each other, a fact that suddenly seemed strange to Samantha. Anne Marie had been fairly silent, too, though she had answered Samantha's questions politely enough, explaining that she was teaching a yoga class at the spa for the summer and would be going to college in the fall. She had offered little conversation of her own, except to admire Samantha's engagement ring and to remark that she wished her hair was as curly as Samantha's—and as colorful.

Privately Samantha wondered why Anne Marie didn't take advantage of the expert cosmetic advice that was surely available at the spa. The girl had potential— her gray eyes were particularly fine and her features were even—but she *was* a bit mousy. Her eyelashes were too pale, her skin a little sallow and her hair was just. . .hair. The proper makeup and haircut would do wonders for her. Later, when she knew Anne Marie better, perhaps she could help her to emerge from her shell.

"Anne Marie will show you where you are to stay," Dr. Birmann said after a rather awkward pause. "I think you will find your chalet comfortable. It is similar to those of our guests. There are two dining rooms in the main building, serving dinner between seven and nine. Please avail yourself of all facilities." He smiled a little stiffly, glancing at his still-silent companion.

The doctor's large competent-looking hands were gripping the steering wheel tightly, Samantha noted, and there was a reserve—a formality—to him that she hadn't noticed during their interview. Whoever the other man was, his presence was having a profound effect on her eminent employer.

"I will not attempt to explain our routine to you now," Jakob Birmann continued. "You will find a copy of our daily schedule in your chalet. For today, please feel free to amuse yourself as you wish. You will perhaps desire to visit friends?"

That was considerate of him, Samantha thought, forgiving him his unnatural manner. He had remembered what she'd told him of her summers on the island. "I *would* like to explore a little," she admitted.

"Very well, then. Anne Marie will conduct you on a tour of the spa at nine o'clock tomorrow morning. Afterward I will see you in my office." His smile had faded altogether now and Samantha realized she'd been dismissed. She put her hand on the door handle, then hesitated as Anne Marie said in a timid voice, "You aren't coming with us, daddy?"

"Later," the doctor said tersely, almost rudely.

A young fair-haired man wearing a beige jogging outfit with an insignia on the jacket pocket opened the car door for Samantha and then carried out her luggage, preceding her and Anne Marie up winding wooden steps to a group of bungalows set in the hillside.

At the top of the steps, Samantha looked back at the station wagon. Dr. Birmann and the thin man were still sitting in the car. The dark silhouettes of their heads were visible behind the glare of sun on the windshield. She couldn't shake the feeling that something was very wrong between those two. Dr. Birmann's abrupt dismissal of her seemed out of character. She wished she could hear what they were saying to each other.

She tossed her head, smiling to herself as her father's voice echoed in her memory: "You're always too curious for your own good, Samantha. Curiosity killed the cat, remember." Her father often used clichés—an occupational hazard in the advertising business. But she *had* been an inquisitive child, she had to admit. She'd always wanted to find out everything there was to know about people, about things, about life.

The young man was waiting patiently, she saw as she turned around at last. He was holding open the door of one of the chalets. Smiling in apology, she hurried across the wooden landing, noticing as she did so that Anne Marie had also stopped to look down at the station wagon. The girl's arms were crossed awkwardly across her chest again, and she was biting her lower lip. Her gray eyes were half hidden beneath her lowered eyelids, but there was a glint to them that reminded Samantha of some small animal caught in a trap. What on earth was going on, she wondered. What strange situation had she walked into?

CHAPTER TWO

THE CHALET was more than comfortable. It reminded Samantha of a first-class hotel suite. There was a fairly roomy sitting room, a bright and airy bedroom, a luxurious bathroom with piles of thick fluffy towels on a white wicker rack.

"This is marvelous," Samantha exclaimed after a whirlwind tour, dumping her tote bag beside the bed.

The young attendant smiled as he set down her suitcases. His name, Matt, was embroidered neatly above the insignia on his jacket pocket, she noticed. He waved her off when she tried to tip him. "Dr. Birmann doesn't allow his employees to accept money," he explained. "He figures he pays us good salaries and that all guests should be treated equally well, so there's no need for tipping."

Samantha's respect for the doctor went up another notch. She hated tipping—felt it was demeaning to the person forced to rely on other people's largess.

Impulsively she signaled to Matt to stay a moment, then checked to make sure that Anne Marie hadn't followed them into the chalet. "What's Dr. Birmann like to work for?" she asked.

Matt tilted his dark head to one side, considering. "Firm, but fair," he said. "As long as you do your job well, he's great." He grinned. "Look out if you goof off, though. Some staff members don't last too long around here.''

"I'll last," Samantha promised.

"Good for you."

She followed him out to the sitting room, where he passed Anne Marie, who was finally coming in, her pretty face screwed up in a frown. "Is anything wrong?" Samantha asked.

Anne Marie shook her head. "Why should anything be wrong?" Her tone was defensive.

"Sorry," Samantha murmured tactfully, then flung her arms wide to indicate the room. "This is gorgeous. When your father told me I'd be living in a chalet, I had visions of a one-room cabin."

She looked around approvingly. All of the materials that had been used in the chalet's construction were natural, and the furniture was light and functional, leaning toward the Scandinavian tradition. The floors were of gleaming oak, scattered with gaily colored wool rugs that accented the earth colors of the room. Dr. Birmann had told her at their original interview that he believed the human body should come into contact only with organic materials, and he had obviously carried this philosophy into the decorating scheme at the spa. The large painting that hung on one wall in the sitting room was an original—an abstract watercolor that seemed to sing with rhythmic color. Samantha found it a refreshing change from the usual hackneyed prints featured in most hotels and motels.

"Where do *you* live?" she asked Anne Marie.

The girl was still hovering near the doorway. She didn't answer until Samantha repeated her question. "Oh, we have a chalet over there," she said distractedly, gesturing off to her left. She turned at last to look at Samantha. "Excuse me, I was thinking about something else." She glanced around vaguely. "My father said I should help you get settled. Can I help you unpack or something?" She didn't sound too keen on the idea. Already she was turning to look out through the open doorway again.

"I can manage," Samantha told her. "I'm just going to unpack the basics, change and take off for a while. You go ahead—I'm sure you have other things to do."

"Well—my father did say...."

"I'm quite capable of taking care of myself," Samantha insisted. She certainly didn't want to have her employer's daughter pressed into service against her wishes.

Anne Marie seemed to detect the slight note of asperity that had crept into Samantha's voice. She flushed and turned back again, looking like a schoolgirl who'd been chastised by her teacher. "I'm sorry. I've been very rude. It's just that I'm worried about...." Her words trailed off, disappointing Samantha, who had hoped for an explanation of the thin man.

"I'll be fine, Anne Marie," she insisted more kindly. "I'd really just as soon take care of myself."

"Oh, well, in that case...." The girl almost bolted from the chalet, stopped on the porch to say, "I hope you'll enjoy working here," in a polite little voice before she shot off down the steps as though she'd just been released from a cage.

Shaking her head, Samantha closed her door. Obviously the arrival of the thin man had caused the Birmanns some kind of problem. But he was *their* problem, not hers. She wasn't going to worry about Anne Marie's agitated behaviour or get offended over the way both the doctor and his daughter had unceremoniously left her to her own devices. Instead she was going to indulge herself, give herself over to nostalgia and the island's magic spell. She would hike to Willow Lake, to the house her parents had rented for those long-ago summers. She might also drop into the island store, to see if old Ben Fletcher was still around. Ben had been the island handyman and gardener and he knew everyone. He would bring her up to date on island gossip if anyone could.

An hour later, dressed comfortably in jeans and a loose white sweater, she hesitated at a fork in the steep trail she'd taken away from the spa, marveling at the peace that had surrounded her as soon as she left the buildings behind. She had forgotten the quality of the silence on the island. Standing there surrounded by trees, she could hear only the occasional cry of a sea-bird, the gentle murmur of wind in the tall evergreens, the crackling sound of some small animal scuttling through the undergrowth on either side of the bark-covered trail.

She breathed deeply of the fresh salt-scrubbed air, then determindedly started up the left fork of the trail. But she hadn't gone more than a few steps before she doubled back and took the other fork, knowing full well that this path wouldn't lead her to Willow Lake. Instead it would cross the point and bring her out on the bluff above Hemlock Cove, the site of Jon's house.

Sooner or later, she rationalized, she would have to bring herself to look down at "their" beach—the beach where she'd often sat alone as a child, chin propped on knees, waiting impatiently for Jon to get tired of scuba diving, while her eyes had scanned the water's surface, keeping a watchful eye on the bubbles that revealed his presence below. It was probably going to be painful to revisit the places connected with Jon, but she might as well get over the worst right away.

Half an hour later Samantha emerged from the woods into the meadow above Hemlock Cove. The rate of her heartbeat had increased quite a bit, but whether that was due to the climb or to the fact that she could see the roof of Jon's house down below, she wasn't sure. The building was almost hidden among the trees. She wondered if anyone was home.

Half turned to go, thinking that she would hike to the lake after all, she abruptly changed her mind. Instead she sat down in the long rough grass, pulled her knees up to her chin, folded her arms around them and fixed her gaze on the spectacular vista of the Cascades, as though the magnificent sight would help make up her mind.

She really had little interest in visiting the house she and her mother and father had occupied during those long-ago summers—even though she had been happy there, pleased to have so much attention from parents who adored her but were often too busy during their work year to spend much time with her. That was the whole point of those summers—a chance for the family to be together without school or work to intervene, as well as a chance to get away from the Los Angeles heat and smog.

They had all enjoyed the island—Samantha and Claudia more than Dwight, perhaps. Claudia had always been delighted to get away for a while from the hectic entertaining their life-style required. While her

husband spent long hours on the telephone, which connected him like an umbilical cord to his beloved office,
she and Samantha had combed the beaches, speculating
wildly on the origins of fascinating things washed up by
the tide. They'd found a piece of a tombstone once—an
ancient chunk of granite etched with the words "beloved wife."

Dwight Austin had spent part of his time fishing for
salmon in the waters surrounding the island. Samantha
smiled, remembering how her father loathed fishing.
He was too active, too sociable to relish time spent sitting in a boat. But his doctor had convinced him that
he needed regular breaks from the frenetic pace of his
advertising agency. And in spite of his lack of enthusiasm, the many fishing sessions that Samantha shared
with him had forged a closeness between father and
daughter.

Affable by nature, Dwight had talked with her about
her life and her activities. He'd also made sure he
described to her in detail the challenges and oppor-
tunities of his beloved advertising business, openly encouraging her to follow in his footsteps—which was all
right with Samantha. Even as a small girl, she'd loved
to visit his office, where she'd sit in a corner, listening
to the people who hurried in and out, backed by the
sound of typewriters clacking, telephones ringing. She
had watched her father adoringly as he paced his huge
elegant office dictating to one of his secretaries; or as
he sat in his big leather chair, feet on the desk, quoting
statistics and promising miracles over one of the many
phones, while he gestured with his cigar. She'd hardly
been able to wait to become part of all that excitement,
part of that mysteriously glamorous world.

Paternally solemn as he held his fishing rod, Dwight had explained to her the necessity of building a strong financial base from which to operate—as he had done. Working with him would enable her to achieve independence, he had said. Of course she would marry someday, in which case she should marry someone who could offer her complete security. Security was very important.

He hadn't suspected that she'd fall in love with Jonathan Blake, even after all the summers the two young people had spent together. They'd always seemed to think of each other as brother and sister. He hadn't once objected to their friendship, though he had reminded Samantha occasionally that Jon and his widowed mother were very poor and that she shouldn't eat meals over there too often. "That boy doesn't have two pennies to rub together," he'd grumbled more than once. "As far as I can see, he'll never amount to anything. All he thinks about are whales and dolphins and seals."

Samantha hadn't argued with her father—she rarely did. She loved him, admired him, respected his opinions. No wonder her announcement that she and Jon loved each other had come as such a shock.

Busy as always, Dwight hadn't noticed how late his daughter returned from those moonlight picnics that final summer, how restless she was when Jon was away. After receiving his bachelor of science degree in oceanography, Jonathan had been taking part in a work-study program at the University of Washington, so he was gone quite often. Dwight *had* noticed that. But he'd had no way of knowing that *because* of their rarity, the times his daughter and Jon spent together had suddenly become more intense, more personal.

Dwight Austin was a practical man. When he was finally confronted with the truth, he didn't rant and rave and forbid Samantha to see Jonathan. Instead he accepted her choice, indulgent father that he was. He was worried though, he explained, because Jon was obviously unable to support her. But she was not to fret; he would see what he could do to help.

Shortly before the Austins were to leave the island, he came up with a plan that he felt was fair to everybody. Two plans, actually—Jon was an independent type; he deserved some free choice. Dwight would personally acquaint Jon with his ideas, he told Samantha, just as soon as the opportunity presented itself.

The opening came in an unexpected way. Jon announced he'd received a wonderful offer—a chance to take part in an extended research project. The project would involve a study of the world's population of whales, marking them, tracking them and doing anatomical studies on any stranded animals that died. He would be out of the country for two to three years.

For a few seconds after Jon made his announcement, there was silence. They were sitting in the living room of the Austin's Willow Lake house, with Jon and Samantha side by side on the big early-American sofa and Dwight opposite in a wing chair. Claudia was visiting a neighbor.

Dwight was dressed smartly in a gray pin-striped suit, for they were leaving the island that day. Samantha was also dressed for travel, in a beige raw-silk suit and an apricot-colored crepe de chine blouse. In contrast, Jon was dressed as usual in cut offs and a wrinkled cotton shirt. He'd come over to say goodbye. He and Samantha had made no plans for the future, but she had hoped to persuade him to visit them in Los Angeles soon. His announcement had taken her completely by surprise. She stared at him, stunned, unable to believe she'd heard him correctly. Two or three *years*!

"And after that?" Dwight asked, tugging at his copper-colored mustache as he did when he was disturbed.

Jon shrugged. "Who knows? I'd like to pursue a doctorate, but I'll have to see how it goes financially. The institute sponsoring the project has the use of government funds to hire me as an assistant while I study. But I won't be making much, so I'll have to wait and see. Whatever I end up doing will be involved some way with mammals. That's where my main interest lies."

Dwight nodded, his expression grave. With his usual thoroughness he had researched Jon's chosen profession and had come away from his study unimpressed. "You probably won't ever make any money worth having," he told Jon. "A lot of oceanographers finish up as glorified technicians or sit in a basement lab punching numbers into a computer. Most research is funded by federal grants, and every penny has to be accounted for. It's not like the space program. Total annual government spending for ocean research comes to about two cents for each dollar spent on that."

Jon shrugged again. He didn't seem at all worried by the prospect of his continuing poverty. "I'm used to pinching pennies," he said cheerfully.

Leaning forward, his hands on the knees of his well-tailored pants, Dwight had looked directly at Jon. "I don't suppose you'd consider coming to work for me instead? You're a good photographer. I could use—"

Samantha reacted as rapidly as Jon did. "Oceanography is Jon's *life*," she cried out.

Jonathan flashed her a grateful glance, then he spoke for himself. After explaining just how strongly he felt about his work, he went on to make several derogatory remarks about the nine-to-five routine. "In any case," he concluded, "I couldn't stand to waste my life making exaggerated claims about unnecessary products so they'd sell at inflated prices." Tact had never been one of his noticeable virtues.

"It's better than being a beach bum all your life," Dwight had lashed out in turn.

In the silence that followed, Samantha was sure her father must have just thought the words—he couldn't have said them aloud, not to Jon.

Jon's eyes were bright with pain and anger and hurt pride. "You assume I can't become a success in my own field?" he'd asked indignantly.

"Not everyone can be a Jacques Cousteau," Dwight pointed out.

"True." There was bitterness in Jon's voice now and Dwight hastened to make amends. "Look, Jon," he said quietly, "I didn't mean to insult you. I'm trying to be *helpful*." He paused for a moment, then spoke again. "I have an alternative suggestion. What do you say to...oh, sixty thousand dollars a year for two-to-three years—yours to do any kind of research you like, as long as it's done here in the States. Call it an investment, until you get on your feet."

"Why would you want to invest in me?"

"Samantha's my little girl. I want her to be happy. You can't expect her to wait around while you go gallivanting—"

"You knew about this?" Jon asked Samantha, cutting off her father's words. He was angrier than she'd ever seen him. His lean face had tightened into a grim mask that she didn't recognize.

She shook her head. "Daddy told me he wanted to help, but not exactly in that way." Hesitantly, she put her hand on Jon's arm. "He's only thinking of our happiness. It's really a wonderful offer. Couldn't you at least think about it?"

Jon looked down at her hand as though it were something unclean, then moved deliberately so that it dropped away. "It takes sixty thousand dollars a year to make you happy?" His voice held a note of disbelief.

Again she hesitated. Obviously she and her father had underestimated his pride, a pride developed through years of almost hand-to-mouth existence. But without the money he would go away—she might never see him again. "At least we could get married," she said at last. "As it is—"

"Who said anything about marriage?" he interrupted.

The words fell between them and seemed to shatter on the floor like shards of pottery. Stunned, Samantha stared at him. He was looking at her as though she were a stranger, his blue eyes icy with an absolute contempt that froze her to the marrow of her bones.

Unable to believe that he could look at her that way, she closed her eyes momentarily, giving in to an old childish belief that if you shut your eyes tight whatever you feared would go away. He *hadn't* asked her to marry him, that was true. She had simply taken it for granted that people who loved each other married each other. "I just thought..." she managed at last, trying to rally from the shock.

"You thought I was for sale?" Standing now, hands

clenched into fists at his sides, he looked down at her as though he had never truly seen her before, as though he disliked...*despised* what he saw. "Did you really expect me to take your father's charity? Did you really think he could buy me for you?"

Shocked by the harsh brutality in his voice, Samantha spoke without thinking. "You didn't mind taking charity from Ethan Collins," she blurted out, referring to the wealthy island man who'd financed Jon's education so far.

The shot hit home. She saw the blood drain from his face, saw him take a breath and prepare to defend himself, then change his mind. "Spoiled little rich girl," he taunted her. "What do you know of life and its necessities?"

Turning to her father, his face pale, he'd added coldly. "Thank you for your concern, Mr. Austin. But I assure you I can manage my own life. I have no need of your interference or your money."

Suddenly aware of her own pride, Samantha had realized he was really saying he didn't need *her*. Standing up, she looked at him helplessly, searching her mind for words that would make everything all right between them again. But his expression closed her out, and she realized there was nothing she could say to bridge the abyss that had opened up between them. She was suddenly furious with him for his arrogance and she lashed out at him blindly, wanting to wound him as deeply as he'd wounded her. "Daddy's right," she said bitterly. "You'll never amount to anything."

His mouth tightened, but he said nothing more. Without another glance at either of them, he had stalked out of the house—and out of her life forever....

Samantha shifted in the long grass, uncomfortably aware that dampness was seeping through the seat of her jeans. If Jon had really loved her, she thought, and if she had been older, more mature, they might have been able to move beyond that terrible argument to a new understanding of each other. But he had cared more for his pride than he had for her. In the end, he had let pride stand between them. Humiliated by his rejection of the love she had so innocently, so eagerly offered, she had left the island in tears, vowing she would never, ever open herself to such pain again. And when, the following year, Dwight had gently suggested that they choose another location for their family vacation—Bermuda perhaps—Samantha had listlessly agreed.

At least her father had realized his wish for her, she thought as she stood up and stretched her cramped legs. No one could offer her more security than could her fiancé. Adrian Westcott, investment banker, was the only and beloved son of the Boston and Hyannis Port Westcotts.

No, it wasn't fair to Adrian to describe him so—even to herself. Deliberately she conjured up Adrian's smoothly shaven face, his always neat, straight dark hair, his intelligent dark eyes. He was a wonderful man, urbane and intellectual and ambitious—and very understanding. What other man would let his fiancée go off like this for six months so she could "get her head together?" Samantha sighed. Adrian did have an unfortunate habit of echoing her father's clichés.

She looked again at the roof of the house below her, trying to decide whether or not to go down to it. As she hesitated, she suddenly noticed movement beyond, on the strip of pebbled beach. Two small children were playing with a Frisbee on the hard wet sand, tossing it without much skill but a greal deal of energy. Their high-pitched voices carried up to her on the wind.

It had never occurred to her that Jon might have married by now, might even be a father. Yet it wasn't reasonable to suppose that such an attractive man would still be single. He must be thirty now; she hadn't seen him for seven years. The children—a boy and a girl—looked about five or six years old. Both had very dark hair, the girl's in a single braid. Jon's hair was light. But of course, their mother. . . .

Samantha wondered why she was suddenly conscious of a sinking sensation. Why should she care after all this time if Jon had married?

The wind was fairly strong up on the hill, making Samantha's eyes sting. The haze that often affected Washington's skies had moved in over the mountains, blotting them from view. She hadn't noticed when they disappeared. She might as well carry out her original intention to hike to the lake, she decided abruptly.

But the children had seen her. For a second they stood staring, then they both waved enthusiastically. Samantha waved back and found that her mind was made up for her. She wasn't going to skulk around the island, afraid at every moment of running into Jonathan Blake.

Before her courage failed her, she started along the rough trail that zigzagged down the face of the cliff, sliding as she rounded the first corner. The islanders were an independent people, who saw no need to make their homes accessible to outsiders. Most of the trails to the beaches would have daunted the hardiest hiker.

Picking her way more carefully, she eventually arrived on the small peninsula where Jon's father had built his house just before going into the army. It wasn't a very big place—two stories, neither of which were a whole lot larger than the chalet she was occupying at the spa. But Eileen Blake had made it cheery with bright curtains and rugs and her own watercolors and sculptures. This small wood-framed house had once been a second home to Samantha.

The children had scrambled up the bank as Samantha descended the trail. Now that they were face to face with her, however, they hung back shyly until Samantha introduced herself and held out her hand. Then they marched forward, shoulder to shoulder, to shake hands with her. They were attractive children, rosy cheeked and sturdy, with friendly open faces and curious dark eyes. Both wore T-shirts and blue jeans.

The little girl's gaze was fixed on Samantha's curls. "You have pretty hair," she said gravely. "The sun was shining on it when you were up on the bluff. I thought you were on fire, but Brian said that was silly. Does it curl like that by itself?"

Samantha laughed. "All by itself."

"Do you dye it? Our mommy dyes hers 'cause she's getting some gray in it."

"No, I haven't had to dye it yet."

"That's good. The dye stuff smells awful."

"Yuck," the boy agreed.

The little girl seemed suddenly to remember her manners. "I'm Tracy," she said brightly. "And this is my little brother, Brian. He's ten minutes younger than me."

That statement brought her a tug on her braid from "little brother," who stood a good two inches taller than she did. A moment later they had wrestled each other to the ground, Samantha forgotten. "Hey, come on, now," Samantha objected with a laugh. "Is this any way to greet a visitor?"

They separated and grinned up at her, then started rolling over and over down the rough grassy bank to the beach, showing off for her, their laughter so contagious that she couldn't help chuckling at their high spirits. At the foot of the slope, they grinned up at her again, their dark eyes sparkling with mischief. And then the boy's glance went beyond her, and she realized he'd caught sight of someone else.

She knew who it was even before a male voice said, "Hello, Sam."

No one else had ever called her Sam. Her heart skidded, stopped beating, started again. Somehow she managed to turn around.

He was standing on the veranda, looking down at her. For just a second his Nordic blue eyes blazed with emotion, then the light in them went out. Straightening, he folded his arms across his chest and gazed at her in an appraising manner, as though he were measuring her in some way.

He was dressed in the height of island fashion—in well-washed, cuffed khaki shorts and shirt, the shirt unbuttoned. His feet were bare, his long elegant toes covered in sand, his hard muscular legs and chest matted with hair that was a couple of shades darker than that on his head.

The past seven years had touched him lightly. His thick sun-streaked blond hair was perhaps a little shorter, and with more shape to it, but it still fell forward over his forehead, softening the sharp planes of his face so that he looked, in those first still moments, as though he hadn't aged a day. He had filled out, though. His shoulders had always been muscular, but now they were broad. He looked more...*solid*, though just as lean; there wasn't an ounce of fat on him. He might have been posing for an advertisement about the benefits of weight lifting, except there was no macho posturing about him. He looked...*comfortable* with his body—healthy and athletic and strong.

A camera, fitted with a telescopic lens, hung on a leather strap around his neck. Whenever Samantha had allowed herself to think about Jon in the last seven years, she had imagined him just like this, complete with camera. It had always been rare to see him without a camera.

"How are you, Jon?" she managed after what seemed an age.

"Fine. And you?" He paused. "You look well."

It seemed they were going to behave politely, distantly. She attempted a laugh that didn't quite succeed. "So do you." she looked around. "Everything looks the same as it always did."

His mouth tightened at the corners. Leaning both hands on the wooden rail that edged the veranda, he lapsed into silence again, still gazing down at her but with no particular expression on his tanned face, no warmth in his blue eyes. Those eyes had always reminded her of sailors', used to staring long distances at endless horizons, so clear they might have been a reflection of the sky.

Samantha was astonished to find that her heart was racing as though she'd run a mile. She ought to move forward, she thought, offer to shake his hand... something. But her brain didn't seem to be transmitting

messages to her feet. She felt cemented in place, as
though she'd suddenly turned into a pillar of salt. There
seemed to be a tight band around her ribs, pressing inward, so that her pulsing heart felt like a wild thing,
unable to break free. She had not thought that seeing
Jon again would shake her so. She had thought she was
prepared—armored with newfound sophistication.

The silence between them seemed to stretch endlessly.
She began to feel foolish standing there, looking up at
him. If he would only smile, move, pick up the conversation again, she could climb the steps, sit down on the old
wooden bench that was still at the end of the veranda.

At the edge of her consciousness, she could hear the
voices of the children behind her. They had evidently
returned to their game, heedless of the drama being
enacted above them.

The children. *Was* he their father? Was their
mother—Jon's wife—inside the house? She wouldn't
ask—wouldn't betray her curiosity.

"It's been a long time," Jon said. Almost immediately he seemed to realize the banality of his words. His
wide mobile mouth twitched into a grimace and he
straightened up, dusting his hands on the seat of his
shorts. For a moment she thought he was going to invite
her up the steps, but instead he lifted the camera strap
from his neck and hung the whole apparatus carefully
from the newel post. For a few seconds he was looking
away from her and she swayed slightly, as though his
steady gaze had held her erect. Her throat hurt as
though she'd tried to swallow a piece of jagged glass.
She was suddenly desperately thirsty. "Aren't you going
to invite me in?" she asked, and was dismayed to hear
an almost arch note in her voice.

He looked down at her again, raising his light eyebrows.

She gave her head a disgusted shake. "I didn't mean that the way it sounded," she said firmly. "I *am* thirsty, though. I could use a cup of your famous camp coffee. I hiked over from the spa." She hesitated. "I'm working there now."

He showed no surprise. "So Jakob told me."

"Oh, you know him?"

"We've become good friends. When he told me he'd hired you as a temporary assistant, I saw no reason not to tell him I . . . used to know you."

"Of course not."

"I was surprised when Jakob told me you hadn't married yet. Your father said you were engaged. Did he mention that I called?"

Samantha stared at him. "When?"

"About a year ago. I'd just returned from Japan. I flew into Travis Air Force Base, so I thought I'd say hello. You were out, with your fiancé—Adrian, is it?"

"Adrian Westcott." She hesitated, at a loss for words. "Daddy didn't tell me."

He nodded as though he wasn't surprised. *Oh, daddy,* she thought, understanding at once why he hadn't told her Jon had called. What would have been the point? But still, if she had known. . . . Would it have made any difference? Of course not. She'd recovered from her childish crush on Jon years ago.

"Your father seemed very pleased with your engagement," Jon said evenly.

"Yes, he . . . approves of Adrian."

"Adrian must be a very successful man."

"He's a banker."

"He must feel secure in your affections to let you go off alone for so long. Can we expect a visit from him?"

"No. I . . . we agreed I should spend this time alone."

"I see."

How could he possibly see? And yet she had the feeling he did understand perfectly. . . that he knew of the doubts that had plagued her ever since she'd agreed to marry Adrian. That he knew she had come here hoping to resolve her emotions, hoping to get rid of those lingering, indescribable yearnings that afflicted her every time she thought of the island.

"I hope you'll be very happy, Samantha."

She was no longer Sam, she noted. "Thank you," she said stiffly.

He was gazing beyond her at the beach now. She studied his averted profile, wondering what was passing through his mind. He had seemed so cold, so distant at first, but there had been a challenging note in his voice through this last exchange. His expression was hard, showing nothing of his thoughts. But his hands were clenched at his sides. He was not as unmoved by this meeting as he was trying to appear.

Suddenly she wanted to touch him. The urge was so strong that she could almost see herself moving up the steps to his side, could almost feel the soft fabric of his shirt under her hand. And then he spoke and she found she hadn't moved at all. The invisible wall he'd erected was still between them.

"Ben isn't here right now," he said. "But I'm sure he wouldn't mind if you helped yourself to coffee."

Puzzled, she stared at him. "Ben?"

He gestured at the house behind him. "This is Ben Fletcher's house now. He took it over three years ago when I inherited Ethan's place."

"Ethan's dead?"

There was genuine shock in her voice and his expression softened slightly. "Why don't you come and sit down?" He gestured at the wooden bench, so she climbed to the porch and sat on it, conscious that he was watching her. He lowered himself on the top step and then turned sideways to face her.

Now that she was closer to him she could see that he had aged a little after all. There were fine lines around his eyes and two more lines bracketed his mouth. There was something else different about his mouth. It had always lifted at the corners even when his face was in repose, but now it curled at one side in an almost cynical manner.

"I'm sorry about Ethan, Jon," she said softly. "You must miss him."

"Yes." He hesitated, then spoke in a gentle musing tone that reminded her forcefully of the kind compassionate boy he had once been. "He died in his sleep. He was very old and his arthritis had worsened, so I couldn't grieve for him too much. I think he was glad to go."

"And he left you his house." She was still astonished.

Jon nodded, smiling faintly and apparently enjoying her amazement. "He left me everything he owned." His voice was casual, but his eyes held an expression she couldn't interpret. Scorn?

She remembered the Collins house, of course. It had been something of an oddity on the island, where houses were mostly small. Ethan had been something of an oddity himself. A retired export-import businessman, the only son of the island's original settler, he had built a large, two-storied, English-style stone farmhouse, tucked away among tall trees on the bluff overlooking

Possession Sound just beyond Hemlock Cove. He had furnished it with rather formal antiques brought from Europe and had hung its walls with paintings he'd acquired at overseas auctions.

The old bachelor, a recluse, had refused everyone's friendly overtures. Yet the islanders had taken a perverse pride in the crazy old man who lived an almost Spartan existence in his luxurious house, hardly ever venturing outside it and not even hiring a housekeeper to take care of him.

Jon had been Ethan's only friend. He had run errands for him, had chopped wood for his fireplaces, had helped the old man dust and clean his many treasures, and had even taken care of him when he was sick. In return, old Ethan had more or less adopted Jon after the boy's father was killed in Vietnam. He had even let go of enough money to pay Jon's way through university, something Eileen Blake, struggling to manage on her pension, would not have been able to do.

Samantha had been a little afraid of Ethan Collins—such a strange, frail-looking old man whose thick white hair and beard were trimmed awkwardly by himself. Accompanied by Jon, she had paid courtesy calls on Ethan every summer, more from curiosity than from anything else. Ethan had always been polite to her, but distant. He didn't care for females, island gossip said. Not that there was anything "peculiar" about that— lots of old bachelors were misogynists. Jon had finally satisfied Samantha's ever-present curiosity by telling her that the old man had been jilted by the one love of his life when he was in his twenties. He had never recovered from the blow to his self-esteem. . . .

"I guess you could say I've come up in the world," Jon said dryly, interrupting her thoughts.

That was a direct crack at her father, Samantha thought, stiffening. Or perhaps it was a direct crack at *her*.

Their eyes met and tension crackled between them. But it was not the sexual tension that had once arced between them, drawing them into each others' arms. There was anger here, and bitterness. He had a right to be bitter, she supposed. But so did she. He, after all, was the one who had thrown her love for him back in her face. *Who said anything about marriage?* The memory still stabbed at her heart.

"As Ben isn't home, I guess I'll go on back to the spa," she said stiffly, standing up.

He'd caught sight of her ring, she noticed. Probably because she'd clasped her hands in front of her and had unconsciously straightened the ring so that the diamond didn't cut into her finger. Why did she suddenly feel she wanted to hide her left hand behind her back?

His glance rose to meet hers. "I'm sure Ben could at least spare you a glass of water," he said cordially. "Why don't you go on in?"

She hesitated. She *was* thirsty. Somehow she managed to get her feet to carry her across the porch. As she drew abreast of him he turned slightly, and she thought for one terrified moment that he was going to touch her. But instead, he merely gave her a smile that seemed forced. "My mother's still living with me," he said. "Why not go up and have coffee with her? You know how she loves company. She's been looking forward to seeing you." A slight emphasis on the first pronoun told her that *he* had not—as though she didn't know that by now.

"I'd like to see her, too," she said with some emphasis of her own.

"Samantha," he said softly, and there was a sudden tender note of protest in his voice that sent waves of remembered emotion through her. She had to restrain herself from taking the step that would bring her close to him, had to clench her fists so that she wouldn't reach out to touch his shoulder.

If only they had never fallen in love, she wished, as she had wished so many times before. If only her fairy-tale fantasy had remained a fantasy! Then they could have kept the friendship that had meant so much to her. He would still be her idol, the adored elder brother she'd never had. If only he hadn't kissed her at the beginning of that summer, that last wonderful, terrible summer.

For what seemed like several minutes, time hung suspended while her body remembered the first time Jonathan Blake had held her close in his muscular arms. She'd finally decided to learn to skin-dive. Though she was a fairly good swimmer, she'd always resisted any kind of diving, feeling claustrophobic at the thought of water closing over her head—an old phobia begun when she'd fallen out of a sight-seeing boat near Catalina Island at the age of three. In the minute it took for her father to rescue her she had panicked and come close to drowning. But at last she'd made up her mind she wasn't going to let fear stop her from doing something she wanted to do. Waist deep in water, flippers on her feet, viewing mask in place, she had taken several deep gulps of air and prepared to put her head underwater.

Jon had stopped her at once, gripping her arms to yank her upright. "First lesson," he'd said sternly. "If you take deep breaths like that, you're filling your lungs with oxygen—which sounds like the thing to do. But at the same time you're losing carbon dioxide, and carbon dioxide triggers an alert that tells you you're running short of oxygen when it's time to come up again. If you destroy that trigger, you could black out.''

Removing her face mask, she'd gazed up at him, still a little shaken by his sudden action. "So how should I breathe?" she asked him.

"Just breathe normally and relax, like this." Still holding her upper arms, he had demonstrated.

As Samantha tried to copy him she'd become aware for the first time of the strength of the hands gripping her arms. Aware, too, of a languid sweetness that was invading her body, setting her flesh tingling, her blood rushing through her veins. "Jon," she said softly, looking up at him, and there was something in her voice that had never been there before—a recognition, a question.

In immediate response the expression on his strong-featured face changed, becoming bemused. Letting go of her arms, he cupped her face in his hands and gazed into her eyes for a long moment. Then he'd touched his mouth to hers, gently at first, and more harshly as they both responded to the passion that suddenly engulfed them. She could remember the way her body had seemed to melt when his hands moved slowly across her breasts.

It was just a summer romance, she reminded herself. It meant nothing, less than nothing, to him.

She saw him frown and realized her facial expression had hardened. "Samantha?" he repeated in a different tone, a questioning tone.

And then one of the children called something from

the beach. She had completely forgotten the children. So, apparently, had he. He started visibly, then turned his head and called down, "What is it, Brian?"

The boy's voice was plaintive. "You promised to take us clam digging, Uncle Jon."

Uncle Jon.

Samantha glanced sharply at Jon as he waved an acknowledgement. He turned back in time to catch her glance and smiled quizzically up at her. He always had been able to read her mind. "They're Lynne's children, not mine," he informed her. "I haven't married yet. Do you remember Lynne? Ben's daughter? She married a flyer from Whidbey Island shortly after you were here last. Greg Lawton. She was hoping he'd show her the world, but instead he left her with two children to raise. Family life didn't suit him, he said."

She was grateful he'd switched to a topic she could feel at ease with. She sat down on the bench again. "Poor Lynne," she murmured, remembering the petulant, unattractive young woman who had driven Ben crazy with her complaints. Lynne must be thirty-five or so now. She'd once told Samantha that she'd marry anybody who would get her away from the island. "This dump," she'd called it. Samantha hadn't been able to understand her attitude. At that time she'd have given anything to stay on the island forever. With Jon.

"Lynne works in a travel agency in Seattle," Jon explained. "She gets over occasionally to see the children. Ben has his hands full with those two. Usually when he has to work he has Suzy McLain in, but there was a sale at Seattle Nordstroms, I understand, and she couldn't resist. So I offered to baby-sit." He smiled.

Samantha had always loved his smile. It began slowly in his eyes, raising his eyebrows, then spread to his mouth, parting his lips puckishly to show even teeth that looked startlingly white against his tan. For a second he looked so much like the Jonathan she remembered that her heart leaped. "You wouldn't know Suzy McLain now," he said with a laugh. "She's seventeen and ravishing."

And probably mad about Jon Blake, Samantha added to herself. Every girl on the island had always been mad about Jon Blake. "Ben is a gardener at the spa now, by the way," he added. "You didn't see him there?"

She shook her head. "I should have known," she said warmly, responding as much to his smile as to her affectionate memories of Ben. "The spa grounds are lovely. Ben hasn't lost his touch." Nostalgia overwhelmed her. "Remember how Ben used to confound us with his magic tricks? I saw that vanishing handkerchief routine done in San Francisco once, but the magician didn't have Ben's flourish. I imagine his grandchildren love magic, too. Does he perform for them?"

"I guess so," Jon said curtly. He had risen to his feet as she spoke and a mask had slipped down over his face, closing out all expression. His mouth, which for a few minutes had relaxed into its old sensitive, sensual familiarity, had returned to a straight, unyielding line. The familiar, humorously quizzical look was gone.

She had trespassed, she realized. She had made reference to their shared past. Why had that made him angry? And what right had he to be that way? Had he been uncomfortably reminded of the rotten way he'd treated her?

She could sense impatience in him now. Probably he wished she would just go. But she must ask, couldn't resist asking, "What about you, Jon? What are you doing now?"

He smiled rather grimly. "Still spending two-thirds of my life underwater. What did you expect?"

But that was a joke, Jon, she wanted to cry—a joke between us. I didn't ever agree with my father that your underwater explorations were a waste of time, something to be outgrown. It was just that there wasn't room in your plans for me. . . .

And yet, it seemed that her father had been right about Jon in one way. He had come back to the island and he was still taking photographs, still bumming around beaches. He might have come up in the world as far as his living accommodations were concerned, but that had been due to Ethan's generosity. His improved circumstances hadn't really been a result of his own efforts.

The quizzical expression was back on Jon's face now, but there was no humor in it. Did he know what she was thinking? "I think I *will* get that drink of water," she murmured, standing up and moving toward Ben's front door.

"Uncle Jon!" Brian called demandingly from the beach.

Jon laughed shortly. "He's not going to give up, is he?" He looked at her once more, his eyes narrowed, showing no emotion at all. "I expect we'll be seeing each other from time to time, Samantha," he said evenly. "I'm often at the spa. I hope my presence won't prove awkward for you."

She swallowed against a sudden lump in her throat, shook her head weakly.

"Good," he said briskly, then waved to Brian and Tracy. "I'm coming," he called, adding in a quieter voice that nevertheless had a shaft of steel in it, "I have no idea what you hoped to accomplish by coming back to the island, Samantha. I can't truthfully say I'm happy to see you. But it ought to be possible for us to behave in a civilized manner toward one another. Don't you agree?" Before she could respond he turned abruptly and descended the cedar steps.

Stunned, Samantha opened the stout wooden door of the small house and closed it quickly behind her, not wanting to watch Jon jump down to the beach. She could remember too well the way he moved—his easy athletic grace.

She leaned against the door for a second, gathering strength, looking blankly around her at Eileen Blake's old oak table with its four wooden chairs, the big old Welsh dresser with the blue-and-white plates lined up on the shelves, the bright rag rugs Eileen had made with her own hands during wet island winters. Standing there, she felt weak with memories, happy memories spoiled forever.

This old family kitchen looked much as it always had, though the whole house had been refurbished and repainted, floors and doors and cabinets replaced. There was even a telephone hanging on the wall near the dresser—Jon and his mother hadn't been able to afford a phone.

Why had she come back? What was it she had hoped to gain—release from the past? Exorcism of old ghosts? Those were the excuses she'd given herself, those were the reasons she'd applied for the job at the spa.

She shook her head impatiently, then walked over to the sink and automatically reached for a glass in the cupboard where glasses had always been kept. They were still there. So was the pain around her heart, the pain she had thought was gone forever. Had nothing changed then? Had the shadow of that former Samantha—that foolish girl—waited here all this time to fold itself around her as soon as she returned?

Abruptly she bent over the sink, gripping its tiled edge as she fought back the threat of tears. Had she really thought that coming back to the island would exorcise all those wonderful memories? Had she believed she could see Jon and not want him with every fiber of her being? Right now, right this minute, she wanted to run out to the beach. She wanted to beg Jon to hold her, to tell her the past seven years of loneliness had been a bad dream, that that last painful scene had never happened. She wanted him to be her friend again. She wanted him to love her.

No.

Straightening, she took a deep breath, let it out. Jon had made it perfectly obvious that he felt nothing for her now, if he ever had. And in reality she felt nothing for him. She loved Adrian—and she was going to marry him. Her physical senses had turned out to have a willful memory of their own, that was all. The silly romantic girl she had been was still alive inside the sensible woman she had become. That was to be regretted, but not dwelt on.

At least the first confrontation was over. And she had survived. In control now, she turned on the cold water and filled her glass.

CHAPTER THREE

EILEEN BLAKE had never been a conformist. What other hostess, Samantha wondered, would offer hospitality in the kitchen of a mansion, pouring strong black coffee from the same old stove-top pot she'd always favored into her own hand-turned pottery mugs. "You haven't changed a bit," Samantha said awkwardly as the older woman sat down at the table and gazed at her with that same direct regard Jon had inherited.

Eileen sipped her coffee without answering, both slender hands clasped comfortably around the cup. She had been unusually silent so far. In the old days she had always rushed into speech, often in the middle of some-one else's sentence. She'd spent a lot of time alone on the island, so any visitor had been treated to a deluge of words immediately on arrival. "Tell me everything you've been doing," she used to demand when Saman-tha arrived for the summer. Then, without pausing, she would launch into a long dissertation about island hap-penings and Jon's latest marine discoveries, completely forgetting she'd asked a question.

Perhaps she *had* changed a little, Samantha thought. But then it was much more likely that Eileen Blake's mind had suddenly focused on something else. She had forgotten that Eileen would often blank out right in the middle of a garrulous discourse while her mind pondered the problems of a watercolor composition still in the planning stage, or a lump of clay that might become the head of a child, or a gull—or an ashtray.

It had never done any good to try to bring Eileen out of what she called her ''fugue'' state, so Samantha now sat as patiently as she could, looking around in admiration at the elegantly streamlined kitchen with its burnished wood cabinets and slate floor.

She and Eileen were seated at a beautiful walnut table with matching high-backed chairs. In the mullioned bay windows that in clear weather framed a heart-stopping view of the high Cascades, including Mount Baker to the north, two cats sunned themselves on the cushioned window seat, curled up in sleepy comfort, eyes closed. One was a young calico, the other a battle-scarred gray tom. On the floor beside Eileen's chair, his graying muzzle stretched out over his mistress's feet, lay a large dog of indeterminate breed and age—a shaggy brown-and-white dog that might have had some collie in his ancestry.

Jon had always loved dogs. He'd had an old labrador retriever who used to follow him into the water and swim tirelessly around his air bubbles, waiting as hopefully as Samantha for him to come up.

The memory disturbed her. For so long she had shut such memories out of her mind. Now that she was back on the island they kept filling her thoughts, as though they'd hovered here in limbo, waiting for her to return.

Hastily she fixed her attention on Eileen again. The artist looked exactly as she had always looked. Her light brown hair was pulled loosely up in a knot on top of her head, and her dress was a loosely fitting camel-colored smock that might have been a duplicate of the home-spun garment she'd been wearing when Samantha saw her last. She must be almost fifty now, Samantha realized. The same age as her own mother, though without Claudia's careful makeup on her lined tanned face, she looked older. That was hardly surprising, considering all Eileen had gone through.

Married straight out of high school, she had lost her beloved husband in the early days of America's involvement in Vietnam. Life since then had been a financial struggle, eased only by her widow's pension and the small amounts she charged for what she called her craft rather than her art. The past three years had probably been easier for her though, since she and Jon had moved into this luxurious house.

"Life stays pretty much the same on the island," Eileen said at last, evidently explaining her unchanged appearance.

She glanced quizzically at Samantha. "I'm sorry I went off for a while there. I was remembering how you and Jon used to come in from swimming, frozen to the bone, and I used to feed you cup after cup of hot chocolate to stop your shivering. Jon always liked marshmallows in his chocolate, but you swore marshmallows cooled it off too much. What a feisty little kid you were! And with such an imagination. All those stories you used to make up. Do you still write? You used to tell me you were going to be the greatest short-story writer of the century."

Samantha shook her head. "I haven't written many stories since college."

Eileen leaned back in her chair. "Too bad. You were pretty good." She grinned. "*You've* certainly changed.

Your hair looks marvelous with all those soft curls. How did you finally manage to tame it?''

"Conditioners are terrific products."

Eileen laughed. ''I remember how it looked when you were a little kid—as wild as if you'd stuck your finger in a light-bulb socket.'' She paused, still studying Samantha's face. ''You really do look great, but...are you happy? This fiancé of yours—does he make you happy?''

Samantha had forgotten that Eileen's speech could be as direct as her gaze. ''Of course I'm happy. Adrian's a wonderful man. Why wouldn't I be happy?''

Eileen regarded her with a measuring expression, her eyes, as hurtingly blue as Jonathan's, narrowed slightly as though they were studying something she wanted to sketch. ''It's your eyes,'' she said at last. ''I remember the first time I saw you. Such a bright, bold little face, trying to look tough so no one would know all you wanted in the world was for people to love you. But your eyes gave you away. Those dark gold flecks made you look...wistful. Marvelous color, your eyes, Samantha. They remind me of an amber brooch my grandmother owned—it used to attract particles of light, then give them back in a kind of subdued glow. Terribly difficult to catch in a painting. I tried several times, remember? And your hair always came out orange. I could never figure out what colors to mix to get that lovely copper sheen. Maybe I'll try again while you're here. I've learned a few things since I last saw you.''

Reaching out in one of her sudden, unexpected movements, she touched Samantha's face with her slightly calloused fingertips. ''Your eyes still give you away,

Samantha," she said brusquely. "You aren't as happy as you'd have me believe."

She dropped her hand, shrugged. "I've no right to pry, of course. I used to think of you as a surrogate daughter and I suppose I still—" She broke off, frowning, then got up to pour more coffee, her tan dress flowing smoothly around her thin frame. "There's an awkwardness between us," she said when she'd seated herself again. "You'll remember, Samantha, that I've never believed in beating around the bush, so let's get this over with." She took a deep breath. "I've never known what happened between you and Jon, and it's none of my business. I do know you fell in love with him that last summer, and I thought for a while that he loved you."

Not enough, Samantha thought as Eileen paused.

"I've never wanted to know what you two quarreled about," Eileen continued. "I didn't want to be forced to take sides."

What she really meant, Samantha thought, was that she didn't want to know if Jon had behaved badly.

"Why did you come back? I know you've got a job at the spa, but what was your real reason?"

Samantha in turn took a deep breath. It had never been easy to deceive Eileen. "I don't really know," she said slowly. "I had the feeling I wanted to get away for a while, until I was sure . . . ."

"Cold feet about getting married?"

Samantha attempted a laugh. "It's not too unusual to have cold feet, is it?"

Eileen grinned. "I wouldn't know. I met my Richard on New Year's Eve, and we were married on January 20. I was afraid he'd get away if I didn't grab him quickly. Aren't you afraid your Adrian will get lonely while you're gone?''

"No," Samantha said with conviction. "He'll wait for me."

"Uh-huh. So why here? Why not Bermuda or Europe or the Rocky Mountains? Why Collins Island?''

"I was happy here," Samantha said simply. "It seemed a good place to think things out."

Eileen's face softened. Her hands reached out to clasp Samantha's. "I hope it works out for you, dear," she said quietly. "I'm sorry I was a bit offhand at first—I guess I was afraid for Jon. He was devastated for a long time after you left. I don't want that to happen again."

"Jon had no reason to be devastated," Samantha protested. "I didn't. . . ."

Eileen made a small movement with her hand and Samantha subsided. Obviously the woman had decided long ago who had been at fault. "Let's just forget it," Samantha said. She was sorry now that she'd come to visit. She almost hadn't, but she'd decided it was better to face the more painful aspects of the past on her first day so that she could relax and enjoy the island. "I didn't come here to—" she began, then broke off. "I just wanted to see you again. You were always so good to me. I couldn't not come to see you."

"I'm glad you did," Eileen said. "Don't mind me, I just wanted you to know where I stood. It's all behind us now." She squeezed Samantha's hands before releasing them. There were traces of clay under her blunt-cut nails, Samantha noticed—a detail of Eileen's appearance that was at once familiar and endearing.

"So now you are working at the spa," she said in a

brisker tone that seemed designed to dispel old memories. "How did that come about?"

Samantha was glad for the change of subject. "A friend told me Dr. Birmann was in San Diego looking for someone to work up here for six months," she explained. "I'd always wanted to come back to the island, so I couldn't resist trying for the job. I drove down to San Diego to see him. He seemed to feel I had the necessary qualifications, so here I am."

Eileen raised her eyebrows dramatically. "What do you think of our handsome doctor?"

"He seems very nice. He's certainly charming."

"That he is."

Her voice was warm, and Samantha darted a surprised glance at her. "We're just good friends," Eileen said hastily. "Actually, I have a...a friend in Seattle who is...." She stopped, laughing. "My friend owns an art gallery, isn't that convenient? He arranged an outdoor show here on the island last summer. Jakob saw some of my stuff and liked it and commissioned a whole slew of watercolors for the spa. Kept me busy for months."

"I think one of them is in my bungalow," Samantha exclaimed. "I didn't think of checking the artist's name, but I admired it as soon as I saw it. It's an abstract pattern of light and shade that seems to flicker and move as you gaze at it."

Eileen nodded, looking smug. "I was going through a Jackson Pollock phase." She smiled. "I do like Jakob a lot. I always did have a weakness for the distinguished European type, and Jakob has such terrifically continental manners. Totally chauvinistic, though... keeps that little girl of his right under his thumb. Poor thing—

she doesn't have a mother, you know. Her mother died when she was born.''

"You're still adopting strays?" Samantha asked affectionately as she took a sip from her coffee.

Eileen gestured at the sleeping cats and the dog at her feet. "Look about you." Her mouth twisted in a wry smile. "I haven't adopted Anne Marie, however, sweet as she is. Jon did the adopting this time.

Samantha looked at her blankly.

"He's very fond of her," Eileen said. "I wouldn't be surprised if he decided to marry her. She is awfully young, of course, but—"

"Has Jon said he wants to marry her?" Samantha asked. She tried to make her voice sound casual, but even to her own ears it sounded strained.

Eileen shot a sharp glance at her but didn't comment. "He won't say one way or the other," she said with a short laugh. "But he does spend a lot of time at the spa when he's home. He and Jakob play cribbage. I'm not sure Jakob is the main attraction, however. Though he and Jon are great friends. They both have an obsession with sea water.''

She leaned her elbows on the table, cupping her chin in her hands, her face pensive. "I never know *what* Jon's plans are," she complained. Then she laughed again. "There I go, rattling all over creation. I never can stick to a subject. We were talking about the spa, weren't we?"

Samantha nodded. "What does everybody think of the spa, anyway?" she asked, obscurely relieved not to be talking of Jon.

Eileen grinned. "We were all up in arms when we first heard about it—you know how islanders are. We were afraid the jet set would try to take us over. But Jakob's clients turned out to be people who value privacy as much as we do, and he didn't mess up the environment or chop down all the trees, so everyone's accepted him. Actually, several islanders work at the spa. He's kept some of our young people from leaving to find work elsewhere, and we're grateful to him for that. He's affected our economy, too—you won't know Carter's store, it's grown so tremendously. Anyway—'' she paused for breath ''—what were you doing before you heard about Jakob?''

Samantha sighed. ''I was working for my father, of course.''

''Dwight still has the advertising agency?'' Eileen chuckled. ''Of course he does—silly question! I remember the way he used to lecture me about turning my talents into profits. Such a dear, dear man, but he could never quite realize that some of us march to the sound of a different drummer. Why did you leave him then? I can't imagine that you two didn't get along.''

''We got along all right, but I didn't enjoy the work as much as I'd always expected to. The hustle and bustle I admired so much turned out to be a lot of sound and fury, signifying nothing. That's the main reason I haven't written any short stories. Writing for the agency dried up my creative juices. I even found myself thinking in slogans. In any case, I felt I needed to get away for a while, to try being Samantha on my own between being my father's daughter and Adrian's wife.''

''Always a good idea,'' Eileen said. ''What does Dwight think about you coming back to the island?''

''He wasn't too keen on it, but he saw that my mind was made up. He's so delighted at my engagement to

Adrian that he doesn't want to argue with me about anything.''

"Afraid you'll change your mind?''

"I suppose so.''

"And will you?''

"No.'' There was more emphasis in her voice than was called for, but Eileen seemed to accept the statement at face value.

"None of us are ever free of the desire to please our parents,'' she said vaguely. She hesitated, sighing. "Though I can't say Jon subscribes to that opinion. I can count on the fingers of one hand the number of months he's been home during the last several years. He won't be content until he's explored every ocean on the planet—and then he'll probably take off to Venus or somewhere to see what's up there. There must have been a mermaid among my ancestors, because Jon is definitely part fish and very much a loner. But still I keep hoping he'll get married and settle down.''

"He looked to me as though he was still wedded to a camera,'' Samantha said neutrally.

"That he is. Some babies are born with a caul, but Jon came into life with a camera around his neck. At least that's the first thing he reached for. He coveted his father's Pentax from the moment he could say, 'I want.' '' She stood up abruptly, causing the dog to open one eye and groan in displeasure. Eileen poked him with her toe and said, "Go back to sleep, Tonto,'' and he settled down again, sighing noisily. Eileen gave her gruff laugh. "Come and see Jon's collection,'' she invited. "He has a lot of cameras now.''

Samantha followed her out of the kitchen without

protest, pleased to have a chance to look at the rest of the house. She'd always admired it.

And still did, she thought, looking around when they reached the huge drawing room. The Collins place was still the most elegant she'd ever seen, far more so than any that belonged to her father's clients and friends. This house had not been decorated by a hired designer. Ethan Collins had furnished it with love, slowly and carefully over a number of years, with an eye to comfort as well as appearance.

Squashy-soft sofas and chairs were drawn into a conversation area around a silky Persian rug in muted shades of rose and blue, centering on an empty fireplace with a finely carved English pine mantel. Distinctive end tables with cabriole legs held lamps with drum-shaped silk shades. On the long coffee table an antique chess set stood ready for play. The effect was of comfortable opulence, heightened by the elaborately framed Impressionist paintings that hung on the paneled walls. At the long windows, lovely loose-weaved curtains, as insubstantial as rice paper, diffused the sunlight and formed an airy backdrop to a lush collection of leafy green plants.

Eileen allowed her a few seconds to gaze around, then led her into the small room that used to be Ethan's den. Here the old man used to retire after his meager dinner, to smoke his pipe and drink exactly one jigger of brandy while he read one of the leather-bound volumes of world history that lined the floor-to-ceiling shelves of the adjacent library.

It was obvious that Jon had taken this room for his own. Oceanic maps and charts covered the walls, and the books piled on the magnificent leather-topped desk were all of a scientific nature. A huge blowup of an underwater photograph stood on an easel in one corner, the colors so accurate, the fish and aquatic plants so stunningly clear that Samantha could almost have believed she was looking down at the scene through the goggles Jon had loaned her that last summer.

On one wall she noticed a small picture she'd given Jon when he was twenty-one—a Japanese woodcut of a boy on a dolphin. She could remember vividly the delighted expression on his face when he unwrapped it, the exuberant hug he'd given her. A hug that had earned him a tart, "Don't get icky, Jon."

Swallowing against a sudden lump in her throat, she turned away.

In the opposite corner of the room was a huge glass-topped case that contained twenty or more cameras, ranging from the original Pentax Eileen had mentioned to an old Brownie box that had belonged to Jon's grandfather. A Hasselblad and an Olympus were among several others Samantha didn't recognize, including what must be the latest in underwater camera gear. Some of the cameras were large and cumbersome, but others were pocket-size. One in particular looked about the size of a cigarette lighter.

"He has acquired a lot," Samantha murmured.

Eileen smiled as she stroked the patina of the veneered cabinet. "Isn't this a lovely piece? Remember the orange crate Jon used to keep his camera and lenses in?"

Samantha nodded, suddenly remembering Jon saying, "I guess you could say I've come up in the world."

"I was really surprised when Jon told me Ethan had left him everything," she said carefully.

Eileen laughed. "You should have heard the gossip on the island! It stunned everyone—Eileen Blake's boy inheriting a small fortune." She hesitated. "It wasn't a huge amount by some standards, I guess, but it sure made a difference to us. It took the islanders a long time to get over it." She smiled reminiscently. "Jon really loved that old man. I guess Ethan substituted for his father in many ways. He looks on this house as a trust. Sometimes he comes in here in the evenings and drinks a tot of brandy, just as Ethan did—a sort of toast to the old man, I suppose. Then he sits and looks at those maps of his with that dreamy look in his eyes, and I know before long he'll be off again." She smiled. "I guess Ethan must have infected him with the lust for travel. My Richard would have stayed on this island forever if the Vietnam War hadn't come along—"

She broke off. "Both Jon and I would have been a lot happier if Ethan had enjoyed the final years of his life more. Such an eccentric old man, wasn't he? That's what comes of living too much alone, I guess. . . Jon says I should let it be a warning to me." She sighed. "I used to get so cross when Jon wouldn't charge Ethan anything for the chores he used to do—God knows we could have used the money. But Jon was adamant. Ethan was his friend, and you don't charge friends for things you do for them. My own fault. . . I always taught him to fend for himself. He almost killed himself working so hard to pay back the loan Ethan had given him for his education. It took him a long time. Such an irony when you think that—"

"It was a loan?" Samantha interrupted, hearing her own voice from the past accusing, *You didn't mind taking charity from Ethan Collins.*

"Of course," Eileen said. "My Jon would never have accepted an out-and-out gift and Ethan knew it. They understood each other, those two. No, Jon paid him back. He was clear with Ethan before the old man died."

She shook her head and led a speechless Samantha back to the hall. As they ascended the graceful staircase and made a tour of the bedrooms, which were as splendidly furnished as the rooms downstairs, she chatted on about some of Ethan's more eccentric ways. "None of the islanders could understand why he wanted all this around him, living alone the way he did. Jon says it was in place of the wife and children he never had. I'm just glad he had Jon to comfort him in his old age."

She laughed. "Jon was horrified when the lawyers told him he was Ethan's sole beneficiary. But there weren't any relatives, so he had to accept the bequest."

Samantha swallowed. How little she had understood Jon, she thought. She'd really half believed, along with most of the islanders, that Jon's devotion to Ethan had been at least partially prompted by his need for money. No one had known that he refused payment for the many chores he'd done for Ethan or that the education fund had been a loan. . . .

She'd obviously vastly underrated Jon's pride, was still not sure she understood it. How could she—she who had never wanted for anything? *Spoiled little rich girl.*

The epithet still hurt, even if it was true, she admitted to herself when she'd left Eileen and had started hiking back across the cliffs toward the spa. Visiting the Collins house had been a journey through a time tunnel into the past, a past she had obviously not interpreted correctly. The journey had been hurtful. As soon as Eileen mentioned Jon's financial difficulties, the pain had seemed as fresh and acute as it had seven years before.

But how could she have known the extent of Jon's pride, she protested inwardly, pausing to catch her breath before descending into the woods. Why hadn't he told her how strongly he felt about making it on his own?

He *had*, she realized ruefully. He had made it very plain. And she, in her youthful, comfortable ignorance, had not understood, had thought he was crazy to turn down her father's offer of money.

Yet what was he doing now? Eileen hadn't mentioned his current occupation, other than to remark that she wished he'd settle down and stop traveling so much, Samantha shook her head and started walking again. Jon's occupation, or lack of it, was no concern of hers. Not anymore.

Jon and Anne Marie, what an unlikely combination that was. But not so unlikely when she thought about it. Jon had become a fairly masterful man. No doubt the ingenuous type of girl appealed to him; she had been that type herself once.

Impatient for letting her mind dwell on Jon, Samantha quickened her pace along the trail. She had handled herself quite well, she thought. Somehow she had managed to refuse Eileen's invitation to dinner without revealing that she wanted to avoid Jon as much as possible. Why had it been so painful to see him again? She had really believed those old wounds were covered with scar tissue. Obviously they were still unhealed—though of course she didn't love him anymore. She was engaged to Adrian. She couldn't love any other man when she was engaged to Adrian.

Later, in her chalet bedroom, she pulled Adrian's framed photograph from her suitcase and set it in a prominent position on the dressing table where she would see it last thing at night and first thing in the morning. Then she sat down and wrote him a long affectionate letter. When she went to bed she counted slowly backward from 1000, reaching minus 250 before her old method of combating painful thought finally worked.

CHAPTER FOUR

AT NINE O'CLOCK the next morning, after breakfasting on Musli, a delicious but not too satisfying mixture of oatmeal, dried fruit and nuts, Samantha opened her chalet door. She'd expected to see Anne Marie, but it wasn't Dr. Birmann's daughter who had knocked so imperiously. Jonathan Blake stood on the porch, looking so big and powerful, so unexpectedly *there*, that for a second her knees failed her and she had to grip the doorjamb to keep herself erect.

"Good morning, Samantha," he said calmly. He was dressed in white chinos and a navy blue knit shirt that hugged the contours of his upper body like a second skin. His face was in shadow, so she couldn't read his expression, but his streaked blond hair gleamed with a life of its own.

"What are *you* doing here?" she managed at last.

"I've been pressed into service. Anne Marie is unwell this morning—nothing serious, a mild indisposition. I was having breakfast with Jakob when she sent word that she wouldn't be able to escort you on your tour of the spa."

"But surely one of the others...."

"Jakob thought you'd prefer me to show you around, since we're such old friends." Was there a note of sarcasm in his voice? "Jakob is a kind man," he added in a chiding way. "His suggestion was meant to be generous." He looked at her curiously, his blond eyebrows raised. "Evidently he felt he'd been rude to you yesterday."

"He wasn't rude exactly—he had some business to attend to, I guess." She paused. "What's wrong with Anne Marie?"

Jon shrugged. "I didn't ask. Jakob was a little terse about it. I think he was annoyed with her."

"He's a bit of an autocrat, isn't he?"

He raised his eyebrows. "What makes you say that?"

"I don't really know. It was just an impression I had. Anne Marie seems a bit—I don't know—timid, I guess."

"She's a little shy, yes. That hardly makes Jakob a tyrant."

"I didn't say he was a tyrant," Samantha objected.

"No? Forgive me, I thought perhaps you were preparing to take up arms on Anne Marie's behalf. As I recall, you did once have the habit of deciding how people's lives should be lived."

The unfairness of this remark struck Samantha speechless. Before she could recover he shrugged apologetically. "I'm sorry, that was rude of me. Are you ready to go?"

She hesitated. Evidently Jon had remembered his promise to act in a civilized manner. She must do the same. During the long hours of the previous evening, she had forced herself to face facts. It was not her happy memories of the island that had brought her back. It was Jon she had to exorcise from her mind and heart, before she could be a whole woman, free to love Adrian as he deserved. And the only way she could perform that exorcism was to act like an adult.

"I don't want to be a nuisance to you, Jon," she said crisply. "If you'd rather not escort me, I can probably find my way around alone."

"I don't mind at all," he said promptly. "I have nothing else to do today."

She frowned at that but felt it wise not to comment. "Well, then...."

He glanced at her as she still hesitated. "Perhaps it would save you embarrassment if we pretend we were only casual acquaintances," he suggested.

She felt heat rise to her face at the dryly humorous quality in his tone, but she managed to reply evenly, "I suppose that would be best." *Oh, Jon,* she thought. *We meant so much to each other once. How can you be so distant?*

"Shall we go then?" he asked, glancing pointedly at her hand, which was still gripping the doorjamb.

"Yes, of course." Somehow she managed to get herself onto the porch and close the door behind her. The tour was going to be very awkward, she thought. There ought to have been some way to avoid spending the next couple of hours alone with a man who so obviously disliked her.

But to her surprise, he chatted easily as they descended the long flight of steps, talking about the weather, which was fairly warm, and even complimenting her on the way she looked in the spa uniform, a chocolate brown blazer with creamy linen pants and a cotton shirt. Perhaps she might manage, after all, to get by without giving her feelings away, she thought—then caught herself up. Giving away *what* feelings?

Halfway across one of the lawns, as they approached the spa's main building, Samantha saw the thin man again. She was unable to stop herself from coming to a halt and frankly staring. The man was still wearing his heavy sweater and white cap. He was working in the rockery, moving a hoe around in a desultory manner, stopping even as she caught sight of him to light a cigarette and gaze off toward the hazy horizon. His mirrored sunglasses reflected the light, concealing his expression, and in spite of the warm sunshine, Samantha felt a coldness at the back of her neck, an almost primitive reaction to the strangeness of the man. He looked out of place with a hoe in his hand, she thought. He was no more a gardener than she was.

She became aware that Jon was looking at her sharply. "Do you know that man?" she asked.

"No. Should I?"

She shook her head. "I suppose he's someone the doctor hired to work on the grounds," she said lamely.

Jon's eyebrows rose. "That *might* explain why he's holding a hoe."

She felt herself flush at the note of amusement in his voice. "There's something about him—" she began, then broke off, suddenly impatient with herself and her weird fancies.

"Don't tell me you still write mystery stories," Jon said, sounding mildly exasperated.

"Not for years, no."

"Wise of you. That sort of activity can make you unnaturally suspicious of people."

Before she could come up with a retort, his hand touched her elbow, impelling her toward the spa, and she had to concentrate all her willpower on appearing unmoved. Yet surely his touch didn't still have the power to affect her? Surely she was just experiencing the unease she'd felt because of the thin man?

She drew in her breath slowly and deeply, determined to act in as casual a manner as Jon. She was not a child any longer, she told herself firmly as they entered the spa. The days of treasuring every loving glance, every brief brush of his fingers were over. In any case, she needed to concentrate all her attention on this tour of the spa. She had a great deal to learn.

She was as impressed by the spa's interior as she had been by its exterior. Last night and again this morning she had eaten her meals in her chalet—something the printed schedule had told her was possible—feeling she'd prefer to wait for her guided tour rather than enter the building alone. Now she looked around earnestly, eager to absorb everything she saw so that she could successfully guide future guests.

The spa turned out to be almost a duplicate of the one in San Diego. Long gleaming corridors led to a wonderland of exotic indoor gardens, shining tiled pools, saunas, beauty salons and exercise and meditation rooms. Much use had been made of natural vegetation, so that every room had a woodsy look to it.

They started on the third floor, where Jon walked in front of Samantha, opening doors, explaining the function of each room, introducing her to the staff members. To her relief, he didn't touch her again.

Most of the attendants were dressed like Samantha, though some wore beige warm-up suits or white shirts and shorts. Several of them addressed Jon as Dr. Blake. So Jon *had* acquired his PhD; she'd wondered about that. All of the attendants were extraordinarily attractive, healthy young people with outgoing, friendly personalities.

"It is necessary for our staff to be good-looking," Jakob had explained at their initial interview. "We must present a good advertisement for the benefits of my treatments, must we not?" Briskly he had added, "This is one of the reasons I am choosing you for this position, Samantha—you are a very beautiful young woman. Not conventionally so perhaps but you possess what I call the plus factor...a special something that makes you stand out from the crowd."

Samantha hadn't been sure how to respond to the compliment. She certainly didn't think of herself as beautiful. The skinny, pert little carrot-haired girl she had been still haunted her memory.

Jon had told her she was beautiful that last wonderful summer, she remembered suddenly, and dismissed the thought at once.

"Nobody seems surprised that you're acting as my instructor," she remarked as they left one of the exercise rooms and approached a wide curving staircase.

"I've helped out a couple of times since Monique left," he said easily. "Anne Marie's yoga classes conflicted with an influx of new guests, and I happened to be in the vicinity. I rather enjoyed introducing the ladies to their new environment. You've done me out of an enjoyable job."

He was managing to perform very well as a mere acquaintance, she thought. How could it be so easy for him when it was so difficult for her? Because he had never really cared about her?

"You surely must have something else to do," she retorted.

He smiled in a rather secretive manner. "Not at the moment. I'm...er, resting as they say in the theatrical world."

She felt a twinge of impatience. More and more it seemed that her father had been right about Jon's lack of ambition. "Resting" was a euphemism for unemployment.

On the second floor, a woman was lying in a bathtub full of green sea mud, another reclining on a bed in a room bathed in infrared light. It's warmth had a soothing effect, Jon informed her. Three young girls who looked like models were sitting in the lotus position on the padded floor of an exercise room, their eyes closed. Farther along the hall, two older but still beautiful women were being tended in a beauty salon, their hair coated with claylike brown substance that Jon told her was an organically based conditioner.

"You're very knowledgeable about the doctor's products," Samantha commented as they started downstairs again.

"Jakob and I have had many long talks."

"You admire him, don't you?"

"Sure I do. He's no quack, Samantha."

"I didn't think he was," she said indignantly. "I was just surprised you know so much about his methods."

"I had him give me a full explanation right at the start." He smiled briefly. "I headed the delegation of islanders who were fighting to prevent the building of the spa. But Jakob was able to convince me that none of his plans would affect the ecology of the island. He'd gone far beyond what was necessary to meet the requirements of the Environmental Protection Agency. I was impressed by his sincerity. We all were."

"When was this?" she asked.

"About two years ago. Jakob had just acquired the land and was starting to build."

"You were home then?"

"For a short time. I was preparing to go to Japan."

So he'd spent a year in Japan. Doing what? Vacationing? Was there no reason for him to work any longer? Why should he if he didn't have to? And what did it matter, anyway.

But she knew it did matter, and the thought was enough to destroy any possibility of ease in his company. "We'd better go on," she said. His eyebrows rose as he registered her cool tone, but he made no comment, merely gestured her ahead of him to a separate single-story wing.

The air here was steamy and tropical due to the heated saltwater tubs. Jon explained to her that sea-water contained gases that alleviated headaches and other stress-related ailments. The doctor had even developed a line of shampoos, soaps and lotions that contained sea algae. Sea algae, Jon commented, contained iodine and Vitamins A and D, which were very beneficial to the skin.

They didn't enter any of the hot-tub rooms, for they all seemed to be occupied. "We mustn't disturb the guests' privacy," Jon said. He glanced at her sideways. "You have to be naked to enjoy the benefits of the tubs," he explained blandly. "Underwater jets massage very energetically, and if you wore a swimsuit the water would splash against the fabric into your eyes."

She could feel heat rising into her face. Could he possibly have forgotten that they had often swum together in the nude that last summer, splashing around in the lake or in the frigid water of the Sound, laughing like children at the thought of how horrified any of the islanders would be if they happened to see them? Could he not hear the echo of that summer's laughter here in this long shining hall?

She stole a glance at his face. He was looking down at her politely, his face utterly devoid of expression. No, he didn't remember.

Samantha strode ahead of him to the wing's exit. "I think I need to sit down for a while and try to absorb all this," she said briskly. "The saltwater may be beneficial for headaches, but my brain is swimming with all the information you've given me. I *am* grateful, though." Deliberately she put a dismissive note in her voice, hoping he'd take the hint and leave.

But he merely nodded. "There is one more room you should see," he said. He gestured ahead. "Then perhaps you'd like a cup of tea?"

She couldn't understand why he was prolonging this. Surely he ought to feel as awkward in her company as she did in his. Surely no one could feel as relaxed as he seemed to be in the presence of an ex-lover. Was he trying to prove that he was a sophisticated man of the world now. . .that their youthful romance had no power to affect him? Eileen had said he'd been devastated. But Eileen was an admittedly doting mother. Any apparent devastation must have been the result of his deservedly guilty conscience. He *had* treated her badly, though he had seemed to think *she* was the guilty one.

Perhaps she was not entirely blameless, she admitted to herself. But if he chose to ignore every echo of the past, there was no reason why she couldn't rewrite it in her own mind.

"Samantha?"

She looked up at him. "All right," she said, not caring if she sounded ungracious.

She preceded him along the hall and into the large dimly lit room he'd indicated. It seemed to be full of shelves holding piles of linens. "I don't really think I need to do a tour of the supply room," she said tartly, but he ignored her. He had closed the door behind them and was leaning against it, looking at her, a speculative expression on his tanned face. His arms were folded, his body tense. Under the dim light his hair seemed to glow.

"Forgive me, Samantha," he said softly. "There's something I have to do."

She should leave. Now. Immediately.

She approached the door. "Didn't you say something about tea?" she asked in a voice she'd intended to be light, but which sounded thick instead. He straightened, smiling in a cynical way that puzzled her. There was a hard look about his eyes.

She reached past him for the doorknob, intent on getting out of the room. Her heart was beating rapidly, and she had the suffocating feeling that if she didn't get out right away she wasn't going to be able to take another breath. As she turned the doorknob, he reached for her, pulling her into his arms. His mouth came down on hers. "No," she said at once.

She tried to struggle free, but he was strong and she was no match for him. Her efforts didn't seem to register, and he didn't for a second lessen the pressure of his lips against hers. The hard light in his eyes had given way to a seductive gleam, and his hands had begun to explore her body, stroking her gently, easing her close to him. Samantha realized quite suddenly that she had stopped fighting him, that she didn't *want* to be free. She wanted to stay right there in his arms.

His mouth was playful on hers now, touching and

withdrawing, his lips firm, then pliant. And her own mouth was responding as she remembered the teasing game they had played together before, her lips following his, opening to his tongue, her own tongue darting to find the tender corner of his mouth.

It was all so familiar, so wonderfully familiar.

Still holding her, he freed her mouth and laid his cheek against hers. "The chemistry still works, doesn't it, Sam?" he murmured against her hair.

Chemistry? She eased herself away from him, looked at him uncertainly.

His fingers reached to play with the soft tendrils of hair at the side of her face. "I suppose I should apologize," he said. "I was just...curious, I guess. I wondered how you felt about me now."

Samantha pulled herself free of his caressing hand, abruptly sickened. "This was some kind of experiment?"

"In a way." He sounded bemused. A small smile was playing around the corners of his mouth.

"I hate to tell you this, Jon," she said hotly, "but your experiment was a failure."

One blond eyebrow rose in a surprised arch that infuriated her. "Was it really? I could have sworn that you—"

"You thought wrong," she interrupted. "I will admit that I couldn't seem to help responding a little, but that was probably because of old affection, which you obviously no longer deserve."

He looked at her with objective interest. "You feel more response to—what's his name, Adrian—than you do to me?"

That peculiar smile was still in place. For a split sec-

ond she considered slapping his face, just to wipe the
smile away. But dignity forbade such an adolescent action.

"Much more," she said. Which wasn't at all true.
Adrian had never managed to call forth the raging fire
that Jon was able to elicit so easily. He'd aroused her,
yes, but some part of her had always held back, resisting
total surrender. She was not going to let Jon know that.
"I love Adrian," she said firmly. "I'm going to marry
him. Whatever was between you and me is gone. As far
as I'm concerned, there is no...*chemistry*, as you call
it."

He looked at her with narrowed eyes, showing clearly
that he didn't believe her. How conceited he'd become,
she thought. He seemed to have developed a confidence
in his powers of attraction that had destroyed his sensi-
tivity to other people.

What did he expect of her? Did he really think she'd
admit to being...affected by him when he'd confessed
he was merely playing with her? *Experimenting?*

"I still feel a certain amount of affection for you, of
course," she said carelessly. "We were very close as
children—we have that whole shared past." She managed a smile. "But I'm afraid my heart belongs to another."

She had the dubious satisfaction of seeing him wince.
Hardly surprising that he would—she'd sounded like a
dime novel.

"Then why did you come back?" he asked mockingly.

"For reasons of my own."

"You're refusing to answer?"

"I am."

"I'll find out, Samantha."

"Is that a threat?"

Again she didn't like the smile he gave her, nor did she like the return of the hard light in his eyes. "Shall we say I'm serving due warning?"

"Of what?"

He laughed shortly. "You never could stand not knowing what was going on in anyone's mind, could you? I must remember that."

She couldn't bear the cynicism in his voice. "I wish we could be friends again, Jon," she said impulsively. "Is it really impossible? Can't we go back to the way we were?"

"When we were children?"

"Yes."

"We aren't children now, Samantha." He hesitated, then shrugged. "I suppose we can try to be friends, if that's what you want."

She frowned, looking at his expressionless face. Somehow she didn't quite trust.... She shook her head impatiently. He was right; she was inclined to be too suspicious of people sometimes. "That's what I want," she said lightly.

His mouth twitched into some semblance of a smile, but he didn't say any more.

She let out her breath. Suddenly she felt wrung out, exhausted from the tumult of emotions that had passed between them. "I believe you suggested tea, didn't you?" she said, trying to lighten the atmosphere.

"So I did." There was still an odd gleam in his blue eyes, but she didn't have the strength to wonder what it might signify. In any case, she knew she had nothing more to fear from him at the moment. Whatever mood had caused him to...attack her like that was now gone.

"Let's just forget the whole unpleasant incident, shall we?" he suggested. "Put it down to a moment of mental aberration on my part."

"Mental ab...." Samantha swallowed the rest of the phrase. She wasn't going to let him provoke her into saying anything she'd regret later.

With all the composure she could muster, she preceded him out of the room, wondering in heaven's name why she felt so disappointed in him.

Outside in the hall, reaction set in, and she started to tremble. She hoped devoutly that Jon wouldn't notice. What on earth had possessed him? He knew she was engaged to someone else.

She chose to disregard the fact that she'd given no thought to Adrian herself until Jon brought him up. Instead she concentrated on getting her wayward physical emotions under control. They *were* only physical, of that she felt sure.

A few minutes later they were seated on a wooden bench in the shade of a tree, drinking steaming liquid from dainty cups. "This is verbena," Jon said. "Hippocrates said it was a cure-all for nervous disorders."

He *had* noticed her trembling. She didn't feel it wise to answer him, so she just nodded curtly and kept her gaze fixed on the terraced gardens. She thought of demanding to know why he'd even *wanted* to experiment with her feelings, but decided instantly that the incident was best forgotten. He certainly seemed to have forgotten it.

But how could he look so *normal*, as though nothing had happened between them? His hair wasn't even disordered. It obviously didn't bother him that they were forced to sit close together because of the curve of the bench—so close that his arm occasionally brushed hers. Not that his nearness bothered her, either. She was in control of herself now and would remain so.

After a moment of silence she managed to remark casually that the tea wasn't as bad as she'd expected. "Though I'm glad Dr. Birmann doesn't extend his enthusiasm for sea algae this far," she added in a voice that was calm enough to satisfy her.

Jon grinned. "Don't be so sure. Some of the guests drink a concoction of powdered kelp dissolved in vegetable juice. Kelp supposedly stimulates the thyroid gland and helps accelerate the loss of excess weight." His glance appraised her casually, almost indifferently. "I doubt you'll need to go to those lengths. You look as though you are in excellent shape."

She glanced at him sharply, but his face held no trace of sarcasm—or anything else. The mask he'd assumed yesterday had descended again.

Why, she thought again. Why had he kissed her? To prove that he still had power over her? Or was his ego not as overweening as she'd thought? Was it in fact so inadequate that he needed reassurance of his attractiveness?

She was saved from having to say anything by the sudden appearance of Anne Marie. The girl was dressed for work in her spa uniform, a duplicate of Samantha's. "There you are," she said in an aggrieved tone, as though they were the ones who had been missing.

"Are you okay?" Samantha asked.

Anne Marie's gray eyes lowered for a moment, then raised to meet Samantha's gaze rather defiantly. "I'm fine now. I had a little. . . hay fever."

That would explain the pink rims around her eyes, Samantha thought, and also the swollen look to her eyelids. But all the same, she could have sworn the girl had been crying. She herself suffered from the same far-from-beautiful results when she cried. Only movie stars, she had decided long ago, could emerge from a crying bout looking starry-eyed and adorable.

Jon had risen to his feet as soon as Anne Marie appeared. He touched her lightly on the shoulder and said, "You're sure you're all right?" There was a fond, almost paternal note in his voice that touched off an irritated response in Samantha. This girl was not a child. He was treating her in the same patronizing manner her father did.

Anne Marie smiled at him, just as fondly.

Jon nodded. "I guess I'll be off then, as long as you're here to take charge of Samantha."

He didn't have to make her sound like a package, Samantha thought resentfully, but somehow she managed to keep her resentment out of her voice and was able to thank him quite coolly for his time and trouble.

Her efforts were wasted on him. He gave her a knowing smile that told her he thought he could see right through her as he always had. "I'll see you later, Samantha," he said easily. "We can discuss our unfinished business at another time."

"I thought it *was* finished," she said harshly.

"Oh, no," he said. "I fully intend to find out why you came back to the island. I have my own ideas, you see."

"And they are?"

"None of your business, my dear."

Without waiting to see her reaction to this, he patted

Anne Marie's shoulder gently, turned and strode away across the deck, apparently oblivious of the admiring glances that followed his tall muscular figure. A few of the spa guests had come out on deck while Samantha and Jon were greeting Anne Marie. As they watched Jon jump down to the lawn the women unconsciously sat up straighter, and one or two of them touched their hair self-consciously. Typical female preening, Samantha thought savagely...and then wondered at her own vehemence.

"What was all that about?" Anne Marie asked wonderingly.

Samantha felt a wave of embarrassment wash over her. They had both spoken as though Anne Marie wasn't even there. What must she be thinking? "Just a silly argument," she said. "Nothing important."

Anne Marie seemed satisfied with the evasive answer. "What do you think of the spa?" she asked, and Samantha relaxed, glad of the distraction and tremendously relieved that Anne Marie had replaced Jon as her guide. She wasn't even going to worry about Jon's motivations, or the meaning of his last remarks, she decided. And she certainly wasn't going to concern herself about the mixture of emotions he had aroused in her in the course of one morning. As for the storeroom incident—as she had told him, she had merely been affected by nostalgia.

"It's wonderful," she said. "I've read about spas, of course, but I had no idea they were so fascinating. Your father's methods are very interesting."

"Aren't they? You'll see a big difference in guests after they've been here a short while. By the time they leave they look and feel fantastic. And daddy gives them lots of information so they can continue to take good care of themselves at home. You must try some of the treatments yourself. Although you certainly don't need them. But they are enjoyable—and fun.''

"Do you use the treatments?" Samantha asked.

"Oh, yes, especially the hot tubs—they really are relaxing." She looked wistful. "I don't get to try out the cosmetic and hairstyling techniques, though. My father believes a young girl should take advantage of her natural looks. There is time later, he says, to look more sophisticated.''

"I take it you don't agree with him."

The girl hesitated. "I can't imagine that I *could* look sophisticated, but I would like to try." She sighed. "I don't think daddy will ever admit I'm a woman. He still sees me as an adolescent.''

Samantha laughed shortly. "I have a father like that myself." Anne Marie looked interested, but she didn't want to talk about Dwight, not right now. Instead she leaned back against the trunk of the madrona tree and gazed out at the sparkling water of the Sound. A small sailboat was speeding across the mouth of the bay, tacking to take advantage of the breeze. The usual morning haze hid the mainland from view, making the island seem more isolated than it really was. Sipping her peculiarly flavored tea and trying not to grimace, Samantha found herself scanning the water for bubbles, reverting to old habits.

Setting her cup down, she switched her mind deliberately to another course. She had been right, obviously, about Anne Marie's father, no matter what Jon said. Dr. Birmann *was* a domineering man. She remembered how satisfied he'd sounded when he described Anne

Marie as an old-fashioned girl. The European influence, she supposed. Poor Anne Marie! But Dr. Birmann was a nice man. He was probably every bit as affectionate as her own father.

All the same, he had acted rather oddly yesterday when she first arrived. There was perhaps something below the surface of Jakob Birmann that was not as civilized as his distinguished-looking exterior indicated.

"We should go in to see my father now," Anne Marie said, as though she'd read Samantha's mind.

Samantha nodded at once and followed the girl into the spa again. Jakob Birmann's suite of rooms was next to the dietitian's office. Jon had pointed them out without taking her there. The doctor wasn't expecting her until about eleven, he'd said. She glanced at her wristwatch—it was right on eleven now.

There was an outer reception room, comfortably furnished with more Sandinavian armchairs and some of Eileen's bright paintings, and a fair-sized inner office that, according to Anne Marie, she would share with Deborah, the bookkeeper.

Deborah turned out to be a twenty-year-old blond bombshell with ravishing green eyes. She gave Samantha a friendly smile and a firm handshake. "I saw you earlier with Jon," she said, smiling. "Jon" seemed to indicate a certain familiarity, Samantha thought. Jon must hang around here quite a lot. And there was something about the woman's smile that told Samantha she was picturing Jon in her mind as she spoke. It was hardly surprising that she'd find him attractive. Most women would.

"A gorgeous man, isn't he?" Deborah continued. "He has such loads of—" she rolled her eyes "—*charisma.*"

"I guess you could say that," Samantha murmured dryly.

"We don't see as much of him as we would like to," Anne Marie said wistfully. "He's forever taking off to the four corners of the Earth."

"Doing what?" Samantha asked.

Anne Marie shrugged. "Well, he's very interested in photography," she said vaguely. "But I don't really understand what he does. He's sort of secretive about it."

"He takes pictures of the oceans," Deborah said. She grinned at Samantha. "I hope you'll enjoy working here. Monique is superefficient, so you should be able to find everything. If not, holler for me. I'm usually back there." She gestured at a desk at the end of the long room, almost invisible under piles of papers and a tabletop computer, then started toward it, muttering something about bringing her filing up to date.

Anne Marie looked at Samantha thoughtfully. "Jon told me you and he knew each other before."

"Yes. I used to spend summers here as a child."

"He must have been a very handsome little boy."

"He wasn't exactly a *little* boy when I met him. He was thirteen when I first came here."

She'd dogged his every footstep that first summer, setting a pattern for succeeding summers—hero-worshiping him, delighted that he didn't seem to mind her companionship even when he had one of the other, older girls in tow.

She became aware that Anne Marie was gazing at her expectantly, evidently waiting for her to say more about Jon. "You like him a lot, don't you?" Samantha blurted out.

Anne Marie nodded and blushed, then darted a quick furtive glance at Samantha's face. "Do you mind?" she asked.

Samantha swallowed. "Why should I?" she asked weakly.

Anne Marie looked down at her hands, which were clasped together in front of her. "He told me you were...more than friends."

Samantha felt a rush of indignation. Jon had had no right to talk about her to the girl. A second later she sighed inwardly. What did it matter? "It was a long time ago," she said gently, trying to cover up the fact that the words had a tendency to stick in her throat.

Anne Marie looked relieved, then wistful again. "He's wonderful, isn't he? So brilliant, so confident—" She broke off and was silent for a moment. "I'd like to talk to you about him someday when we have more time."

"Sure," Samantha said, almost choking on the word.

Anne Marie nodded once, then glanced sideways at Samantha. "Why is Jon so cross about you coming back to the island?"

Samantha sighed. Evidently Anne Marie had not accepted her explanation after all. "I don't know," she said carefully. "We used to be good friends, but I guess he doesn't want to bother with me anymore."

Anne Marie looked puzzled. As well she might, Samantha thought. That was hardly a satisfying answer. But what could she say?

After a moment Anne Marie shrugged and smiled. "I hope you and I can be friends," she said.

"So do I," Samantha replied warmly, and meant it. She was feeling very drawn to this awkward young woman, though she must be careful not to encourage her to talk too openly about Jon. She wasn't quite sure she could take that, especially after what had just occurred.

"Your father is waiting for us," she reminded Anne Marie.

The girl flushed again. She really was very young and ingenuous, Samantha thought as she followed her into her father's office. She'd have a terrible time if she got mixed up with a complicated man like Jon.

The doctor's office was a large room, simply but attractively furnished in earth tones like all the rest, the sunlight's glare diminished by vertical narrow-slatted blinds.

Dr. Birmann greeted Samantha with a warm handshake and a charming smile, all traces of yesterday's stiffness banished from his manner. He'd replaced his suit jacket with a short white cotton coat, but looked no less well dressed and distinguished. "You have enjoyed your tour?" he asked.

Samantha nodded. "I'm impressed," she told him. "I can see that a couple of weeks here as a guest would be a marvelous experience."

He nodded approval. "I'm glad you feel this. It is necessary that you communicate enthusiasm to our guests—and I am pleased your enthusiasm will not be feigned."

He indicated a chair for Samantha in front of his desk, smoothed his already immaculate white jacket, then sat down and leaned toward her, his handsome face earnest. Without further small talk, he began to outline her duties, which he had summarized for her at their first interview.

She would work five days a week, with Fridays and Saturdays off. New guests often arrived on Sunday, he explained. Besides the usual secretarial duties, she was to greet all guests on arrival, help them to get settled in and then escort them to him for a thorough physical examination. After that she would guide them through the spa and introduce them to the various experts designated for their care and comfort.

"We have a slightly different approach here," Dr. Birmann said. "We wish to emphasize the benefits of relaxation and moderate exercise, rather than strenuous activity. Here we have no tennis courts or calisthenics. Our guests are not encouraged to jog. We begin with a brisk morning walk that is slightly uphill, to promote cardiovascular fitness, but our walks include time to stop at vantage points to admire the scenery, to look at the trees and shrubberies and birds. And, of course, we teach yoga and meditation."

"How do you determine the program for each individual?" Samantha asked.

He nodded approval at her interest. "If someone needs to lose weight, the emphasis will be on exercise and proper nutrition. If she has a skin problem, then more time will be scheduled with our beauticians. If she merely needs some freedom from stress, the emphasis shifts to meditation, yoga and *thalassotherapy*."

"Saltwater baths."

"With underwater massage, yes." He smiled at her. "You will find no television here—I hope that will not disappoint you?"

Samantha smiled. "I'm more of a reader than a TV viewer."

"Good." He stood up.

Hesitantly Samantha rose to her own feet. Was the interview over so soon?

"I'll have quite a bit of dictation for you," he said. "Anne Marie has been assisting me, but she hates typing. I'm sure she'll be happy to turn over her extra duties to you."

Smiling to take any sting out of his words, he glanced at his daughter, who had remained standing near the door. She smiled in return. Obviously she adored her father, in spite of her complaints about him.

The doctor returned his gaze to Samantha and for some reason hesitated before speaking again. "It is possible I may also ask your assistance with some publicity for the spa."

She hadn't expected this—had hoped that sort of work was behind her. She hadn't enjoyed it when she worked for her father and. . . .

"Nothing onerous," the doctor said hastily, evidently seeing the change in her expression. "I will explain later. Now Anne Marie will take you to lunch."

"I would like to speak to you first, daddy," the girl said. "I didn't have a chance yesterday, you were so busy with—" She broke off, started again. "I really want to know why you—"

The doctor raised his hand in a silent warning. "Very well," he said tersely. "I can give you a few minutes. Perhaps, Miss Austin, you will wait outside?"

"I'll wait in the reception room," Samantha said, making a hasty exit. The doctor's whole manner had changed the moment his daughter made her request. For a moment there he had looked. . .hunted. And his voice had revealed his impatience. He was not a man who liked to have his actions challenged. Was Anne Marie going to question him about the thin man, she wondered as she stood in the reception room, gazing idly through open French windows that overlooked the side grounds. It was none of her business, of course, but she definitely sensed a mystery. And her inquisitive mind wouldn't let her rest until she found out what that mystery was, she knew.

The grounds were as lovely here as they were at the front of the spa. Beyond a smooth expanse of lawn, which was interrupted only by two large circular rose beds, a narrow footpath wandered away among trees, wild-rose bushes and ferns, probably joining up with other pathways in the woods. The lawn was immaculate and weed free, the paths of a recent mowing evident in wide ruler-straight bands across its width. Ben Fletcher's work, she had no doubt—Jon used to say you could use a lawn Ben had mowed to demonstrate parallelism.

Even as she thought of Ben, she saw his short stocky figure limping across the grass toward her. He was dressed in green overalls, carrying a coiled loop of garden hose over one shoulder. He saw her at almost the same moment and stopped to stare, rubbing his free hand over his sparse gray hair. Then he quickened his step, his weathered features arranging themselves into the unique expression that on Ben's face was intended to be a smile.

Samantha had always loved Ben's face, which had always reminded her irresistibly of a bloodhound's. Ben had the same overhanging brows, the pouched sorrowful eyes, the drooping expressive lines that gave to his face and to the dog's a perpetually mournful cast. She had recognized even as a child the kindness and intelligence that shone from Ben's eyes, the lively good humor that sparked his speech and belied his lugubrious features.

"It *is* you, Samantha," he exclaimed as she stepped out of the room to join him. "I wasn't sure for a second there, though I didn't think two people could have hair that color." He took her outstretched hands in both of his and held them warmly, while his dark eyes studied her face. "It's good to see you. You've been gone away far too long."

"It's good to see you, too, Ben," she assured him. "How are you?"

"Touch of rheumatism now and then. I'm not getting any younger." He shrugged and changed the subject—he'd never been one to dwell on his ailments. "What did you think of my grandchildren? Sassy little brats, aren't they?" The pride in his tone told Samantha exactly how fond he was of them.

"They're lovely children, Ben."

He relented. "That they are. But wearing, I have to tell you." He averted his eyes. "Lynne doesn't get over to see them too often lately. It's a worry to me."

Samantha made a sound of sympathy and he shrugged, casting off his sudden depression. Glancing down at her hands, still clasped in both of his, he said, "I heard about your engagement from Eileen. Is he a good man?"

"He is."

"I'm glad to hear it." He gave her his familiar mirthless grin, lips folded inward. "That's some diamond ring you've got there. What you need is a box to keep it in."

With a sudden movement he released her hands,

reached into her blazer pocket and pulled out a matchbox that she'd never seen before. Bowing, he presented it to her with all of his old flourish.

Samantha laughed delightedly and hugged him, hose and all. "You always could fool me, Ben," she exclaimed. "Now I know for sure I'm back on the island."

He raised his heavy eyebrows at her, then his face dropped into its usual solemn lines. "It's hard to think of you engaged to some city feller. I always thought you and Jon would end up together, the pair of you on the island for always." He sighed. "I worry about that boy, haring around the world like a satellite rattling through space."

She seized the opening. "What is he doing now, exactly?"

Ben shrugged. "I don't know. . .*exactly*. Used to be he told me all about his trips. But the last few years he's only told me where he's been. . .England, Japan, Russia, China. There aren't many places he hasn't visited. But I don't know what he's doing. He's a lot more closemouthed than he was, Samantha. You saw him at my house, I understand."

"Yes. I went to visit Eileen, too." She looked away from his deceptively mild gaze.

Ben sighed. "I wonder sometimes why Jon never looks really happy. It's not as if he's stuck with a homely face like mine and can't help himself." He shook his head. "Ah well, he's lonely, most likely. I know how that is. Jon's like Kipling's cat—he walks by himself. Being alone's necessary of course for everyone, sometimes, and there's nothing wrong with being alone if it's what you choose. But when it's thrust upon you it's not so hot. After Lynne left—"

He broke off and Samantha guessed he was thinking about the past. That seemed to be everyone's favorite pastime just now, she thought bitterly.

After a moment his face brightened perceptibly. "Jon and the doctor have surely cottoned to each other. Word is Jon's interested in the doctor's daughter. What do you think about that?"

"Now, Ben," Samantha chided. "Don't tell me you still like to gossip."

He looked totally unrepentant. "Gossip's the lifeblood to an island," he said. "Bets are already down on whether Samantha Austin's engagement will last now she's seen Jon Blake again." He looked at her slyly. "Be a pretty good catch for you now, Samantha. He's a lot better off than he used to be."

"That doesn't make any difference to me," she said firmly. "My engagement will last. You can tell everyone I said so."

He chuckled in the back of his throat, the closest he ever came to a laugh. "Won't do any good," he said. "Everyone remembers how you and Jon used to skinny dip in the Sound when you thought no one was looking, so they don't put much account into some other man they've never seen."

Suddenly conscious that his conversation was getting into dangerous areas, Samantha looked beyond Ben, away from his sly gaze. She'd intended to comment on the spa's grounds, but then a different subject presented itself. At the edge of the woods the thin man was chopping away at a patch of tall weeds with his hoe, looking immensely awkward. "Is your helper new on the job?" she asked.

Ben turned to follow the direction of her gaze and

snorted. "Hatched yesterday, if you ask me. I don't reckon he's ever held a real job in his life, unless it was sitting behind a desk. Absolutely useless, he is. I've almost made my mind up to complain to the doctor... waste of good money paying a no-good loafer like that."

"What's his name?"

"Tom Greene." There was a derisive note in his voice. "If you ask me he made that one up... got a foreign accent you could cut with a knife." He sighed. "Look at him! If he moved any slower he'd turn into a statue. Well, he won't last long. Dr. Birmann's got no patience with slackers." He turned back to her with a mournful grin. "I'd best be off, Samantha, or I'll be getting my walking papers, too. It *is* good to see you. You'll come visit, every chance you get?"

"Of course I will."

"Brian and Tracy will be pleased. They've quite taken to the lady with the orange hair." He chuckled, then reached into his overall pocket for his pipe, pulling out with a surprised air the same box of matches that Samantha had slipped back into *her* blazer pocket not a minute before. "Well, you're getting pretty slick yourself," he teased, then lit his pipe and went off around the corner, his head surrounded by a cloud of smoke, leaving Samantha smiling after him.

Her smile faded as she looked again across the lawn at the thin man. He was holding the hoe like a golf club now, making fierce sweeps at the tall weeds, following through with surprisingly graceful movements. Now there was an activity that seemed natural to him, she thought. He'd obviously be at home on a golf course. And Ben had confirmed her opinion that he wasn't a manual laborer. Why was he pretending to be a gardener? But unemployment was high everywhere right now. Perhaps he'd lost an executive position and had to take what he could get—which was something to be admired. Except that she couldn't bring herself to admire him, especially remembering the fear he'd inspired in the doctor. Who was he, she wondered again. And what was he doing here?

CHAPTER FIVE

AFTER A DELICIOUS BUT EXTREMELY LIGHT LUNCH that left her wickedly planning a trip to Carter's store for some private stockpiling of food, Samantha spent the afternoon with Anne Marie, talking to the various experts employed by Dr. Birmann. There was a dietitian, a biofeedback technician, and other specialists in various skills, from aquapressure to body wraps to massage.

She was especially interested in the biofeedback techniques and was given a demonstration by the instructor, an enthusiastic young man who reminded her of a gym teacher she'd had in school. The man taught her that she could monitor her own state of relaxation simply by holding the bulb of a small thermometer between her thumb and index fingers and checking it after ten minutes of meditation. He also introduced her to an electronic exercise bicycle that monitored her pulse rate. She was pleased to note that her temperature and pulse rate were within normal limits, showing that she had recovered from the morning's stress.

Each of the experts in turn gave her a small course in their specialty, and by the end of the afternoon she felt like a computer that had been stuffed with facts and then switched off. She didn't seem to have a clear thought about anything.

She needed some time outdoors, she decided when

Anne Marie finally left her alone. Changing into jeans and a plaid shirt, she set off into the woods behind the chalets, taking an old island trail that she knew about rather than one of the spa's contrived walkways. This trail, if she remembered correctly, should bring her out on a promontory from which she'd get a good view of her favorite mountain, if the haze had dissipated as it often did in the evening.

Her memory had not let her down. After a half hour's brisk walk she emerged onto a headland and saw to the southeast beyond the mainland, the magical sight of Mount Rainier, sharply etched like a child's cardboard cutout against the clear blue sky, visible from its snow-covered peaks and glaciers to the tops of its twilight-blue foothills. Above it a lens-shaped cloud, formed by strong updrafts, shaded its topmost white contours like a cap. For a long time Samantha sat on the rough grass, filling her gaze with the mountain's serene beauty.

Refreshed, pleased that she hadn't wasted her time dwelling on Jonathan Blake, she eventually wended her way back between the trees toward the spa, intending to see if dinner in the dining room offered more calories than she had enjoyed so far.

She had walked for fifteen minutes when she heard voices on the trail ahead of her. The path was narrow and she stepped into the long grasses at one side, meaning to let whoever was approaching have the right of way. It was a moment before she realized that the voices weren't coming any closer, and a moment more before she realized they weren't speaking in English. They were male voices—two of them—and one had the rhythm and intonation of Dr. Birmann's. Even as she recognized his voice, he raised it until he was almost shouting at his companion. The other man responded more softly, in a nervous way that made Samantha feel self-conscious about eavesdropping, even though she couldn't understand a word. She didn't even recognize the language. It wasn't French or Spanish or Italian. It seemed to have a Slavic flavor...Polish perhaps?

For a few seconds she hesitated, wondering whether to return to the promontory until Dr. Birmann and his companion finished their discussion or argument or whatever it was. But then she noticed a small trail leading away from the main path and took it gratefully, hoping the woods were thick enough to hide her from the men's view. Though why she should worry about being seen, she had no idea, except there was something in the other man's voice, some note of caution or unease, that made her feel he would not be glad to see her. It was the thin man, she felt sure, and her suspicion was confirmed a moment later when she glanced sideways and caught a glimpse of the man's white cap between the trunks of a group of alders. He and the doctor were standing very close together, fortunately facing away from her. As she went on her way, the thin man said something in a very low tone and the doctor exploded again. *"Nyet,"* he shouted. And again, *"Nyet."*

Well, that took care of that mystery. No one who'd ever read espionage novels could mistake what language that word for "no" belonged to. The two men were speaking Russian.

Which was odd, considering that the doctor was originally Swiss.

Samantha shook her head as she emerged from the woods and headed toward her chalet, chastising herself for her old habit of building mysteries. What difference did it make if the men *were* speaking Russian? Russians *had* left Russia over the past decades—possibly the thin man was a Russian émigré who had known Dr. Birmann in Switzerland. Perhaps they'd gone to school together or something.

In which case, why would the doctor employ the man as a gardener?

Enough, Samantha scolded herself.

By the time Dr. Birmann emerged from the woods, alone, she was sitting on the small porch of her chalet, treating herself to a cup of coffee. Matt had shown her, on request, how to use the small beverage-making machine in her bathroom and had brought her in a supply of instant coffee.

So she wouldn't appear to be watching for the doctor, she fixed her gaze on a pair of violet green swallows that were swooping and gliding above the lawn next to the spa's main building. The sun shone on their gorgeously colored backs, striking all the colors of the rainbow from their layered feathers. The spa was silent now—the guests must be in the dining rooms. She should stir herself into going down, too. But it was peaceful here, and the air felt cool against her skin and she could smell the roses. A small gray squirrel sat at the base of a nearby oak tree, chattering away, apparently scolding her.

From the corner of her eye she saw Dr. Birmann coming up the steps. She felt suddenly guilty about drinking coffee, but the doctor didn't seem to notice what she held in her hand. His face was rather flushed, she noticed. Was that due to his exertions or to remnants of his anger at the thin man? *Tom Greene.* Why would a Russian have a name like Tom Greene? But she didn't *know* he was Russian, she reminded herself.

"I forgot to invite you to have dinner with us," Dr. Birmann said when he was close to her. "I hope you haven't made other arrangements, or eaten already."

"Neither," Samantha said, smiling, about to stand up until the doctor motioned her to stay where she was.

"You have enjoyed your first day?" he asked.

"Immensely. Though I'm not sure how much I've absorbed."

"It will make sense to you after a while," he assured her. "May I tell Anne Marie to count on you for dinner, then?"

"I'd love it."

"Good." He smiled at her with a return of that overwhelming charm that had so impressed her at their first meeting. "Ask someone to show you to our chalet. It is not far. We usually dine at eight, but please come for cocktails at seven-thirty."

About to turn away, he suddenly flashed a very warm smile that took years off him. "Do not worry, Miss Austin. We dine quite well. Only good healthy food, of course, but I am addicted to French cooking, and we will have a fine saddle of lamb *en croûte* for you. My housekeeper is a wonderful cook." He chuckled. "I understand you have been served a dieter's meals by mistake so far. Anne Marie's mind must have been on other matters. I apologize. I do not expect my employees to exist on 850 calories a day—I ask too much of you all for that."

Samantha smiled, letting her relief show. "I was afraid I was going to turn into a shadow of my former self!" she admitted ruefully.

He laughed out loud, his color totally restored to normal. Then he started down the steps at a pace that would have been remarkable in a much younger man. So his face had not been flushed from exertion.

Stop it, Samantha, she told herself again, and blanked out her mind while she finished her coffee. Then she went inside to change into a peacock blue silk dress that she thought might be suitable evening wear at the spa.

The doctor's chalet turned out to be a much larger version of her own, with the addition of a formal dining room whose sliding doors had been opened to enlarge the living area.

The first person she saw as she entered was Jon, sitting next to Anne Marie on one of two long sofas that flanked the large picture window in the east wall. It hadn't occurred to her that he might also have been invited to dinner. She wished he was anywhere but here, but she supposed she'd have to accept his presence. He certainly looked debonair in a well-cut dark gray suit that contrasted dramatically with his sun-streaked blond hair. A crisp white shirt and a faintly striped tie completed the picture of an urbane man-about-town, not an image she had ever associated with Jonathan Blake. He looked at her and lifted his martini glass in silent acknowledgement as she entered, but he didn't smile. Samantha felt a spasm of nervousness and found herself clutching the skirt of her dress, bunching the silk fabric in both hands like a shy little girl.

Luckily, within a second or two the doctor took her arm and drew her toward his other guests. He had invited one of his instructors, Barry, the biofeedback specialist, and his bookkeeper, Deborah, probably to make Samantha feel more at ease, she realized. Again she appreciated his thoughtfulness, and she sat between the two tall good-looking people and talked with them over cocktails, which she was relieved to find were the normal variety and not some concoction of herbs.

They had both come with the doctor from San Diego and were both enthusiastic about the Pacific Northwest. Deborah had once considered going into archeology, she told Samantha, but an automobile accident had injured her back slightly and decided her on a less strenuous occupation. She was still interested in archeology though, and she'd recently visited an established dig on the Pacific Coast. While Jon and Dr. Birmann and Anne Marie conversed, she entertained Samantha and Barry with stories of the dig's history.

Samantha was interested—Indian culture had always fascinated her. But she was acutely aware of Jon on the other side of the glass-topped coffee table, and she kept stealing glances at him, covertly, she hoped.

She couldn't remember ever seeing him so elegantly dressed. He was really a remarkably attractive man, even if his features weren't perfectly even. Actually, it was that very imperfection that gave his face its rugged charm. She found herself watching his mouth as he talked enthusiastically to the doctor and Anne Marie, who was seated between the two men. His mouth had lost the bitter twist she'd noticed since her arrival on the island. She'd never seen a mouth as strongly marked as Jon's. She could remember vividly how it had felt on hers that morning. No one since Jon had kissed her so expertly, so sensitively. The first time they ever kissed it was as if they had been born knowing how to please each other, how to draw heat from each other's lips and. . . .

Horrified at the direction of her thoughts, Samantha deliberately switched her gaze to Anne Marie. The girl was looking up at Jon with a solemn but admiring expression on her face. She was wearing a white dress with a ruffled bodice and full sleeves—very pretty, but more suited to a twelve-year-old. Her long fine hair was drawn back at the nape with a satin ribbon that intensified the youthful effect.

Jon was including her in his conversation with the doctor, but she seemed to be perplexed by the subject matter, which, Samantha determined by eavesdropping, had to do with international sea laws concerning offshore petroleum development.

"...and, of course, the clay from the landslide had sealed out all oxygen, so that the artifacts were found in near-perfect condition," Deborah was saying when Samantha remembered her manners and began paying attention again.

Deborah's rather sharp-featured but effectively made-up face was alight with enthusiasm, and Samantha regretted that she'd missed so much of the story. But the other woman hadn't seemed to notice her inattention.

"What kind of artifacts?" she asked, glad she'd at least caught something to question.

Deborah launched herself into eager descriptions of baskets and weapons and whale skeletons, and Samantha forced herself to listen properly, though she wished she could continue to eavesdrop on Jon's conversation—she'd read a little about the subject and would like to have heard his views.

She had the opportunity to listen to him a bit later, however, when they had all begun tackling the excellent lamb and salads and the delicious full-bodied red wine that accompanied the food. Jon was seated opposite her, next to Anne Marie, with Deborah on his other side. And when Deborah again mentioned the huge whale bones she had seen, he began talking about whales, which had always been a favorite subject of his.

It was his first sighting of a whale in its natural environment that had decided him on a career in oceanography. At the age of sixteen, diving in the waters off San Juan Island, he had unexpectedly encountered a young killer whale that had shown great curiosity about this two-legged fish. The whale had swum around him in the clear water, looking him in the eye in what Jon swore was a friendly, even humorous way, bumping against him several times as though encouraging him to play before swimming off, presumably to join fellow whales. Samantha could vividly remember the expression of awe and excitement on Jon's face when he told her of the incident.

She remembered also an occasion when he had taken her to Kalaloch on the Olympic seashore and they had watched a pod of gray whales migrating far out to sea. They had quarreled good-naturedly over the use of Jon's old binoculars, which he'd bought at a flea market somewhere. Later she'd bought him an expensive, more powerful pair. He'd accepted them gravely, thanking her for her kindness in a tone that was sincere yet at the same time held a hint of resentment. Even then she should have recognized his pride.

She had drifted off into memory again, she realized, suddenly coming back to her surroundings. Jon was talking now about a time he had gone out with Icelandic herring fishermen in order to study the killer whales that always surrounded every boat. He had made several trips, preparing to help in the capture of one of the whales.

"You captured a whale?" Samantha exclaimed, surprised and horrified.

Jon's blue eyes met hers across the width of the elegant dinner table that was set with silver and crystal and a bowl of Ben's roses. He smiled crookedly at her, then glanced at the others. "Sam remembers that I used to be totally opposed to interfering with wild creatures in their natural habitat," he explained.

Sam. He'd called her Sam. She was shocked by the elation that went through her, and she rushed into speech to cover up her reaction. "Don't tell me you've changed your mind? How could you? You used to get furious at the very thought of animals in cages or hunting of any kind... especially whale hunting."

"I'm still opposed, Samantha," he said sternly. "Even if I wasn't, the methods of killing are abhorrent to me. How anyone can club a baby seal to death...!" He paused, grinning crookedly. "Let's not get me started on that!"

He looked at Samantha. "The whale we caught was for a Dutch research institute. I've learned that there's a good case to be made for maintaining wild creatures in oceanariums as long as they are kept under humane conditions. Through research we achieve a better understanding of the creatures who share this world with us. And understanding leads to conservation. Sea-life shows do have their uses. Once people watch the whale and the sea lions, and they get an idea of their sense of humor and their sparkling intelligence, they could surely never harm one in the wild. They might even begin to worry about the preservation of such marvelous creatures."

"I have a friend at Sealand," the doctor remarked.

Jon turned toward him. "I remember, you told me about him. He's a chef in one of the restaurants there?"

Dr. Birmann nodded, but he hadn't really seemed to hear Jon's response. He was gazing thoughtfully into space, a piece of cheese in his hand, halfway to his mouth, apparently forgotten. After a second of silence he roused himself, ran his free hand through his iron gray hair and smiled apologetically at Jon. "I'm sorry, I was wandering in my mind. I did not mean to interrupt you. I am most interested in your whales. How did you go about catching one? They can be quite vicious to humans, can they not?"

Jon shook his head. "Mostly they're victims of a bad press. All I've seen of whales leads me to believe they're unlikely to become aggressive toward humans unless provoked. We tend to forget that man is an alien in the whale's environment. Any cruelty is ours, not theirs. It's true that killer whales will attack just about anything in the sea if they are hungry—even other bigger whales. But they seem to have a special interest, even an affection, for the human race. There's no eyewitness account of one ever hunting down and eating a human being, but there are several accounts of a man falling overboard into water filled with killer whales and not being harmed by them. They definitely seem to like people and to trust them. The killer whale we caught stayed far calmer than I would have done under similar circumstances."

Everyone laughed, and he went on to describe the special cradle his team had used to lift the whale from the sea into the boat, and the care taken in its transportation. After that he told his now-rapt audience of the depredations caused among mammals by man. "A huge percentage of our whales was destroyed before we even started worrying about them," he said. "Even now God knows how many dolphins are trapped and killed by fishermen. There are nets designed to allow dolphins to be released, but they aren't used everywhere, unfortunately. The prospect for any kind of sea life is not good—and it's not just a case of prohibiting hunting. To raise a public outcry to save the whales, or the seals or whatever, is fairly simple. Much more importantly we have to work at preserving the ecosystems in which these creatures live. So much damage is caused by chemicals and agricultural pesticides and untreated human sewage dumped into rivers and carried out to sea. The coral reefs are actually sick, and much of the bottom life on the continental shelves has been destroyed. Many of the world's shorelines are dying. I get infuriated when I see the damage. Man may have started out needing to fight nature in order to survive, but now it is essential that we protect it. If we kill off our oceans, we ourselves won't survive. Human beings are at the top of the endangered-species list."

He paused and shook his head, raising both hands in apology. "Sorry, I have a tendency to get on my soapbox without being asked."

Anne Marie was gazing up at him, her gray eyes bright with admiration. Samantha didn't blame her— she had an idea her own eyes were shining, too. This was the Jonathan she remembered—the crusader, intense and dedicated. "You should never apologize for speaking out," she said impulsively.

"Ah, you have a champion, Jon," Dr. Birmann said with a smile.

"Sam was my first champion," Jon said softly, looking at her.

She'd pleased him, she saw. He'd always had an endearing expression when he was pleased—an expression she'd never forgotten because it was uniquely his: a kind of shining that started way at the back of his blue eyes and moved slowly forward until his eyes were brimming with affection.

For several long seconds it was as though no one else was in the room. Samantha's gaze was caught and held by that so familiar expression of affection on Jon's strong-featured face. All hostility between them was gone for the moment. His eyes held steady on hers, and she felt a warmth—a familiar warmth—stealing through her veins. "I'm glad you still care," she said quietly.

"I will always care," he replied, and for a moment she thought in confusion that he meant he still cared for her. But then he laughed and said lightly, "That doesn't mean I should dominate the conversation," and turning to Dr. Birmann he asked a question about some aspect of the spa program. The talk became general once again.

Samantha listened with interest, though she was not yet knowledgeable enough to contribute. A part of her mind was still back there with the look on Jon's face, however. So often over the past few years she had seen his face in her mind, looking at her like that, as though she had pleased him immeasurably. She was suddenly overwhelmed by the enormity of her loss.

But almost immediately the defense mechanisms she'd perfected over the years went into effect, and she reminded herself that she could not go through life constantly probing the wounds of the past. In any case, Jon was no longer the rather shy young man she had once loved so desperately. There was an aura of—what was it—power? authority?—about him that was relatively new. Whatever it was, she wasn't sure she liked it, even though she had to admit it enhanced his physical appeal.

About an hour after dinner Deborah and Barry stood up to leave. Samantha rose with them, but Dr. Birmann asked her to stay a while—he had something he wanted to discuss with her, he said.

Obediently she subsided onto the living-room sofa that he indicated and waited with a strange feeling of trepidation, while he saw Deborah and Barry out. Meanwhile Jon poured liqueurs for her and for himself, and mineral water for Dr. Birmann and Anne Marie.

There was cause for trepidation, she soon realized. The doctor, it seemed, had asked Jon's help in preparing a brochure to be used in advertising the spa. Jon had agreed to photograph the various facilities, though he insisted he couldn't guarantee the results as he was totally unqualified in that particular area. "Anne Marie is going to be one of the models," Jon told Samantha as he seated himself next to her. He glanced at the girl with that same fond paternal expression that had irritated Samantha earlier in the day, and they exchanged a smile. Anne Marie's face was adoring, Samantha noticed.

Dr. Birmann leaned forward on the sofa he was sharing with his daughter. "We cannot photograph our guests, you understand," he explained. "Most of them are already suffering from overexposure, so to speak. They come here because I promise them privacy. And I do not wish to use professional models because I feel such pictures have the air of a stage set about them. However, I wish to make plain that these brochures will not be distributed haphazardly. They will be sent to potential clients on request only. I want such people to see they need not be great beauties in order to benefit from our program. This is why I have agreed that Anne Marie pose for Jon's photographs."

"Thanks a lot, father!" Anne Marie said with ironic stress, surprising Samantha with her unsuspected spirit.

Jon laughed. "Not very tactful of you, Jakob. Especially when you are about to ask Samantha to participate."

Samantha looked at the doctor, eyebrows raised. "You are?"

"If you would not mind. I do not think it is right for Jon to photograph Anne Marie alone. Barry and Deborah have agreed to take part, but I would like you to be with her, also."

He *was* old-fashioned, Samantha thought. What was she supposed to be, some kind of chaperon? She turned to look at Jon. "Won't this cut into your time?"

"I have time on my hands right now, Samantha."

"No whales to save?" She couldn't resist letting a mildly sarcastic note show in her voice. She was feeling quite exasperated with him again. Surely with his knowledge and skills he shouldn't be wasting his time hanging around the island, taking photographs of mud packs and electronic bicycles.

His eyebrows had risen. For a second tension sparked between her and Jon, bringing a return of that challenging hostility to his eyes. But when he spoke his voice was even. "There are always whales to save," he said easily. "But everyone needs time off once in a while."

"You still haven't told me what kind of work you're

doing now," she pointed out. "I take it you haven't given in to the nine-to-five ethic yet?"

"Hardly." He hesitated, and she knew at once he wasn't going to answer her question. She stared at him defiantly, waiting. His gaze met hers, just as directly. Once again she lost consciousness of others in the room. She realized of course that Dr. Birmann and Anne Marie were still there, quietly listening, but they seemed insubstantial, far-off. It was suddenly very important to her that Jon answer her question. What she really wanted, she admitted to herself, was for him to laugh carelessly and say he didn't really do anything anymore. That would justify the insult she'd hurled at him seven years ago. *You'll never amount to anything.* Had she really said that to Jon?

"As I told you before," he said at last, "I'm resting right now."

He was determined to evade her curiosity, it seemed. "And after you have... rested?" she asked, managing to sound fairly indifferent.

"That is yet to be determined." There was a chiding note in his voice that she remembered of old. *Don't be nosy, Sam,* he was saying, as he'd used to say.

"As I *am* at liberty," he continued, his blue gaze still fixed on her, "I'm perfectly willing to help Jakob with his project. What about you?"

Samantha hesitated, feeling very disappointed that he'd refused to respond to her probing. He was right, of course; it was none of her business. All the same....

She had to make a decision. If she agreed, she would be committing herself to time spent in Jon's company. Did she really want that? Anne Marie would be with them, she reminded herself. And wasn't it necessary for her to see Jon anyway, if she was ever going to rise above the clutch of those tentacles of memory that kept reaching out of the past? Why else had she come back to the island?

"Surely your fiancé wouldn't object?" Jon asked in a challenging way.

"Of course not," Samantha retorted, but at heart she wasn't so sure. Adrian *was* rather conservative. He had a hang-up about privacy. People who were constantly being photographed for newspapers or magazines were just making exhibitions of themselves, he often remarked. *His* family believed in keeping a low profile. She sighed—Adrian and his clichés again. She would really have to persuade him to try to be more original in his speech.

She became aware that Jon was still gazing at her, still waiting for her decision. How intensely blue his eyes were against his tanned face. He really seemed to want to photograph her. Wouldn't it be churlish to refuse? She was the one who'd suggested they try to be friends. She had no real choice, anyway. Jakob Birmann was her employer, after all. "Okay, I'll do it," she said hastily, before she could change her mind.

Jon nodded and turned toward the doctor, releasing her from his intense gaze. But not before she had seen the triumphant gleam in his eyes. Why had he wanted so badly for her to agree? So that he'd have a chance to be with Anne Marie? Given the doctor's overprotectiveness, that could be a likely reason. Or was some other motivation at work here? Was he still pursuing the unfinished business he'd talked about? She was suddenly convinced she should have refused Dr. Birmann's request.

But she couldn't deny that she was just as suddenly looking forward to the photographic sessions. She'd had no idea this was what the doctor had in mind when he mentioned publicity. "It should be fun, don't you think?" she asked Anne Marie.

Anne Marie wrinkled her nose. "I suppose so. Usually I don't like to be photographed. But Jon is very good. Perhaps he will make even me look beautiful."

"You *are* beautiful," Jon said at once, and the girl smiled at him gratefully, with a look in her eyes that did indeed give her a sudden beauty. There was something else in her eyes, Samantha thought suddenly. Was it admiration...or love? She remembered that Eileen thought Jon might marry this girl. Did Anne Marie think the same thing? Did Jon?

CHAPTER SIX

"JUST PEDAL AWAY," Jon said. "Forget I'm here. Relax."

Relax, Samantha echoed sardonically to herself while her legs worked like pistons. Jon had made quite sure that she was *unable* to relax.

She and Anne Marie were riding twin exercise bicycles, while Jon, dressed in a tank top and matching white shorts, darted around them, now crouched down, now looming over them, now yelling at them from across the room, aiming his camera at them from every conceivable angle, his finger triggering shot after shot.

The two young women were dressed alike in blue leotards. Identical blue bandannas, twisted into slim ropes, circled their foreheads in sweatband fashion. There all resemblance ceased. Anne Marie was obviously at the peak of condition. Samantha had thought *she* was in fairly good shape, but Jon had set the tension on this bike to the maximum, and her muscles were screaming objections every time she forced her legs down.

Anne Marie looked cool and comfortable, her slender back straight, a slight smile on her lips. Made up by a cosmetologist for the occasion, she looked very pretty and much more grown-up. Samantha, in contrast, felt hot and sweaty. She could feel a faint film of perspiration on her upper lip. Any second now Jon would call a halt so that he could gently wipe the perspiration from her face, or adjust her posture or the positioning of her hands on the bike's handlebars. He'd seized every possible chance to touch her since they'd begun these photography sessions. This was their fourth in two weeks. When Jon had photographed her lying down in the infrared room, he'd adjusted the folds of her terry-cloth robe every few minutes, folding back the hem to expose one leg from the knee down, loosening the sash so that the upper edges of her robe parted to show the swell of her breasts. "Just a little cheesecake," he'd said lightly, his fingers lingering against her flesh just long enough to ignite small explosions of heat throughout her body.

Deborah, posing in shirt and shorts as an attendant, had noticed the gesture. Her penciled brows had risen almost into her hairline, embarrassing Samantha tremendously. And Anne Marie, watching from the sidelines, had laughed at Jon's humor, then smiled in a conspiratorial manner at Samantha, as though inviting her to share her admiration of his wit.

When he'd photographed her emerging from a bathtub full of green sea mud, her hair pinned in a knot on top of her head, he'd fussed with the towel she'd clutched to her chest, "trying to make it look more natural," he'd insisted. Natural! His fingers had trailed across her bare skin, accidentally of course, every time the towel began to slip, until she was sure the finished photographs would show sensual patterns drawn in the thick green mud, revealing bare patches of blushing skin.

The yoga sessions had provided him with another opportunity for amusement. In the lotus position her legs weren't close enough to the floor, he decided. Anne

Marie had agreed. So he had to push them down, stroking them into place. Then her posture wasn't as erect as it might be. His fingers had probed between her shoulder blades, massaging tension from her back...so he said.

And every time he touched her, her body responded with a fiery urgency that refused to be controlled. He knew it, too. He knew exactly how he was affecting her and was repeating his teasing gestures as often as he could find excuses to do so.

Why? What possible satisfaction could he find in knowing that he could still arouse her physically? She was constantly relieved that at least he didn't know no other man had ever been able to arouse her in quite the same way.

"You can stop pedaling now, Samantha," he said softly, and she realized with a start that he was standing very close to her, holding, as she'd expected, a small square of toweling with which he proceeded to mop her face. She knew by now that it was useless to protest that she could handle such jobs herself. He'd already explained, very politely and several times, that she might smear her makeup and they would have to start all over again.

Anne Marie had dismounted from her bicycle and was sipping water from a glass Barry had handed her. She was sitting on a bench at the side of the room, talking to the young man while she drank, not looking toward Samantha and Jon.

"Why are you doing this?" Samantha hissed at Jon.

His blue eyes regarded her innocently as he adjusted the knot of the sweatband behind her head, his fingers "accidentally" tangling in her hair, brushing against her scalp with tender, gentle motions she could feel down to her toes. "I guess it must be boring for you to have to put up with such a perfectionist," he said easily.

"You know perfectly well what I'm talking about, Jon Blake," she said through clenched teeth as his hand trailed the length of her spine, supposedly straightening her from her slumped position.

With a satisfied smile, he brushed a curl of hair back behind her ear, delicately caressing her earlobe at the same time. Then he backed off and took a picture of her scowling at him.

A moment later he was calling Anne Marie back to work, helping her on to the bicycle as though she were a fragile doll.

Swearing under her breath, Samantha dismounted and joined Barry at the side of the room. "He's a hard taskmaster, isn't he?" Barry commented. "I guess he's trying for realism."

"He's trying to drive me crazy," Samantha muttered, but luckily Barry had chosen that moment to call some advice to Jon and didn't hear her.

For the rest of the session Jon ignored her, concentrating instead on photographing Anne Marie. He barely glanced at her as he left them to go home to dinner. He was deliberately trying to keep her off balance, she felt sure. But she was no closer to finding out why.

Every muscle in her body was aching as she toiled up the steps to her chalet. Her job at the spa kept her busier than she'd expected. She'd become a sort of girl Friday, doing all kinds of odd jobs for Dr. Birmann. Not that she minded. She quite enjoyed the work and enjoyed being around the doctor, whose expertise she

was coming to admire more and more. And she'd
made friends with some of the spa guests. But her
schedule left her little time for physical exercise. By
the time her day ended she was exhausted by all she
was learning, and she wanted only to crawl into bed
with a book. On her days off she had walked, but not
vigorously. Mostly she'd wanted to roam the island,
and as she'd often been accompanied by Brian and
Tracy she'd had to adjust her pace to theirs. All of this
meant that the photographic sessions had demanded
physical efforts from her that her body wasn't
prepared for. Today's session especially had worn her
out.

Dinner in her room, she decided. Later she'd read
one of the new paperbacks she'd picked up at Carter's
store, then she'd soak her aches away in one of the
spa's tubs. Dr. Birmann had told her to feel free to use
one whenever she wanted to. Tonight she'd take him
up on his offer.

There was a letter from Adrian waiting for her in the
box beside her chalet door. She pulled it out and admired his firm, very legible handwriting on the envelope. But she didn't open it right away. Later, she
thought, setting it down on the coffee table. It would
be something to look forward to before she went to
sleep. She could pretty well guess what he'd have to
say. She'd received four letters from him over the last
two weeks, letters that meticulously recorded his activities and refrained from asking her if she was missing
him. Adrian didn't believe in questioning the person
one loved. If someone wanted to say "I love you," or
"I miss you," they'd say it, he always insisted. Demanding proof of affection was a sign of insecurity.

She was sorry there was no letter from her mother. Claudia's letters were always bright and chatty and cheering, and she could use a little cheering up. But she could hardly expect her mother and father to write very often—they were on vacation in Europe this summer, and probably still a little upset that she hadn't gone with them.

She sighed to herself as she stripped off her leotard and jeans and pulled on a comfortable robe. She had to get used to being on her own, being independent. That was one of the primary motivations behind this trip.

"You're a big girl now, Samantha," she said aloud as she headed for the phone to call for her dinner. She had chosen her solitude, after all. She thought of Ben saying that being alone was necessary sometimes for everyone. There was nothing wrong with being alone.

It was close to ten o'clock when she let herself back into the spa. Most of the guests would be relaxing in their chalets by now, she knew. She checked in with the attendant on the first floor just to let someone know she was in there—a house rule. Dr. Birmann didn't want anyone staying in a tub too long alone as there was always a possibility of fainting, even though the tubs weren't kept much above body temperature.

She took off her clothes in the dressing room, tied up her hair with a rubber band and padded naked across the tiled floor to the circular tub sunk in the center of the room. After testing the temperature with her toes, she slipped into the water to sit on the ledge that served as seating halfway down the tub. She felt immediate relief as the warmth soothed her sore muscles.

Languidly she reached over and opened the air valve, activating the switch that controlled the underwater jets. Then she slipped down until only her head was above the bubbling saltwater. She had positioned herself in front of one of the jets so that it massaged her aching back. It felt marvelous.

Within a few minutes the room was cloudy with steam and smelled strongly of salt. Samantha tipped her head back, looking up at the wide panes of glass set into the ceiling. It was dark outside now—she could see her face reflected in one of the windows, looking misty and amorphous, like the photograph of a ghost.

She felt completely relaxed, her legs and arms lifted and floating. When the door opened she thought it was only the female attendant coming to check on her. It was not until the door closed again and she sensed someone's presence in the room that she lifted her head.

Jonathan Blake was standing next to the tub, a surprised expression on his face. There was something contrived about his surprise, she thought.

"What are *you* doing in here?" she demanded.

He raised his eyebrows and held up a camera. "Just getting some shots of the equipment while it's not in use."

He'd exchanged his shorts for blue jeans, his tank top for a white knit shirt. His hair looked damp, as though he'd recently emerged from a shower. He positively glowed with golden health and well-being.

"This equipment *is* in use," Samantha snapped, overwhelmingly conscious of her nakedness, though she was confident that Jon could not see her body clearly beneath the water. Just to make sure she reached out to a second switch that brought more bubbles up from the ledges.

She saw him smile crookedly, as though he'd recognized what she was doing. He had knelt down at the opposite side of the tub. He wasn't looking at her, had barely glanced at her so far. His attention was on the thermometer, which he'd pulled out of the water on its rope.

"You've no right to be here, Jon," Samantha said.

"No? Probably not." He was still gazing at the thermometer, turning it over in his strong brown fingers as he examined its plastic case.

"Did you follow me here?" she asked indignantly.

"Why should I do that?"

Her feet pressed tightly against the bottom of the tub, hands clenched into fists on her thighs. Somehow her nakedness seemed more pronounced in contrast to his fully clothed body. She was quite sure he was aware of the same contrast. "I can't understand why you're deliberately provoking me," she said coldly.

"Provoking you?" He glanced at her without interest, then shifted his gaze slightly to one side of her. "That's where the water flows into the skimmer," he said conversationally. "The water makes an interesting pattern, doesn't it? I wonder if I could get it? Tricky lighting, but worth a try."

Lifting the camera, he looked through the viewfinder, adjusting the focus with infinite care. "I hardly think a shot like that will be useful in the brochure," Samantha said as he lowered the camera and smiled benignly at her.

"Possibly not. Sometimes I just shoot extra little details for my own amusement."

"Is that what you're doing? Amusing yourself? At my expense?"

He raised his eyebrows. "Really, Sam, don't you think you're being a bit sensitive?"

"*Sensitive!* All through the photo sessions you've been making excuses to touch me, to goad me. And now you're trying to...humiliate me, just because I'm...."

"Naked?" His voice held just a tinge of amusement. It was a cruel amusement, Samantha thought.

He stood up and stepped backward to the door. Samantha thought he was going to leave, but instead he lifted the camera again and refocused it—on her. "Just let me get a couple of shots as long as I'm here, okay?" he said easily.

He peered around the camera. "Could you manage a smile for me, Samantha? The tub is supposed to be a pleasant experience, you know."

She gritted her teeth and smiled ferociously. The camera clicked a few times. Then Jon thanked her with a sardonic smile. "I'm sure those will be great," he said.

He started wandering around the room, opening and closing the dressing-room door, examining the large serrated leaves of the plants set here and there, opening a cabinet to peer with interest at a pile of towels, getting himself a drink from the small water fountain. Samantha watched him warily, willing him to leave. She was beginning to feel waterlogged. Much more time in the tub and she'd be wrinkling up like a prune.

"You don't look very comfortable," Jon said from behind her.

She couldn't, wouldn't crane her neck to see what he was doing. From the corner of her eye she saw him reach to switch off the air pump. "Too many bubbles," he said. "Your hair is getting wet." Gently he gathered up the few strands of hair that had escaped, tucking them into the rubber band, his fingers moving skillfully, delicately. "Such pretty hair," he murmured. His hands cupped her head, and she had to steel herself not to lean back against the pressure.

It seemed a long time before he relaxed his grip and stood up. Even then Samantha could still feel the touch of his fingers burning against her scalp. She heard the camera click again and wondered what on earth he was photographing.

A moment later he appeared again beside the cabinet, where he stood for a minute looking at her with such objective interest that she felt like a lab specimen under a microscope. "Perhaps I should join you," he said abruptly, setting his camera down on the cabinet top.

"You wouldn't dare."

"Wouldn't I?" He tugged the hem of his knit shirt out of his pants.

In spite of her astonishment, Samantha couldn't help noticing and admiring the play of muscles across his back as he pulled the shirt over his head, folded it neatly and laid it on the cabinet top. When he turned to face her, his fingers were fumbling with his belt buckle. There was a curiously enigmatic smile playing around his mouth now. His eyes were cool and watchful.

"Jon, please," she said, afraid he really meant to strip in front of her.

His eyebrows raised. "You surely aren't bothered by the thought of my nudity, are you, Sam?" he asked. "You *have* seen me before, after all."

"That was...not the same."

"Of course not. But as I recall, you decided there wasn't any chemistry between us now, so there's no need to be self-conscious, is there? We can just enjoy a good soak together, for old times sake." He lowered his jeans, lifting one foot to shuck off his shoe as he pulled the fabric down.

"There's an attendant on this floor," she said nervously, despising herself for using the lame excuse. Why didn't she just order him to leave?

"Not anymore there isn't." He'd completely removed his jeans now, was giving them the same careful attention he'd given his shirt. Now he was reaching for the waistband of his briefs. "Maria was anxious to go to her own chalet for the night. I assured her I'd tell you she was closing up shop. We're supposed to lock up on our way out."

"Then you *did* know I was in here?"

Not at all put out that he'd given himself away, he nodded.

"And you did follow me here?"

"Guilty, I'm afraid. Seemed like a good chance to get some extra shots."

He stood naked before her, that same ambiguous smile inviting her to admire the perfection of his body. How could she not? He was golden brown everywhere except for a brief strip of white where his swimsuit had protected him from the sun. The thickly matted hair on his chest and abdomen and legs, though darker than that on his head, was tipped with gold, gleaming under the light. He was not at all affected by her presence, that much was clear.

Heart pounding, she averted her gaze, but not as quickly as she should have done. She heard him chuckle. "So shy, Samantha? How you've changed."

"I think you'd better leave," she said at last, but to her dismay, her voice lacked conviction.

"*I* don't," he said, stepping into the water and settling himself on the ledge opposite her. "It's great, isn't it? Did you notice the scattering of pine needles on the glass up above? Looks like one of my mother's abstract designs, don't you think?"

Automatically she glanced upward, and saw to her horror that the dark skylights mirrored not only her face but also her entire body...and Jon's. A twist of emotion churned in her stomach, and she had to force herself to tear her gaze away.

She glared at him. "Why, Jon? Why are you deliberately provoking me?"

"I'm sorry." His smile held no apology, only a polite perplexity that had to be faked. "I'm just trying to be friendly—I thought that was what you wanted." He shook his head. "As for the photographic sessions, you must understand that it's difficult for a photographer to pose his model without touching her from time to time. Anyway, you did say you felt nothing for me, so I don't see why my touching you should distress you." His voice was eminently reasonable. Samantha was beginning to feel her reactions had been very childish. Which was probably what he intended her to feel.

"There's certainly no reason why you should be bothered by my presence in this tub," he continued smoothly. "You really shouldn't think of a hot tub in sexual terms, Samantha. I know several people who own them, and believe me, it's not unusual for them to invite friends to share the pleasure of a good soak. I really don't understand why you're so disturbed. If my kiss didn't bring any response, I don't see why my naked body should. You can't even see me now, anyway, unless you insist on looking up at the skylights.''

Infuriated, Samantha tried to decide what it would take to persuade him to leave her alone. But quite suddenly and completely she realized that he wasn't going to leave no matter what she said—which left her only one alternative. Gathering all the dignity she could muster, she said evenly. "Very well, then, if you won't leave, I shall have to.''

Without pausing long enough to feel embarrassed, she stood up and climbed out of the tub. Hurrying over to the cabinet, she grabbed a towel, which she hastily pulled around her. At the door to the dressing room she couldn't resist turning to check Jon's reaction. He was looking directly at her, his face unreadable. "You're so very beautiful, Sam," he said softly, without a trace of his former irony.

Her breath caught in her throat. For just a moment she stood very still, and the air between them was charged with all of the excitement that used to be. She was abruptly conscious of the softness of the towel next to her soft flesh, remembering, as surely he was remembering, another time, another place....

Willow Lake on a summer night when the moonlight had seemed to bathe the island with an unearthly glow. She'd stood in just this way, with only a towel around her, waiting for him to emerge from the lake. He'd gazed at her, treading water, his face as solemn as it was now. And then with a burst of vitality he'd come roaring out of the water, lunged for the towel before she could guess his intentions and pulled her, laughing, down onto the soft sweet-smelling grass.

The damp air of the therapy room had curled his hair over his forehead, making him look as young as he'd looked then—an effect intensified by the lack of cynicism on his face. His blue eyes looked at her and into her, and he knew everything about her—just as he always had. And there was, for a fleeting moment, regret in his eyes.

Abruptly Samantha remembered that this was not that long-ago summer of their love, that there was still between them the memory of lacerated feelings and shattered emotions. Her expression must have changed, hardened again, for his own mouth curled at one corner. He seemed once again to be about to say something she wouldn't want to hear, and she retreated hastily into the dressing room, where she locked the door. Her heart, which had seemed to stop beating for that one long minute, now started up again at twice its normal speed.

There was within her a feeling of deep sadness—sorrow for what had once been, for what might have been, what was. Jon *had* deliberately provoked her, for some reason of his own. She had known that all along, yet still her traitorous body had betrayed her by responding to his glances and his innuendoes. That one glimpse of him before he stepped into the tub had been enough to set her pulses clamoring. Chemistry, he'd called the dynamic, mysterious force that was still between them, drawing them together even while their words drove them further apart.

She was going to fight that chemistry, she decided as she stood under the shower, sluicing saltwater from her skin. She would continue to deny it until she'd conquered it—just as she would continue to resist his deliberate provocation. It didn't matter *why* he was teasing her so cruelly—all she had to do was ignore his attempts to upset her. Whatever game he was playing required two participants; she would quite simply refuse to rise to his bait.

Feeling calm and strong of purpose, she put on her clothes and let herself out of the dressing room. He'd already dressed and was standing by the door, which he opened as soon as she appeared.

Not looking at him, she strode past him and started along the hall to the exit. He followed, reaching around her to open the door. Once again, this wing of the spa seemed airless, and Samantha was glad to emerge into the freshness of evening. "Good night, Jon," she said firmly as soon as he had locked the door.

His hand touched her elbow. "I'll walk you home."

"That isn't necessary." She was proud of the calm tone of her voice, apparently unaffected by the heat that surged through her at his touch.

"Yes, it is," he said just as firmly.

Samantha took a deep breath but refused to enter into another argument. Apparently docile, she allowed him to guide her along the footpath and up the steps to the chalet area. He didn't speak again, and he seemed somehow subdued.

At her door, she said once again, "Good night," and this time he didn't demur. His grip tightened momentarily on her elbow, creating havoc with her nervous system, then his hand dropped away and he went past her and down the steps.

Her knees feeling suddenly weak, Samantha forced herself to open her door and go inside. But when she had, she leaned back against the door and let all the pent-up breath escape from her lips. *God help me,* she thought, and the thought was almost a prayer.

CHAPTER SEVEN

LESS THAN HALF AN HOUR AFTER SAMANTHA RETURNED to her chalet, the telephone rang. Instantly she decided it was Jon, calling to apologize for his behavior. And he certainly should.

"Hello," she said cautiously into the receiver, her heart pounding stupidly in anticipation of his voice.

But it was Anne Marie who answered her, and her voice sounded strained. "I know it's late, Samantha, but could I possibly come over to see you? I've got to talk to someone or I'll go out of my mind."

Samantha hesitated. She couldn't bear to listen to Anne Marie prattle innocently of her admiration of Jon, not right now. But there had been a desperate note in the girl's voice. How could she refuse? "Of course," she said as graciously as she could. "I'll make us some hot chocolate. I was just going to have a cup."

She'd just finished stirring hot milk into the chocolate powder when she heard Anne Marie's timid knock on the door. The girl was standing on the porch, dressed in jeans and a T-shirt emblazoned with the spa's logo. She looked unhappy and defenceless and very, very young, and Samantha's heart went out to her. "Come on in," she said warmly.

"You're sure it's all right? You weren't in bed?" She

was looking at Samantha's terry-cloth robe, poised to turn away if she had changed her mind.

"I was just relaxing," Samantha insisted, drawing the girl into the room and gesturing toward one of the two armchairs. After closing the door and serving the chocolate, she seated herself opposite the girl and waited.

It was a few minutes before Anne Marie could bring herself to begin. Then she suddenly blurted out, "When did you last see Tom Greene?"

"The assistant gardener?" Samantha's voice sounded as surprised as she felt.

Anne Marie nodded, and Samantha sipped her hot chocolate, trying to remember. "A couple of days ago, I think," she said at last.

"You didn't see him leave?"

"No." She looked enquiringly at Anne Marie's pinched face, noticing for the first time that the girl's eyes were red rimmed. Was Tom Greene the reason for Anne Marie's "hay fever" that first day? "I didn't even know he was gone," she said.

For some reason her words disturbed the girl's tenuous hold on her composure, and she burst into tears. Sighing, Samantha set down her cup, took Anne Marie's own cup from her nerveless fingers and replaced it with a tissue. Kneeling beside her chair, she gently rubbed the girl's hunched shoulders for a moment. "Don't you think you'd better tell me what this is all about?" she suggested sympathetically.

Anne Marie nodded, blew her nose and tried to compose herself. "I'm so worried, you see. And daddy won't tell me— I don't know what to think."

"You aren't making sense, dear," Samantha said gently, sitting back on her heels. "Suppose you start at the beginning."

"You won't tell my father I talked to you?"

"My lips are sealed."

Her attempt at humor seemed to have the desired effect. Anne Marie took a deep breath and started to talk more rationally. "When we were in San Diego...about five years ago...he came to see us."

"Tom Greene?"

Anne Marie nodded. "That's not his real name, his original name. At least I don't think it is."

Samantha shrugged. "People who come here from other countries often anglicize their names to make things easier."

The girl looked a little less worried, as though that thought comforted her. "Well, anyway, Tom Greene came to see us in San Diego a couple of times, and one day he and daddy had a big argument." She glanced at Samantha rather furtively. "I listened in, but I couldn't understand what they were saying, because they weren't talking in English."

Were they speaking Russian, Samantha wondered.

"All I could understand was this woman's name— Esmée Taylor, one of daddy's regular clients. I don't know why they were talking about her. She's very rich, or at least her husband is—he's got something to do with electronics. Computers, I think." She paused, then sighed. "I asked my father what Tom Greene wanted, but he wouldn't tell me. He just said I was not to worry about Tom Greene because he wouldn't be coming again."

"But he did. He came here."

"The day you arrived. Yes."

"Your father was upset again?"

"Very. He and...Mr. Greene had a terrible argument, but I didn't get any names out of it this time."

"But you did eavesdrop again?"

Anne Marie looked a little sheepish. "Well, I was worried so . . . ." Her voice trailed away.

All of what Jon had once called her Nancy Drew instincts were awake and intrigued. She'd *known* there was something fishy about that man!

"I guess they must have resolved their argument," she said to Anne Marie. "Your father gave him a job."

Anne Marie's smooth forehead furrowed in a frown. "There was something funny about that, too. Daddy said people had seen Tom Greene arrive, so he couldn't just hide him away. That's why he put him to work in the grounds." She hesitated. "When he said that, it seemed as though he was speaking out loud without meaning to. You know how people do sometimes?"

Samantha nodded. "I don't think Tom Greene was a very good gardener, either."

"No. Later on daddy said it wasn't working out. He said he'd have to think of something else—and then Tom Greene disappeared."

Samantha's stomach contracted. "What do you mean . . . *disappeared*?"

"Well, I asked Steve Cory if he'd flown him off the island and he said no. And then I remember Jon went to Seattle yesterday to get some things for Eileen, so I asked him if he'd taken him with him in his boat. He just looked at me and said, 'Who?' And then he said he hadn't gone in his boat anyway, he'd flown with Steve."

Samantha hadn't known Jon owned a boat, unless Anne Marie was referring to the old tub he used to have. No, that couldn't be—that old boat would never make it to Seattle. Whether he owned a boat or not was irrelevant anyway. "Tom Greene could have taken the ferry," she pointed out.

"I thought of that but I—well, I know a couple of the boys who work on the ferry and I asked them. . . ."

"Did you ask your father where Greene had gone?"

"Of course."

"What did he say?"

"He said he'd got him a job at Sealand on Vancouver Island."

Samantha looked at the girl, exasperated. "Then what are you worried about?"

"Well, I just . . . I can't understand why daddy would give him one job, then find him another when he doesn't . . . like him. When he's afraid of him."

"Dr. Birmann is afraid of Tom Greene?"

"Yes. I can't explain how I know that, but I knew it in San Diego and I know it now. And I'm afraid daddy might have told me a lie just to shut me up."

"You don't believe Tom Greene is at Sealand?"

Anne Marie shook her head miserably.

"Then what to you think happened to him?"

When she swallowed visibly and averted her eyes, Samantha felt a tremor of alarm. Surely Anne Marie didn't think Jakob Birmann had . . . *done away* with Tom Greene? "Your father said he had a friend at Sealand," she pointed out. "What could be more natural than that he'd ask him to get Tom Greene a job?"

"When he wasn't a good worker?" Anne Marie said skeptically. "Why should he?"

Why indeed.

"Well, if I were you, I wouldn't worry about it,"

Samantha said soothingly. "If your father says that's where he is, then I'm sure—"

"But I have to *know*," Anne Marie interrupted. "Otherwise I'm going to wonder always if daddy is mixed up in—well, if he's done something he—" She broke off, evidently feeling she'd said too much. She was holding something back, Samantha felt sure, something she didn't want to tell. And she must really be worried, to go around asking everyone if they'd seen the man leave the island. Dr. Birmann would hardly be pleased if he ever found that out.

Samantha sighed. "I don't really see what we can do," she said slowly.

"I thought perhaps...." Anne Marie hesitated, looking at her with a hopeful expression in her gray eyes.

"You thought maybe *I'd* go to Sealand and find out if Tom Greene is working there?" she asked, suddenly realizing what Anne Marie had been leading up to.

"Would you, Samantha? I'd go myself, but if he *is* there and if he sees me and tells my father...." Her voice trailed away.

"I don't even know how I'd get there," Samantha said.

"You can take the ferry to Seattle and catch the Princess Marguerite to Vancouver Island. It leaves at eight every morning and comes back the same day. There's a layover of about five hours. You'd have plenty of time to take a cab to Sealand and check.... And nobody would wonder—you'd just be sightseeing...."

"You've got it all worked out, haven't you?" Samantha interposed dryly.

The girl had the grace to look sheepish. "Well, yes, I thought—"

"That's okay, Anne Marie." She hesitated. "Why don't you ask Jon? You say he has a boat."

"Yes, he keeps it at the marina." She looked down at her hands, which were clasped in her lap. "I thought of that, but Jon might be cross with me for interfering. Anyway, if Tom Green *wasn't* there, and Jon thought something had happened to him, he might feel he'd have to go to the...authorities."

"I might feel the same way," Samantha pointed out.

"Oh, no, I'm sure it couldn't be anything.... Anyway, if I just knew for sure he wasn't there, then I could make daddy tell me." Her tears had started again, and Samantha knew she couldn't hold out against the girl's obvious distress. Privately she thought Anne Marie was probably exaggerating the situation, but then again, she herself had wondered about the "thin man," and she was really curious to know what had happened to him.

"All right," she said after a few more seconds of thought.

Anne Marie flung her arms around her, almost unbalancing her from her kneeling position. "Thank you, Samantha," she cried. "I knew you would be my friend, I just knew it!"

"Hold on," Samantha said, extricating herself and moving over to her own chair. "I won't be able to go until I have a day off, which isn't until Friday."

"That's all right. Just as long as I find out one way or another, sometime." She looked at Samantha gratefully. "I'll pay all your expenses of course," she added.

Samantha smiled. "That won't be necessary. I've no objection to taking the trip for my own sake. I might even ask Brian and Tracy to go along with me. They'd enjoy an outing like that.''

Anne Marie was smiling tentatively now. Samantha was glad she'd been able to allay the girl's fears a little— she just hoped she wasn't getting into something that would prove embarrassing, or even worse, for the doctor. She'd come to admire him a lot, she realized, and she was also, obviously, becoming very fond of Anne Marie. Which would be very ironic if Anne Marie and Jon did decide to marry someday.

Samantha was annoyed with herself for the immediate negative response this thought evoked in her. She was going to marry Adrian; why shouldn't Jon marry, too?

And yet, after Anne Marie had left—full of gratitude and finally convinced, after many promises, that Samantha wouldn't reveal her real reason for going to Sealand to anyone—she admitted to herself that she hated the idea of Jon and Anne Marie getting together. Was she just feeling protective, afraid that Anne Marie was in for some heartache if she got involved with Jon. Or did she, in some recess of her subconscious mind, feel that Jon still belonged to her?

But that was nonsense, she told herself sternly as she prepared for bed. She was just naturally concerned that Anne Marie might get hurt as she had. After all, Anne Marie was only eighteen to Jon's thirty-five. And she was a very young eighteen—as young as Samantha had been. . . .

She was drifting off to sleep when she remembered she still hadn't read Adrian's latest letter. But she was too sleepy to do anything about it by then.

THE NEXT EVENING, dressed in her beach outfit of scooped-neck T-shirt and shorts, Samantha hiked across the point to Ben's house in Hemlock Cove. She found Brian and Tracy sitting on a driftwood log on the beach, excitedly planning their fourth of July celebration, which was to take place on the following Sunday. To hear Brian tell it, they were planning enough pyrotechnics to light up the entire island, but Ben assured Samantha that their festivites would all come out of one average-size box of "safe and sane" fireworks and would concentrate mainly on a hot dog and marshmallow roast. The thought of such glorious food, conspicuously absent from the spa's menus and probably forbidden under pain of exile for life, was enticing to Samantha, and she readily accepted Ben's invitation to join them for the day. Dr. Birmann had already suggested she switch one of her days off so she'd have the holiday free.

"Will your mother be here?" she asked the twins and could have bitten her tongue when their faces fell.

"Lynne's going to Hawaii for the weekend," Ben explained.

Samantha felt a spasm of anger with the always-absent Lynne. How could she desert her children this way?

"We'll have a great time," she told the twins, who responded with tentative grins that widened hopefully when she said, "I have an invitation for you, too." She sat down between them on the log, kicked off her shoes and put an arm around each of them. "How would you like to come with me on Friday to Vancouver Island— on the Princess Marguerite?"

A double war whoop left no doubt of the children's reactions. "We can go to the Underwater Theatre," they shouted together.

"And the waxworks museum," Tracy added, her round face bright with anticipation.

"Ride a double-decker bus," Brian contributed.

Tracy leaned against Samantha, dreamy eyed. "Tea in the Empress Hotel with lots of little sandwiches."

"The English Village," Brian suggested.

"Butchart Gardens!"

"Whoa!" Samantha cried, laughing. "I'm planning a day trip, not full-scale emigration. I thought we'd go to Sealand and see the whale show. That's probably all we'll have time for."

The two almost identical faces clouded slightly, but then they exchanged a glance and nodded. "Okay," Brian said generously. "I guess we could do that."

"I should warn you, Samantha," Ben said solemnly. "The last time Lynne and I took these two monsters on the Princess Marguerite they terrorized all the passengers. There wasn't an inch of that huge boat they didn't get into or onto or inside of. They even invaded some of the private state rooms. You really think you can manage?"

"Manage what?" Jon's voice asked behind them.

Samantha's hands pressed hard against the smooth driftwood log as though it were the only stable thing on the beach, and she fixed her gaze on the distant mountains, hoping the sight of their lofty peaks would calm her. Why did her nervous system always over-react when he appeared on the scene, she wondered angrily.

Luckily she had a few minutes to regain control of herself; Brian and Tracy had leaped up and were climbing all over Jon, excitedly telling him of the proposed trip. "Are you sure you know what you're doing?" Jon asked her when the twins finally let him get a word in.

She looked up at him as he stepped across the log. Khaki shorts and open shirt again. Bare feet. Blond hair unruly, finger combed. The usual quizzical expression combined with a thoughtful look in his blue eyes.

"Now, Jon," Ben interrupted before Samantha could respond. "Don't you be talking Samantha out of it. I have a day off Friday, too. The thought of a day off without these two. . . ."

"I've no intention of talking her out of it," Jon said. He squatted down in front of Samantha, sitting cross-legged on the pebbles, leaning back easily on both hands, a twin on each side of him. He'd always been good with children, for he treated them like intelligent people, never talked down to them, rarely lost patience with them. Tracy was leaning against him, Brian looking as though he wanted to but wasn't quite sure if he should. Jon solved his dilemma by straightening up and putting one arm around him, pulling him close. "You do remember it's a holiday weekend?" he asked Samantha.

She looked at him blankly.

He grinned. "Have you any idea how many people travel up to Victoria on the ferry on holiday weekends?"

She shook her head. "I've never taken a ferry. Daddy took me up a few times, but—"

"Over a thousand people," Jon said. "And most of

them will have bought advance tickets, so you'll have to wait until they're all on board before you can even buy a ticket—*if* there are any left. Besides which, you'll have to catch the 6:30 ferry from here, or maybe the 5:30 in case there's a bigger crowd than usual—the weather's supposed to be good.''

"I don't have any trouble getting up in the mornings," Samantha said tartly.

"And then you won't have much time on the island— it takes forever to get a cab if you want to go anywhere out of the city.''

"You *are* trying to talk her out of it," Ben said gloomily.

"Not at all! I'm merely pointing out how much more enjoyable the trip would be if I take them in my boat. That way we can make our own schedule. We don't have to worry about ferry timetables and—''

His words were cut off as each child attempted to get an affectionate stranglehold on his neck. "Oh, boy," Brian was shouting. "Will you really, Uncle Jon? Will you really take us?''

"Now that's a fine idea," Ben said with a sideways, measuring glance at Samantha.

Tracy was glowing, holding on to Jon as though she'd never let go. "We'll have time for tea at the Empress," she said happily. "I love Uncle Jon's boat," she told Samantha. "It's got the neatest little place downstairs in the front where you can sleep, and a little kitchen and everything.''

"That's the bow, not the front," Brian said sternly. "And you don't call a kitchen, a kitchen when it's on a boat. It's the galley. And you don't say downstairs, you say below.''

Jon tousled the little boy's hair and looked at Saman-tha, blond eyebrows raised. "No glad cries from you, Sam?"

"I don't—I'm not—" She broke off, annoyed with herself for two reasons—one, the rush of pleasure she felt when he called her Sam; the other, the fact that she couldn't come up with a single argument. How could she say no when the twins were so excited? And yet how could she agree to spend a whole day with him, most of it in the confines of a boat? Heaven only knew what plans he might have this time.

That he had plans of some kind she was sure. There was a definitely speculative expression in those innocent blue eyes of his, a crooked smile playing around his mouth. Not a nice smile; there was more than mischief there. He'd manipulated her again, just as he had manip-ulated her into agreeing to the photographic sessions. And now he was waiting for an argument—*expecting* an argument—so that he could destroy her excuses one by one. Could she suggest Anne Marie join them? No. Anne Marie didn't want to be seen by Tom Greene.

There was only one way to handle this, she decided. She couldn't refuse, so she must just accept as gracious-ly as possible. His attempts to provoke her couldn't suc-ceed unless she allowed them to. "How very kind of you, Jon," she said with barely an edge of sarcasm. "I'm most grateful. Of course we'd love to come with you."

His smile was genial to the point of brilliance, show-ing all his even white teeth. "I knew you'd find the invitation irresistible," he said.

Outraged, Samantha swallowed the angry retort that had leaped to her lips. With a consciously sweet smile, she said merely, "What time should we be ready?"

His eyes met hers and narrowed slightly. Then he nodded as though conceding victory. She had the feeling he'd followed her entire line of reasoning and was already planning his next move. But he answered her, naturally enough, "That depends on how much you want to see."

"I'm mainly interested in Sealand."

She thought he was going to question her about that, but after a slight pause he merely shrugged. "Okay, if you want to see the whale show we should leave the marina about seven in the morning. That'll get us to Oak Bay Marina in time for the first show, and still give us time for some sightseeing in Victoria afterward."

The matter seemed to be settled. As she listened to Jon calmly making arrangements with Ben about time sequences, Samantha wondered if she'd overreacted... misjudged him. Perhaps he did just mean to be kind. Perhaps he only wanted to save her the hassle of fighting through holiday crowds. And yet every once in a while she caught him glancing at her, and behind the familiar humorously quizzical expression there seemed to be a hint of something else. *Enmity?* Why should he feel enmity? But there did seem to be something vaguely hostile in his glances. Logic to the contrary, she had a feeling of unease, as though her psychological antennae were signaling danger.

The twins absolutely refused to go to bed at the proper time. They wanted to stay on the beach and discuss every aspect of the upcoming trip. For a while they tried to persuade Jon to bring Tonto along, but he finally managed to convince them that the dog wouldn't appreciate the opportunity as he was not a good sailor.

Darkness was falling by the time Ben decided he'd been lenient enough. Standing up, he picked up a stick that was lying nearby and pointed it at the still-excited children. "This is a magic wand," he said sternly. "When I say the magic words you will both rise and walk directly into the house and up to the bathroom to brush your teeth." He waved the stick over their heads and solemnly pronounced, "Shoo!"

Brian and Tracy giggled, then glanced at each other and nodded. Standing, they stretched out their arms and turned like robots. Climbing up the bank, they walked stiffly toward the house, side by side, arms still extended, obviously trying to look like sleepwalkers.

"Winkin' and Blinkin'," Ben said fondly. "Which makes me Nod, so I'll be off, too." He narrowed his eyes at Jon. "Why don't you take Samantha for a walk on the beach?"

"Ben!" Samantha objected, but he ignored her and waved his "magic wand" over her head. "You have no choice," he intoned solemnly. "My magic will force you to obey."

"That's good enough for me," Jon said, standing up, and no matter how she might hate herself later, Samantha found it impossible to miss the chance to be with him for a little while.

She was too damned weak, she decided as she strolled along with him near the water's edge, carrying her shoes.

A full moon was rising over the Cascades, silvering a path across the water, etching mystery into the woods on shore. How many times had they watched the moon rise together, Samantha wondered. And the sun. This beach held so many memories. When she was eleven or twelve she'd thrown a pail of saltwater over him as he lay sunbathing on the sand, mad at him because he was too lazy to go clam digging with her. He'd chased her all the way around the bay and up the cliff on the other side before he caught her, wrestled her to the ground and threatened to give her a spanking. She'd thrown a couple of mock punches at him. What a tomboy she'd been.

How many mornings had they stood side by side in the gentle surf, fishing for bottomfish? Or raced each other along the beach, each swearing they could outdo a four-minute mile?

So many shared memories lingered among the cluster of rocks here, that pile of driftwood there. Young voices still haunted the edges of the clouds.

They were walking in the water now, splashing slightly, kicking up small spurts of water to sparkle in the moonlight. Surely it was near here, Samantha thought, that he had taken her in his arms that first time.

She realized Jon had stopped walking. He was staring morosely across the water at the mainland, his profile, when she glanced at it, filled with sadness that made her wonder if he was remembering, too.

"It's so fantastically beautiful," Samantha said, gazing at the lights on the mainland and beyond at the upper peaks of the Cascades, now luminous in the moonlight.

He nodded, turning to look at her. "So are you, Samantha."

She caught her breath, then she looked at him again and saw that his expression was now the skeptical one she'd come to dread. "I'd better get back," she said hastily.

He raised his eyebrows. "Afraid I might make advances again?"

"I certainly don't *want* your advances, as you call them," she said hotly.

"No?" There was that mocking quality to his smile again. Was he deriding her or himself? "I leave you quite unmoved, do I?"

Without warning, he took her shoes from her hand and dropped them to the sand, then pulled her abruptly into his arms, his mouth seeking hers without waiting for permission or giving her a chance to object. He kissed her brutally, his tongue forcing her lips apart when she would have clamped them shut. Shuddering as the sheer physical impact of his kiss sent heat flaming through her body, Samantha tried to pull away, but she was no match for his muscular strength. He held her easily, taking no notice of her struggles, his mouth moving lazily over hers now, his tongue resolutely exploring, demanding, awakening. . . .

"No," she cried out, wrenching her mouth free of his. "Don't do this, Jon. I hate it."

"You didn't hate it once," he said harshly.

"That's because—oh, what's the use—there's no love in you now, Jon. Once there was, or there seemed to be. Now you just want to prove you can still attract me. I don't know why."

"Don't I attract you? You still attract me." He was still holding her tightly against him, his hands clamping her hips to his, giving her proof that his passion was not pretended.

Her eyes searched his face, looking for some clue to his true emotions, looking for love. There was none there. His face was shadowed, but even in the moonlight she could see that his eyes were narrowed in speculation. "What is it you want of me, Jon?" she asked desperately, aware that even while she protested the heat was increasing in her body, molding her against him even more closely than his hands insisted.

"No more than you gave me before."

"Jon," she protested, but he shook his head impatiently and wouldn't let her speak. "You didn't answer my question," he said grimly. "Do I still attract you?"

"No," she said at once, chilled by the almost menacing note in his voice.

Incredibly, he laughed. "No?" he echoed. His hands slid wantonly up her body, sliding easily over the thin fabric of her T-shirt, moving under her arms to cup her breasts. "You don't enjoy this now?" His thumbs brushed across the tips of her breasts, and she felt their immediate response. Hooking his fingers in the scooped neckline of her T-shirt, he stretched it out and slid his hand beneath to her bare breast, in a swift maneuver that brought her blood pulsing to meet his touch. At the same time his mouth touched against hers, his breath blowing lightly into her, evoking yet another erotic response, so strong she had to clutch his shoulders to stop herself from swaying forward. "No," she said weakly, despising herself for the weakness.

His eyes looked into hers. "You always were a poor liar, Sam. That 'no' sounded remarkably like a 'yes.' What if I were to tell you that I love you, that I've never stopped loving you. Would that make a difference?"

For a split second she stared at him, feeling herself tremble. Could it possibly be true? But then she saw the sardonic gleam in his eyes, the twist of bitterness in his smile and knew he was mocking her. She felt abruptly sickened. Her emotion must have showed in her eyes, for his own darkened. "You really don't want me to do this, do you?" he said softly, all mockery gone from his face.

"Not like this, Jon, not when you hate me so."

"You're quite sure? You don't want to lie with me on the sand and make love in the moonlight with the mountains watching? We used to enjoy that so much, don't you remember?"

She did remember. Every nerve ending, every sense that she possessed remembered, had always remembered. But he was making sordid something that had been beautiful, and she despised him for that.

Coldly she looked at him, and his hands dropped away from her. Without a word she turned her back on him, straightening her clothing and stuffing her wet sandy feet into her shoes.

"Samantha," he said abruptly, and she stopped, waiting for whatever it was he had to say, though she was determined not to be influenced by it or to accept any apology he might offer.

But he didn't speak. He came up beside her and took her hand in his. She let it lie there limply, and he gripped it as though he were angry again. It was her left hand. When his grip tightened, her ring cut into her fingers, but she didn't pull free. Physical pain was preferable to the pain that was threatening to split her in two.

He had felt the shape of her ring, apparently, for he lifted her hand and looked at her. "I'd forgotten," he said in the same harsh voice he'd used earlier.

"Obviously," she said icily.

He let her hand drop. "I'm not going to apologize,

Sam,'' he said evenly. ''You wanted that as much as I did—for a few minutes, anyway.''

''If you say so,'' she said flatly, and had the dubious satisfaction of seeing him flinch.

There was a moment's silence, then unexpectedly he asked in a matter-of-fact voice, ''How did you get here? To Ben's I mean?''

''I walked.''

''Then I'll drive you back. We can climb up here and walk along the road to the house.''

About to tell him it wasn't necessary for him to see her home, she changed her mind. Protestations hadn't got her anywhere before, and she was suddenly feeling too weary to argue with him anymore.

Lights shone out of the house when they came up to it, indicating Eileen was at home. Jon didn't suggest they go inside, however, for which Samantha was grateful.

His car turned out to be a BMW—oddly enough the same kind of car Samantha drove when she was home in California. She didn't tell him so. He'd probably make some sneering remark about being able to afford something as good as hers.

They were silent as he drove toward the spa. Jon seemed to have withdrawn into himself as he had the night he escorted her back to the chalet after the tub incident. As they turned down the winding driveway to the spa, he broke the silence, his voice perfectly level and courteous in tone. ''You'll still let me take you to Victoria on Friday?''

About to protest that she certainly would not, Samantha weakened again. The twins were counting on going on his boat; the explanations would be impossible. ''If you could remember your promise to act in a civilized manner, I might still consider it," she said as he stopped the car.

"Then I'll pick you up here." He glanced at her quickly, then away. "All right, Sam, you have my promise." There was no emotion in his voice now.

Allowing herself only a brief nod in his general direction, she climbed out of the car.

It was only later, when she was wearily preparing for bed, that she remembered the original purpose of the trip to Vancouver Island. Hunting for Tom Greene was going to be extremely difficult with Jon along. Even more difficult would be the mere fact of being in his company. If only he would stop provoking her so! He had made a promise, but she didn't have a lot of faith in it. There had been an odd expression in his eyes when he'd glanced at her.

She sighed wearily and got into bed, pulling the covers up tightly under her chin. No matter how she looked at it, Friday was going to be a difficult day.

CHAPTER EIGHT

JON'S BOAT WAS A BEAUTY—a sleek white cruiser named *Aegir*, which Samantha recognized as the name of the Norse god of the sea. The divided cabin layout—forward space with a galley, dinette, double berth and small head, separated from an after cabin—was immediately below the canvas-topped bridge deck and an open sun-deck aft. Jon had transformed the after cabin into a small but efficient-looking lab, she noted as she helped load supplies onto the boat. She had a quick glimpse of a complicated maze of glass tubes linked by rubber tubing, a microscope, plastic containers and several long skinny nets hanging on one wall.

Brian and Tracy immediately made for the helm, but Jon shooed them out and sat them on a companion bench, with stern instructions to stay put until they were under way. Surprisingly, they obeyed, sitting very still in their bulky orange life jackets, watching with wide-eyed interest as Samantha and Jon cast off. Samantha enjoyed the once familiar tasks, helping Jon with an ease born of familiarity and a love of boats. She did spare a thought for the old wooden tub Jon had inherited from his father—a freight-train caboose, he'd called it. It had rolled violently in the mildest swell, its ponderous weight showing a tendency to bury its nose in the sea. They had loved that old boat, in spite of its obvious flaws, and had spent many happy hours churning away on Puget Sound, somehow managing to avoid being swamped or dumped overboard.

This was quite a change, she thought, looking around at the neat galley as she prepared breakfast. The *Aegir* handled beautifully, planing smoothly over the slightly choppy water, as stable a boat as she'd ever ridden in. The lab in the aft cabin confused her, though. It would seem to indicate that Jon was still working. Why was he so secretive about his work? Was the miniature lab simply a hobby, and all this evidence of luxury due to Ethan's bequest? Had Jon turned into some kind of playboy since Ethan's death?

After breakfast, which they ate on the bridge, the twins, already worn out with their early rising and excitement, crawled into the double berth and went immediately to sleep. Huddled together, still wrapped in their clumsy life jackets, they looked like a couple of plump pumpkins with blue-jean legs and sneakered feet. Again Samantha wondered how Lynne could abandon them, as she apparently had. She might just go to see Lynne in Seattle, she thought. But she'd better not mention the possibility to Jon or he'd accuse her of interfering again.

After she'd cleaned up the galley, she brewed coffee and took it topside to Jon, who accepted it gratefully, and casually indicated space beside him on the bench. She was at first a little embarrassed at the lack of space between them. Once settled, however, Samantha looked around, admiring the uncluttered control station with its good visibility in all directions, its comfortable benches on top of sturdy lockers, its racks for scuba gear, its mind-boggling array of instrumentation and navigational gear.

"Quite a change from the old caboose, isn't she?" Jon asked, echoing her earlier thoughts.

"Yes, but—" Samantha sighed and broke off.

"I miss her, too," Jon said softly.

For a moment there was an old feeling of accord between them. Relaxing, warmed by the coffee, Samantha opened her cream-colored ski jacket, pulling the tab of the front zipper all the way down. Jon evidently noticed her movement. He leaned forward to open the vents at the base of the windshield. "Too much?" he asked.

Samantha shook her head. "Just right."

Without warning, tension invaded the cockpit along with the breeze. To her dismay, Samantha was suddenly aware of Jon in every fiber of her being. She could feel the pressure of his thigh against hers, sense the energy in the muscular bulk of his body so close to hers. He was wearing white jeans and a blue crew-neck knit shirt, a tan down-filled vest being his only concession to the biting chill of the morning. His blond hair was ruffled slightly by the breeze filtering through the vents. One hand held his coffee mug, the other gripped the wheel... gripped it fairly tightly, she saw. His long legs, stretched forward in an apparently relaxed attitude, were tense, too. He was as aware as she was.

She stole a glance at his face, and immediately wished she hadn't. He was looking at her speculatingly, not at her face but at her hands. She had set down her coffee cup in the rack provided, but hadn't realized that her hands were twisting together, pushing her engagement ring round and round on her finger.

"You have a habit of doing that, you know," Jon said in a conversational tone. "One might think your ring doesn't fit comfortably."

"It fits very well," she said defensively.

"Uh-huh." There was a teasing note in his voice.

Samantha searched her mind for a change of subject, finally coming up with one that might help settle Anne Marie's problem. "Does Dr. Birmann ever come out with you on the boat?" she asked, carefully not looking at him.

"Occasionally. Why do you ask?"

"I wondered if he liked fishing."

"Mmm...." There was a suspicious note in his voice, but he didn't question her further. After a moment he volunteered the information that Dr. Birmann was *not* a fisherman but that he did like to get out on the water from time to time and even borrowed the boat occasionally when Jon was away.

Samantha nodded indifferently, hiding from him the fact that her mind had immediately seized on his last remark. Jon had been gone for one day; Anne Marie had told her he'd flown into Seattle with Steve Cory to take care of some errands for Eileen. So if Jon had been gone, Dr. Birmann could have taken Tom Greene out on his boat.

"You're very thoughtful," Jon said.

Samantha almost jumped, but she managed to smile vaguely. She must put Tom Greene out of her mind, she decided, or Jon would become suspicious. He'd always had the ability to see right through her. "I was just enjoying the day," she said evenly. "It's lovely, isn't it?"

She looked away from him as he agreed, determined to concentrate on the scenery and nothing else.

The saw-toothed line of the Olympic Mountains was clearly visible in the west, looming above the Olympic Peninsula. To the east, a ribbon of snow, still edging the tops of the Cascades, glittered in the sunshine, Mount Baker towering above.

Unexpectedly, she *was* enjoying herself. She felt suddenly, tremendously glad to be alive, her senses almost unbearably sharp. The air smelled invigorating, tangy with salt. The small amount of breeze released by the open vents seemed to caress her face, making it feel as clean as though she'd just emerged from a cold shower. Ahead of the boat a pair of gulls circled, calling a guttural *kuk-kuk-kuk*, their pink feet tucked neatly against their snowy underparts. The sky shone with a clear blue light. The land on either side was dotted with houses and small farms. Dark evergreens, clustered like thousands of meticulously worked French knots on an embroidered picture, mingled with alders and maples to shadow the edge of the water, graying the shallows into mystery, contrasting them with the bright ebullient blue of the water closer to the boat, which itself was tossed with the sparkling white foam of the wake. On the starboard side they were passing a shoreline she recognized. "Is that still part of Whidbey Island?" she asked, trying to dispel with words the peculiar tension that was still alive in the cockpit.

Jon glanced to his right and nodded as he set down his empty cup. "We're about to pass Admiralty Head. And that's Port Townsend on the Olympic Peninsula, coming up to port." He paused, glancing at Samantha. "We went there once, remember? You wanted to move into one of those old Victorian houses."

Why was he reminding her of times best forgotten? He'd seemed to resent it when she did the same. Of *course* she remembered Port Townsend. . . .

On a sight-seeing trip funded by Jon's sale of some

marine photographs to a local newspaper, they'd spent a night in what was called the Garden Suite of one of those old houses, recently converted into a hotel. They had reveled in the rightness of the old-fashioned brass bedstead, the flowered wallpaper, the open fire, the marble-topped washstand. They'd made love by firelight, shadows flickering across their bodies as they moved and turned together, his breath mingling with hers as they kissed, his hands tracing erotic passages across her willing flesh. They'd made a game out of the dancing shadows, kissing each other wherever the shadows touched their bodies, moving frequently so that more places were outlined in the fire's glow, secret places that must be explored and caressed with fingers and lips and tongue, places to be whispered over, marveled over as they deliberately slowed their explorations, stretching time and tension between them until their passion flared so violently that it could not be contained.

Jon's long-fingered hand touched hers and Samantha jerked back to her surroundings, to the realities of clear sky and scudding water and the brisk brightness of morning. Automatically she made a move to withdraw her hands, but his own clasped them tightly, holding them imprisoned in his grip. "You're doing it again," he said lightly.

She felt heat rising to her face. She had indeed been twisting her ring again. She'd thought of Adrian, she realized. Contrasting him with her memories, she'd thought of the way *he* kissed her—affectionately, with skill, but without stirring her to the depths as Jon stirred her. She'd thought she lacked that consuming passion because she was grown up now, more restrained. She and Jon had certainly not shown any restraint that last summer, yet she had never felt guilty about their love-making. She loved him, he loved her. Neither of them was the promiscuous type. Their lovemaking had seemed so right, so meant to be.

Was it possible, she wondered abruptly, that she just wasn't able to feel passion for *Adrian*?

Unnerved by this traitorous thought, she pulled her hands free and glared at Jon. "It's just a habit," she said firmly. "It doesn't mean a thing."

He grinned. "I wonder if Freud would agree." He glanced at her sideways. "When are you going to admit that you're still attracted to me?" he asked in a deliber-ately exasperated voice. "That gesture you make is ob-viously a subconscious desire to throw away that monstrous rock and go after me again."

"It's nothing of the sort," she protested.

"Isn't it?" Before she could guess what he was about to do, he glanced swiftly to all sides, evidently making sure the shipping lanes were empty. Then, with one hand holding the wheel firmly in place, he stretched his left arm around her, pulled her close and kissed her—at first gently, then with rising passion, his tongue insistently in-vading her mouth, which had parted involuntarily with surprise. She murmured a protest that sounded feeble even to her own ears, something about his promise to behave. She was not surprised when he ignored her. In-creasing the pressure of his mouth, he drew from her lips that same instantly responding heat that had always flared between them.

There was a tightness, a warm melting contraction between her thighs. Somehow her arms had wound themselves around his waist, feeling the soft yielding down of the vest he wore, stealing upward beneath it to the knit shirt that covered but did not disguise the ridged muscles of his back. Her breasts were pressed against the unyielding strength of his chest, and she could feel their firm outlines as though there was no clothing between them. His hand was wound in the curling mass of her hair, not pulling, not tangling, but pressing insistently, urging her closer, as his mouth urged her to submit to him and to her own aching longing for him.

She sensed no anger in him this time—no mockery, no desire to cause her pain. This was a time out of mind, a time from the past when love had come easily to both of them, when passion had governed their every move.

His hand moved again, stroking roughly down her spine against the bulk of her ski jacket, lifting the knitted hem, seeking entry beneath her thin cambric blouse. And it was on the bareness of her back, its coldness a shock against her unnaturally heated skin, making her shudder in a way that was again familiar— a shudder not due to the cold at all but to the caressing, reassuring pressure of his hand, her lover's hand. "Jon," she murmured against his mouth. "Jonathan, Jonathan, Jon."

It was an old litany she murmured, an old cause of laughter between them, this unconscious alliterative repetition of his name. She felt his hand tense as he recognized it, and then his mouth eased away from hers. Blue eyes blazed into hers. "Say it," he ordered. "Say you still want me. Tell me you love me."

If he hadn't demanded them, the words would have been there on her lips, eager to tumble out into the crisp morning air. But now she recognized again that look of triumph in his eyes and knew that this was what he'd been leading up to all along. All his provocation, his sometimes apparently senseless teasing of her, his actions on the beach the other night, had been intended to bring her to this admission.

Even though she recognized all of this in one fleeting moment, even though she knew without any doubt that his motives were not at all admirable or honest, she was almost ready to say the words that would tell him he had succeeded in awakening all of her dormant love for him. She was almost ready to admit that he hadn't even needed to go to these lengths, that she had recognized at once that she still loved him as she would never love any other man.

But then fate intruded in the person of young Tracy Lawton, who had evidently awakened and was shouting for permission to come up.

For one second more Jon continued to hold her close to him, his hand tensely possessive against the flesh of her back. His face was turned away from her, for Tracy's intrusion had obviously reminded him of his duty to navigation. But in an instant he would face her again, she knew. She could feel the tension in his back muscles, straining under her hands as he waited for her answer, and she felt too the reminding pressure of Adrian's ring against her finger, crushed between Jon's tight-fitting shirt and his vest.

Sanity prevailed. "Why, Jon?" she asked softly. "Why do you want me to make a confession like that? Why is it so important to you?"

She saw his mouth tighten, felt his hand lose its pressure against her back. That was not the answer he'd wanted to hear. Within another second he'd straightened himself, allowing her trapped hands to release themselves. A moment later they were sitting stiffly side by side, both looking ahead at the sparkling water. Samantha felt suddenly as weary as though she'd rowed the boat this far. "Why Jon?" she repeated, as Tracy shouted once more.

Jon delayed answering her. He thumped twice on the deck beneath his feet with the heel of his shoe, then made some minor adjustment to one of the instruments in front of him. Then he sighed. "It doesn't matter, Samantha," he said with forced lightness. "It just seemed to me that we're both suffering unnecessarily, physically speaking. I have to get you out of my system somehow. Probably the sensible thing to do would be to go to bed and get it over with."

Swallowing, Samantha prepared to deliver a blistering response to show him just what she thought of this humiliating suggestion. But then Tracy's voice called again, closer this time, and she turned to see her's and Brian's dark heads appearing through the open hatch behind her.

Both children had awakened refreshed and full of high spirits, and Samantha had all she could do to keep them from falling overboard in their eagerness to examine every fascinating object on deck. There was no opportunity for Jon to talk to her again, or vice versa; no chance for privacy in which to argue with him.

It was a frustrating situation, made more so by the fact that Samantha's renewed knowledge of her love had been blasted apart by his proposition—his *indecent* proposition. She had the feeling he'd laugh if she called his suggestion indecent. After all, they had certainly "gone to bed" with each other before. But there was a big difference now. She could never bring herself to make love with a man who wanted her only because of some spilled-over memories fo the past—unfinished business, as he called it. She couldn't pretend to be a prude, not where Jon was concerned, but neither could she be intimate with a man who didn't love her, as Jon most patently did not.

By the time they arrived in Oak Bay Marina and Jon was chatting affably with some customs officials on the dock, she had managed to calm her traitorous senses and had almost succeeded in convincing herself that she couldn't have revealed her true emotions to Jon. Nor had she really felt them. He had caught her at a weak moment, that was all, caught her while she was mentally questioning Adrian's feelings for her. She didn't really still love Jon; after that revolting suggestion, in fact, she almost hated him. And so she was safe now, armed against his insidious attraction for her body—her physically hungry body.

It had not been easy to arrive at this decision. She had felt terribly rattled for a long time, though somehow she'd managed to deal with Brian and Tracy and their countless questions. Gradually, however, her pulse had slowed, her heart had stopped hammering against her rib cage, and she had achieved at least a semblance of calm.

Jon had evidently experienced no such difficulty. He had immediately, at the twins' appearance, become "Uncle Jon" again—a smiling good-natured man without a care in the world. He had even managed to meet her angry gaze several times without comment or response, treating her as he treated the twins, with friendly all-pervasive charm.

Damn you, Jon Blake, she thought as she assisted the twins onto the dock and helped them off with their life jackets. *What kind of game are you playing? And how best can I thwart you?*

She wanted revenge, she realized. Revenge for his arrogant assumption that she would agree to make love with him so as to "get her out of his system." And revenge she would have, somehow.

"Truce?" Jon murmured after they'd both stowed their jackets aboard and he was escorting her toward the entrance to Sealand.

She glanced at him uncertainly. He was smiling in a disconcertingly friendly way. About to make some angry reply, she hesitated. The twins, both skipping excitedly ahead, had no idea there was any dissension between them. She couldn't spoil their day by staying angry with Jon, at least not noticeably so. "I guess so," she said grudgingly at last, and his hand squeezed her elbow, his grip warm through the thin russet cotton of her blouse.

She was pleased that she felt no physical response to his touch this time. Anger was a good strong emotion, she thought, a good defense against weakness. She would hide it from the children for now, but she would keep it alive until she could decide what form her revenge would take against Jonathan Blake.

Without obvious haste, she drew her elbow free and smiled tightly at Jon's enquiring face. "For the sake of the children?" she asked bitingly.

"Of course not," he said. And that ambiguous reply served to worry her for the next few hours.

Jon was a thoughtful guide. He explained, with absolute patience and interesting anecdotes, the habits and life-styles of the octopuses, wolf eels, salmon and other creatures on view through the giant underwater windows in the lower part of the Sealand building.

The twins were tremendously impressed to learn that he had once captured a huge octopus in Puget Sound, a gift for the aquarium at Tacoma's Point Defiance Zoo.

"I was in no danger," he assured them. "The octopus is a very timid creature. This one did turn bright red with rage and frustration, but didn't attempt to hurt me. Octopuses can't hurt anyone, anyway. Unfortunately they're sometimes confused with giant squids, who have claws on their tentacles. But even giant squids, though they will attack whales and certainly *look* fearsome, live at depths remote from man and don't bother him at all."

Brian gazed at the large Pacific octopus that was clinging to the window of one of the undersea grottoes, the rows of suckers on its tentacles plastered like suction cups against the glass. "Yuck," he said loudly. "*I* wouldn't want to touch it."

Jon ruffled the boy's dark hair, smiling. "It's not at all unpleasant. The main thing I had to be careful of was not to hurt it. I'll lend you a book about octopuses, Brian. You'll find they are the most misunderstood of creatures. They're really quite wonderful and marvelously equipped for survival. They aren't at all the evil quarrelsome creatures movies and adventure stories make them out to be. Mostly they just want to be left alone."

"Tell us about some other animals," Tracy demanded, and Jon went on to tell them about sharks he'd swum with when testing out a new type of wet suit meant to protect divers from shark attack.

He was at his best when talking about the oceans and their inhabitants, Samantha thought. He had obviously lost none of his love for the sea.

As Jon and the twins strolled, engrossed, throughout the huge aquarium, she took the opportunity to look around her more thoroughly, even going back upstairs to buy a guidebook for the twins—a good excuse to look into the office and see if Tom Green was there. He wasn't. She hesitated, wondering if she should question the girl who'd sold her the guidebook, but somehow she couldn't bring herself to do that. If he *was* there, the girl might tell him she wanted to see him, and then what would she do?

Jon had noticed her brief absence. He raised his eyebrows questioningly, but seemed satisfied when she held up the guidebook. After a few more minutes it was time for the show, and they emerged into the pool area to find it crowded with sightseers. Jon managed to find room for the twins by the rail that surrounded the sea-lion pool, but Samantha hung back. While everyone else laughed at the antics of the sea lions as they responded to the commands of their trainer, she idly looked around. Several employees were engaged in various tasks, she noticed, but none of them remotely resembled Tom Greene. Most of the attendants were young.

At the side of the whale pool was a wooden fence and a door marked Animal Care Dept., Authorized Staff Only. She watched it for a while, but no one went in or out. Tom Greene could be behind that door, she thought. How could she find out? Why hadn't she realized what an impossible task Anne Marie had set for her? How could she get away from Jon long enough to really explore the place?

The sea-lion show had ended, and the twins were tugging at Jon's hands, eager to get to the whale pool while there was still room at the rails. Jon looked at her quizzically. "You've no interest in sea lions?" he asked.

"Of course I have," she replied stiffly. "There wasn't room for me. But I saw quite a bit—that alarm-clock act is really something, isn't it?" Luckily she'd managed to see that much.

Jon nodded and made no further comment, but she noticed him watching her thoughtfully as they took up their positions at the rail around the whale pool. Samantha had chosen to stand by a white railing, which the commentator assured everybody was the least likely place for a spectator to get wet. Brian and Tracy persuaded Jon to stand farther along at a gray rail, though he balked at the blue rail, said to be wettest of all.

The show began with Haida, the killer whale, swimming the length of the pool waving one pectoral flipper at the crowd, much to the delight of all the children. Then he poked his huge head out of the water and "talked back" to his trainer for a while, showing all his teeth, his high-pitched keening voice sounding like human yodeling. After that he began to swim again, surfacing every once in a while to flap his enormous tail against the water and splash some of the spectators, who screamed with mingled astonishment and delight. Tracy and Brian hung on the railing, eyes round with wonder, faces bright, obviously longing for their chance to get wet. Jon himself stood back a little, evidently not as anxious for a bath. The children seemed to especially enjoy Haida's impression of a motor boat, managed by snorting through his blow hole as he zoomed the length of the pool. His impression sounded very realistic and brought applause from the crowd.

Remembering her quest, Samantha kept glancing behind her at the door marked Animal Care Department, so she almost missed Haida's most spectacular trick. Luckily she turned back just in time to see five tons of streamlined black-and-white whale leap vertically into the air, completely clearing the water at the center of the pool. It was an awe-inspiring sight—he was a magnificent creature.

There was a second of thunderstruck silence before the resounding splash of the whale's reentry sent the crowd scurrying away from the barrier, most of them too late to escape the huge fountain of water displaced by the whale's body. Tracy and Brian had achieved their wish, Samantha saw. Though not soaked, they'd managed to get fairly damp, and they were laughing and clapping with glee. Even Jon was smiling as he shook water from his hair. Another leap, and another, and the crowd was applauding enthusiastically. Samantha herself was so caught up in admiration of the whale's instant response to his trainer's whistled commands as well as his obvious enjoyment of the herring treats that rewarded him each time that she forgot her primary purpose in coming to Sealand. But as the show drew to a close, she remembered again and realized she would have to think up some excuse to leave the others for a while.

It was Haida who provided her with a reason. Having spent a few minutes lazily circling the large pool, the whale evidently decided it was time for some mischief of his own. Without any whistled command, he suddenly raised his huge head as he drew level with Samantha's position, rolled one small but intelligent eye at the people standing there, then spat out a full mouthful of water, straight over the crowd. Samantha saw what looked like a wall of water coming toward her, backed rapidly up to the wooden fence behind her and could go no farther. A second later she was drenched from head to toe.

Jon and the twins joined her at once, the children chortling, Jon with a concerned expression though his eyes were twinkling. "I thought this was supposed to be a safe area," Samantha sputtered.

"Somebody forgot to tell Haida that," Jon said gravely.

Samantha frowned with mock anger at the still-laughing twins, who weren't anywhere near as wet as she was, and then an idea occurred to her. "I'd better find a rest room," she said to Jon as he tried to mop her blouse with a pocket handkerchief—an exercise in futility. She was aware, even before she followed his quizzical gaze, that the thin cotton, which had received the full force of the water, clung to her body, revealing every curve of her breasts. But she ignored the wave of embarrassment that followed the realization. "I can't go around like this," she said evenly. "I look like a drowned rat."

"You do rather," he drawled, transferring his handkerchief to her dripping hair, one hand lifting her chin to hold her head steady.

Samantha swallowed an angry retort. She was not going to respond to his teasing again, she reminded herself. Moving her head free of his far-from-gentle ministrations, she suggested to the children that they go back into the aquarium while she tried to get herself dry.

It took her about ten minutes to restore some semblance of order to her appearance. Her hair would finish drying once she was back in the sunshine, she decided. So would her blouse. She'd held it under the air dryer for a short time, afraid to hold it there too long in case it wrinkled beyond redemption. Once it was on again and she'd repaired her makeup, she felt she was at least presentable.

Avoiding the aquarium, she managed to find an alternative route to the pool area and headed that way, determined to open the forbidden door to see what was on the other side. If anyone caught her, she could just say that she was curious, she decided.

Subterfuge proved to be unnecessary. As she passed the Stellar sea-lion pen, she saw a man washing a window down a passageway to her right—a window that jutted out in front of the seabird cliff. She paused and then backed up to station herself behind a post at the corner of the sea-lion pen, watching through the double set of windows to the other side. The man was Tom Greene. He was still wearing the same blue sweater and white cap, the same sunglasses. And he was wiping the window of the seabird cliff with the same enthusiasm he'd shown for hoeing at the spa, making desultory movements with a wad of paper towel, apparently unconcerned that he was making streaks on the glass.

As she stared at him, safely concealed behind the post, he took off his hat and glasses and ran the back of his hand across his forehead as though he were overheated. As well he might be in that bulky sweater.

His face looked familiar to her. How could that be, she wondered—she'd never seen it uncovered before. But there was something about his eyes.... She couldn't see their color clearly from this distance, but they seemed strangely luminous, like quicksilver—unexpectedly attractive and familiar looking. Why familiar? The memory was just beyond her grasp. She tried to pull it into view, but couldn't.

Why did he keep his eyes covered all the time anyway, she wondered. Did the sunlight affect them? Evidently so. A moment later he replaced the glasses, settled his cap back over his graying brown hair and went back to wiping the window.

"What the hell are you up to, Sam?" Jon's voice asked from behind her. She was so startled that she jumped and hit her forehead on the thick glass of the sea-lions' window.

Trying desperately to think of an excuse, she turned to face him, but found he wasn't looking at her as she'd expected. Instead he was squinting through the glass, looking at Tom Greene. "That man worked at the spa for a while," he said slowly. He frowned at Samantha. "You asked me about him. What's going on?"

"I just...I was only...." She was saved by the appearance of the twins, who had decided they were hungry and were demanding fish and chips from the nearby snack bar.

Samantha started feverishly talking to them about the show they had seen, keeping up a barrage of conversation so that Jon would have no chance to question her further.

At least she'd accomplished her objective, she thought as they all entered the snack bar. She could tell Anne Marie that Tom Greene was perfectly safe and apparently healthy; Dr. Birmann had told his daughter the truth. Though she still couldn't help wondering....

Determinedly she put Tom Greene out of her mind. She didn't have to worry about him anymore. Now if she could just think of something to tell Jon when he questioned her again, as she was sure he would....

What bad luck to have him recognize Tom Greene. If not for that, she could have told him she was just watching the birds. But he *had* recognized the man. And he had seen her skulking around the corner of the sea-lion pen.

She would tell him the truth, she decided. There was no reason not to now. Relieved, she set herself to enjoy the remainder of the day, which went all too quickly for the twins.

Jon took them to Victoria, and she marveled as she used to at the magnificent old Empress Hotel, draped in ivy, majestically commanding the harbor scene. The children, forced to choose among all the entertainment available, voted for a city tour on a double-decker bus, a trip through the wax museum and a shopping expedition that netted them some new toys and a Toby jug for Ben. Finally showing signs of fatigue, they didn't argue when Jon decided it was time to go home.

Samantha worried that they were so tired they would need another nap right away, but they were happy enough to sit on a bench in the control station, eagerly asking questions about the various places they passed. It was a couple of hours before they gave in to the combined effects of fresh air and excitement, but they still refused to go below. Instead they leaned against each other, gradually slipping down onto the covered bench until they lay there in a heap, arms and legs dangling.

Samantha brought up a couple of blankets to cover

them, and coffee for herself and Jon. The presence of the children had so far prevented any return of tension in the cockpit, and Samantha was feeling quite relaxed and even pleasantly sleepy when Jon suddenly asked, "All right, Sam, out with it. What were you up to?"

There was a patronizing sound in his voice that made her stiffen. Maybe she wouldn't tell him the truth after all. "I was looking for you," she said. "I just happened to see that man and thought he looked familiar."

"Uh-huh. He's not the reason you wanted to come to Vancouver Island?"

She hesitated, not wanting to tell him an outright lie.

"Come on, Sam," he urged, leaning forward over the wheel but looking back at her over his shoulder, both eyebrows raised. "This is me, remember? I *know* you. You weren't interested in making the trip for any reason but to get to Sealand—I figured that out right away. You expect me to believe it was a coincidence that you saw that man there? What is he to you? And why didn't you want him to see you?"

Samantha sighed. She might as well come clean, she decided. Looking away from him at the distant shoreline, she told him of Dr. Birmann saying he'd got a job for Tom Greene at Sealand.

"And you didn't believe him?"

"Well...." She hesitated. "There was something funny about the whole thing." Carefully she tried to explain the odd circumstances of Tom Greene's arrival on the island, Ben Fletcher's comments about him, his sudden disappearance.

When she was done, Jon laughed and sat back, flexing his shoulders as though they ached a little. "Rub my back a bit, would you?" he suggested.

She glanced at him suspiciously, but he wasn't looking at her. All his attention was directed ahead of him. "Please, Sam," he said. "I've got a hellacious cramp. I've put in quite a few hours at the wheel today—all of it for you."

Grudgingly, not sure if he was trying to start something again, she began rubbing his back with as objective a touch as she could manage. "Not outside my vest, for heaven's sake," he objected. "I can't feel a thing."

Obediently, determined not to give him cause to think she was afraid to touch him, Samantha slipped her hands under the down vest and began massaging his back more firmly, gritting her teeth against the annoyance she felt over his request.

After a moment he glanced at her again. "You haven't changed much, have you, Sam? Still looking for mysteries. I wondered why you showed sudden interest in the possibility of Jakob using my boat. Why did you think the good doctor had lied?"

"I didn't. Well, actually, it was Anne Marie. She was worried."

"You checked on this guy because Anne Marie asked you to?"

"Yes."

"You didn't *seriously* think Jakob was up to something criminal, did you?"

"Not exactly, but...."

"I know. There was something funny about it." His voice was impatient now, and her hands stilled against his spine. After a moment she withdrew them; he didn't seem to notice. He hunched forward, evidently thinking over what she had told him.

She stole a glance at his profile. His mouth was tight, his eyes narrowed. At last he said angrily, "You really are the limit, Sam. You and Anne Marie have taken a bunch of perfectly innocent happenings and worked them up into a mystery that has no foundation in fact. I remember now that she did ask me if I'd taken someone to Seattle. I had no idea who she was talking about. But I'm sure she'd never have thought of pursuing the matter if you hadn't encouraged her. She knows as well as I do that Jakob is a respectable and honorable man." He paused. "Don't you think it's time you grew up?" he added caustically. "What if you hadn't seen what's his name—Tom Greene—at Sealand? Would you have decided Jakob had done away with him?"

It did sound ridiculous, Samantha realized. But then Jon hadn't seen Anne Marie's worried face, hadn't heard her tell of Tom Greene's previous visit, and of her father's subsequent alarm. Nor had he heard the two men arguing so violently in the woods behind the spa. Did Jon know that his friend spoke Russian, she wondered.

"I merely wanted to relieve Anne Marie's anxiety," she said coldly. She was especially furious that he didn't believe the trip had been Anne Marie's idea, but she wasn't going to expose herself to further ridicule by insisting. Actually she felt a bit guilty that she'd betrayed Anne Marie's confidence—though she hadn't told Jon the whole story by far.

"Are you satisfied now?" he asked tartly after a while. "Or are you going to check up on Tom Greene again? Don't ask me to take you if you are."

"I didn't ask you this time," she pointed out.

"So you didn't. And if I'd known what you were up

to, I'd not have volunteered. I thought you were being very kind, taking the twins off Ben's hands for a day. I didn't know you were using them for nefarious reasons of your own.''

"Nefarious—" Samantha broke off. "I didn't *have* to take them with me," she pointed out.

"No, but they were good camouflage, weren't they?"

As this was exactly the thought that had occurred to her, Samantha subsided, deciding she wasn't going to continue this senseless argument. She'd really angered him, she saw. He didn't like the idea of her having suspicions about his friend. He was loyal, that was certain, at least to everyone except her.

Jon made no attempt to continue the futile argument, either. For a long time he paid no attention to her. She might well have been one of the pieces of equipment on the boat.

And that was just fine, she decided as Collins Island came in sight. At least his annoyance had prevented him from making any further advances to her, and for that she was glad. She was still smarting over his earlier remark. *Go to bed and get it over with.* He'd pay for that. She was quite determined that he would pay.

For the rest of the journey she amused herself by plotting her revenge, thinking up and discarding several schemes and arriving finally at the conclusion that she'd play it by ear. Jon quite obviously still had physical feelings for her—sexual feelings—and he was determined to prove that he was not alone. He wanted to prove that she was still sexually attracted to him.

Very well, then, what if she went along with him? What if she *appeared* to respond to him, and then at the last moment showed she was strong enough to walk away before anything happened between them? It was not a fully conceived idea, but it held some promise of revenge. Jon would be furious, she thought, and the thought pleased her.

She would think about it, she decided. She would definitely think about it.

CHAPTER NINE

ANNE MARIE must have been sitting in her front window with binoculars trained on the parking lot. She arrived at the chalet at the precise moment Samantha reached the top of the steps. "Did you see him?" she demanded in a stage whisper.

"Yes," Samantha said wearily. "He's fine. He's employed at Sealand. There's nothing to worry about."

Anne Marie's petite body slumped with relief against the doorjamb. Samantha hoped that would be the end of it, but Anne Marie wandered into the sitting room behind her and sat down without being asked.

"I saw Jon bring you home," she said. There was a question in her voice.

Samantha had gone to tidy her windblown hair in front of the bathroom mirror. She was glad Anne Marie couldn't see her face. Might as well confess, she decided. It would be all over the island by the next day. "Jon took me to Victoria in his boat," she said. "We brought the twins with us."

There was a silence. Samantha took a deep breath and walked back into the sitting room. Anne Marie was sitting tensely upright in one of the wooden-armed chairs, staring in Samantha's direction, her face crumpled. "How could you, Samantha?" she wailed. "I *told* you I didn't want Jon to know."

"I didn't have any choice. The twins told Jon we were going. He offered a boat ride and the twins went crazy over the idea."

"Did Jon know *why* you were going?"

"He thought it was a sight-seeing trip."

As Anne Marie started to slump with relief again, fairness made her add, "He knows now, however."

"Oh, Samantha." The tears started again.

Samantha sighed. "Look, Anne Marie, I'm sorry I had to tell him, but I really didn't have any choice. He not only saw Tom Greene and recognized him, he saw me watching the man."

"Does he know the trip was my idea?"

"Not entirely. I told him only the essentials. You don't have to worry. He blames me for the whole thing. He thinks I'm preternaturally nosy."

Anne Marie brightened. "I'm sorry, Samantha. I do appreciate your going and everything. I guess what I'm upset about is that you went with Jon. I mean, you used to be such great friends and I think he still likes you. He hasn't been the same to me since you came back."

She was sitting up again, a defiant expression on her face. "I know I'm not as, well—as *glamorous* as you or anything, but before you came Jon and I were, well, we were pretty close. He even took me out on his boat with my father sometimes, and he *wanted* to take me out alone. But now...."

"You could have gone with him," Samantha said wearily, sitting down in the other chair. "I suggested that, if you remember."

"But I didn't want him to think I was being stupid."

"So now he thinks *I* was being stupid. It doesn't really matter, does it? You don't have to worry about me where Jon's concerned, anyway. There's nothing between us now.''

Anne Marie looked more genuinely apologetic. "I'm sorry, Samantha," she repeated, this time with more sincerity. "It must have been awkward for you. I really am grateful. And I'm sorry I snapped at you. I guess I was relieved that Tom Greene's all right." She paused and added sheepishly. "I guess I was jealous, too." She took a deep breath. "I might as well tell you, I'm in love with Jon.''

Samantha swallowed. "Does he know that?"

"Oh, yes, I'm not very good at hiding things." There was a cheerful, almost smug expression on her childlike face now.

Samantha felt a mixture of emotions, none of which were very commendable. "You don't have to be jealous on my account," she said neutrally.

"I see that now. But Jon is such a wonderful person, it's hard for me to believe he really likes me. I'm so ordinary and he's so special and clever and handsome and—"

"For heaven's sake, Anne Marie, he's not some kind of god.''

"He is to me," the girl said warmly. "We really did become very close, Samantha. He's been much more than a friend to me." She hesitated, and Samantha was half afraid she was going to reveal something more, half afraid she wasn't.

"I'm very tired," she said abruptly.

Anne Marie stood up at once. "I'll go then. But I want you to know I really am grateful."

"Okay."

Still the girl hesitated, a little tight-lipped suddenly.

"You're definitely not . . . you really don't still care for Jon? That way, I mean?"

"Not in any way," Samantha lied.

"Because I wouldn't want to think he was, well, cheating on me."

It took a moment for Samantha to register the implications of that remark. When she did, she felt sickened. "Just how close *are* you and Jon?" she asked.

All at once Anne Marie seemed very anxious to be gone. She hovered by the door for a moment and then turned back looking somewhat furtive. "We're very, very close," she said firmly, and then she opened the door and left.

Samantha sat with her head back, eyes closed. She was beyond thought, she decided. The events of the day had worn her out. Perhaps things would look better in the morning.

But when morning came and she was back working in her office, she was as confused about her own feelings as before. In spite of what Ben had said and Eileen had implied, Jon had given no indication that he was interested *sexually* in Anne Marie, not yesterday when they talked about her, or before that. He'd seemed to act more like an elder brother to her, a rather patronizing elder brother. And if he and Anne Marie were all that close, why would he make advances to *her*?"

"I'll never understand men," she told her typewriter.

"Don't even try," Deborah's voice said from the other end of the room.

JULY 4 WAS HOT—the hottest Fourth of July in thirty years, the islanders said. There was no breeze—a thick haze had settled over the island. All the mountains were invisible. Weather forecasters talked about a low-pressure area and pronounced solemn warnings about storms.

In the spa rockeries the leaves of the rhododendrons drooped in spite of the sprinklers Ben had started early in the day. Day lilies had popped into rich coppery orange bloom, seemingly overnight, and the bright yellow flowers of hypericum—St. Johnswort—glowed with an unearthly light against the thick green carpet of their leaves.

Samantha and the twins escaped the heat in the always cool waters of the Sound, swimming and splashing and playing water games of the children's devising until Samantha felt waterlogged and collapsed in a lawn chair beside Ben. For a long time they sat without talking, just relaxing, watching Brian and Tracy romping in the shallows like a couple of Charles Kingsley's water babies.

In the later afternoon Ben set up a hibachi and a picnic table on the veranda, and they toasted hot dogs and buns that tasted deliciously of burnt charcoal, and marshmallows that melted golden brown on their tongues. Samantha and the children kept on their damp swimsuits. The temperature seemed to have increased. So had the humidity. The sky was thick, white and glaring, exerting pressure on the earth and making Samantha feel lethargic.

She keet glancing at the sky, hoping there wouldn't be a storm. The horizon to the southwest had darkened considerably, and she'd caught an occasional glimpse of lightning and heard the faint threatening rumble of thunder in the distance.

Once in a while she found herself looking up toward

the bluff, toward the Collins place—the Blake place now—though it was hidden among the trees. She wouldn't have been surprised to see Jon clamber down the hillside to join them for their meal—she'd carefully refrained from asking Ben if he was invited. But he hadn't come, and Samantha convinced herself the emotion she felt was relief.

After dinner the twins talked Ben into demonstrating card tricks, and he proceeded to dazzle them at the wooden picnic table, making them roar with laughter at his apparent consternation when aces moved from four piles into one, or he turned up cards that matched those selected by the children from another pack. He also produced missing cards from unlikely places, including a folded card from the wet tangle of Tracy's braided black hair.

The children would have kept him going all evening, but at last he professed himself "all tricked out." Still they wouldn't let him stop until he'd performed their favorite rising-card trick.

His face set in its usual mournful lines, he produced a fresh pack of cards and held them up, requesting various cards to rise from the deck. Miraculously, they did, until he ordered the queen of hearts to put in an appearance. "Looks like we can't get the queen to come out today," he said sadly.

"You have to ask her nicely, grandpa," Brian shouted, showing he knew the rules of this trick as well as Samantha did.

Obediently Ben obliged, using the flowery phrases of an Elizabethan courtier. And of course the lady immediately jumped out of the pack and into his hand, delighting and mystifying the children. Samantha enjoyed the trick as much as they did, even though she now knew the secret of the hidden silk threads attached to the cards.

"Let that be a lesson to you, Brian," Ben said with a sidelong glance at Samantha. "If you want girls to like you, you have to talk sweetly to them. They like that kind of stuff."

Brian made a gargoyle face. "Yuck," he said. "Who wants girls to like them? Girls are yucky."

Tracy punched him on the shoulder, then ran off down the steps with Brian in hot pursuit. After wrestling around in the grass for a while, they rolled on down to the beach, then went peaceably off together to see what the last tide had brought in.

Samantha laughed. "Brian's part of the new generation, Ben. He'd rather tell a girl what he honestly thinks and take his chances, instead of beguiling her with flowery phrases."

Ben nodded, still shuffling cards hand over hand. "And you, Samantha?" he asked gently. "Are you always so honest yourself?"

Samantha eyed him suspiciously. He'd put the cards down as he voiced the question and was regarding her directly with his mournful dark eyes, a fond expression on his lined face.

"What's that supposed to mean?" she asked.

Ben put his large hand over hers on the picnic table, completely covering it. "I was watching you, girl, the other day when Jon suggested taking you out on his boat. You still love him, don't you? But you're not about to let him know it."

"Of course I don't love him," Samantha protested. "I'm engaged to Adrian, remember?"

Ben gave her his mirthless grin and sat back. Reaching into the pocket of his jeans for matches, he lit his pipe, taking several minutes in the process. "Adrian?" he repeated gravely. "Oh, yes, *Adrian*. The city feller."

"That's the one."

Ben shook his head. "You're not being honest with yourself, Samantha. I know love when I see it. There was a lot of it between my Catherine and me, enough to stop me settling for second best after she died. Are you sure you're not settling for second best, agreeing to marry this Adrian person?"

Samantha squirmed uncomfortably on the bench. "Adrian's a good man, Ben, I told you that."

"I remember. But I saw the way you looked at Jon, too. And I think you're not facing the truth."

"It doesn't make much difference," Samantha blurted out. "Jon doesn't have any feelings left for me anyway. He's forever provoking me, deviling me."

"You think he'd bother if he didn't still care about you?"

"Look, Ben—"

He raised his pipe, forestalling her protest. "Okay, girl, I'll shut my mouth. Just remember though that people's words don't always reflect their feelings. Pride gets in the way, and he's a proud man, is Jon. You hurt him badly once. He's still smarting, I've no doubt. He'll have to get beyond that before the two of you can get together again."

"What about the way *I* was hurt," Samantha protested. "I didn't want to end it. It was Jon who—" She broke off, realizing Ben had provoked her into saying more than she'd meant to. "You're still a wily old fox, Ben Fletcher," she said lovingly.

He nodded. "That I am. But I'll say no more. Just

remember that sometimes it's best not to say anything when things aren't going well between two people who love each other. Sometimes it's best to just let things happen, to give them a chance to happen. And to be honest. Honesty is always the best.''

Remembering the way she'd plotted revenge on Jon, Samantha felt ashamed of herself under Ben's direct scrutiny. But Ben hadn't witnessed Jon's assault on her senses on the boat, she told herself. And he hadn't heard Jon suggest they "go to bed and get it over with." He had no idea of the true situation, after all.

"Are you enjoying your job at the spa?" Ben asked as she hesitated, trying to decide if she should respond to his last remark.

Relieved at the change of subject, Samantha smiled. "I'm amazed how fast the days go by. I really enjoy meeting all the new people, even if some of them are a bit... supercilious. I've made several friends, too—a Mrs. Delaney and Liz—" Samantha broke off. She'd been about to tell Ben about Liz Vandervort, and that would have been a breech of ethics. Liz Vandervort had arrived fairly recently to rest and recuperate following face-lift surgery. A well-known beauty and renowned Washington hostess, married to a politician, she had chafed under her enforced solitude in her chalet. The face-lift was a secret. Mrs. Vandervort was registered at the spa as Margo Smith; she had arrived at night. Only Dr. Birmann, Anne Marie and Samantha knew her true identity.

Taking pity on the woman's boredom, Samantha had visited her whenever she had time. She'd played scrabble and backgammon with her and sat for long periods listening to her tales of Washington life. Liz had spared no details.

From the sound of it, Washington life was not for the fainthearted. According to Liz, she was busy from sunrise to late at night, attending club activities or accompanying her husband to political or social gatherings. She'd given up her own career as a fashion consultant so that she could volunteer for community activities and work in political campaigns. It had been a mistake to give up her career, she told Samantha. After all her devotion, her husband had recently acquired a mistress—a young mistress, which was the reason for Liz's face-lift. Not a very good reason, Samantha thought. She had nothing against face-lifts, but she felt the only reason for taking such a drastic step was to improve the way you felt about *yourself*. It seemed to her that having a face-lift in the hope of saving a marriage was like having a baby for the same reason—it wasn't too likely to work. However, she liked Liz and hoped her marriage *would* work out.

Samantha became aware that Ben was waiting for her to continue. "Dr. Birmann is really nice," she said hastily. "He's always concerned that I might be working too hard. It was his suggestion that I switch my days off so I'd be free today, even though he had some new people arriving this morning. He said he could manage them himself for once."

Ben nodded. "He's a thoughtful employer all right. I've found that out for myself. He understands my whole problem here with the twins and lets me make my own hours."

"So he should. He won't find a better gardener anywhere." Samantha was tempted for a moment to ask Ben what he thought about Tom Greene going off so suddenly, but she decided that was a subject best left alone. "I'm learning a lot about exercise and nutrition," she said after a while. "I'm going to be in much better shape when I leave here than I was when I came."

"You look pretty good to me," Ben said, scowling at her over his cloud of pipe smoke.

Samantha laughed. "There's always room for improvement."

"If you say so." He tapped out his pipe in an old metal ashtray and put it down, looking at her soberly. "You don't think you'll be tempted to stay on when Monique comes back? I have an idea the doctor might want you to."

Samantha shook her head. "I've only contracted for six months. Besides, I have to get back home, to get ready for my wedding."

As she saw Ben's heavy eyebrows raise, she rushed on, "I wouldn't want to go on doing such work anyway, Ben, even though it's fun. It's not too... meaningful."

"Nothing wrong with helping people look as good as they can," Ben said firmly. "I've never agreed with those who think it's foolish vanity that brings people to places like the spa. You have to look your best if you're going to have a good opinion of yourself. I'd enroll myself if I thought it would do any good. Only thing that saves me is I've already got a damn good opinion of myself—seems to be built in. And I don't apologize for it. If you don't have a good opinion of yourself, who *can* you like?"

Having just had similar thoughts, Samantha wasn't about to argue with him. It did seem to her, though, that some of the spa's guests were far too dedicated to their own beauty, to the exclusion of anything else. Which was hardly a healthy attitude. "I didn't mean I thought the *spa* was worthless,'' she said slowly. ''It's just that I feel I could be doing something that would have more meaning for me.''

She was surprised to find herself voicing thoughts to Ben that she hadn't realized she had. She'd thought she was quite happy with her work at the spa, had thought her nagging sense of nonachievement was due to her still-confused emotions about Jon.

''Will you go back to working for your father, then?''

She made a face. ''No. That palled, too. It was too... mercenary.'' Actually she'd found herself remembering Jon's disparaging remark and agreeing that making exaggerated claims for unnecessary products so they'd sell at inflated prices was no way to spend a life.

''I'd like to do something more...more useful,'' she concluded lamely.

''You used to write, I remember.''

''And want to again. I thought I'd get started here, but so far I haven't had time.'' That wasn't strictly true, she admitted to herself. She'd had the time, but she'd felt too rattled, too unsure....

''A bit confused, are you, Samantha?'' Ben asked kindly.

She smiled at him with affection. ''It shows, doesn't it? Don't worry about me, Ben. I'll get myself sorted out one day.''

''I hope so, girl. I'd like to see you happy, and no matter how happy you say you are, I don't think you're settled yet.'' He patted her hand gently. ''Don't you go throwing that Adrian in my face now. I'm determined to see you back together with Jon again, and I won't be argued with.''

Samantha sighed. ''Ben, you don't understand—''

"That's what Lynne used to tell me all the time. But it's surprising what a bit of old age will do for you. I understand a lot more than I'm given credit for."

Suddenly curious, Samantha was about to question him about Lynne and her continued absence from the island, but Brian and Tracy returned before she could do so. Tracy pointed out that it was starting to get dark and it was definitely time to get out the fireworks. Already in the distance they could hear the sound of firecrackers, and once in a while a rocket exploded somewhere on the mainland, showing bright fountains of color that were visible even through the now-lowering haze.

Obediently Ben went to get the box of fireworks, and Samantha and the children went into the house to change into shorts and T-shirts.

Samantha had hoped the evening might bring clearer weather, but when she returned to the veranda, a wind had come up and black clouds were boiling in from the southwest. Directly above, the sky had a fierce brilliance to it. In the patch of garden at the side of the house, Ben's marigolds looked luminous in the odd light.

"Looks like we may be in for it," Ben said as she joined him on the beach. "We'd best get this over with and get the kids inside. They'll never forgive us if we get rained out."

Luckily they managed to use up all the fireworks before the wind grew too strong. Brian and Tracy most enjoyed the sparklers, which they handled with great care, managing all the same to whirl them around and around, "writing messages to shipwrecked sailors," they said. They also enjoyed the writhing black "snakes" that Ben lit for them, apparently deciding they were as much a part of his magic as his earlier card tricks. They kept the few rockets until the end and greeted each shower of light with appropriate screams of glee.

By the time the fireworks were done with, the wind had come up with a vengeance, and after a cup of coffee with Ben inside the house, Samantha decided she'd better get on her way back to her chalet.

She didn't realize her mistake until she'd reached the top of the winding path up the cliff and was halfway across the meadow. It was only then that the first drops of rain splattered on her unprotected head. She'd be soaked by the time she got back to the spa, she realized as she walked on, wondering if she should return to Ben's house. The sky was inky black now and turbulent. She did have a flashlight that Ben had pressed into her hand, but its light wasn't much use against the complete darkness that had come with the rain. As she hesitated at the edge of the woods, a flash of lightning forked across the sky, lighting up the entire area with an eerie glow. Immediately afterward, a crack of thunder reverberated above her head.

She glanced back toward the cliff. It would probably be wisest for her to return, but then she'd disturb the children, who'd finally become sleepy. And Ben had looked tired as they drank their coffee. If she went back down, he'd feel obliged to sit up with her until the storm passed.

She'd been wet most of the day, she rationalized—a little rain wasn't going to hurt her T-shirt and cut offs. She was cautious enough to start out along the main road rather than hike through the woods, though, and was glad she'd made this decision when another clap of thunder and lightning flash split the night sky and the rain increased. Head down, she started to run, the beam of the flashlight bobbing on the road in front of her.

After a few minutes she developed a mild stitch in her side. Hot dogs and marshmallows, she thought ruefully—not very good conditioning before a run. She kept up a fairly rapid pace all the same, anxious now to get indoors. She'd never been afraid of storms, but she recognized that it was fairly stupid to be running around in the middle of one. She should have gone back to Ben's right away, she realized as the rain started coming down even harder. It was going to take her some time to get to the spa this way, but it would have been even more foolish to take the shorter trail through the woods. She'd known several instances in her childhood when one or more trees had been struck by lightning.

She was absolutely drenched when she saw the lights of a car coming toward her. She'd given up trying to protect herself from the rain by hunching down, so she saw the lights from some distance away. She hoped the car belonged to someone she knew, someone who would take pity on a drowned rat and give her a ride down the hill to the spa. She stopped running and looked hopefully toward the driver through the wet curtain of her hair, feeling relieved when the car slowed and came to a stop beside her. Without hesitation she pulled open the passenger door, pausing only when she saw that the driver was Jonathan Blake.

"Get in, Sam," he urged. "You're letting all the rain in."

"It doesn't make any difference," she said as she climbed in and pulled the door shut behind her. "I'm going to soak your upholstery anyway."

"What the hell are you doing out in this?" he demanded. "I thought I was hallucinating when I saw you. I didn't think anybody was stupid enough to jog in a downpour like this."

"Pretty stupid to drive in it, too," she rejoined. She was damned if she'd explain her decision not to go back to Hemlock Cove. "I was on my way home from Ben's," was all she offered.

She peered through the windshield, realized they were driving into Jon's driveway. "I guess you can turn around here," she suggested.

"Turn around nothing," he said. "I'm not going any farther in this. You can stay here until the storm's over, then I'll take you back to the spa."

She didn't argue. It would be nice to see Eileen. She'd visited her a couple of times but had been afraid to come too often in case Jon thought she was chasing after him. Eileen would probably make her some hot chocolate, she thought, which right now sounded very inviting.

She didn't realize until she was in the kitchen, dripping all over the slate floor with Eileen's dog busily sniffing at her wet sneakers, that Eileen wasn't anywhere in sight. And knowing Eileen, if she'd heard Jon's car arrive, she'd have come downstairs right away, making sure he hadn't come to any harm in the storm.

"Where's your mother?" she asked.

Jon was looking through a cabinet, for towels, it turned out, and didn't answer for a second. Then he smiled at her as he handed her one. Once again she didn't quite like the quality of his smile—there was something else beyond it, she thought, something that verged on hostility if not outright dislike. "She's in Seattle," he said easily. "I took her over in the boat this morning. We spent the day with Peter Darrell—he owns an art gallery."

Samantha bent her head and started rubbing her hair with the towel. "Oh, yes, she told me about him," she said vaguely after a while. Then realization struck her. They were alone in the house. "She didn't come back with you?" Her voice emerged from the folds of the towel with a definite squeak.

"My mother is a grown woman, Samantha," Jon said gravely.

She pulled the towel from her head and glared at him. "I didn't mean that," she said. "I meant—" She broke off and disappeared under the towel again. It seemed safer.

"I would suggest a hot shower," Jon said. "I'll lend you a robe. A glass of brandy wouldn't hurt, either. I'm going to have one. By the time I got *Aegir* under cover I was getting nervous myself, though luckily the storm didn't hit until I reached the marina."

"I don't need any brandy," Samantha objected at once and then realized she was being childish. "A shower does sound good, though. I'll take you up on it."

She mustn't act as though she suspected his motives in bringing her here, she decided. If she acted as though it was perfectly normal for her to be here under the circumstances, which it was, then he'd have to see that she was not to be trifled with.

He did show unmistakable signs of wanting to trifle. When she came out of the downstairs bathroom, wearing one of his robes, a sensuously soft burgundy-colored kimono that would have been fairly short on him but reached respectably past her knees, he'd lit a fire in the drawing room. A couple of snifters of brandy sat on the coffee table in front of one of the long sofas as well, gleaming golden in the firelight, the only light in the room. It was a scene straight out of a romantic movie.

Jon was sitting at the end of the sofa, long legs stretched out toward the fire, looking suitably posed for the scene, his hair shining, his face shadowed into mystery. At least he hadn't been too obvious—he hadn't slipped into something "more comfortable" but was still dressed in the tan jeans and white polo shirt he'd been wearing when he'd picked her up.

Eileen's old dog was nowhere in sight. "I put Tonto and the cats in my den," he said when she looked around. "It's a little more soundproof in there—they were feeling nervous, too."

He patted the cushion beside him, but she pretended she hadn't seen the gesture and sat on the floor on the other side of the table, reaching up to switch on a lamp before picking up her glass.

Jon made no comment, but from the corner of her eye she saw his mouth twitch when she turned on the light.

"I decided the temperature had dropped enough to warrant a fire," he said after a while. "You looked as though you might be feeling chilled. Are you warmer now?"

"Mmm," Samantha murmured, feeling more relaxed now that she'd established a boundary between them. The fire *was* a good idea—the temperature had dropped considerably. The rain was really beating down now, and the thunder and lightning showed no sign of letting up, though the noise of the storm was muffled in here.

Maybe she'd misjudged his motives in setting the scene. Maybe he *was* just concerned about her health. He'd always been thoughtful that way.

Gradually she became even more relaxed, as Jon talked easily about his day and about the man his mother was visiting. Apparently he'd forgotten his annoyance with her over the Tom Greene incident. He seemed to have a lot of respect for Peter Darrell and was genuinely pleased that his mother had found someone compatible.

In return she described her own Fourth of July, making him laugh with her descriptions of Tracy and Brian's porpoise imitations, Ben's card tricks and the children's antics with their sparklers.

It was becoming quite cozy in here, she decided. Because of the room's size, the fire didn't seem unpleasantly hot, but it did give out a comforting warmth, aided and abetted by the brandy—Grand Marnier. Both smelled wonderful—the fire of fresh scented fir logs, the liqueur of cognac and oranges ripened in the sun. There was something almost decadent about sitting in a warm room while the elements raged outside, she thought contentedly.

Relaxing, she leaned back against the sofa opposite Jon, soothed by the low murmur of his voice as he told her about a show Peter Darrell was arranging for Eileen. She was feeling sleepy, she realized, which was not really surprising.

And then, after a fork of lightning seemed to crackle through the elegant room, followed by a truly horrendous crack of thunder, the light above her head went out.

For one confused moment, she thought Jon had reached over to turn it off, but even as she opened her mouth to protest, she saw he hadn't moved. "Looks as though we've lost our power," he said, trying out the lamp beside him and getting no response. "Good thing I lit the fire."

Samantha didn't answer. She was suddenly aware, as Jon looked at her, that her relaxation had fled with the light. Even though the fire gave out plenty of illumination, there was a different quality to firelight—a romantic, sensuous quality that was affecting her in a way she'd sworn she wouldn't be affected again.

Jon, with his usual insight, had evidently realized this when she failed to speak. A small smile turned up the corners of his mouth and his eyes, shadowed again, seemed to gleam with triumph. "Why so nervous, Sam?" he asked gently.

She wanted to reply, wanted to tell him hotly that she most certainly was not nervous in any way, but she seemed to have lost her voice. She could only look at him, remembering again the night they'd spent in Port Townsend, when firelight had flickered over them just as it was doing now, remembering Ben saying, "Sometimes it's best just to let things happen."

Jon's eyes seemed to darken as he gazed at her. And then, with one fluid movement, he came over and knelt beside her on the rug. "Samantha," he murmured.

At some time she had set down her brandy glass. She had no memory of doing so. She just suddenly realized that her hands were empty, and it seemed perfectly natural to rest them on each side of Jon's face. One of his hands immediately covered one of hers, moving it so that his lips could deposit a kiss on her palm. And then his other hand was reaching for her, twining itself in her still-damp hair, pulling her head close enough for a kiss.

Afterward, she seemed to remember that she had sighed once, very softly, before going into his arms. And she also remembered thinking confusedly that this was after all what she'd planned—to go along with him the next time he made advances to her. In revenge. Hadn't she had some intentions of revenge? How silly. She loved him! She had always loved him. All that mattered to her was that she was in his arms and he was kissing her very delicately and softly, as though he didn't want to startle her, kissing her as only Jon had ever kissed her, knowing exactly when to increase the pressure of his mouth on hers, when to decrease it, when to draw away from her mouth and turn his attention to her throat.

"Let's pretend," she said against his hair. "Let's pretend that I'm eighteen and you're twenty-three and it's all new between us."

"Yes," he whispered in response.

Her hands pressed his head closer to her, touching his hair, feeling the crispness of it under her fingertips. She could smell the cleanness of it, the unmistakable man scent of him, composed always of a certain element of saltwater and fresh sea breezes, heady to her senses, uncluttered by any cologne. He'd always refused to use cologne.

Outside the storm raged on, muted by the throbbing of her pulse in her ears. She was only vaguely aware of the still-rumbling thunder and the sound of rain drumming on the rooftop, counterpoint to her pounding heart.

Jon had gently removed the robe from her body. Now

he took off his own clothes, without haste, looking at her with an intense all-consuming gaze as he did so, so that she hardly noticed what he was doing.

For a moment he hovered above her, looking down at her, his muscular arms and shoulders illuminated in the glow of the fire behind him, his face in shadow.

She was afraid he was going to insist once again that she admit she wanted him, but instead he said softly, "You understand that I'm not going to let you leave until the storm is over?"

"Yes," she whispered, her fear evaporating as excitement took its place.

"You understand that you are here alone with me, that no one will hear you if you cry out, no one will come to the door, or call on the telephone?"

She thrilled to the memory of the words, repeated verbatim from that long-ago summer when they'd first made love in Jon's old house. Afterward Jon had explained to her that he'd wanted her to be sure there was no turning back if she once gave her consent. She had given it gladly then, gave it just as gladly now. "I understand," she said.

She thought he smiled, but couldn't be sure. His voice resumed speaking as soon as she answered him. "I'm going to make love to you very slowly and very thoroughly," he said. "I'm going to give you my utmost concentration and attention. I'm going to convince you that you want only me, you have never stopped wanting me—there is no other man in your life nor ever will be. Do you understand all of this?"

For just a second, no, not even that, a fraction of a second, she felt there was something in the words he'd used that should alarm her, make her hesitate. But the feeling passed as quickly as it had been born and again she answered, "Yes."

To her surprise, he rose then and walked to the side of the room. Naked, he was elegantly graceful, as self-possessed as though he were fully clothed. For a moment she felt confused by his desertion of her, but then she saw that he had opened a cabinet to reveal a stereo system. Picking out a cassette, he slipped it into a portable tape deck, which he set on top of the cabinet.

A moment later familiar music filled the room, music from a movie they'd seen together—a song they'd loved years before. Barbra Streisand singing "The Way We Were."

His choice seemed almost too appropriate, too deliberately intended to suit the occasion. She glanced at his face uncertainly as he lowered himself beside her, but the firelight had washed it clean of any expression. "Do you remember, Samantha?" he asked, looking down at her, and her suspicions melted away and she reached for him, allowing the music to enfold her as he enfolded her, letting the lyrics speak to her as his mouth closed over her lips, his body pressed warmly against hers.

A moment and he raised his head again. "Slowly," he reminded her. He began to touch her, delicately, his fingers light as a whisper across her breasts, her abdomen, her thighs, tormenting her with his unnatural restraint.

She felt a mixture of emotions—wonder, excitement, love, fear... fear because she couldn't see his face clearly, still couldn't be sure of his motives. Somewhere in the back of her mind, she could hear Anne Marie's voice saying, "Very, very close." So far, she realized, Jon hadn't said anything about love. And he seemed too...

solemn. Yet perhaps it was only a trick of the firelight that made his eyes seem so clear and cool.

Behind him Streisand sang softly. They were both moving now, the firelight burnishing their bodies with a pagan glow. They moved slowly, familiarly, fingers and lips caressing, touching, moving over the shadowed portions of themselves in the sensuous, sensual game they had played together so long ago, exploring each other. Once they had known every inch of one another's bodies—now there were small changes to be noted, touched, commented upon.

"Your breasts are bigger," he murmured as his hands cupped and stroked them, his fingers delicately brushing against her nipples, arousing her to sensuous torment.

"Half an inch," she admitted with laughter in her voice.

One of his hands trailed down her body, pressing gently against her abdomen, lingering erotically over her hipbone on the right side. "What is this?" he asked, peering down at the place his fingers had discovered.

"I had my appendix out—two years ago."

He moved to caress the small whitened scar with his lips, kindling a rush of sensation that tightened her thighs. At once his hand touched gently on the triangle of copper-colored hair, but his touch was not intended to arouse, more to gentle her. "Slowly," he repeated.

Her fingers had found a scar on *his* body—a long jagged ridge of tissue on the back of his upper thigh. "Shark," he said tersely as her expression queried him.

She shuddered at this proof of near tragedy, but he gave her no time to dwell on it. "My own fault," he said. "I was encouraging a shark to attack, one who really didn't want to. I was wearing the new-style scuba suit I told the twins about. It was supposed to protect me. Didn't quite work out.''

"Hell of a way to earn a living," she said lightly to cover her horror.

She'd said the wrong thing. Momentarily his body stiffened. But then he almost visibly forced the tension away and laughed. "Isn't it?" he agreed.

And then his mouth found hers again and all conversation ceased, the only voice in the room that of Streisand, now heartrendingly ending her song, the softened final notes trailing off into silence as the tape ended.

Outside, trees were whipping back and forth in winds of gale force, creaking and groaning as though they were about to be uprooted forcibly from the earth. Rain lashed the windows and thunder boomed and rolled across the turbulent sky. None of it seemed threatening to Samantha. Rather it seemed a mere background for their rising emotions.

Jon's mouth was savage now against her own, as though he too were part of the storm, part of the violent music. His hands caressed her roughly, familiarly, moving over her constantly, touching, always touching until she caught his hands with her own and held tightly to them, glorying in their rigid strength and in her own power to stop them, teasing him by relaying back to him his instructions to move slowly. He didn't allow her triumph to live long. Lifting his head, he raised her hands with his, first covering her knuckles with passionate kisses, then stretching her arms above her head and holding her hands there with one of his, while the other stroked her shuddering body urgently, almost angrily, his fingers tensing against the hollows of her shoulders, the swollen thrust of her breasts, the arch of her back, trying to pull her closer though there was no space between them, rolling with her until they lay on their sides, locked together in an embrace that would surely never end.

There was a feeling of oneness between them, a feeling of bonding, a partaking of each other. He was making her feel she was the only woman in the world for him, the sexiest, most desirable, most wonderful lover he'd ever known. And she was responding with all the love she felt for him, wanting him to know that he, in his turn, was the only lover in the world for her—the only man who could make her lose control like this.

Spasms were spreading all through her body. She could not have controlled them if she wanted to, and she didn't want to. For now the rain seemed to have entered the room and was pounding over her—and her blood was one with the rain, singing through her veins, throbbing in her ears and throat, filling her with its erotic rhythm until she couldn't breathe. She was drowning, they were both drowning—two sea creatures turning and floating in an abandoned dance of passion.

And then the fire crackled and flared briefly, illuminating Jon's face and upper body as he positioned himself over her.

He was not smiling. His eyelids drooped halfway over his eyes, giving a somber expression to his face. "Samantha?" he asked and she nodded, giving final consent, her hands moving up his arms, across his shoulders to the back of his neck.

She felt the tightening of his smooth, firm masculine flesh as her fingers moved over it, heard the swift intake of his breath as her hands traveled upward into the thick

There was a feeling of oneness between them, a feeling crispness of his hair, exerting pressure, pulling him down to her.

She could feel the power between them, stronger than it had ever been, having been heightened by the passion of their preliminary play, and she knew an aching need that could not be assuaged by anything less than total intimacy. She wanted him. She wanted to *contain* him.

The somber expression had fled from his face. His blue eyes blazed passion down at her. His face was the face she remembered, loving her, wanting her. "I've waited so long, Samantha," he murmured.

As he gathered her close in his arms, she answered him, as though the words had been wrung from her, "So have I."

And for some unknown reason he hesitated again, as though her words had brought an involuntary stillness to his body. He continued to hold her, his arms cradling her, but he made no attempt to take possession of her. Silently she waited, suddenly uncertain again, as unmoving as he, though the tension in her body was screaming for release.

The fire had burned down to a subtle glow, some part of her mind noticed. There were no more leaping shadows, only a gleaming, almost phosphorescent light that cast a harshness over the two of them lying intertwined on the rich silken carpet.

The rest of the room, the restrained and elegant furniture, the paneled walls, was in darkness. It was as though they lay upon a stage at the center of the universe and nothing else existed in the world. He was so still. Why had he stopped? He was still holding her, but loosely, as though at any second he would let go.

And slowly, as they lay there, the storm diminished, the thunder became a muted grumble in the distance, the lightning a mere flicker of gentle light beyond the loosely woven drapes over the big windows.

Samantha moved at last, struggling gently to disengage her body from his, one hand rising to touch his face. "Jonathan," she whispered. "Is something wrong?"

He didn't answer, and a tremor went through her body—a tremor of fear.

Rolling away from her, he sat up. "Are you cold?" he asked in a carefully controlled voice. "I guess the fire's gone out." He laughed shortly. "Very symbolic."

There was a note in his voice she couldn't understand. It chilled her. Lifting herself on one elbow, she touched his bare shoulder. "Jonathan?" she said again, tentatively.

"I couldn't go through with it," he said. His voice held a note of disbelief.

He was kneeling in front of the fireplace now, and he began adding kindling to the embers, blowing gently on them until they flamed and he could add another log to give them light and warmth.

She waited, afraid to speak, her eyes studying the rigid line of his spine. After a few minutes he laughed again, but there was still no humor in the sound. "Funny," he said softly, almost to himself. "I guess I really believed in the old saw that revenge is sweet, but it isn't at all."

"Revenge?" she whispered, bewildered. Then, as horrified understanding ripped through her, she sat upright, staring at his back. "You intended this as revenge?"

He didn't turn to look at her, didn't move at all.

"Why, Jon?"

She saw a convulsive tremor pass down the side of his neck as though he'd swallowed—hard. He lowered his head for a moment, then stood up and moved to the sofa. Picking up his clothes, he began to dress, still not looking at her, not speaking.

Feeling suddenly self-conscious, she reached for the robe he'd loaned her and pulled it on, fastening the sash tightly around her waist, hoping it would help hold her together. She didn't understand what had happened, and wasn't sure she wanted to. She felt as though something inside her was beginning to tremble—that if he didn't speak soon—explain—that part of her would shatter into a thousand pieces.

He'd sat down on the sofa and looked into the fire, his face set in harsh lines that were unfamiliar to her.

Mute, she sat on the opposite sofa and looked at him, keeping her gaze steady until the force of it made him look up. When he did, his eyes were empty of expression. His voice, when he spoke, was slow and tentative, as though he were speaking half to himself.

"I knew the moment I saw you that you were still in my blood. I didn't want that. You've caused me enough pain. I wanted. . . revenge. I made up my mind you were going to want me again, and I would take you as coldly, as deliberately as I could, and then tell you exactly what I had done."

The words seemed to hang in the air for a moment, echoing against the walls. It was as though the room had turned into a dark cavern lit only by the flickering firelight. As if from a great distance, Samantha heard a log splutter as sap bled from it into the flames. She felt frozen in time, unable to speak or move. And then anger flared through her like a sudden tropical fever, burning through her veins to her brain in a burst of white heat. Just as she had suspected, he had deliberately provoked her so that he could use her to give him back his pride.

"Are you satisfied now?" she demanded in a choked voice that didn't seem to belong to her.

"Not as I thought I'd be." He sounded bewildered, uncertain. "I couldn't go through with it, Sam, I...."

"Is that supposed to make everything all right?"

He stood up, frowning, looking as though he were about to approach her. Quickly, she got up herself and moved behind the sofa, feeling she needed a physical barrier against him. "This whole...encounter, was carefully thought out, wasn't it?" she said through her teeth. "I guess you didn't plan it for tonight—the storm just happened to offer an opportunity. If it hadn't, you'd have made your own opportunity, wouldn't you?" She drew herself up straight, masking the trembling of her body, forcing her voice to sound even. "Here's something you didn't plan, Jon," she said icily. "I suspected your motives all along—they were terribly transparent. But I didn't really believe you could be so cold-blooded. I guess I didn't want to believe it. In the end, I—" She broke off. She'd come perilously close to telling him she'd come to believe instead in the whole rebirth of love and passion between them.

"I hope I'm well and truly out of your blood now," she continued with hardly a pause. "I wouldn't want to cause you another moment's discomfort."

"Sam," he protested, looking as though he were just beginning to awaken from some kind of trance.

"My name is Samantha," she said coldly, trying to gather composure around her like a shield, knowing that if she didn't she would burst into tears. She wouldn't, couldn't, give him the satisfaction of knowing his ruse had succeeded. "As a matter of fact," she went on, enunciating every word, "I plotted a little revenge of my own. I didn't take kindly to your remark about going to bed with me so we could get whatever it was over with. I decided right then that I'd go along with you the next time, find out how far you were prepared to go. And now I know...."

She'd shaken him, she saw, even though she'd lied. She'd known even as she planned revenge that there was no way she could go through with such a scheme. But he had been able to do so, or had at least come close to doing so.

She looked at him directly, noting the shocked expression in his eyes with satisfaction, noting also, in spite of herself, the way the renewed firelight was playing on his hair, softening the taut lines of his face.

Then she saw that doubt had entered his eyes and he was shaking his head. "You seriously expect me to believe you weren't responding to me?" he asked abruptly. "You're that good an actress?"

"I am." She paused, then plunged on, knowing if she didn't, if she allowed full realization to dawn on her, she would fall apart and surrender all dignity, all pride. "We went to bed, if you'll pardon my using your euphemism. And we *almost* got it over with. As far as I'm concerned, it *is* over. We should both be satisfied now. I came back and found out my father was right. You haven't amounted to anything, wealthy as you seem to be."

His face blanched and she knew she'd hurt him. Good, she thought. "Something's got twisted in you, Jon," she said evenly. Then she turned on her heel and stalked from the room, striving for a dignified exit in spite of the comical picture she must present in his over-large robe.

She heard him call her name as she fumbled her way into the bathroom in the dark and closed the door, but she didn't answer him. With shaking fingers she pulled on her T-shirt and shorts, flinging his robe into the corner. Before leaving the bathroom, she drew in a deep breath. She had to hold together, she told herself, at least long enough to get back to the privacy of her chalet.

After two more deep breaths she felt strong enough to cope and opened the door.

He was waiting for her, a tall dark shadow against the firelit doorway to the drawing room. As though it too had been waiting for her, the chandelier above the high wide hallway and curving staircase unexpectedly blinked on, startling them both with its brilliance. The electric power had returned. The house seemed to hum with renewed life. For a second they stood blinking at each other. Jon's mouth was set in a straight line, his blue eyes narrowed against the light. Samantha's face felt rigid. "You'd better drive me home," she said coldly. "It's late and I have things to do—letters to write." She had no idea why she'd said that.

He came toward her, a sardonic expression twisting his mouth. "Love letters to Adrian?" he asked with grim sarcasm.

"I owe him a letter, yes."

He frowned but said nothing more. Walking around

her, giving her a wide berth, he opened the heavy front
door and gestured her through it.

The storm had passed. The night air felt cool and
clean. There was only a mild breeze now, setting the
trees swaying gently against the sky. Far above a few
stars showed through the ragged remnants of the
clouds.

She heard a slight rustle of clothing beside her and
was afraid Jon was going to touch her, but he was hand-
ing her a sweater. She accepted it and draped it around
her shoulders as she climbed into the car.

He didn't speak for a few minutes. Neither did she.
She felt she had nothing more to say. She concentrated
on the swishing sound of the car's tires against the as-
phalt, the powerful hum of the engine, staving off
thought.

As they reached the turnoff to the spa, he stirred beside her. "I could call you a liar, Sam," he said softly,
adding as she stiffened, "but I won't. I've acquired
some gloss of sophistication in the last seven years. I try
not to hurl insults at women now. But I know you're not
telling me the whole truth. When I touched you back
there. . . ."

She couldn't believe he was still trying to get her to
admit she'd wanted him. "I don't want to hear any
more of your triumphant male braggings," she said
frostily. "If you want to prove how irresistible you are,
go see Anne Marie. I'm sure *she'll* welcome you."

"What the hell does Anne Marie have to do with
us?"

"That's for *you* to decide. *I* don't ever want to see
you again."

"Samantha—"

"Just stay away from me, Jon Blake," she said stonily.

To her relief, he relapsed into silence for the rest of the drive. Outside the spa's main building, he didn't turn off the ignition; she made a hurried exit and strode off toward the wooden steps as quickly as she could. She was halfway up them when she heard him close the door she'd left open, and at the top before he drove away.

Not looking down, she fumbled for her key in the pocket of her shorts and opened the door. Somehow she managed to get inside and close the door behind her before she started to shake. For a long time she couldn't stop shaking.

CHAPTER TEN

A LONG TIME AGO, when Samantha was ten, she had been struck by a rock while helping her father mow the lawn. The rock had fractured her left ankle, and she had spent endless weeks with her leg encased in a plaster cast to her knee. She'd hated the cast, longed for the day it would come off so that she could run and jump and swim and be free.

But to her dismay, when the plaster was finally removed she could not place her foot on the floor without pain. It was as stiff and cold and immovable as though some of the plaster had seeped inside her bones, making them rigid. The doctor had told her to use her foot gradually, accustoming it to bear her weight a little at a time. Weeks had passed before she could walk normally again, without a limp.

Now her whole body felt as her foot had felt then. It was as though the essence that was Samantha had seeped out of her and in her place was something that hurt constantly even while she moved and talked and functioned. Her limbs and body and heart felt bruised and sore and she didn't feel. . . balanced. She was afraid that if she moved too fast she would stumble and fall.

It was natural she should feel this way, she supposed. Bones that had been fractured needed time to become whole, flesh that was bruised could not become flexible right away. Shattered emotions were no less slow to heal.

She was typing a daily schedule for a newly arrived guest when Dr. Birmann arrived the next morning. He regarded her thoughtfully for a moment, then invited her into his office and gestured her into a chair.

Samantha felt uncomfortable. She knew how she looked this morning—haggard. All color and life had fled from her face. But to her relief, he made no comment as he seated himself, merely asking her if she'd had an enjoyable holiday.

She managed a smile that felt frozen. "Thank you, yes. I spent the day with Ben and the children. It was fun."

He nodded, still looking at her with a clinical eye. "You are happy here?"

For a horrible moment Samantha was afraid Ben had said something to him about her feelings of dissatisfaction, but almost immediately she realized Ben would never betray a confidence. "Everyone's very kind to me," she said evasively.

Again he nodded, looked for a second as though he were going to question her further, then shrugged and smiled. "I wish you to know I am pleased with your work. You pay great attention to detail, and you've gone beyond your duties to make my guests comfortable."

Samantha's smile was more genuine this time. "You must have been talking to Liz Vandervort."

"I have heard your praises sung by Madame Vandervort, yes, and several others, including Thelma Delaney."

Thelma Delaney, an interior designer whose "beat," as she called it, was Beverly Hills, had recently gone through a traumatic divorce from her husband of thirty years. She too had taken to Samantha and had filled her ears with lurid accounts of her husband's bizarre behavior. How she'd managed to stay married to the man for so long was beyond Samantha. "They are both nice women," she said to the doctor.

He nodded and was about to speak again when the phone rang. Excusing himself, he picked up the receiver.

Samantha looked away, giving him token privacy, her gaze traveling over the framed diplomas on the walls. What a kind man he was, she thought. So many employers offered only criticism. Even her own father had been somewhat stingy with praise.

Glancing back at the doctor, she noticed he was doodling on a pad on his desk, making neat little boxes with words in them, joining the boxes together in parallel rows. Her own doodles were less structured—she had a habit of drawing hearts and flowers as she talked on telephones. Eileen was right about her, she thought with a tinge of bitterness—she'd always had a tremendous need to be loved. Why was that? Her parents had certainly loved her. But of course, parental love was not enough for anyone.

"Mrs. Delaney told me a few days ago that she would like to adopt you," Dr. Birmann told her when he hung up the phone.

She laughed, surprising herself—after last night she hadn't thought she'd ever laugh again. "I think I'm beyond the age of adoption," she said lightly.

"Nevertheless...." He paused, again looking at her. She averted her eyes and he said briskly, "However, pleased as I am by your work, that is not why I called you in here. We have no new guests expected until

Thursday. A small hiatus. So I wish to invite you to accompany me to Seattle for a couple of days. A Dr. Lawrence Hodgkins is conducting a seminar at a medical convention there. He has some new ideas on vitamin and mineral depletion that interest me. I need you to take notes, as I understand he does not allow tape recording in his seminars. It seems he sells his own tapes of his speeches.''

His eyebrows rose, inviting her to share the amusement that glimmered suddenly in his gray eyes. ''A profitable idea, don't you think? Perhaps I shall steal it from him.''

He was trying to cheer her up, she realized. She made an effort to respond to his good humor, but her face felt stiff. Dr. Birmann gave her an encouraging smile and returned to his brisk manner. ''Actually, the seminar lasts only one and a half days, but it begins early tomorrow, so I think it best we fly into Seattle this evening. We will return Wednesday night. I have some. . . .'' He hesitated, the humorous expression leaving his face so abruptly that for a moment he looked older than his years. Older and. . . worried, *desperately* worried.

''I have some business to attend to on Wednesday afternoon,'' he concluded. There was a strain in his voice, and a somewhat furtive, almost hunted expression on his handsome face.

Samantha worked at keeping her sudden interest out of her voice. ''Well, of course, I'd love to go,'' she said at once, thinking that this was true—it would be good for her to get away from the island—and Jon's proximity—for a while. But then fairness prompted her to add, ''Wouldn't you rather take Anne Marie? I'm sure she'd love a couple of days in Seattle.''

Dr. Birmann made an impatient gesture with his right hand. "You know how such conventions are—too many men away from home. It would not be a good place for a young girl."

Did he think *she* was an old lady, Samantha wondered.

"But she'd love the trip," Samantha argued. "It must get boring for her sometimes, it's so isolated...."

"She has told you she is bored?"

"No, I didn't mean to imply...." For a moment she floundered, but she had determined that when the opportunity arose she'd speak up for Anne Marie, no matter what the situation might be between the girl and Jon Blake. She plunged on, ignoring the doctor's rather forbidding expression. "It's just that I think, well, I really think Anne Marie should have a little more freedom. She so wants to grow up, to become a woman— and she looked so lovely for our photographic sessions."

"So Jon told me."

"Oh." Samantha swallowed, but pressed gamely on. "She could be a stunning young woman if—"

"If I were not such a poor father, holding her back."

"I didn't mean...that wasn't what I intended...." She was floundering again, sure she'd offended him, but then she noticed that the twinkle had returned to his gray eyes and he was quite obviously enjoying her discomfort.

"Dear Samantha," he said. "I appreciate your championship of my daughter, but I must tell you I have already had such truths pointed out to me by our mutual friend Jon. He gave me a similar lecture on Saturday, pointing out that I have always preached that a woman's search for beauty is not due to vanity but to a need for self-confidence in a changing world, and that I was not practicing what I preached in my own home. He showed me the proofs of the photographs he took and I was forced, reluctantly, I must admit, to agree with him that my daughter is a beautiful young woman—not just a fairly pretty girl. I have given Anne Marie permission to consult with our makeup and hair experts in order to improve her appearance.''

Deflated, Samantha could manage no more than a limp, ''I see.''

Dr. Birmann laughed. ''I suspect a conspiracy between you and my friend Jon. Am I right?''

''Not exactly. . . I didn't realize Jon was going to talk to you. He seemed to disagree—'' She broke off, aware that she was letting him know she *had* discussed his treatment of Anne Marie wtih Jon.

She took a deep breath, tried again. ''I'm sorry, Dr. Birmann. I like Anne Marie very much. I felt that she wasn't too high on self-esteem and. . . .'' Why was she pursuing this, she wondered. She wasn't too high on self-esteem herself today.

Dr. Birmann leaned across the desk and patted her hand gently. ''There is no need to apologize, my dear. It is difficult for a father sometimes to admit his daughter is growing up, especially when she is all he has. But I now realize the error of my ways, I promise you. I intend seeing that Anne Marie receives more attention, also. She has a birthday soon. I will take her into Seattle for dinner then.'' He stood up, his usual signal that the interview was over. ''However,'' he added in a soft yet determined voice, ''I am not yet ready to expose her to the advances of some of my esteemed colleagues. I have attended such gatherings many times.'' He smiled. ''I am sure that you, on the other hand, have the tact and wisdom to protect yourself. And that ring on your left hand will offer some protection also, do you not agree?''

Automatically Samantha glanced at her ring. Adrian's dark hair and patrician features flooded her mind, and she felt a sinking sensation she didn't want to examine too closely. "I guess you're right," she murmured.

Dr. Birmann came around his desk to escort her to the door. "We leave at six," he told her. "I will send someone to pick up your luggage. Casual clothing will be sufficient. We will not stay for the official banquet."

Samantha nodded. She was suffering from a mixture of emotions as she returned to her desk, and was relieved that Deborah had apparently gone off for her herb-tea break. She sat for a while staring at a large split-leaf philodendron that stood near the doorway, not really seeing it, struggling to sort out her thoughts.

Jon had spoken to the doctor about Anne Marie. Why? Compassion? Or self-interest? *Very, very close,* Anne Marie had said.

She sighed. What did it matter now, anyway? She glanced again at her left hand. What was she to do about Adrian? She had intended to write him last night, though not with love, as she'd led Jon to believe. Examining her turbulent emotions where Jon was concerned, it had become obvious to her that her feelings for Adrian had never been as strong as they should have been. Nor were his for her. He loved her madly, he'd told her when he'd proposed. But as soon as they were engaged, he'd acted as though they'd already been mar-

ried for years—as though passion wasn't quite...
respectable.

Yet he'd loved her in his way. And she had loved
him—warmly, *comfortably*. This love had seemed
enough for her at the time, but she realized now that it
wasn't enough. So why had she postponed writing the
letter and why was she still wearing his ring? Was she
afraid that if she gave him up she'd have no one? Possibly, if she confessed to Adrian that she had almost
given herself to another man, he would forgive her.
He'd remarked once that passion often seemed to make
people behave like fools. How right he had been! He
would probably chide her, tell her that she'd acted very
foolishly but no harm was done.

And of course, she didn't *have* to tell him anything.
He would never suspect her. She swallowed. Why was
her mind considering such possibilities? She *couldn't*
stay engaged to Adrian after what had happened with
Jon. Even though they had not indulged in the final intimacy, they had come very close. She *had* wanted him.
No matter how she denied that to him, she couldn't
deny it to herself. Nor could she deny any longer that
she still loved him.

She remembered a slogan connected with one of her
father's advertising campaigns—"She's a one-man
woman." Apparently, the description fitted her—even
though "the man" had rejected her again.

For a second pain threatened to overwhelm her, but
she gritted her teeth and forced it down. *You've caused
me enough pain,* he'd said. He had suffered, too, it
seemed. But how could he have sought revenge in such a
way? Did her pain count for nothing?

She was suddenly, fiercely, glad she had denied her

response, glad she'd admitted that she too had entertained thoughts of revenge, glad she'd told him she never wanted to see him again.

What did he think of her this morning, she wondered. Was he satisfied with himself, pleased that he'd managed to hurt her? Or had he believed her finally when she insisted her responses had been faked? She hoped so. At least if he believed that she was left with some semblance of pride.

Round and round her thoughts traveled, getting nowhere. "Work," she muttered to herself, switching on her typewriter with a decisive click and hunching over it as though in this way she could close herself off from her own mind. By the time Deborah returned, she was pounding away at the blessedly monotonous task of filling out responses on a printed form.

Deborah glanced at her curiously, probably intrigued by the fury of her attack on her machine—Samantha was usually a cautious typist who rarely had to use the lift-off tape on her IBM. But she returned to her own work without saying anything, much to Samantha's relief.

A few minutes later, she called diffidently. "D'you suppose you could give me a hand?"

Samantha glanced across the long room. Deborah was peering at her from behind her computer, an anxious expression on her pretty face. "I'm missing thirty dollars in Dr. Birmann's personal-checking account," she explained. "I've gone over and over it and it won't come out right."

She handed Samantha a sheaf of checks when she came over to her. "If you could read these off, I'll check them on the computer screen." Her green eyes lingered a second on Samantha's face as she sat down. "Have you got a headache? I've got some aspirin in my desk."

"I'm fine," Samantha said shortly. "Let's get on with it. The first check is for Frederick and Nelson's— $38.45."

"Right."

She'd hurt Deborah's feelings, she realized. She really had to put aside her personal problems for a while. "Elliott Ramsey, DDS—$105," she said in a milder voice. "Dr. Birmann had his teeth cleaned, right?"

"Right," Deborah said, smiling. "Took me forever to get him to go for that checkup. Why are doctors such fools about their own health?"

She sounded mollified and Samantha managed a smile, which helped even more. For another minute they worked steadily through the stack. The doctor had written a lot of checks in the previous month.

A checking account was very revealing, Samantha realized for the first time. Going through the list, she could tell almost everything Dr. Birmann had done in the last few weeks. He'd had a haircut in Seattle. Why wouldn't he use the facilities at the spa? Too personal? He did tend to keep a distance between himself and his staff. He'd taken suits to the cleaners, bought a new pair of shoes, sent flowers to someone.

Near the end of the pile was a check for five thousand dollars made out to Jonathan Blake.

Samantha stared at it after she'd called out the amount.

"Find something?" Deborah asked.

"No. I just wondered...."

Deborah giggled. "So did I. It's the fifth one. Five

housand a month for five months. A dowry for Anne Marie, do you suppose?''

''Maybe it was for the work he did for the brochure,'' Samantha suggested, realizing even as she spoke that the doctor had requested the brochure just after she arrived, and anyway, the figure was much too high.

Deborah shook her head, blond curls bouncing. ''Nope. Jon wouldn't let the doctor pay for that. It was a favor, he said.''

Five thousand dollars a month for five months. Twenty-five thousand dollars. Why?

She turned the check over. *For Deposit Only, Jonathan Blake.* Odd, definitely odd. And definitely not her business.

''Weisfield's Jewelers,'' she read from the next check. ''Two hundred seventy dollars and eighty-five cents.''

''That's it!'' Deborah exclaimed, looking over her shoulder. ''That's a watch for Anne Marie—it's her nineteenth birthday on Sunday.'' She made a disgusted sound with her tongue and teeth. ''I should have known—I do it every time. The doctor makes his sevens in the European way, see, with a line across the number. I read it as a four. Thanks, Samantha.''

''You're welcome,'' Samantha said automatically as she returned to her own desk. Five thousand dollars a month, she thought again. What on earth was Dr. Birmann paying Jon *for*?

LATER IN THE MORNING she decided to visit Liz Vandervort, to let her know she wouldn't be putting in an appearance for a couple of days. Liz would cheer her, she felt sure—she was always so cheerful herself.

But she found Liz in a pensive mood, staring at herself

in the mirror, trying to arrange her dark hair to cover the scars where her surgeon had clipped away hair before making the necessary incisions. "My hair looks so thin," she wailed as soon as Samantha entered the chalet.

"It will grow back," Samantha assured her. "And it isn't thin at all." She searched for more reassuring words but couldn't come up with any. Liz was looking a lot better than she had when the bandages first came off, but the suture lines were still mildly inflamed behind her ears and across the top of her head, and her eyes and cheeks were still bruised looking. She still managed to look very attractive, but she certainly wasn't the raving beauty Samantha had seen pictured in newspapers. Though Dr. Birmann had assured her she would be even more beautiful than before in just a few more days.

"You *feel* better, don't you?" Samantha offered at last.

"Gosh, yes," Liz said with a shudder. "Believe me, love, if I'd had any idea there was pain involved, I'd never have gone through with it, even for Harold. A little discomfort, that damned plastic surgeon told me." She made a face at herself in the mirror, then turned around on her dresser stool and stood up, looking at Samantha with a grin, her usual good spirits evidently restored. "Don't mind me, I've got a case of cabin fever, that's all. I haven't spent this much time alone since—" She broke off, tilting her head to one side. "What's wrong, love? You look as if you've gone through a little discomfort yourself. That fiancé of yours giving you trouble?"

"Something like that," Samantha said, averting her eyes from the woman's sharp glance.

Liz settled herself on her bed, leaning back against the down pillows and smoothing her cloud of white negligee around her. "Come tell mama," she ordered, patting the bed beside her.

Samantha sat, but shook her head. "Nothing to tell."

"Did Adrian finally decide he was a fool to turn you loose?"

Liz had delivered herself earlier of the opinion that Adrian was crazy to let a girl like Samantha go off on her own for six months. "He should have dragged you to the altar the minute you said yes," she said now. "Eighteen months! Whoever stays engaged eighteen months nowadays? The man's mad."

"It's mostly my doing," Samantha objected. "I'm the one who kept postponing the wedding. I just wanted to be sure...."

Liz snorted. "If you want my opinion, and you're going to get it whether you want it or not, you don't want to marry the man at all."

"That's the conclusion *I've* reached," Samantha agreed. "I've decided it's not fair to Adrian to stay engaged to him, especially since—" She broke off, but not soon enough. Liz's bright green eyes, undimmed by the bruised flesh around them, sparkled immediately.

"Someone else, is there?" she asked.

Samantha laughed shortly. "I didn't know you were clairvoyant."

"Can't live in Washington without becoming something of a witch. Come on, love, tell me all." Her eyes narrowed. "Could this have something to do with the stalwart gentleman who escorted you to your chalet a few nights ago? He looked like quite a hunk, even in the dark." She laughed at Samantha's astonishment. "I take walks at night, love. I have to get out of this shack sometimes."

The idea of anyone referring to the luxurious chalet as a shack brought a smile to Samantha's face, and Liz applauded its appearance. "That's better. Now, do you want to talk about it?"

Samantha shook her head, though she was tempted to pour out the whole story into Liz's sympathetic ears. "It's too complicated," she said finally. "And it's over. And besides...."

"Besides, it's none of my business," Liz finished for her. "Don't worry, love, I won't pry. But believe me, if there's anything I've learned in my...." She hesitated, patting her face. "...well, let's say in my over forty years of experience, it's that love is the most important ingredient in any human relationship. The storybooks may *seem* to exaggerate its importance, but they don't. Love, or the lack of it, is at the center of everything. I truly believe that. Anyway," she added with a suddenly mischievous grin, "without love, it's impossible to put up with any man. So if you don't love what's his name—Adrian—then you certainly mustn't marry him. And if you do love the hunk, you should go after him."

"He turned out to be...not lovable," Samantha said with a tinge of bitterness in her voice. "I guess I'm just not fated to fall in love with the right man."

Liz grinned again. "You know, there's a theory that people who fall in love disastrously have brains that produce more phenylethylamine than most. Phenylethylamine promotes the effect of birds singing, bells ringing, all the symptoms of love, whether it's really there or not. The same chemical is present in chocolate, which may be why love-starved people eat lots of it. I know I do. Maybe we should send someone out for a couple of candy bars and drown our sorrows."

She smiled approvingly as Samantha laughed, then slid off the bed and gestured Samantha to follow her into the sitting room. "Come on, love, end of lecture. Let's play scrabble and take my mind off my face and yours off your heart."

With that she spent the next hour being so outrageous with her choice of words on the scrabble board, so determinedly vivacious, that Samantha was charmed into forgetting herself and her misery, though she did find, after she'd left Liz's chalet, that the woman had helped her make up her mind to take one course of action. As soon as she returned from Seattle, she would write to Adrian and break off their engagement. She had a suspicion that Adrian's heart would not be broken too badly. Which in itself said a lot about her relationship with Adrian, she thought as she packed her suitcase later.

She felt enormously relieved now that she'd reached a decision. At least the episode with Jon had shown her how much less emotion Adrian aroused in her. She ought to be grateful to Jon for that, she supposed.

CHAPTER ELEVEN

UNFORTUNATELY THE SEMINAR PROVED TO BE RATHER DULL. Samantha had hoped it would be interesting enough to take her mind off herself, but it had not been designed with the layman in mind, and there was a lot of the eminent doctor's material that made no sense to her at all, though she dutifully copied down everything he said.

Toward the end of the last session, she found herself in a state approaching torpor. She had not slept well the previous two nights, though the hotel bed was very comfortable. Try as she might to crowd Jon out of her thoughts, he remained with her. She had lost him once, and then life had seemed to offer her a second chance. But that chance had not been fulfilled—she had lost him a second time, and she didn't know if she could bear the pain of it.

"If you love him, go after him," Liz had said. If only it was that simple. But she couldn't even decide *how* she felt about him. One minute she hated him for what he'd done, the next she ached to be near him. Was that love?

A round of applause startled her. She glanced quickly at Dr. Birmann and found to her relief he hadn't noticed her inattention. She looked at the last sentence she'd written.

"In contrast to that of Vitamin B12 and calcium, absorption of phosphorus is not known to depend on spe-

cific substances comparable to intrinsic factor or Vitamin D.'' What on earth did that mean? And more importantly, what had Dr. Hodgkins said after that?
Something about pathologic sequelae, whatever that
was. ''I'm afraid I didn't get the last part,'' she whispered to Dr. Birmann.

He glanced at her notes, then smiled at her. ''It is of
no consequence. You have the most important facts.
His closing remarks were simply a summing up of the
whole.'' His glance became sharper. ''Are you unwell,
Samantha? You look quite pale.''

''I didn't sleep too well,'' she admitted.

''Nor I. The city noises. . . .''

She let that stand as her own excuse and managed to
get through luncheon without losing attention again. As
Dr. Birmann had warned her, during the two day seminar some of the other doctors had paid her far more attention than she welcomed. One in particular, a tall,
balding, rather antiseptically handsome young doctor
from Tacoma, had pressed her several times to have a
drink with him—in his room, she suspected. At lunch,
he offered to take her sightseeing around Seattle, but
she declined as graciously as possible, telling him Dr.
Birmann had work for her to do.

''I *don't* have need of you this afternoon,'' Dr. Birmann told her as coffee was served. Luckily he had
spoken quietly and the young doctor didn't overhear.

''I was making excuses,'' Samantha murmured.

''Ah, I see.'' He glanced at her sideways, obviously
amused. ''What will you do with yourself then?''

''I thought I'd take the monorail to Seattle Center,
maybe ride to the top of the Space Needle. It's a lovely
day, so I should be able to see all the mountains.''

Dr. Birmann was shaking his head. "The center will no doubt be crowded. Schoolchildren on summer vacation. You might enjoy more a visit to Pike Place Market and the waterfront."

"I'm more interested in the center," Samantha insisted. "I'd like to see what's been added to the Pacific Science Center since I was there last, and I understand from Eileen Blake that the old Food Circus has been remodeled. I always liked to go there and—"

"What about the Underground tour," the doctor suggested. "You know, the original Seattle was built in a boggy spot and the current buildings were later constructed right on top. The tour begins at a turn-of-the-century tavern, called Doc Maynards, in the Pioneer Square area, which was the heart of the city during the Alaska gold rush. A guide takes you below ground to see the old storefronts and sidewalks. You would enjoy such a tour, I'm sure."

"But I want to...." About to persist, Samantha hesitated. There was something more in the doctor's expression and voice than a mere desire to ensure her enjoyment of her free afternoon. He was trying to talk her *out* of going to the Seattle Center. Why?

"Maybe you're right," she said carefully, watching his face. "The tour does sound like fun."

At once the muscles of his face relaxed, as though he were feeling relieved. Why was it so important to him that she not go to Seattle Center? Whatever the reason, she wasn't going to argue any longer, but she wasn't about to have her recreational activities dictated to her. The center had always interested her. Built for the Seattle World's Fair in 1962, the handsomely landscaped grounds contained a coliseum, an opera house, ice arena and high-school football stadium, as well as the Science Center, various museums and galleries, an amusement park and the Space Needle, which offered spectacular views from its observation deck. She wouldn't say any more about the center to the doctor, she decided, she'd simply go there.

At first merely puzzled by the doctor's insistence, she became even more curious when she saw him at the other end of the monorail car soon after she'd boarded. So—he was going to the center himself—the monorail didn't lead anywhere else. But the center covered seventy-four acres; surely there was room enough for both of them. Why hadn't he wanted her to go? Was he meeting someone, perhaps, someone he didn't want her to see him with? Tom Greene? Her interest quickened. It was always possible, of course, that the charming doctor was simply meeting a woman. But somehow she didn't think so.

Luckily the car was crowded, and she was careful to keep herself out of sight, mainly in order to prevent embarrassment. And when the monorail car reached its destination, she held back for the same reason and stayed well behind the doctor as he strode toward the exit.

No one met him at the foot of the concrete ramp. And he didn't seem inclined to wait for anyone. He turned right and headed straight up the sloping walkway past the Center House in an unwavering line to an open phone booth on the corner.

Okay, he was going to make a phone call. Ashamed of herself for spying on her employer, Samantha was about to turn away toward the Science Center, but then it occurred to her to wonder why the doctor could not have made his call from the hotel. Even more curious was the fact that he didn't pick up the receiver. He just stood very still for a moment, then he lifted one hand to touch the perforated metal wall at the back of the open booth.

A second later, he was backing out of the booth, going around the corner and down a pathway that led past the Flag Pavilion to the plaza where every state's flag snapped briskly in the breeze. Her curiosity growing by the minute, Samantha followed slowly, ambling along in the middle of a group of tourists from California wearing jeans and T-shirts.

He seemed to be heading for the International Fountain. Perhaps he was meeting someone there. No. He was sitting down on the wide rough ledge that edged the huge sunken concrete bowl, apparently intending to sit and watch the central fountain's plumes of water as they soared and dipped and soared again in time to music.

Now that really was strange, Samantha thought. She had noted on several occasions that Dr. Birmann was fussy about his clothing. He was always immaculately dressed and took pains to stay that way. She had often watched him smooth his jacket before hanging it carefully on a padded hanger in his office, and had twice observed him dusting off a bench on the spa's patio with a paper napkin before sitting. Now there he was, in his beautifully tailored and probably expensive navy blazer and gray slacks, sitting on the edge of the concrete bowl like any jean-clad visitor.

All of this was none of her business, she chastised herself. She should simply turn smartly around and go on her way toward the lacy soaring arches of the Pacific Science Building, leaving the doctor to amuse himself in any way he saw fit.

Yet still she hesitated at the corner of the Flag Pavilion. Something about the doctor's behavior this afternoon bothered her. His walk to the fountain had not been the aimless wandering of the usual Center visitor. There had been purpose in it—as though he'd taken a sighting from one of the flags in the plaza and aimed for that particular spot.

After a moment she walked on across the grass, hoping the tourists ambling beneath the widely spaced trees would help to hide her from view. The doctor was leaning forward now, running his hands along the front of the ledge, under the ledge, leaning precariously forward. Watching from beside a maple tree with a fairly large trunk, Samantha took an involuntary step forward, almost afraid he would lose his balance, then she froze as the doctor suddenly straightened and stood up, clutching something in his right hand that she was sure he hadn't been holding before. Something fairly small and cylindrical—a container of some kind. Black. Metal or plastic. As she watched, he glanced at it, then slipped it into his trouser pocket with a furtive gesture that reminded her of one of Ben's sleight-of-hand tricks. Then he casually dusted the seat of his pants, turning as he did so.

Hastily Samantha stepped to the other side of her tree. It would be more than embarrassing if the doctor were to catch her watching him now—she had the distinct feeling that he would be extremely angry.

He went by her, fairly close, walking briskly. She tried to tell herself she was acting like an idiot, imagining some kind of mystery in the doctor's actions, and it was certainly time she came to her senses. At the same time, she found her feet were in motion again, carrying her back up the tree-lined walkway behind the doctor as he once again headed for the phone booth. He still didn't make a call. Again his hand touched the back wall, then moved to the other side. A second later he was out of the booth and moving in the direction of the Space Needle.

Leaving the safety of the large shrub in a concrete tub that she'd ducked behind, feeling unimaginably ridiculous by now, Samantha continued to follow him until he turned, not toward the Space Needle but back up the ramp to the monorail.

An odd sequence of actions, she thought. Though of course, if she were to watch almost anyone in the center, she could probably make a mystery out of perfectly innocent actions. Strangely, though, something in the doctor's behavior had stuck her as familiar. An idea was hovering in some corner of her mind, about to make itself known. Hesitating beside a popcorn stand, heedless of the people milling around her, she watched the monorail car leave the terminal, heading back downtown. Only then did she move, heading rapidly back the way she had come. Entering the phone booth, picking up the telephone receiver as though she were about to make a call, she scrutinized the back wall thoroughly. Nothing. She'd had half a notion that the doctor might have left a message for someone there. But he hadn't.

Hanging up the telephone, Samantha began to turn away, feeling vaguely relieved. But as she did so, sunlight glinted on something in the upper-left corner of the booth. She studied it. A pin was stuck in one of the perforations—a roundheaded pin of the type dressmakers used. Quite suddenly the events of the past few minutes fell into place.

Not long ago she had read an espionage novel written by one of her favorite authors. One of the characters in the novel, a spy, had picked a piece of adhesive tape off a brick wall outside a public building. It had been placed there by another man as a signal that something had been left for the spy at a prearranged place. The spy had gone there, to a cinema, retrieved a package from behind a cistern in a men's toilet, then returned to the wall and replaced the strip of tape in a different place, this letting his colleague know he had picked up the package. She had thought at the time that it was a remarkably simple but effective method of passing on material without risking a meeting.

What could Dr. Birmann have picked up? And who had left it for him? And why?

As she mulled over the questions, she remembered the sound of Dr. Birmann's voice emphatically saying "Nyet" to Tom Greene. A chill ran the length of her spine, and she felt cold in spite of the heat of the sun on her head.

No. It was impossible. Dr. Birmann was a respected doctor. He couldn't possibly be a Soviet spy. Such things didn't happen in real life.

Yes they did. Fairly recently, a young man had been caught peddling information on CIA spy satellites to Russia. An ordinary-looking young man. An American. Dr. Birmann hadn't even been born in the United States, which made it even more possible that....

"Excuse me," a voice said beside her as someone jostled her.

Startled, Samantha looked into the face of an elderly lady who was smiling apologetically at her. She was astonished to discover that she was standing at the foot of the ramp to the monorail, with no memory of getting there.

She might as well go back into town, she decided as she murmured her own apologies. She wouldn't be able to concentrate on the displays at the Science Center in her present frame of mind.

What she should probably do, she thought as the monorail car whisked back toward town, was to forget the whole thing and chalk it up to her own vivid imagination, which had built a few odd incidents and a few remarks from Anne Marie into a major mystery.

But she knew herself too well to believe she could just forget what had happened this afternoon. In any case, Dr. Birmann's odd behavior had made her forget her own problems for a while—and that was to be encouraged. If she kept her mind busy with this mystery, she wouldn't think about Jonathan Blake.

For a while she wandered around downtown Seattle, not really noticing much of anything, her mind teeming with ideas, each one seeming crazier than the last. Even if Dr. Birmann was really a Russian, she realized, he wouldn't necessarily be a spy. Someone had said once— a client of her father's she thought—that Russians in this country didn't spy, they hired other people to do the spying for them. People like Tom Greene, she wondered.

She wasn't getting anywhere. She couldn't seem to think constructively. When she stepped off a curb and was startled by the sound of a car horn, dangerously close, she decided that for safety's sake she'd better put this afternoon's events into the back of her mind until she returned to the island.

It was too bad she hadn't thought of getting Lynne's

office address from Ben. This would have been an ideal opportunity to see her and perhaps try to persuade her to spend more time with the twins. She and Lynne had never been close friends—the eleven-year age gap had made a difference. But they had always got along fairly well, and Samantha was sure she could introduce the subject of the twins' welfare in a tactful way.

But she *hadn't* thought ahead, so for the rest of the afternoon she might as well concentrate on sightseeing and try to put herself in a frame of mind where she could greet Dr. Birmann without giving her earlier activities away.

She remembered suddenly that both Dr. Birmann and Deborah had mentioned Anne Marie's birthday was coming up. Glad to have something innocuous to occupy her mind, she entered the closest department store. After a short time there, she wandered out into the streets again, determined this time to pay attention to her surroundings.

She had always loved Seattle, which she thought must surely be one of the most livable cities anywhere. Increasingly sophisticated, a center for the arts and music, the city had managed to retain its feeling of the great outdoors. Fitted between a lake and the inland sea of Puget Sound, with mountain ranges in the distance on either side, the city offered something for everyone. At no time was a resident far from water, and glimpses of the Sound and the tree-covered islands and high mountains offered themselves from various vantage points on the hilly, bustling urban streets—a combination that would be hard to equal anywhere.

Samantha enjoyed the hard physical exercise of walking the steep streets down to Pike Place Market and on to the waterfront, and she was pleasantly fatigued by the time she joined Dr. Birmann in the hotel lobby. As she'd expected, she did feel a little embarrassed when she saw him, but her awkwardness lasted only a moment. He seemed to be rather subdued, but he greeted her cordially. They talked mostly of the seminar they'd attended as they made their way back to the island. At his suggestion, they took the ferry. "Such a lovely evening," he pointed out. "We should not waste it." They stood by one of the upper rails, enjoying the summer breeze and the beautiful scenery. The July 4 storm had washed away the usual summer haze, and all the mountains were visible, seeming to tower higher than ever under the blue evening sky.

At only one point did Samantha feel really uncomfortable. That was when Dr. Birmann questioned her about her sight-seeing activities. No, she told him, she hadn't taken the Underground Tour, but she *had* explored the waterfront and the market. The market had changed, she said. There seemed to be more craft booths and antique stores than she remembered and not so many stalls offering fresh farm products.

She was afraid he would ask her directly if she had gone to Seattle Center after all, but he seemed satisfied with her answers and dropped the subject.

And now that she was with him, her suspicions seemed insane. She looked at him as he stood against the rail, his iron gray hair ruffled by the breeze. In his well-cut blue blazer, gray slacks, immaculate white shirt and carefully knotted dark tie, he looked exactly what he was—a professional man of some means, a caring, knowledgeable physician. There was great dignity in the blunt-cut features, assurance without arrogance in his posture. A nice man, a kind man, an honorable man.

And yet . . . what other interpretation could she put on for his actions of the afternoon, especially in the light of what Anne Marie had confided? In some way Dr. Jakob Birmann was involved in something that was *not* honorable. She was surer of that than she'd ever been of anything. He seemed to be deep in thought now, his eyes staring straight ahead of him, apparently not seeing the passing landscapes or the pristine outlines of the mountains.

Samantha sighed inwardly. She had thought when she'd first returned to Collins Island that she might be able to solve her personal problems. She had hoped, naively, that she would take one look at Jon Blake and decide he held no attraction for her. She had meant to revisit the magic places of her youth and find they had lost their enchantment—after which she could return happily to an uncomplicated life as Mrs. Adrian West-cott. Instead her emotions were more tangled than ever where Jon was concerned. She'd decided she couldn't live with Adrian. And she had stepped into a situation that belonged in the pages of a novel or in some television play. At the moment she had no idea what she was going to do about any of these situations. It was ironic in a way. She'd left home wanting to take control of her own life for a while. She was obviously unable to do that. What a mess she'd made of everything. What an absolutely unholy mess!

First things first, she decided when she reached her chalet. She couldn't do much about Dr. Birmann until she'd had a chance to think things through. Probably she would never be able to do anything about Jon. But Adrian was a different matter. She'd delayed long enough.

After dinner she attempted several letters, all of

which she tore up, recognizing finally that writing to him was a cowardly way out. At last, taking a deep breath, she called him at home.

"Hello, Samantha," he said warily. "How are you?"

He sounded moderately pleased to hear from her, she decided—not delighted, which was hardly surprising considering the way she'd left him. "Your latest letter arrived safely," he added when she didn't respond for a moment. "You received mine, I hope?"

"Of course." Why on earth had she called him, how could she phrase. . . ."

"I had a letter from your father yesterday. He and Claudia seem to be having a nice time."

"Yes. I guess they are." He wasn't going to ask why she'd called him, even though they'd agreed she wouldn't telephone him. They'd decided letters would be their only contact until she sorted herself out. Adrian would wait, she knew, for her to explain. She'd thought, early in their relationship, that his patience might balance her impatience, but it hadn't worked that way. The more patient he was, the more she felt like throttling him with her bare hands.

She took a deep breath. Might as well get it over with. "I've been thinking, Adrian."

"Yes?"

"Well, I've decided. . . ." This was even harder than she'd expected. "I've decided it would be best if we broke our engagement."

Silence.

Then, "I see." More silence. Nothing but the hum of long distance. "Is there someone else, Samantha?"

"No, not exactly. It's just that. . . I'm not really the kind of wife you need."

"You may be right, Samantha," he said unexpectedly. "This jaunt of yours *was* rather juvenile—this search for yourself or whatever it was."

"Yes, well, I'm sorry, Adrian."

"You're sorry." There was a chill in his voice. "I suppose there's no point in trying to get you to change your mind. As you know, I've never believed in using coercion."

Perhaps it might have been better if he had, Samantha thought, but she didn't say so aloud. "I'm sorry, Adrian," she repeated. Why didn't he shout at her, beg her, why didn't he at least try.... Did she really want him to do that? No. But if he had just been a little more emotional, perhaps she might have loved him more, perhaps she might never have wanted to come back to the island, might have forgotten Jon....

"I'm damn disappointed in you, Samantha," Adrian said coldly after another long pause. "Your father is going to be disappointed, too."

He hung up.

Dammit, she wanted to shout, *my father wasn't the one who was going to marry you!* She almost called him back to say so but managed to restrain herself.

She sighed as she climbed into bed. Adrian had his pride, his stiff upper lip as he called it. Probably he was very upset, but he'd never let her know that. She would never know how her call had really affected him.

At least it was over. And she was free. There was relief in that.

CHAPTER TWELVE

IN ITS USUAL UNPREDICTABLE MANNER, Washington's weather had changed again. After a week that had included extremes of heat, a storm and breezy springlike sunshine, whoever was in control had decided to throw in a little winter for a change.

When Samantha left her chalet on Friday morning, she remembered a quotation—Mark Twain, she thought: "I spent one of my coldest winters one summer on Puget Sound." She was glad she'd worn a heavy sweater over her jeans and blouse. The wind out of the north was cold enough to make her eyes sting as she hurried across the lowest terraced lawn in front of the spa. Above her head, slate gray clouds stretched to the horizon, showing not a single patch of blue sky.

"Rain by nightfall," Ben told her when she came across him weeding in the rockery. "After that, maybe some warmer weather."

"I hope you're right," Samantha said.

She hesitated for a second, wondering if she should confide in Ben her suspicions of Dr. Birmann. But then she reminded herself she'd decided there was only one person she could possibly discuss this with.

No matter how much she personally might want to avoid Jon, he was the one person who might conceivably be able to tell her what to do.

"I'll see you later, Ben," she said, and left him to his work.

Jon wasn't home. Eileen greeted her at the door with the news that he'd taken his boat to Seattle to bring some guests out to the house.

"I won't keep you then; you must be busy," Samantha said, turning away.

Eileen objected at once. "They aren't houseguests," she said. "Some kind of business meeting," she added vaguely. "Come on in, have coffee at least. They won't be here for an hour or more, and I've been hoping you'd come by. I complained to Jon just the other day that I wasn't seeing enough of you. He said you were pretty busy," she added over her shoulder as she led the way to the kitchen and lifted the coffeepot from the stove. "I'm glad you two have been able to get friendly again. It would be a shame if you were permanently estranged."

She sat down opposite Samantha at the big walnut table and smiled fondly.

Samantha squirmed uncomfortably under Eileen's direct blue gaze, remembering the last time she was in this house—with Jon. Did Eileen know she'd come here the night of the storm, she wondered. She didn't think so. Eileen's eyes were totally without guile. Feeling an explanation for her presence was probably called for, she said hastily, "I just wanted to ask Jon's advice about something."

"Oh?" There was a question in Eileen's voice, but when Samantha didn't respond she got up and busied herself getting out cream and sugar and a dish of cookies that smelled wonderfully of cinnamon.

Tonto wandered into the kitchen and draped himself

over Samantha's right foot. The two cats were in their usual places on the windowseat, the calico sleeping, curled in a ball, the scarred old tom looking out at the dreary sky, his tail twitching from side to side.

Samantha bit into one of the cookies and tried to decide what she should do now. She'd worried all day yesterday about Dr. Birmann's behavior in Seattle. It had been difficult to concentrate on her tasks, and she'd had a lot of work to do after her time away. She hadn't even noticed Anne Marie was wearing a little foundation and mascara until the girl pointed it out and asked her opinion. "Very nice," she managed when prompted. "You could probably use even more, especially around your eyes."

"I didn't want to shock daddy too much right away," Anne Marie had confessed. "I thought it best to start slow. But I do think I look less virginal now. I felt silly looking virginal when—" She broke off.

The implication was there again—she wanted Samantha to think she'd had at least one affair. With Jon?

"You look great," Samantha murmured neutrally. At the moment she had more important things to think about. Her thoughts had already left the girl and were circling around her father again.

In the evening Deborah had come over to her chalet to visit for a while and talk some more about archeology, and she hadn't left until late.

Once in bed Samantha had gone through that whole afternoon in her imagination, visualizing every step the doctor had taken, every move he had made. And she had decided the implications were definitely too serious to keep to herself.

Now, having keyed herself up to a meeting with Jon,

she felt frustrated. She'd have to wait, she supposed, until Jon's meeting was over, then try to catch him alone.

"Jon's guests will be leaving the marina around five," Eileen said as though reading Samantha's mind. "They have to catch a plane. I don't mind telling you," she added as she seated herself, "I'm a bit worried about this whole thing."

"What whole thing?" Samantha asked, wondering if Eileen could possibly know something about Dr. Birmann.

"Jon hasn't told you?"

"How can I know if I don't know what you're talking about?"

Eileen grinned. "Isn't that just like me? Jon says I'm the only person he knows who *expects* other people to know what's on my mind. Peter agrees—he's always teasing me about...." Her voice trailed away and her face colored a little. "I'm doing it again. What was I... oh, yes, Jon and his meeting." She frowned and put down her coffee cup. "Jon said I wasn't to tell anyone, so I'd better not talk about it, if he hasn't told you himself."

"I guess not," Samantha agreed, totally bewildered now.

"So anyway, what have you been up to?" Eileen asked briskly.

Not surprisingly, Samantha felt an immediate flash of guilt, but she covered it up by commenting on the cookies and then, acting on a sudden impulse, added, "I'm thinking of writing a mystery novel set in this area—well, Seattle anyway."

Eileen looked interested. "What's it about?"

"I'm not sure yet. I had this one scene come into my mind that seems to be pivotal—a drop scene I think it's called—but I haven't figured out how to use it yet."

Taking a deep breath, telling herself she wasn't really *deceiving* Eileen, she launched into an account of Dr. Birmann's odd actions at Seattle Center, pretending they were part of a fictional plot.

"What's in the container," Eileen asked as soon as she was through.

"I haven't decided yet."

"Well, it has to be something to do with espionage with a scene like that."

"That's what I thought," Samantha said weakly. For a moment she felt sick. This wasn't fiction. This was real life. Dr. Birmann. . .surely he couldn't really be an enemy of the country, working against it? Surely. . . .

"Microfilm," Eileen said positively. "There are all kinds of military and strategic installations in Washington State. Pictures of documents, secret documents. Our man is going to sell them to the highest bidder. Or something."

"I don't know, Eileen," Samantha said, wishing she hadn't brought up the subject, deciding she'd better slow down Eileen. "I've an idea all of this has been done too many times before."

"So you have to come up with a gimmick—a twist—to make it seem new." Eileen's blue eyes were sparkling now. She'd entered into the game with zest. Only it wasn't a game, Samantha reminded herself again.

"Could you make one of the characters a woman maybe?" Eileen went on. "I can just see her with one of those tiny little cameras, photographing papers on a desk—one of those little desk lamps on."

Samantha could visualize the scene herself. She'd seen it several times in movies.

Unbidden, a memory came to her. Shifting slightly, she looked toward the hall that led to Jon's den. He owned a miniature camera. What did he use it for? He could hardly take pictures of whales with a camera that size.

She dismissed the thought. Jon owned all sizes of cameras for all kinds of purposes.

Eileen was still rattling on, her ideas getting wilder and wilder. Samantha sat back and let her go until at last she ran down and apologized with a laugh. "Here I am writing your story for you."

"I don't know why I even brought it up," Samantha said carefully. "The more I think about it, the more trite it sounds."

And things became trite because they were true, a voice inside her said. Espionage did take place in real life. She had *witnessed* an act of espionage, she was sure of it.

She managed to lead Eileen into a discussion of her sculpture and the show Peter Darrell was planning for her, and as soon as she possibly could she made her excuses and left.

After visiting the twins for a while and confirming for herself that Suzy McLain, who was baby-sitting them, was indeed as ravishing as Jon had said, she borrowed an old five-speed bicycle of Lynne's and cycled around the island's old roads, reacquainting herself with parts she hadn't managed on foot. The old house at Willow Lake was occupied for the summer by a family from Idaho—she'd discovered that on one of her exploring trips with Tracy and Brian. So she didn't bother to go back there.

The rain Ben had promised hadn't materialized by five o'clock. Encouraged by the continuing dry weather, she had ranged farther afield than she'd intended. Of course, she admitted to herself, she must have known subconsciously all along that her ramblings were leading her toward the marina.

She was there watching some fishermen unload their boat when Jon drove up in his BMW. She was standing beside the Marina Restaurant, the bicycle parked beside her. She saw him get out of the car, dressed in his boating clothes—white jeans and navy blue crew-neck sweater—and her heart thumped painfully against her rib cage.

He wasn't smiling. For selfish reasons she was glad of that.

She made no effort to conceal herself, but he didn't see her. Which wasn't really surprising. The restaurant was some distance up the hill, and he was concerned with opening doors for his passengers.

She blinked with surprise when they emerged from the car. Three men dressed in business suits, carrying briefcases. There was an aura of the city about them—an aura of purpose, of power. They looked out of place, almost alien—an odd contrast to the denim-clad fishermen who were now walking along the pier to the shore, carrying large plastic bags that bulged from the weight of the salmon they'd caught.

She saw Jon greet the fishermen, saw them nod in response, and heard a word or two pass between them. Why was she standing here making herself suffer by watching Jon? How graceful he was. He was incapable of making a clumsy or unbecoming move. He leaped easily aboard his boat—the other men looked awkward, almost ludicrous in contrast. Apparently they weren't accustomed to boats. Jon was seating himself at the helm now. She should leave. Obviously it was going to be some time before Jon returned. She calculated—an hour to Seattle, an hour back. He might even decide to spend the night.

Still she couldn't tear herself away, not even when *Aegir* purred rapidly out of the harbor and headed south.

After some time she went into the marina coffee shop and drank some coffee. Then she went outside and sat on a bench, watching boats come in one by one as the clouds thickened and darkened, heavy with the promise of rain.

At last *Aegir* appeared in the distance, and she stood up and went down to the dock to help Jon tie up.

He didn't seem surprised to see her. He regarded her coolly for a second, then went about his tasks. "Have you been waiting here all this time?" he asked as soon as *Aegir* was secure.

He *had* seen her earlier then. But he hadn't acknowledged her presence. There was pain in that to add to all the other pain. "I wanted to...I need to talk to you," she said. "Not about us," she added as his eyes darkened. "It's something...I need some advice." She attempted a smile that didn't quite come off. "It's probably nothing, but I'm worried."

His blue eyes studied her face. Then he frowned. "It's serious, isn't it?"

"Yes."

"Then by all means let's talk." There was kindness in his voice—a distant kindness. Taking her arm as they walked along the dock, he gestured at the restaurant with his free hand. "How about dinner? Mom served a huge lunch, but I'm ready for something more. Could you stand some of Charlie's Crab Louie? It's still the best in the west."

A twist of pain went through her. Years before they had celebrated all happy events by eating Crab Louie at the elegant Marina Restaurant, which on a clear day offered a panoramic view of Puget Sound and the Olympic mountains.

"We're hardly dressed for it," she demurred.

Jon shrugged. "Charlie won't mind."

Samantha didn't offer any further protest. At least they could talk in relative privacy in one of the restaurant's plush booths.

Charlie greeted them himself, beaming all over his round ruddy face as he led them to a corner booth. "It's great to see you two together again," he assured them. "Samantha, I heard you were back. You can't know how much I've missed your pretty face. You always used to brighten up this old place of mine." He was glancing from Jon to Samantha, his brown eyes bright, his weathered face creased into a network of wrinkles by his smile.

Under the circumstances Samantha felt discomfited by his enthusiasm, and she was afraid he'd hover over them throughout the meal. But as soon as he'd consulted with Jon and the steward over the wine they'd drink with dinner, he left for his kitchen, giving Jon a monstrous wink as he left, as if to indicate he knew exactly how their conversation would go.

If he only knew, Samantha thought, feeling suddenly, contrarily, that she wished he had stayed after all, making it impossible for her to talk to Jonathan about Dr.

Birmann. For now that the moment was upon her the story seemed insane again—impossible to tell, especially to Jon, whose very presence was setting up a clamor in her blood, deepening the pain around her heart.

Jon looked at her across the table, his eyes steady and cool and incredibly blue, reflecting the light from the wall lamp. "Okay, young Sam," he said softly. "Out with it. What's bothering you?"

The room seemed to lurch as she felt herself slipping backward through the years. In just such a way Jon had always greeted her when she was a child and had suffered some hurt, real or imagined. The transition from adult reality to remembered childhood lasted only a second, but it was enough to disorient her, so that for a moment she couldn't speak.

"Hey," Jon said gently. He reached across the table and clasped both her hands in his, warming her, bringing her back to the present. "Are you all right?" There was tenderness in his voice.

Swallowing hard, she carefully slid her hands from his. "I'm sorry, I guess I didn't remember to eat today."

He wasn't listening to her. He was looking at her hands, her left hand in particular. "You forgot to wear your ring?"

She glanced at her empty finger, covered it childishly with her other hand. "It's not important." She didn't want to explain to him her reasons for breaking the engagement, couldn't bear to see that look of triumph gleam in his eyes again.

"You *are* worried, aren't you?" He was looking at her face now, his expression cynical. Then he shook his head. "Never mind, we'll get to it. You said you hadn't eaten. Here." He plucked a packet of crackers from the basket on the table, opened it and handed it to her with the dish of butter. His manner was brisk now. Perhaps she'd imagined that brief moment of tenderness. Or else it had no real meaning. Jon had always been quick to sympathize with anyone who seemed unwell. She mustn't start reading any feeling for her into his words and actions. She'd been trapped by that error before. She was here because she was concerned about a mutual friend—nothing more.

Calmed by this thought, she was able to begin to tell him, lucidly and with composure, what she had witnessed at Seattle Center.

At some time the steward appeared with wine. She stopped speaking while Jon sampled it and nodded to the man to pour. A few minutes after, another waiter brought their crab. Neither of them made any attempt to eat.

At first obviously startled, Jon very quickly wiped all expression from his face. He didn't interrupt at all, though there were times when he seemed about to. From time to time his gaze brushed her face, but she couldn't tell what he was thinking. Only a slight frown furrowed the tanned skin above his nose.

When she was done he didn't speak for a while. He gazed out of the window as though he was trying to absorb all she had told him. This time she had left nothing out. She had told him of the argument she'd overheard between the doctor and Tom Greene; she had explained Anne Marie's concern, her own instinctive and negative feelings about the man. She had even remembered and passed on Anne Marie's story about the original argument between the two men.

The silence lengthened. Several people had come into

the restaurant, but they were seated some distance away—Charlie's doing—and she could hear only a murmur of their conversation. Rain was running steadily down the restaurant windows, obliterating the view. At last she began to eat her crab, though she had no appetite for it.

Finally Jon stirred. He picked up his fork and looked at it, then judiciously selected a piece of crab. "Okay," he said. "I'll take care of it."

Whatever she'd expected him to say, this wasn't it. She stared at him for a moment, then demanded. "What do you mean, you'll take care of it. What will you do?"

"I'm not sure yet. I've got to think about it. There has to be some explanation."

Impatience with him surged through her. "What possible explanation could there be? You surely aren't going to talk to Dr. Birmann about it?"

"Why not?"

"But Jon, if he is involved in something...subversive, you'll be warning him."

"He's my friend, Samantha."

She put down her fork and stared at him. "I can't let you discuss this with him. I'll go to the authorities myself before I'll let you do that."

"But for heaven's sake, Sam, there *has* to be an explanation." He stirred the food on his plate, not really seeing it, apparently thinking hard. "Try this for a scenario. Jakob goes to Seattle Center, decides to make a phone call, but once he's in the booth he changes his mind. So he wanders over to the fountain and sits down to think about it. Maybe there's a woman on his mind. Maybe this Esmée Taylor you mentioned earlier. Maybe he and Tom Greene have fought over this woman. Maybe he's not sure if he should call her—she's a married woman, you said. So he sits there. Maybe he has coins in his hand for the phone call. When he stands up, he puts the coins in his pocket...."

"It was a container, Jon. I saw a container, the kind film comes in."

"It might have contained pills. Maybe he has to take pills from time to time, who knows? So he goes back to the phone booth, still undecided, fiddles around in there, sees this pin you are sure is so significant, pulls it out and sticks it back—sort of thing anyone might do if they are cogitating. But he still can't bring himself to make the call, so he goes back on the monorail."

"But why would he go all the way to Seattle Center just to make a phone call?"

"I know someone who went all the way to Vancouver Island just to spy on a man who was none of her business." He waved aside her protest. "Okay, I agree, that was uncalled for. If there is a woman, and she's a married lady, he might go all that way to call her simply because he's overcautious."

"He spoke Russian to Tom Greene, Jon."

"I speak a little Russian myself. I've been to Moscow a couple of times." His mouth twisted sardonically. "I even speak Dolphin. That doesn't mean I am one. In any case, he might have been saying *not yet*. You do tend to have a vivid imagination, Sam."

Samantha stared at him blankly for a few minutes. She *knew* the word she'd heard was *nyet*. She felt tremendously disappointed in Jon. She had been so sure he would help her. Instead, he seemed determined to discredit her story. If his recital of that ridiculous "scenario" was anything to go by, he wasn't even going to take her seriously. He was tucking into his crab now as though the problem had been taken care of.

She took a deep breath. "You know damn well I'm right, Jon Blake. There's something odd about the whole thing."

He glanced at her and away, but not before she had seen in his eyes a concerned expression that told her he *did* agree with her. But he continued to argue. "Jakob Birmann is an honorable man, Samantha. I'd stake my life on it. Apart from anything else, he's a very visible man. It would be ridiculous for someone in his position to get involved in something as overt as you're suggesting."

"Anyone can make a mistake. He might have been rattled. By Tom Greene perhaps."

"Anyway, he's an American citizen. He became an American citizen years ago before he married. His wife was American. Anne Marie...."

"Do you know he's an American citizen, or did he just tell you so?"

He sighed. "Okay, Sam. I said I'd look into it."

"How?"

He looked at her with grim amusement. "Persistent, aren't you?"

When she didn't answer but kept her gaze fixed on him, he sighed again. "I have a friend, Mike Summers, in the FBI in Seattle. We shared a dorm room in college. I'll talk to him, see if he can check out the doctor."

"When will you call him?"

"I'll go to see him. I can't make insinuations against a respected man on the telephone. Mike's a good guy; he'll keep it confidential."

She sat back. "If you're willing to go to the FBI then you *do* believe something's wrong."

When he hesitated she leaned forward. "You *do*, don't you?"

"I believe *you* think something's wrong." He regarded her skeptically. "And as I certainly don't want you running around Seattle hurling accusations right and left, I have no choice but to talk to Mike."

She felt heat rise to her face. His voice held such *disdain*. But she refused to let him see that he'd hurt her. "You won't mind if I come with you, will you?" she asked casually.

His eyes met hers and narrowed. "I'm well aware of your low opinion of me, Sam, but I didn't know you didn't trust me."

She hesitated, shocked by the bitterness in his voice. Evidently he interpreted her hesitation to mean she *didn't* trust him. Briefly, a flush stained his cheekbones and his gaze hardened. His jaw was tight, his mouth an unyielding line. For a second he stared at her, his eyes blue as ice seen through snow. Then he laughed shortly. "Okay, Sam, I'll take you along—if you're sure you can stand to be with me." His eyebrows raised. "I'm surprised you're even talking to me."

"I came to you because I need your help, Jon," she said wearily. "If you don't want to give it to me, I'll understand. There's no need for us to fight over this. We've done enough fighting."

"Another truce? Okay. How about tomorrow? Is that soon enough for you?"

She flushed again at his sarcasm, couldn't resist offering some of her own. "Thank you, Jon, you're very gracious." She hesitated. "I do have another day off tomorrow. Will your friend be available on a Saturday?"

"He owes me a favor. He'll be available." He paused. "We'll have to take my car over on the ferry. I had a little engine trouble with *Aegir* tonight. I don't want to take her out again until I've had a chance to check her."

His voice was still clipped, as though she'd tried his patience. He thought her suspicions were nonsense, obviously. Did he think she *wanted* to discredit Dr. Birmann? Perhaps he even thought she'd exaggerated the situation just so she could be with him.

Or was there another reason for his offensive manner? For a moment there, she'd suspected he did believe her, yet might be prepared to cover up for the doctor. But that was silly. Why would he do that?

She sighed. He had agreed to take her with him to the FBI. What else had she expected of him? Had she secretly hoped he'd take her in his arms as he used to and tell her softly that he would help her in any way she wanted him to help her? Perhaps she'd even hoped he might apologize to her for treating her so badly the other night. That certainly didn't seem very likely now.

The thought crossed her mind that she'd committed herself to spending another day with him, and that might be difficult when he obviously despised her. Especially as, to her dismay, she was finding it difficult enough to sit here with him now. She literally ached to reach out and touch his hand where it lay on the table. Such a lean tanned hand, with such long graceful fingers. Strong fingers that could be incredibly gentle and delicate on her body. Impatient with herself, she averted her gaze. Hadn't she learned yet that it was foolish to indulge in daydreams?

Nevertheless, now that her concern for Dr. Birmann had lessened a little, she was becoming strongly aware of the close intimacy of the booth—an intimacy that was strengthened by the darkness of the window, which reflected them both. From the corner of her eye she could see her own bright hair in the rain-blurred glass, Jon's fair head opposite, shining under the lamplight. He had sat back in the booth now and was studying her left hand expressionlessly. He hadn't asked her again about her ring. Why should he when he obviously didn't care.

Oh, Jon, she thought suddenly, unexpectedly, *how can I live the rest of my life without you?*

A heartbeat later, he lifted his gaze and looked at her quizzically as though she'd spoken aloud. Hastily she applied herself to her dinner and began talking very rapidly about ferry schedules and the need for secrecy. "I don't want to alert Dr. Birmann," she said breathlessly. "And if my suspicions are unfounded, as you seem to think, I don't want him to know I suspected him. You won't tell him, will you?"

"I won't tell him."

He didn't speak again, but the silence between them seemed to shriek with her unspoken thoughts. For what had come clear to her as she looked at him was the fact that her love for him was hopeless. It wasn't ever going to be returned.

CHAPTER THIRTEEN

THEY MET MIKE SUMMERS in a tavern, which seemed a strange choice of rendezvous to Samantha. It was Mike's choice, Jon told her, as was the time of their meeting—late in the afternoon.

"I didn't tell Mike what we wanted to see him about," Jon explained. "He's probably expecting this to be a social meeting."

Samantha was favorably impressed by Mike's appearance. He was as tall as Jon, dressed in a tan three-piece suit that emphasized his lean build. His brown hair was neatly trimmed and parted, cut short to tame its tendency to curl. He was clean shaven, clean cut, everything an FBI agent was supposed to be. When Jon and Samantha entered the tavern, he slid from a high stool at the bar and gestured them to a table at the side of the room, giving Samantha a boyish grin that made her warm to him at once. She held out her hand when Jon introduced them, and he kept it in his for a second longer than was necessary, his glance appraising her figure in her slim white linen dress and matching jacket in a way that was obviously admiring, but not annoying.

He was an attractive man, she thought. She was amazed he was Jon's age, for he looked no more than twenty-two or twenty-three. "Clean living," he said when he caught her unbelieving gaze on him. She smiled at him.

"How's everything going?" Jon asked him after the waitress had taken their order.

Mike gave an exaggerated sigh. "Don't ask. If I have to deal with one more whacko who comes into the office with a crazy story, I'm going to start climbing the walls."

"You're not getting out in the field?"

"Not at the moment. Company policy, you might say. We all have to take a turn at the office. It's the democratic way."

"Well, I'm afraid you have one more whacko to deal with," Jon said lightly, glancing at Samantha in a sidelong sardonic way that infuriated her.

Mike groaned. "Hang on a sec then." He took a deep draught of beer, then grinned at Jon. "Okay, shoot."

"It's not my story," Jon said. "Samantha?"

He wasn't going to help her, that much was obvious. Samantha took a courage-inducing sip of the white wine she'd ordered and sat up very straight.

Mike was looking at her curiously, his brown eyes steady. As she hesitated, he gave her an encouraging smile.

She took a deep breath and started in on her story, beginning with her arrival on the island and striving to keep conversations and events in proper chronological order, hoping that she would at least impress the young FBI agent with her lucid account.

Mike kept his gaze fixed on her as she talked. He was a good listener. He was possibly a good poker player, too, for his face showed no reaction to what she had to say. Toward the end of her story, Samantha's voice faltered a little. In the face of Mike's attentiveness, she felt foolish recounting impressions, hearsay and conjecture. She could hear a voice in her head demanding, "Just give me the facts, ma'am, only the facts." There were few facts in her account, she realized. "I expect you think I'm nuts," she said into the silence that followed her conclusion.

Mike frowned and took another swallow of beer. "Not at all," he said politely. "I think you are a concerned citizen. We could use more of them."

For a while he moved his beer glass around on the square oak table, spreading and swirling the water that had melted from his frosted glass. "Not much to go on," he commented at last. "For one thing, if your doctor friend *is* mixed up in something...subversive, he was pretty careless and that's not too usual."

Samantha felt more foolish than ever. "Jon says I have a vivid imagination," she admitted.

"Maybe so." He paused. "Could you describe this Tom Greene for me?"

She did the best she could, realizing that the sunglasses and concealing cap sounded a bit too melodramatic. "I did see his eyes once," she concluded. "He has rather nice eyes, large eyes. Sort of luminous—and...." She hesitated.

"Go on," Mike said.

"Well, it was just—his eyes reminded me of someone, but I couldn't pin the memory down."

"Some movie star, maybe?"

"I don't think so."

More silence. Then Mike glanced at Jon and raised his eyebrows before turning his level gaze on Samantha again. "What I *can* do is put the computers to work on your friend," he said. "I can at least find out if he is a citizen, which I'm sure he must be. A doctor...he'd have to go through licensing and so on."

"He went to medical school in California," Jon interrupted.

Mike's eyebrows raised again. "He's lived in the country that long?" He pursed his mouth in a wry grimace. "Well, at least I can find out if he comes from wherever he's supposed to come from."

"Switzerland," Samantha supplied.

Jon added the name of the town.

"Uh-huh." Mike glanced at Samantha. "I'll check him out, okay?"

"I do like Dr. Birmann," she said quietly. "I don't want to make trouble for him. I'm really hoping you'll find everything's all right. I mean...."

"Don't worry. I can do this on the qt as the Brits say."

"Thank you."

He smiled warmly. "You're welcome. I'm always happy to set a pretty lady's mind at rest."

"He does think I'm nuts," Samantha said glumly after Mike had finished his beer and left.

Jon shrugged. "He's cautious."

"What if he finds out Dr. Birmann *doesn't* come from Switzerland?"

He frowned. "I don't think that's too likely. Let's not speculate, okay?" He glanced at his watch, then back at her. "You in a hurry to get back?"

Surprised by his amiable tone, she looked at him warily, trying to ignore the fact that he looked so attractive in his well-cut suit that her body was responding to him in its usual traitorous manner. "Why?" she asked.

"Don't be so suspicious. We're supposed to have a truce, remember? I thought we might stop in to see Lynne. She's quite possibly working late. She often does. And her travel agency's only a few blocks from here."

Samantha hesitated. "I've wanted to see Lynne, but...."

His mouth tightened. "For heaven's sake, Sam, I know you don't want to spend time in my company, but you got me into this thing with Jakob and I'm willing to see it through, even though I'm very reluctant to pry into a friend's private affairs. Don't you think you owe me something for that? All I want to do is visit an old friend for a few minutes. A mutual friend. Is that too much to ask?"

"Not at all," she said stiffly. "I'll be happy to go with you."

And that was at least partly true, she thought as she walked with him up the hill a few seconds later. There had always been pleasure in just walking alongside Jon. Their steps matched as they always had; even as a child she'd had long legs. And the sun was shining. Yesterday's rain, which had dwindled to a drizzle in the morning, had disappeared by the time they left the island. Now only a few fluffy clouds marred the blue of the late-afternoon sky and the breeze was fresh off the water. Shoppers were hurrying along the busy streets, arms loaded with packages. Traffic was heavy. The city bustle, combined with the return of good weather, lifted her spirits. She suddenly felt very glad to be alive.

They had to wait some time at the light before they could cross the street. Jon didn't take her arm as they crossed, as she'd half expected him to. She stole a glance at his profile. It was set, almost grim. Nothing had changed. Jon's love for her had disappeared years ago, he'd made that crystal clear. The pleasure went out of her. And the thought occurred to her, out of the blue, that she hadn't asked Mike Summers for his ID. What if he wasn't really a federal agent? What if Jon had arranged with him to meet them just to shut up Samantha?

A visual image, almost forgotten, presented itself in her mind. A check for five thousand dollars made out to Jonathan Blake, signed by Jakob Birmann. At once she rejected the image. That money had nothing to do with this. Her imagination was running away with her simply because she was offended by Jon's skeptical reaction.

She sighed. Truce or no truce, anger and suspicion kept coming between them. And she didn't want it to.

She glanced at him again. He was still looking straight ahead. She realized she wanted to touch him, to see him smile. She wanted to be his friend again. She wanted—

Impatiently she broke off her thoughts. She was letting herself be affected by his physical presence again. Jon had treated her abominably. She had treated him no better. Too much had been said, too much had been done. There could be no going back. And dammit—she *still* wasn't sure she trusted him.

"Jon," she said tentatively, intending to question him more closely about Mike Summers. But they had reached the travel agency, which occupied the lower floor of a soaring tower of concrete and glass. Jon opened the door and ushered her in, and she put her suspicions out of her mind.

Lynne didn't look at all as Samantha had expected. Following the twin's candid comments about her dyeing her hair, and what Jon had told her about her failed marriage, coupled with her own memories of Lynne's dissatisfaction with her lot in life, she'd half expected to see a sour disappointed woman, a matronly type fast approaching middle age.

Instead she was faced with a pleasant-looking woman with natural-looking black hair that curved around a lively, if rather plain face. Exact replicas of the twins' dark eyes shone with pleasure as they lighted on Samantha and Jon.

"Samantha Austin," Lynne exclaimed, coming around her desk to greet them. "Gosh, you're prettier than ever. The kids told me you were gorgeous and they were right." She took Samantha's hands in both of hers, looking at her with a pleased smile. "You've been good to my kids. I'm grateful."

"They're adorable children," Samantha said warmly. "I hadn't realized how much they look like you. You've changed, Lynne."

"Gained a few pounds in the right places and a lot of self-respect is all," Lynne said with a laugh. She released Samantha and hugged Jon exuberantly. "You, you stinker, you promised to take me to lunch sometime soon. How long has it been since I saw you? Two weeks? I'd decided you'd gone off to Timbuctu or the shores of Gitche Gumee or somewhere."

Jon laughed. "Last time I came in some brute with shoulders like an ox glared at me the whole time, so I thought I'd better stay away for a while."

"Oh, that was just my boss. Regular slave driver he is. Anyway, that's no excuse."

Jon grinned. "You're probably right. I get on that island and I don't want to leave it." He sighed. "I'll have to be going soon enough."

"Another one of your trips?"

He hesitated. "A little different this time."

Samantha felt his words strike her with the force of a blow. He was going away. Soon. He hadn't mentioned that to her. Why should he?

She felt empty with anticipated loneliness. She couldn't let him just walk out of her life again. She couldn't.

"Samantha?" Lynne said.

They were both looking at her oddly, as though they'd already spoken to her and she hadn't heard them. "I'm sorry," she said hastily.

Lynne grinned. "You were off in a world of your own there." She gestured them both into chairs and seated herself behind the desk, looking from one to the other, a knowing smile playing around her mouth. "Jon and Samantha. It's like old times."

Samantha winced. "How are you, Lynne?"

"Just fine. Well, I get along. You wouldn't know me now, Samantha. I've become a regular workaholic. Look at me, the only one here." She waved a hand at the empty chairs and cleared desks in the large room. "Everyone else has gone off for the weekend and here I sit."

"The twins told me you went to Hawaii recently," Jon said. "So it's no use trying to make us feel sorry for you."

"Hawaii. Ugh. You should have seen the group I had to take that weekend. Bunch of so-called businessmen. Acted like juvenile delinquents. Waikiki may never be the same again."

"Tracy and Brian missed you," Samantha said. "They wanted you there for the fireworks."

She could have sworn there was no note of censure in her voice, but Lynne looked at her with a suddenly cool glance that reminded Samantha of the rather unfriendly girl she'd once been. "You think I didn't miss *them*?" she asked. She glanced at Jon. "She hasn't changed, has she?"

For a moment Jon looked as though he were about to object to Lynne's tone of voice, and then he shrugged. "Maybe not."

Samantha felt her face flame. "I wish you wouldn't discuss me as if I wasn't here."

"You *aren't* here, Samantha, not in the real world." Lynne's voice was quite kind now, which gave Samantha a feeling of humiliation.

"What on earth did I say?" she demanded.

Lynne shrugged. "It wasn't what you said. It was your attitude." She shook her head, reached across the desk to pat Samantha's arm. "I'm sorry I sounded off like that. I heard in your voice what I hear in other people's voices. Condemnation. I know exactly what you've been thinking, Samantha. You've been thinking that it's a lousy mother who never visits her children, who goes off to Hawaii for July 4 and disappoints her kids, who leaves her old dad to take care of her responsibilities."

Samantha swallowed and glanced helplessly at Jon. He was leaning forward now, watching her closely. "What Lynne's trying to tell you, Sam, is that she loves her children. She'd spend all her time with them if she could. But she's trying to make extra money here by taking on extra work so that she can afford to go to school nights."

"I'm studying to be a certified public accountant,"

Lynne explained with pride in her voice. "At first this job was ideal. I commuted every day and spent weekends at home. But things keep coming up on weekends—seminars, trips. So I had to make a change. I'm staying with a girl friend right now because class lets out too late for me to catch the ferry." She shook her head. "This last month's been a doozy. Shortage of staff because of summer vacations. But I've talked to the kids every day on the phone, and I should be able to get home tomorrow for a while. Once I get established I'll go back to commuting."

She hesitated, sighed. "It would probably make more sense to get an apartment in town, but I'm afraid living in the city wouldn't be so good for the kids. I'd have to leave them with a strange baby-sitter." She lifted her hands in a helpless gesture that moved Samantha. "At least on the island they're safe. Once I'm in business for myself, I might be able to get some private tax work at home."

"I thought you hated the island," Samantha said hesitantly. She was almost afraid to speak, feeling that she'd already made a fool of herself. Obviously she hadn't understood Lynne's situation at all. She hadn't taken time to *try* to understand but had rushed in to condemn her without knowing all the facts. *Spoiled little rich girl,* echoed her memory. *What do you know of life and its necessities?*

"I used to," Lynne said, smiling, her cheerfulness evidently restored. "People change, Samantha. I guess I can't blame you for thinking I was avoiding the old place," she added. "But the truth is, I'd go back to it like a shot if I could get a job there. Isn't that ironic? I had to get away from the island to find out how much I loved it. And how much I loved my dad. He's been ter-rific, taking on the kids at his time of life.'' Her smile became rueful. ''I made a mess of my life for a while,'' she admitted. ''But I'm straightened out now. I want my kids to have a chance—a good college education, all the breaks. It takes a hell of a lot of money to raise kids nowadays, so I have to work. Dad can't keep us all on what he makes—not above a bare existence, anyway. And he's getting close to seventy. It's time he retired.'' She grinned at Samantha. ''I thought of trying to get a job at your spa, but I'm hardly the glamour type, so I have to stay in Seattle for a while and try to make the best of things.''

''It won't be long now,'' Jon said softly.

She smiled at him. ''I know it. I keep telling the kids to hang in there a while longer, and they'll have their mom back again.'' She turned to Samantha. ''I have to tell you, this guy saved my sanity when Greg walked out on me. Greg left me in debt up to my eyebrows, that's another of my little problems. Jon wanted to help me out, but no way could I let him do that. I'm every bit as proud as he is. But he's a good guy,'' she added, smiling warmly at him. She glanced at Samantha again. ''Sorry I got miffed.''

''It was my fault,'' Samantha protested. ''I didn't understand.''

''No reason why you should.'' She arched her eye-brows, her brown eyes dancing. ''Do you have anything to tell me? According to what dad's been saying over the telephone, you two are an item again.''

''For once the island telegraph is mistaken,'' Jon said before Samantha could respond. ''Samantha is en-gaged, didn't Ben tell you?''

Lynne looked at her enquiringly, and Samantha managed what felt like a sick grin. But she had no desire to get into a discussion of her erstwhile engagement right now, and Lynne evidently sensed her feelings, showing she was more sensitive than Samantha had been.

Jon was standing up. "We'd better get going and let you go back to work."

Lynne looked down at the pile of papers on her desk and groaned. "I do have a lot to get through. I'm glad you came by, though." She glanced at Samantha. "No hard feelings, I hope?"

"None at all."

"I'm really grateful to you for helping out with Tracy and Brian."

"I know." Samantha stood and followed Jon to the door. "I wish you luck, Lynne," she said awkwardly. "If I can do anything to help...."

Lynne smiled. It was a tired smile but a game one. "I'll get by. As Jon said, it won't be long now."

"I've been very stupid," Samantha said in a small voice as she and Jon headed back down the hill toward the ferry parking lot.

Jon didn't say anything for a second, long enough for her to decide he agreed with her. "You didn't know the circumstances," he murmured at last.

"At least I could have asked somebody why she wasn't home with the twins. I could have thought about the fact that she had to make a living. It just didn't occur to me—" She broke off, then blurted out, "I've led such a ridiculously sheltered life. I know you think of me as a spoiled little rich girl, and I guess I was. But I've been trying to change that, Jon, honestly. I've been trying to make a living of my own, to be independent.''

"Why?"

She was taken aback by the terse syllable, and she stammered a little when she replied. "Because, well, because I didn't like the way my father was trying to run my life. He meant well, but I suddenly realized I'd always done everything he expected me to do. I knew I couldn't do much about it as long as I was dependent on him for my income and everything. That's one of the reasons I left home.''

"My mother said you didn't enjoy your work. You felt it wasn't too honest?" He was looking at her sideways, and she remembered his estimate of her father's business. She'd felt insulted then, for her father's sake, but now....

"The people are honest," she said slowly. "But some of the claims they make for products—and the information that's often left out...." She paused. "My father's an honest man. He really believes in what he's doing.'' She laughed shortly. "Which may not reflect on him too well, I suppose.''

"Uh-huh." At least he didn't say I told you so.

"So you left your job and you left home," he mused aloud. "Is that why you got engaged to Adrian? To escape?''

She shook her head. "Escape is too strong a word. I love my parents, but I knew if I was ever to be my own person, I had to get away. And I had to find work that had more...value.''

She hesitated, decided to be honest. "Adrian was part of the problem, not the solution.''

Jon stopped walking and looked at her with startled eyes. "I think you'd better explain that."

"I'll try." She breathed in deeply, spoke rapidly. "My father likes Adrian a lot. He introduced him to me, encouraged me to see him. And I was very attracted to him. He's a very attractive man—a decent man. The only real problem was that I couldn't seem to feel for him what I...."

"Feel for me?"

They had reached the parking lot. Jon had a strange expression on his face now, one she couldn't interpret— almost a calculating expression. Was this more of the same, she wondered wearily. Was he trying again to coerce her into admitting she still cared for him, still wanted him? Why? So that he could throw her feelings back in her face again?

She was suddenly weary of speculation and suspicion and false pride. She could hear Ben's voice in her memory saying, "Honesty is always the best." Whatever the cost to her pride, she was going to be honest from now on.

"I haven't ever felt for anyone one-tenth of what I feel for you," she said slowly and emphatically.

"My God, Samantha...." There was for a moment a look of wonder in his eyes, and then he blinked and gazed at her directly. "I noticed you spoke of Adrian in the past tense. And you're still not wearing his ring."

"I sent it back to him."

"Sam...." Abruptly he looked around, then raked his fingers through his hair in a characteristic gesture of impatience. "Why the hell are we standing on a street corner trying to hold a conversation as important as this?" He frowned, apparently thinking hard, then raised his eyebrows. "Would it upset the truce if I asked you to have dinner with me again? We could go to the Space Needle restaurant, catch a later ferry. Maybe we can talk a few things out. I've obviously misunderstood. We could at least try to clear the air. What do you say?"

She hesitated. So far, talking hadn't improved anything. Probably if she spent more time with him, she'd simply be storing up more pain for herself. It would be far more sensible to return to the island now. "I've never eaten in the Space Needle," she said slowly.

The light started at the back of his eyes, moved forward until it threatened to spill over. The part of her that had been bruised and hesitant stirred inside her, fluttered and showed signs of life. "I'd like to have dinner with you," she said.

"And we'll talk?"

"We'll talk," she promised.

CHAPTER FOURTEEN

"DID YOU KNOW that I fell in love with you when you were sixteen?" Jon asked.

Samantha stared at him. The statement had come unexpectedly in the middle of her remarks about the view from the tall Space Needle. They had finished their dinner of Pacific Northwest salmon accompanied by salad and wine. For the past hour and a half they had talked as they should have talked the first day they met again, like the old friends they were, reminiscing, with a good deal of laughter, about the days when she was a little girl and he an adolescent boy.

They had both eaten with good appetite, having had to wait. They hadn't been able to get a reservation until 8:30; the revolving restaurant five hundred feet up the slender structure was a popular place to dine.

To fill in time they'd wandered the amusement park in the center and then backtracked over the route Dr. Birmann had taken. By some unspoken mutual agreement they hadn't commented on the circumstances, and Samantha was no more sure than before that Jon believed the doctor's behavior had been suspicious.

"*Did* you know I loved you that early?" Jon repeated and Samantha found she was still staring at him blankly. How devastatingly attractive he looked in the glow of the lamplight. The waitresses had been more than attentive.

She shook her head. "You didn't tell me."

"I knew when you gave me the picture of the boy and the dolphin for my twenty-first birthday. Possibly I knew it before, but it seemed a revelation at the time. You weren't just my weird little friend anymore. I loved you. I almost gave it away. I hugged you, remember?"

Samantha looked at him, smiling, charmed by the memory. "I told you not to be icky," she recalled. "What a brat I was."

He smiled ruefully. "You were only sixteen. And still a tomboy. I told myself I could wait until you were older, more grown up." He paused. "It wasn't easy. I tried dating other girls, but all I could think of when I was with them was your face, that tough little grin you had when you were feeling scared and didn't want anyone to know it—the way you'd stick your chin up when someone made you mad. Yet there was such innocence in your eyes—a rare quality even then."

"But I did grow up, Jon."

"Yes. I saw that when I was teaching you to skin-dive. I saw you suddenly become...aware. I've never forgotten that moment—knowing you'd discovered love at last."

"It was a wonderful summer."

"Until it ended."

There was a silence between them. Samantha looked out of the windows. Darkness was gathering rapidly. Lights shone below like strings of precious gems, orange and amber and white. This portion of the restaurant was circling slowly toward a view of Elliott Bay and West Seattle. A ferry was progressing majestically toward the terminal, its bow cutting through still water that looked as smooth as black ice. Over her left shoulder she could see the ghostly outline of Mount Rainier in the distance. Rising almost two miles above its foothills, it seemed to float in the sky, far beyond the tall lighted buildings of downtown.

She looked back at Jon and found he was still gazing at her, his blue eyes dark around their centers, his face tense. She felt suddenly, acutely nervous as she began to suspect what was coming. Half unconsciously, she braced her shoulders, saw him note the gesture. One corner of his mouth twitched in something that was not a smile.

"You hurt me more than I've ever been hurt in my life, Sam," he said softly.

"I was hurt, too," she pointed out, immediately defensive.

"I didn't know that then, or at least, I refused to acknowledge it. All I could see was that you and your father were belittling everything I'd ever believed in, everything that I was. You've never been poor, Sam—you've never known what it's like to stand in front of the person you love and have nothing to offer."

"You had a great deal to offer."

A crooked smile touched his mouth. "You didn't seem to think so."

"I was only eighteen, Jon. I was suddenly seeing you through my father's eyes, and I was afraid you'd never really loved me. I got the impression it didn't matter anyway. There didn't seem to be room in your plans for me."

"There wasn't," he said flatly. "I was in debt up to my ears—to Ethan. I had no idea where the money would come from for the rest of my education. Yet I couldn't accept your father's charity. It would have meant giving up...myself."

"So you gave up me instead."

"I didn't think I had any choice. I couldn't ask you to marry me, not with my total lack of prospects at the time. You appeared not to want anything else."

"You didn't offer me anything else."

He winced and she made a small movement with her hand. "Perhaps we shouldn't pursue this, Jon," she said hesitantly. "Perhaps it's better just to bury the past, to try to be friends in spite of it."

He shook his head and began to speak, but one of the waitresses had decided their coffee cups needed refilling and he sat back, waiting politely until she was through. Then he leaned forward, his face earnest, eyes troubled. The subdued lamplight made his fair hair luminous, emphasizing the healthy sheen of it.

Samantha felt a tug in the region of her heart. He looked about nineteen years old.

"I couldn't believe it when you let me walk out of that house," he said, returning at once to their conversation as though she hadn't protested the subject at all.

"*I* couldn't believe *you'd* walked out," she rejoined.

His frown deepened. "Don't you see, Sam, I felt as though you'd rejected everything I stood for. I felt... *humiliated*."

"There was no need..." Samantha began, but he stopped her with an impatient gesture of his right hand. "Let me finish, Sam, please. I'm trying to explain what led up to...why I acted the way I did...on July 4. I know you don't want to dig into the past, but we have to clear it away or we can't—"

He broke off, turned his head to gaze unseeingly out at the night sky. Then he went on, speaking rapidly, as though afraid she'd interrupt him or argue with him again. "I went through a rough time for a while. I told myself I hated you and your father and your father's money and that I was going to go far away from you and prove I could be a success all by myself."

He laughed shortly, a bitter sound, and glanced at her. "I suppose I should thank you. You were responsible for the driving ambition that sustained me during the years I was gone. They were bleak years, Sam. I loved the work, but God, I worked hard. Most of my time was spent in cramped crowded quarters on uncomfortable unstable boats. I froze and I baked and I didn't get enough sleep, and I kept driving on and on, determined I wouldn't contact you until I had something to show you, something to offer you."

He paused for a long time, his gaze averted from her again. At last she thought he wasn't going to continue. "Jon?" she prompted.

He nodded, sighed deeply. "At last I decided I was ready to get in touch with you. All the money I'd inherited from Ethan wasn't enough, you see. I had to wait until I had something of my own to show you, something tangible, concrete. When I thought I had, I left Japan, got a lift into California with the air force and I telephoned you."

Samantha swallowed. "And daddy told you I was engaged to Adrian."

He nodded again. She wanted to protest then, demand to know why he hadn't insisted on speaking to her. But some instinct warned her that she should wait until he was done.

"I stood in that phone booth for an hour," he said in a musing tone. "God, it was hot at Travis—about ninety-five. The booth had glass walls, and I almost roasted before I realized I had to move.''

He looked down at his hands, loosely clasped on the table, glanced at her, then away. ''What finally came to me there was the knowledge that *I'd* rejected *you*, by insisting I hadn't asked you to marry me. Then I'd compounded my stupidity by expecting you to be there waiting for me to come around, to get over my injured pride. I realized I'd lost you altogether. It took me a long time to accept that. But I finally began to. And then you came back.''

Samantha looked at his averted face, seeing the lines of strain bracketing his mouth, the shadowed sadness in his eyes. How could she have thought it was cynicism that had carved those lines? How had she not recognized pain when she had seen enough of it in her own eyes?

She leaned forward, about to confess to him why she'd come back to the island, but then she hesitated again, wanting him to finish, to tell her why he had felt a need for revenge after all that time.

When he spoke again, his voice had changed, hardened. ''You stood there,'' he said. ''You stood there in your cashmere sweater and your designer jeans, flashing your huge diamond to show me you could get a rich husband to take care of you, and then you looked around at that shabby little house and at me in my shabby clothes and you said, 'Everything here looks the same,' in that cool cultured voice of yours, and I felt all the old anger explode inside me again.''

''But I didn't mean. . . .''

He raised one hand, stopping her protest in midsentence. "It doesn't matter what you meant. I wasn't thinking. I was *feeling*. I was Eileen Blake's poor little boy again—the one the neighbors used to give cast-off clothing to, and outgrown shoes. The one Ethan Collins kindly paid tuition for, so he could try to make something of himself. No matter that I'd paid Ethan back, no matter that I could at that moment have bought and sold the whole island—or at least a good portion of it. None of that counted. All my newfound confidence had disappeared with that one remark from you. It seemed clear to me then that you'd come back for one reason only—to confirm to yourself that I hadn't achieved any success at all."

His hands had knotted into fists and he was sitting rigidly upright, his jaw tightly clenched. "The trouble was that the moment I saw you I knew you were still a part of me, that I'd never be free of you. And you were engaged to someone else. I was furious with you for coming back, for disturbing the peace of mind I'd finally achieved. Afterward, when you left to go visit my mother, I made up my mind that I was going to hurt you the way I'd been hurt."

"You succeeded, Jon," she said bitterly.

To her horror, her statement seemed to surprise and please him. His face cleared and his hands relaxed. Reaching across the table, he took her hands in his, looked deeply into her eyes. "Finally," he said on a long breath.

Bewildered, she stared at him, her hands tense in his, afraid even now that he still wanted to hurt her, still wanted revenge.

"Samantha, my dear," he said slowly, "you told me you'd plotted revenge yourself. Are you telling me now that you lied? Are you saying your response to me was as genuine as it seemed at the time?''

What did he want from her, his pound of flesh? Did she have to admit her need of him so that he could have his moment of triumph? About to deny her feelings once more, she looked down at their joined hands and remembered her vow to be honest. ''I did feel vengeful for a moment,'' she said slowly. ''But only for a moment.''

He sighed. ''And Adrian? Is he truly out of your life?''

''I think I probably hurt him a great deal,'' she said in a low voice. ''It wasn't fair of me to encourage him, to agree to marry him. I think I always knew I couldn't go through with it, even though I . . . cared about him.'' She took a breath, let it out. ''He had to compete with your ghost, Jon. I couldn't ever forget you.''

His hands gripped hers so tightly she was afraid he'd crush her fingers. ''Why the hell didn't you tell me that right at the start?'' he demanded, then made a sound of disgust. ''Don't answer that. Of course you couldn't tell me. I was too busy playing my damn games, covering my own tracks, protecting myself and my stupid pride.''

She had raised her eyes to meet his. His eyes were blazing with self-disgust. ''Can you forgive me, Sam? Can you see how it was with me?''

She hesitated. ''I understand that you were more hurt by our breakup than I'd realized. I guess I can see why you felt you deserved some revenge.'' She paused, trying to reach into herself for truth. ''Obviously we were both at fault. We threw away what we had.'' She hesitated, looking at him. ''Do you still want to punish me for

what I did to you when I was eighteen, because if you
do—''

It was his turn to interrupt. "God, no," he said fervently. "I didn't even want to at the time, but again I
was too proud to admit it even to myself. But if you'll
remember, Sam, I couldn't go through with it. The
reason was simple enough. I kept seeing you as I used to
see you. I kept feeling the way I used to feel. That first
moment we met; again in the tub when you stood there
with that damn towel around you, looking like some fey
water sprite, and I remembered Willow Lake. Again
when I kissed you on the beach, and on the boat—and
at my house when you looked at me in the firelight.''

He gave her a rueful smile that still had a trace of pain
in it. "When I told you I'd waited so long, that was
truth coming through. I'd rehearsed those words. I
meant them to be an ironic expression of my patience—I
was getting my own back at last. But the words didn't
come from my mind, they came from my heart, for I
knew in that moment that I'd been provoking you because all I wanted, ever, was to have you in my arms
again. I might have started out planning to get even, but
I couldn't control my own response.''

He looked down at their hands, still clasped together
on the table, then back at her face. "You said to me, 'So
have I.' I began to suspect then that in spite of all your
denials you'd wanted to be with me all those years, just
as I'd wanted to be with you. I'd tried to get you to say
so, but you were too damn stubborn, or suspicious, to
tell me.'' He paused, looking at her. "Will you tell me
now?''

"That's why I came back," she admitted at last. "I
couldn't get you out of my mind. I told myself it was the

island that was haunting me. But I knew as soon as I saw you that the island had nothing to do with it. It was you I missed.'' She paused. ''Why the hell didn't you tell me the truth that night?'' she asked, giving back his question. ''You say you realized it then.''

''You wouldn't let me,'' he said simply. ''I was about to when you told me you'd also been after revenge. You said you didn't want to see me again—and you were going home to write to Adrian. I'd forgotten until that moment that you were going to marry someone else. But I remembered at once that you'd told me you loved him, so I thought I'd been mistaken—you didn't want me after all.''

She closed her eyes momentarily, then looked at him again, moving her hands so that they were outside his, touching lightly. ''We've been pretty stupid, haven't we?''

''Yes.''

''More coffee, sir?'' the waitress asked.

They were both startled. Their hands jerked apart. ''I...er, no, thank you. I...we'll take the check now.''

Samantha was amused. She'd never heard Jon stammer before. As the woman sorted through a pile of checks Samantha glanced out of the window again. The restaurant was overlooking Lake Union and the University District now—it had performed half of a revolution since they'd finished eating. She hadn't even noticed. Half an hour seemed a short time to cover seven years of waste. She had a feeling they hadn't yet taken care of all the problems between them, but at the moment she couldn't remember what they might be.

Half an hour, she thought again. It must be getting late.

Even as the thought occurred to her, she saw Jon glance at his wristwatch as he returned his billfold to his pants pocket. He made a muffled exclamation, then looked at her with a quizzical grin. "We've missed the last ferry, Sam."

"Oh." She caught her breath. "I guess we could call Steve Cory and charter his plane."

"We could, yes." He was sitting very still now, his gaze holding hers.

She felt a sudden constriction in her chest as though she'd forgotten how to breathe. It wasn't at all an unpleasant sensation. She realized that the bruised stiffness she'd been suffering from all week had eased, gone away. As it had when she'd hurt her foot, she recalled, feeling suddenly light-headed. She had, after all, learned to walk again.

Jon's blue gaze was intent on her face. "I have to be at work by nine in the morning," she said slowly, almost reluctantly.

He reached across the table for her hand, lifted it to his lips. Her gaze followed the movement, settled on his mouth. Such a beautiful mouth. Lightly he brushed a kiss across her fingers. She felt the touch of his lips course through her veins, felt her blood run warm all the way to her toes. Her heart had started to beat erratically, rapidly.

"There's a ferry at 8:00 A.M.," Jon said.

Their eyes met.

She nodded.

He turned her hand over, pressed a kiss deep into the palm, then released it gently and stood up. "Don't go away," he said softly. "I have to make arrangements for a new beginning."

She watched him stride from the room, admiring, as if for the first time, the confident way he moved. Across from her was a mirrored divider. Intent on Jon, she hadn't noticed it before. As she sat there, waiting, she studied her reflection, trying to see herself as Jon saw her.

Her hair had been blown by the breeze; copper-colored tendrils were curling over her forehead and in front of her ears. Her eyes, shadowed by the lamplight, seemed darker than they were, but they were shining—the flecks of gold more noticeable than usual, perhaps because of the lighting, perhaps because of the exhilaration that had swept through her when she and Jon exchanged that one loaded glance. Her cheeks were pink, though she'd applied no blusher. Her mouth seemed fuller, riper, eager to be kissed. She looked, she decided, exactly what she was, a young woman in love—a young woman with an assignation with the love of her life.

Jon returned before she had time to miss him. "I've booked a room at the Carlisle," he said, leaning over her.

Her heart thumped once, then she was calm.

They rode down in silence in the outside elevator, along with several other people who'd been visiting the observation platform at the top. Outside the foyer, Jon took her arm and held her still for a moment, looking directly into her face, his blue eyes intent. "You're sure?" he asked.

She wasn't, not completely, but she didn't want to think rationally right now. She was feeling again, and she wanted to go on feeling.

"I'm sure," she said, and there was no hesitation in her voice.

CHAPTER FIFTEEN

THE CARLISLE was Seattle's one remaining Grand Hotel—in the original meaning of the word. Built on the waterfront at the turn of the century, it featured huge chandeliers, sumptuous antique furnishings, high ceilings, and carpeting two inches thick. Recently remodeled to include more up-to-date plumbing and kitchen facilities, it had lost none of its old style.

Their room was on the ground floor, overlooking the Sound. Samantha caught a glimpse through the tall windows of lantern light glinting on water, before Jon moved past her and closed the light drapes. They were both suddenly, unaccountably shy. "I guess I'll take a shower," Samantha said after they had looked mutely around the gracious room for a couple of minutes.

It wasn't until after she'd dried herself that she realized she had no robe with her. Feeling rather silly, she wrapped the largest towel around herself, tucking it securely over her left breast, and emerged from the bathroom with her white dress and jacket and underwear over one arm, her high-heeled shoes gripped in one hand. She'd pinned up her hair with a clip she'd found in her purse and then had forgotten to let it down. She should have brushed it, she thought, catching a glimpse of herself in the dressing-table mirror. It was a mass of curls that framed her face in tumbled disorder.

Jon made no comment when she appeared. He smiled rather tightly at her before going hastily into the bathroom himself. Evidently he felt just as tense, she decided as she hung her clothes neatly in the closet. When he came out, she saw he'd draped a towel around his loins.

He laughed when she glanced at it. "Me Tarzan, you Jane," he joked.

She tried to smile, but her face felt stiff and unnatural. For a moment they stared at each other, she with her back to the ornate dressing table, he in the center of the room at the foot of the enormous canopied bed. His blond hair shone in the light of the one lamp they'd left burning. What a magnificent body he had, muscular, yet lean—tanned to a golden brown.

Without knowing she was going to, she stretched her hand out in a helpless, almost childish gesture. At once he moved toward her, taking her hand and pulling her hard against him. Cupping her face with his hands, he began to kiss her mouth, his own lips gentle but insistent and curious, as though he were trying to first discover and then to absorb the essence of her into himself.

She was trembling when he released her. Deliberately he set her away and studied her face. She wanted to fling herself back into his arms, to press warmly against him, but she sensed that he had a need to wait, perhaps a need to savor his own restraint.

He was not smiling. His face looked solemn, almost somber. Moving slowly, as though he didn't want to frighten her, he raised one hand to touch her neck, sliding his fingers up the side of her head until they found and loosened the clip that held her hair. At once it tumbled down around her shoulders in a fragrant mass.

He looked at it with approval. "Promise me you'll never cut your hair," he said softly.

She nodded wordlessly and he resumed his study of her, his gaze finally moving down to the towel that was still wrapped around her. Smiling gently, he lifted the tucked-in corner and let the towel drop to the floor. She stood naked before him, still silent, letting him take his time as he seemed to want to, while his gaze roamed her body as though he were trying to relearn every curve, every shadow, and imprint them on his memory again.

"I thought of you so often," he murmured. "Curled up on a hard, hideously uncomfortable bunk on some ship or other, I'd let you walk into my mind just as you are now. I'd look at your glorious body and imagine myself touching your soft bright hair and your warm yielding flesh, and I'd forget that there were lumps in the mattress and my legs were jackknifed for lack of space, that there was a smell of fish and mildew in the air. All night I would hold you and love you. In the morning the loneliness was more than I could bear."

Gently she silenced him with her fingers against his lips. "Let's not think any more about those mornings, those nights," she pleaded softly.

"Samantha—"

She shook her head, swayed toward him. "Those years don't exist," she insisted. "Tonight is seven years ago. There have been no quarrels, no recriminations, no loneliness."

For a moment, seeing the frown, she was afraid he was going to protest this wiping away of the past. But this was the only way they could come together, the only chance for them to recover the love that had once been theirs.

"This is the fantasy you want?" he asked, his voice gentle.

She nodded.

"Then it will be mine, too."

He smiled at her, the lamplight turning his eyes to blue flame. His hands had moved to caress her bare shoulders, their palms barely touching her skin, making her tremble. Releasing her, he freed the towel from around his waist, then pulled her to him, his hands like steel against her bare hips, holding her fiercely against him, their bodies so close they might have been one. A second later his mouth searched out hers, and he kissed her with a delicate restraint that awakened a turmoil of familiar emotions throughout her body. Her hands moved across his back, stroking, touching, delighting in the feel of hard smooth muscle, firm masculine skin.

His mouth still on hers, he lifted her carefully and laid her down on the bed, somehow managing to draw back the covers at the same time. Then he was lying beside her, holding her, his mouth now playful, teasing her with tender, infinitely slow kisses, his lips gently brushing against hers. Her hands moved over him again, and she gloried in the smooth long curve of his hip, the lean indentation of his waist, the firm contours of his back.

He had lifted himself on one elbow so that he could gaze down on her. She looked up into eyes that were dark with passion, deep blue as the ocean's depths. Smiling, she placed one hand against the soft glinting hair on his chest, feeling against her exquisitely sensitive palm the rapid beating of his heart. His mouth curved in a sensual smile. "Can this be chemistry?" he asked.

She laughed softly. "Something like that."

His smile deepened for a moment, then was gone. He was looking at her mouth now, and he raised one finger to trace her lips tenderly. "You are so lovely, Sam," he murmured.

She lifted her hands to wind them around his neck, attempting to pull him down against her, her flesh aching for him. But he resisted her. Instead he lowered his head to her breast, gently touching the swollen tip with his tongue, teasing it erect, making her gasp with a mixture of excitement and frustration over his deliberate pace. With her hands tangled in his hair, her fingers remembering the familiar crispness, she fought to press his head close and brought her body hard against his, which was half covering her now.

Murmuring soft protests, he resisted the pressure, leaving a line of gentle kisses across her flesh as he moved his attention to her other breast, his mouth soft and pliant, his breath warm against her skin. He would not be rushed, it seemed, and at last Samantha, smiling mischievously, accepted his leisurely pace and even encouraged it, relaxing purposely against the soft sheet, her hair spread out in a tangled mass on the pillow. She forced her body to control its urgency, to hold back even a trace of response. Two could play this game, she thought with impish pleasure.

In a moment he recognized her deliberate withholding. Lifting his head, he smiled wickedly in acknowledgement of her playfulness, then bent his head to her breast to circle its aching tip with his tongue. "Can you resist this?" he whispered.

She felt her own smile deepen. "Of course."

"And this?"

His tongue trailed a line of fire from the nipple to the soft underswell of her breast, his lips nipping gently at the curving flesh.

"Easily," she murmured, and he laughed softly at the lack of breath in her response.

Struggling for control, she looked up at the canopy above the bed. On its underside the lantern light, glimmering through the thin fabric of the window drapes, wavered and danced, creating patterns of moving light as the dock on which the lamps were fastened swayed in the waves. Watching them, mesmerizing herself so that she could more deliciously delay her response, Samantha imagined that she was floating down some untroubled stream, looking at sunlight through the leafy overhanging branches of a tree. Fully in control of her emotions now, she felt at ease, serene as Jon's mouth delicately brushed downward across her abdomen and his hands stroked her with that same restrained deliberation. He wanted to touch every inch of her, it seemed, and she allowed him access, turning lazily as his hands commanded so that he could brush feathery kisses up the length of her spine, lingering against the back of her neck, his hands combing through the tangle of her hair. Slowly, gently, his tongue rimmed the edges of her ears, his hands sliding down one arm to find her hand and bring it to his lips as he turned her again. Delicately he took her fingers into his mouth one by one, tasting, teasing the flesh with his tongue.

His eyes were narrowed with concentration, his face solemn, almost somber. Beneath the drooping lids, his eyes were dark with an emotion that astonished her with its intensity, drawing from some deep well of feeling inside her body an answering tender rush of breathless wonder.

"Anything?" he queried, his gaze holding hers, eyes brightening with loving amusement.

"A little something," she admitted breathlessly, and then stopped breathing completely when he gently pressed his body against her, lifted and pressed again.

"Don't hurry," he commanded, his eyes laughing now. "I'm a very patient man. I can quite happily spend my time celebrating you."

There were spaces between his words, too. His breathing had quickened, and she could feel the warmth of it against her mouth.

Her hand touched his face, her fingers sliding over the hard cheekbone, across the sensuous rasp of cheek and chin to light on his mouth and trace the upward curve of his lazy smile. "Don't I get to celebrate?" she asked softly.

The lines bracketing his mouth deepened in sensual enjoyment. "Feel free at any time."

And suddenly she was no longer compliant, a passive object to be stroked and kissed and touched. Raising herself, she brought her mouth over his, her tongue entering delicately between his lips to caress the sensitive skin inside, flirting with him at first, teasing him, then gradually thrusting deeper and deeper in an intrusive demanding kiss that called forth a fierce response from his entire body and brought him up off the bed to crush her to him. But she pushed him gently back. "I'm not through yet," she protested.

He lay back obediently, passively, smiling at her, and she began to explore his body as he had explored hers. Her hands moved urgently over him, seeking out the sensitive places, the secret places, meant only for her to explore. Her mouth followed her hands, her lips savage against warm taut flesh. There was no more holding back. All self-imposed control was gone. She felt a tremor run through him as she kissed his body hungrily, and marveled at her power. Heard him moan softly and gloried in her domination.

But her triumph didn't last for long. Calling her name on a long sighing breath, he gathered her up and captured her mouth with his. Eagerly, blindly, their lips met and parted and met again, and now they were both murmuring incoherently, without real words, only broken syllables that formed a private language of need and love and passion gone out of control.

Cupping her hips with his lean strong hands, he lifted her close and moved against her, bringing her to such a state of quivering awareness that she cried his name aloud, and the lights reflected on the canopy burst like shooting stars and fell all around her, burning her skin. A second later she realized that the white heat searing her flesh had nothing to do with the lights. This heat came from inside her and was building to unbearable pressure yet again, lifting her against Jon's hard body. Smiling triumphantly at her, he lifted himself up and over her, until his face shut out the light. "Darling Samantha," he murmured, lowering his weight on her, his mouth once more seeking her own.

And now there was no gentleness in him at all. His mouth was fierce against hers, calling forth an answering primitive fierceness she'd forgotten she possessed— a fierceness that sent wave upon wave of sensation through her body, lifting it again and again to arch against him, her hands and mouth as demanding, as violent as his. She knew him so well, could anticipate his every move, every touch of his fingers. Her wish had come true. The lonely empty years were gone. There was only joy in the familiarity of his body against hers, excitement in the remembered touch of his flesh, of his hands made impatient with desire. This wasn't a new beginning, but a continuation—the old shadows were gone and there was no more pain, only a mindless ecstasy as he took possession of her.

Beyond his head the dancing patterns of light blurred and shimmered like sunlight on the sea. He held her still for a moment, his hands powerful on her body. Then he moved again. In a return to fantasy she imagined that she and Jon were soaring upward together through the ocean, easily at first, and smoothly, then more roughly as they fought the resistance of the waves. They were two swimmers struggling together, trying to reach the surface so that they could breathe again, struggling upward on a thrusting swell of passion, suddenly breaking through into a wash of blinding light.

How clear the light was, she thought wonderingly. How bright the stars.

A moment's mind-shattering explosion seized his body and hers and welded them together in a fury of sound and movement, and then they were sliding down again, still locked together, sinking slowly, spiraling reluctantly back to the depths of the sea.

It was a long time before they let go of each other. Slowly their breathing returned to its usual calm rhythm, slowly their heartbeats steadied.

At last Jon lifted his head away from hers and looked at her, smiling tenderly. "I guess this means we're friends again," he murmured.

Laughter bubbled up inside her. "I guess it must," she agreed.

"I think another shower would be a good idea."

"Me, too."

His head came up and he grinned at her, looking so much like the boy who lived in her memory that her heart contracted. "Together," he suggested, mischief showing clearly in his eyes.

They made a game out of their shower as they had made games out of all shared experiences in the past, soaping each other carefully, sensuously, their hands drawing patterns on each other's body with concentrated artistry. Giggling like children, they turned the shower head to massage and held each other while the water beat against them so torrentially that they had difficulty standing upright and had to clutch each other and the soap rack to keep from falling.

Samantha's hair was a mass of tightly tangled curls when they finally emerged. Jon's was plastered close to his head. Soaking wet, dripping runnels of water onto the hotel bath mat, they embraced again, kissing gently, tired now but content.

They took turns drying each other with meticulous care, rubbing their bodies until they glowed. And then they fell into bed together and slept almost immediately, holding each other close through what remained of the night.

Samantha awakened when the first light of dawn glimmered through a crack between the thin drapes and touched gently on her eyelids. She was still clasped tightly in Jon's arms. Her right arm ached dully where it lay trapped beneath his body, but she had no desire to move. Pleased that she'd awakened before him, she gazed at his face, the fingers of her left hand lightly tracing the line of his lips, curved in a satisfied smile even in sleep. A moment later he opened his eyes and gazed at her. "I dreamed I made love to you last night," he said softly.

She smiled. "That was no dream, that was reality."

He sat up and grinned down at her. "What time is it?"

She rolled over, rubbing her arm surreptitiously to ease its cramp and glanced at her watch on the bedside table. "Five o'clock."

He reached for her, lifting her in his arms and brushing her lips lightly with his. "Love or breakfast?" he queried.

"Isn't it too early for room service?"

He rubbed his nose against hers. "Probably."

"Then we don't have a decision to make, do we?"

His arms closed around her and his mouth grazed against hers with a lazy delicacy that awakened every nerve cell in her body. Moving slowly, his hands began to caress her, his touch intoxicating her senses. "Did you know that the French prefer to make love in the morning?" he asked softly, his mouth against her hair.

"*Vraiment?* Truly?" she asked.

He laughed. "*Parles-tu français?* You speak French?"

"*Je parle amour.* I speak love." Her voice was light, teasing, and either the tone of it or the words themselves seemed to bother him a little. He gazed at her for a second, seemed about to speak, then evidently changed his mind. Pulling her close, he nibbled at her ear, then kissed the pulse that had begun to beat rapidly in her throat. Again he tormented her with his restraint until she lay back and moved her hands across the long muscles of his back, exerting pressure so that he was forced to come down against her. He entered her gently, moving slowly, arousing her to new heights of sensation. For the first time she learned that lovemaking could be measured, orderly, restrained—that it was possible to extend the time spent on each small gesture, each loving touch, as though it had been choreographed into a dance set to music.

When it was over she felt replete, contented, satisfied. Jon held her tightly to him, rolling with her until they lay side by side, arms and legs entwined, resting in the calm aftermath of lovemaking. For a long time they didn't move, didn't speak.

Then she stretched lazily against him, reveling in the feel of the cool morning air against her naked body. Sometime in the night Jon must have opened a window. He'd always liked to let in the sea breezes when they were available. A creature of the sea, she thought fondly, hugging him. A merman, happier in the water than on land. She laughed inwardly at the absurd fancy. Was there such a creature as a merman, even in fantasy? Was there even such a word? She opened her mouth to ask him, then saw that his eyes were closed.

She studied his face for a few minutes as she had when she first awakened, her gaze roaming over the strong features, the tanned smooth skin, the chiseled perfection of his mouth. And suddenly, without warning, like a shadow stealing across the sun, a thought moved forward from some forgotten corner of her mind and presented itself as a question. In all his murmurings, had Jon said he loved her? Had she said she loved him? Wasn't it important that they say the words—the magic words?

In the summer of their love, Jon had seemed to delight in saying them. It seemed to her in retrospect that he had whispered them to her with every other breath. Was there still a part of him that was holding back from her? And was she in turn holding something back from him? Could she still not trust him completely?

She did love him—she knew that for fact. What was between them was no mere chemistry or aura or magnetism that worked only from the body and not from the brain. She *loved* him. Why then couldn't she tell him so?

Suddenly chilled, she reached for the top sheet and blanket, which had been pushed halfway off the bed in the heat of their passion. Dragging them up, she tucked them securely around the two of them to ward off the cold.

Jon held her close, his mouth against her hair, his breath warm and sweet against her forehead. For a little time longer she let herself rest against him, trying to block out the disturbing thoughts that had come alive in her mind. But they wouldn't be denied. His breathing was even now. Surely he wasn't going to sleep?

"Jon," she said hesitantly. She felt him smile. "Are we going to be all right?" she asked him softly.

He stirred against her, kissed her lightly on the cheek. "I thought we did okay," he said with amusement in his voice.

"I didn't mean that. I meant—" She wanted to ask him how he felt about her now, but she was afraid.

Instead of finishing her question, she clung to him, hoping he might volunteer the words she so badly wanted to hear. After a while his mouth found hers and kissed it. "Don't you think we did okay?" he asked lightly, his lips sliding gently down to her throat. Was he looking for the same reassurance?

She opened her mouth to tell him she loved him, but the words wouldn't come. For the length of a heartbeat he lay very still, then he raised his head and looked at her. "Samantha?"

She gazed at the face of this man she loved so much and willed herself to tell him so.

His eyes clouded for a second, then cleared and he grinned at her. "All right, Samantha, what's bothering you now?"

She drew a breath of air deep into her lungs, realizing abruptly what was wrong. As long as suspicion darkened her mind, she couldn't freely confess her love for him. "Mike Summers didn't show me any ID" she blurted out.

He looked astonished. "So?"

"How do I know, how can I be sure, that he's really with the FBI?"

"Because I said so?" He was still half smiling, but the smile didn't reach his eyes.

She wanted to stop then, wanted to tell him she was just being silly, that she hadn't meant to ask such a foolish question. But something seemed to drive her on, to force her to put into words the suspicions that had come to her the previous day, so that he would deny them, and in denying them restore her trust.

"Do you believe there's something odd about Dr. Birmann?" she asked.

"For God's sake, Sam!" His mouth tightening, he lifted himself away from her. Kicking aside the bedclothes, he sat on the edge of the bed, his back turned toward her.

"I have to know, Jon," she said hesitantly.

He didn't turn around. Sighing audibly, he seemed to consider for a moment, then he said, "No, I don't believe there's anything odd about Dr. Birmann. As I said before, I'm sure there must be an innocent explanation for what you saw." He paused. "Does that satisfy you?"

"Who were those men who came to see you on the island?" she asked, surprising herself. She hadn't known she was going to ask him that.

He swung around, obviously startled, and stared at her. The coldness that had struck such fear in her so often before was back in his eyes. "Isn't anyone immune from your nosiness?" he asked.

She sat up abruptly, the sheet and blanket pulled up under her arms, her hands gripping them tightly. "Why won't you tell me?" she demanded.

"Because it's none of your damn business and because it's—" He broke off, shook his head as he leaned over and kissed her, one hand reaching to stroke her hair. "Sam, darling, let's not do this again." Tenderly tucking a strand of hair behind her ear, he smiled. "How did we get started on this, anyway?"

The tension had gone out of him. She wanted to put her arms around him and hold him again, but she couldn't seem to stop. "Please, Jon," she pleaded.

He sighed. "Okay. I'm not going to make a big thing out of this. Those men were acquaintances of mine. They came to ask me to do some work for them. They asked me a couple of months ago, actually. This visit was to find out if I'd made up my mind to accept."

"What kind of work?"

He regarded her steadily again, then his lips parted, and she thought he was going to answer. Instead he suddenly straightened up and said a violent word that she'd never heard him use before. "Damned if I'm going to let you give me the third degree," he said coldly. "What's all this about, Sam? Just what is it you've got on your mind?"

She hesitated, but she was committed to a course of action now. She had to know. She had to be sure. "I helped Deborah with some bookkeeping a while back," she explained. "I saw a check made out to you by Dr. Birmann. It was for five thousands dollars. Deborah said there'd been five of them."

"And you decided the good doctor was paying me off for some reason?"

She squirmed uncomfortably. "I'm sure there must be an explanation."

"Uh-huh. Let me get this straight now—there's a sequence here. If Mike's not in the FBI, then I must have produced him merely to get you off my back. Is that what you think?"

She bit her lip, hesitated, then nodded.

His eyes narrowed. "You also want to know about my visitors. You think they were suspicious-looking characters?"

"Not suspicious exactly. I just wondered—"

"Jakob paid me twenty-five thousand dollars," he went on without waiting for her to finish. "So you've decided I must be involved with Jakob Birmann, poor innocent Dr. Birmann, in some kind of subversive activity. Have I got everything right so far?"

"Dr. Birmann is *not* innocent!" she said, her voice rising aggressively. "I saw him, Jon. I know...."

"You know nothing, Sam. You're conjecturing. And you're slandering my character as well as his. My God, girl, what on earth do you think I did for that twenty-five thousand dollars?"

"I don't *know* what you've been doing, that's the whole problem. Whenever I ask, you evade my questions. You're evading now." She was sitting very straight, the sheet and blanket clutched to her chest. "You've got to admit, Jon, that you've been very secretive and—"

"I don't have to admit a thing," he said, standing up. "Tell me now, is that everything? Is there any other little suspicion rattling around in your mind?"

"Jon, I . . . ." She hesitated. A pulse was hammering in her throat. But she wasn't going to back down now. She had to know. "There *was* one other thing," she said bluntly. "Your mother showed me your camera collection. There was a miniature camera there. I tried to think of what you could use it for and I couldn't . . . ."

He laughed, but there was no amusement in the sound. "You're really the limit, Sam, you know that? My mother told me about the book you were planning— the plot you discussed. Tell me, which came first, the book idea or Dr. Birmann's escapade? Are you trying to fit the known facts into some fictional scenario in your head?"

Exasperated, she shook her head. "I didn't have any plan for a book. I was sounding your mother out, telling her what I'd seen to see if her interpretation agreed with mine. And as a matter of—"

He waved her to silence. "Here's an answer for you, Samantha. Try this one for size. I don't use half of the cameras in my collection. I've picked them up over the years because they interest me. The small one you're talking about I bought in Japan, as a curiosity, nothing more. There now, does that make you hesitate? Does that make you wonder if you haven't used your lively imagination once too often?''

"That still doesn't explain—"

"I'm not explaining anything more.'' He was glaring down at her now, and she couldn't seem to get enough oxygen in her lungs.

"I brought you here," he said in a quiet voice that cut into her with its sharp intensity of feeling, "because I hoped we could learn to love each other again. Instead of that, you. . . .'' Words apparently failing him, he stalked off to the closet, jerked his clothes from their hangers and started putting them on.

"Where are you going?'' she asked.

"I'm going to find myself some breakfast.'' He glanced at her with no expression at all in his eyes. "Don't worry, I'll see you get to the ferry in time. I wouldn't want you to be late for your job with your *trusted* employer.'' The sarcasm in his voice cut her to the core.

"Jon!'' she protested. "Can't we talk this over? I didn't mean to insult you. And of course I don't really suspect you of anything. It's just that everything sort of added up and I have to know—''

"You don't have to know a damn thing," he said through his teeth. "I should have known better than to get mixed up with you again.''

Fully dressed now, he ran his hands through his hair, tidying it. Then he started toward the door. "Jon, please,'' she called after him.

He hesitated for a second, then turned around and

looked at her. "Okay, Samantha," he said calmly. "I'll believe you don't really suspect me of being an enemy agent. I'll accept the fact that you were just curious about the money Jakob paid me. I'll even forgive you for spying on me and my guests. As for my recent activities, I'll be happy to explain them to you. When I suggested we come here, I meant to tell you the whole story, because it's going to break this morning and I wanted you to be the first to know. I was actually looking forward to telling you. But I'm afraid your approach leaves too much to be desired. I'm damned if I'll tell you anything right now."

He took a deep breath and went on before she could say a word. "What I can't forgive, what I will never forgive, is that you could use me in such a way. It's perfectly obvious that you only agreed to come here with me in order to satisfy your curiosity about me. I suppose you thought if you let me make love to you I'd come clean. You never could bear to have someone keep something from you, could you?"

With that, he opened the door and went out, closing it sharply behind him.

Too shocked by his accusation to speak, hardly able even to breathe, Samantha sat as he'd left her, staring at the door, trying to will her body to stop shaking.

SHE SAT THERE for what seemed a long time, until an alarm clock ringing somewhere in the hotel reminded her that she'd better get moving.

She was out of the shower, dressed and made up, standing in front of the dressing table brushing her hair when a knock came at the door. Breath held, she opened the door to find not Jon but a waiter pushing a room-service trolley.

That was thoughtful of Jon, she thought as he set down a breakfast tray on the table near the window. Or was it? Was this supposed to make it clear that he didn't want her to join him for the meal?

Automatically she sat down and looked at the plate of bacon and eggs, for which she had no appetite. Someone had included a folded newspaper on the tray. Picking it up, she scanned the headlines as she poured a cup of coffee from the small pot provided, not really taking anything in. She hadn't had much sleep. She was tired as well as soul weary.

As she gratefully sipped the scalding coffee, she turned the first section of the newspaper over—and froze, the cup still pressed to her mouth. From the front page of the second section, a large photograph of Jonathan Blake looked up at her.

The photograph was excellent. Jon was standing amid large rocks on an unrecognizable ocean shore, looking out to sea like some latter-day explorer contemplating the vastness of the world. He was wearing shorts and a cotton safari shirt, his sleeves rolled up. His hair was unruly as usual, ruffled by the wind. He looked so attractive, so virile, that her breath caught in her throat.

Hastily she shifted her gaze to the text. Jon had apparently written a book entitled, *Destruction*. The research had taken him four years. According to the columnist, the book contained a remarkable collection of photographs, shot all over the world, and an economical text that together with the pictures formed a stunning indictment of mankind's destruction of the earth's oceans. The end of the world, according to Jonathan Blake, would come not from nuclear holocaust, but from the pollution and neglect of the greatest resource left.

There was one quote from the book. ''We are facing the greatest challenge of history—to clean up our oceans before we kill their ability to produce our life-giving oxygen. For if we cannot breathe, what else matters?''

There was a short biography of Jon, whom the columnist called, ''one of the breed of youthful, dynamic and highly intelligent scientists who are endeavoring to understand the whole spectrum of man's interaction with the sea.'' As well there was a quote from a University of Washington professor who had evidently been one of Jon's teachers. ''It is vital to spread knowledge of the oceans' importance to human survival,'' said the professor. ''Jonathan Blake is one of a rare group of scientists who have the ability to communicate their theories and discoveries to others in simple, shocking and immediately understandable terms.''

The book was destined to become a best-seller, the article predicted, and was sure to join such books as Rachel Carson's *Silent Spring* as required reading for any intelligent reader who was concerned about the future of the planet. The author had already sold reprint rights to a paperback publisher, and the book would also become a two-part miniseries for television.

A final note said that Jon was one of the founders of the International Pollution Control Commission, which was rapidly becoming recognized throughout the world.

Stunned, Samantha stared at the newspaper, suffering from a mixture of emotions. Pride was uppermost, but she was also conscious of her own shame. *How she had misjudged him!* There was anger in her, too. Why hadn't he simply told her what he'd been doing? Why let her think he'd become some sort of wealthy playboy since Ethan had died? Lastly came a kind of nervous apprehension. What on earth was she going to say to Jon when she saw him again?

She still hadn't decided this last question when he called her at 7:20 to say he'd pick her up in fifteen minutes at the Carlisle's front door. His voice was cool and even. He hung up before she had a chance to reply.

Still nervous, she glanced at his face as she got into the taxi. His expression told her nothing, and his polite, "Was breakfast okay," gave her no clue as to what he might be thinking of her.

"I read the newspaper," she said hesitantly as they drove toward the ferry landing. "I'm...I don't know what to say."

"You don't have to say anything," he rejoined calmly. "I sent the paper to you merely to satisfy your curiosity in one respect at least."

"It's a remarkable achievement, Jon," she said quietly.

"Thank you."

"Why were you...was it really so necessary to be secretive about the book? I should have thought you'd be proud...."

"My publisher felt it was best to keep quiet until it was in print," he said evenly. "They felt if the accusatory nature of the book became known too early, pressure might be brought to bear on them to stifle it. It hits a few industrialists and governments in the economy, where it really hurts." He hesitated, then added carelessly, "The trip I mentioned to Lynne is connected with the book. I'll be traveling the country, doing some promotion, lecturing in various cities. My publishers are anxious for as much publicity as possible now, so that there's no possibility of the book getting suppressed by anyone whose interests it conflicts with.''

"It sounds like a very controversial book," Samantha offered.

"It is." He smiled briefly, wearily. He was tired, too, she observed. "I've never been one to step aside from controversy," he said. "I'm even expecting potshots from some scientists. Who do I think I am, setting myself up as an authority and a doomsayer—that sort of thing."

"Jon, I really don't know how to...."

They had reached the ferry landing, and the boat was already in its slip. Jon was kept busy for a while, lining up the car in the slot assigned him by one of the crew. Then he suggested they go above to one of the lounges, rather than outside on the deck, as neither of them had brought warm coats. They might perhaps have another cup of coffee, he suggested. His manners were, as always, impeccable. He assisted her up the steps, opened doors for her, went to fetch the coffee after seating her. She had no idea how to penetrate his cool distant facade. It *was* a facade, she felt sure. There was a tightness around his eyes and mouth that told her he was having difficulty maintaining the pose.

Once the ferry was under way, she tried again. "You told me a while back that you'd called me when you came back from Japan. You said last night that you hadn't felt able to contact me until you had something of your own. Was that...."

"The book, yes. I was going to show you the manuscript and the publisher's acceptance. I suppose I thought it might impress you with my worth."

"I was always impressed by your worth, Jon. All the same, you should have insisted—"

"Your father seemed to feel I was the furthest person from your mind."

He had raised an impenetrable wall against her. It was hard to believe that last night and again this morning he'd made love to her with such tender care. Had he simply wanted her physically and taken the opportunity to get her "out of his blood?" Surely if he loved her at all, he would be willing to meet her halfway?

"The paper said you were a founder of the International Pollution Control Commission," she said at last, not knowing what else to say. "How did that come about?"

He stirred his coffee, his gaze fixed on some point over her shoulder. "I've always known it wasn't enough to worry about saving any particular species of sea creature," he said slowly. "We have to preserve the environment in which they live. A few years ago I began an in-depth study of the composition of seawater and the elements it contains, including the effect of foreign matter such as oil or other pollutants."

He sighed, then went on more briskly. "At a conference I met some scientists who shared my concern and sense of urgency—an Englishman, two Japanese and a Russian woman. We pooled our information and ideas and called ourselves the International Pollution Control Commission. Put simply, we've created an international human-resource center that includes engineers, lawyers, economists and independent scientists. This group makes sure that people—politicians who are involved in making decisions about the environment, for example— are aware of the possibly disastrous results of their policies, and are also provided with alternative suggestions. The general public is also kept informed of those legislators who are farsighted enough to press for reform. The book is part of this, of course.''

"I read about your commission," Samantha exclaimed when he paused. "I had no idea that you. . . it started in England, didn't it?"

He was looking at her now. He'd lost his withdrawn air, but he wasn't really seeing her as herself, Samantha felt. She was merely an audience interested in his views.

He nodded. "We had a lot of cooperation from the British government and the fisheries department. And we've set up a program in Japan." He paused. "Recently I was invited by a group of politicians to set up a similar center in this country." His gaze sharpened suddenly on her face and became sardonic. "My trio of mysterious guests," he explained crisply.

"Are you going to accept?" Samantha asked, not wanting him to dwell on her stupidity.

He sighed. "I haven't made a final decision yet. I'd hoped to get back eventually to my own first love—the study of mammals. I'm not really cut out for politics. But I've been thinking it over, trying to decide where my duty lies."

He laughed shortly. "That sounds pretentious. I guess I really mean I have to decide where I can be most useful. As I told you, I've been resting—I hadn't had a vacation in seven years. This seemed a good time to consider exactly what I want to do in the future. However, I was fairly encouraging to my mystery guests. I think I'm probably going to agree."

There was a silence. Then Samantha said slowly, "Can you ever forgive me for the things I said?"

He looked at her gravely. "I don't know, Samantha.

Having thought of myself as a crusader bent on saving the world, it's a bit difficult to swallow accusations that I might be involved in something as shoddy as espionage.''

She wasn't sure if he was teasing her or not. It seemed to her that the derisive tone in which he'd made the rather pompous-sounding statement indicated he was mocking himself rather than her.

She looked at him uncertainly, and after a moment he reached out and patted her hand. "Don't look so upset with yourself, Sam. After all, I may yet turn out to be in cahoots with Jakob, in spite of all my high-sounding principles. Perhaps you'd better withhold judgment until we see what Mike has to say.''

She felt herself flush at the renewed sardonic note in his voice. But he hadn't explained Jakob's payment to him, she thought. And she still didn't know for sure that Mike was with the FBI. She no longer entertained any doubts as to Jon's sincerity about his work, but even so, she was confused about some aspects.... And obviously Jon was unable to accept that *she* might be right about something. He was patronizing her as though she were a child.

"Well, I do want to apologize for the things I said,'' she said carefully. "And I want you to believe I didn't agree to spend—to go with you so that I could find out—''

She broke off as he looked at her with raised eyebrows, skepticism showing clearly on his face. What was the use, she thought despairingly. Evidently he was still mistrustful of her motives. If only they could go back to the simple acceptance of each other they'd had in their much younger days, how much easier their relationship would be! How could she convince him that her suspicions had nothing to do with the emotions he aroused in her? How could she persuade him that she loved him, that she had gone with him to the Carlisle *because* she loved him and for no other reason?

She couldn't, she realized, as he turned away from her to look out of the ferry-boat window toward the saw-toothed line of the Olympic mountains in the west. If she blurted out now that she loved him, he'd make some snide remark about her being impressed by his achievements and his worldly success. She had kept her true feelings from him for too long, and she had lost him for a third time, this time forever.

CHAPTER SIXTEEN

ANNE MARIE WAS SITTING at Samantha's desk when she hurried into her office. The girl looked very bright, almost sparkling, making Samantha feel even more weary in contrast, though she'd taken the time to wash and change into her spa uniform.

"What happened to you last night?" Anne Marie asked cheerfully. "Liz Vandervort was looking for you."

"Liz Vandervort?" Samantha echoed blankly. *Concentrate,* she ordered herself. *You have a workday to get through.* "I'll go check on her right away and see what she wants." She started to turn away.

"She isn't here," Anne Marie said, halting her. "Her husband called last night and said he couldn't get along another day—or night—without her. She plastered on some makeup, slapped on a wig and flew out on the first available cloud—which masqueraded as Steve Cory's airplane." She grinned. "She wanted to say goodbye to you."

"I'm sorry I missed her."

"She left you a message." Anne Marie picked up a small white envelope from the top of Samantha's desk and handed it to her.

Curious, Samantha opened it. "Don't forget," Liz had written, "if you love him, go after him."

Samantha had to blink back tears as she slid the

small sheet of paper back in the envelope. If only life was that simple, she thought. If only. . . .

"I wanted to see you last night, too," Anne Marie said. "I wanted to invite you to my birthday party."

Samantha summoned a smile. "I almost forgot," she murmured, reaching into the bottom drawer of her desk. She pulled out a brightly wrapped package and handed it to the girl. During her sight-seeing tour of Seattle after the seminar she'd bought a beautifully arranged makeup case for Anne Marie. Covered in creamy leather, it opened up to reveal compartments for eye and cheek colors, lipsticks and foundations, tubes of mascara and shaped cutouts for brushes of various sizes and shapes. Consulting with one of the spa cosmetologists, Samantha had filled the case with cosmetics suited to Anne Marie's coloring and skin type.

The gift earned her a rib-crushing hug and an enthusiastic flow of gratitude that only ceased when Samantha retreated to another chair and said, "What's all this about a party? Your father told me he was going to take you to dinner in town."

Anne Marie shook her head. "That's what he meant to do. But Eileen Blake offered to host a party for me tonight and daddy agreed. Eileen's friend Peter Darrell is coming, and Jon will be there, of course, plus Barry and Deborah." She turned to wave at Deborah, who had walked in. Deborah gave her a grin and wave in turn. "Even my father will have a date—Thelma Delaney said she'd go as his partner. He doesn't usually socialize with the guests, but he likes Thelma—she makes him laugh." She paused for breath. "I asked everybody where you were last night, but nobody knew. I even went down to Ben Fletcher's, but there was nobody home. Did you go off somewhere with them?''

Obviously Anne Marie hadn't seen Jon drive her home this morning after the ferry docked. With luck, no one else had seen them, either—the spa had just begun to stir when she returned. She'd managed to whisk into her chalet before the first group of early-morning walkers emerged from the woods.

"I was out and about," she managed lightly.

"Jon was gone, too," Anne Marie said innocently. "But Eileen said she'd tell him about the party this morning. He called a little while ago to say he'd be there. You will come, won't you, Samantha?''

"I can't," Samantha said at once. The words seemed to have been wrung out of her. She hurried to improvise an excuse. "I promised Ben I'd look after the children."

Anne Marie's face clouded. "Oh." She brightened. "I could always invite them, too. Eileen said I could have as many guests as I wanted as long as I let her know before she starts the lasagna. Have you ever tasted Eileen's lasagna? It's heavenly."

"Those children would cause havoc at your party," Samantha pointed out. "They aren't really house-broken yet. Besides," she added as a clincher, "I'd be the odd one out."

"We could find a dinner partner for you."

Samantha summoned all her energies into forming a smile. "I don't think so. It's sweet of you to ask me, but really, much as I hate to miss your party, I think I'd better keep my promise to Ben."

"Oh, well, if you insist." Anne Marie looked genuinely disappointed and Samantha felt guilty for deceiving her. She *would* go and entertain the twins later, she vowed to herself. Ben could probably use a restful evening.

"You'll manage fine without me," she said gently. "After all, you'll have Jon all to yourself." Where, she wondered, had she found the strength to tease the girl in that particular way?

Anne Marie was smiling sunnily now, her brief disappointment forgotten. "It will be good for daddy to see me with Jon in an adult situation," she said happily. "I do believe he's coming around. I think his main worry has been that Jon is older than me—but what's eleven years, after all? So silly. My father was older than my mother, and he's always told me how happy *they* were. And he's *really* fond of Jon, so I think it's going to work out. Why, he even contributed to Jon's swamp because he thinks so highly of him and his ideals."

"Jon's swamp?" Samantha echoed, feeling she'd missed some transition here.

Anne Marie nodded. She was contentedly examining the contents of the cosmetic case, clucking over each new find. Her voice was absentminded. "Jon didn't tell you about it? I'm amazed he didn't dun you for money—he's ruthless when he's working on a project like that." She gave a joyful cry of discovery and held up a pink-topped jar. "I love this shade of blusher. Gosh, Samantha, this is the most wonderful thing anyone's ever given me, except for my new watch, of course. Did you see it?" She twisted her wrist for Samantha's inspection.

Samantha resisted the urge to throttle her. "A project like what?" she demanded.

"The swamp? Oh, it's some piece of land out near Olympia. Some construction company wanted to buy it and build condominiums on it. It has a super view of the water. But Jon heard about it and he says that swamp is a perfect ecosystem, whatever that is, and so he started preaching at all his friends, persuading them to put money into a special fund with some conservation organization so they could buy it and save it. Daddy's putting in $30,000 all together. So that must mean he approves of Jon, right? Now all I have to do is convince Jon that I'm the girl he's been looking for all his life."

Tense with shock and renewed shame, Samantha nevertheless managed to respond. "I thought you implied to me that you'd already convinced Jon of that."

Anne Marie's smile was sheepish. "Jon's never really looked on me as anything but some kind of kid sister," she confided. "I pretended to myself that he was really covering up stronger feelings. I guess some of the pretense slipped out when I talked to you about him."

Obviously feeling a little embarrassed now, she glanced at her watch, exclaimed, "Gosh, I have to go. I'm supposed to get my hair done." She glanced at Samantha once more. "You're sure you can't come tonight?"

"I'm sure."

"Well, then. . . ." She closed the cosmetic case, slipped it under her arm, stood up and bent to kiss Samantha's cheek. "Thank you, Samantha," she said softly. "You're a good friend."

Samantha sat still after the girl had gone. Deborah

had followed her out, murmuring something about a tea break. The office was quiet, though she could hear the busy hum of the spa around her—people talking softly somewhere close by, the soft rattle of a supply cart rolling down the hall.

She felt stunned. Not only had Jon's motive in accepting the money from Dr. Birmann been innocent but it had also been altruistic. And she had indirectly accused him. . . .

She drew in her breath sharply, fighting the urge to lay her head on the desk and give in to tears. Probably the next thing to come her way would be proof that Dr. Birmann's expedition to Seattle Center had some perfectly obvious and innocent explanation, too. She wished she could creep away into some deep dark hole and never let Jon see her again.

THE LAST THING she felt like doing that evening was exposing herself to the twins' exuberance. But she had lied about her plans in order to avoid confronting Jon, so the least she could do was to alleviate her guilt by carrying through on her vow.

Immediately after dinner, she hiked over to Hemlock Cove, where she found the twins on the beach playing Frisbee again. They were delighted to see her, full of high spirits. Their mother had visited them that day, bringing with her a new Frisbee that glowed in the dark. "We're going to try it out tonight," Tracy confided.

"After grandpa goes to bed," Brian added.

Samantha made a mental note to alert Ben to the twins' plans and then challenged them both to a game, hoping she could tire them enough that they'd go right to sleep at the proper time.

Brian took her up on her challenge at once, backing off rapidly so he could skim the Frisbee in Samantha's general direction. Catching the plastic circle on a rebound from the bank, she sent it whizzing to Tracy, who missed it but ran cheerfully after it into the edge of the Sound. When she threw it, dripping wet, back to Samantha, the game was on in earnest. Samantha gave it her best, sending low curving throws to Brian, high overheads to the little girl, running to catch the returns. She concentrated so hard on the game and the physical release of energies formerly used to berate herself that she didn't hear Brian's protests until they'd gone on for some time.

"You're throwing too hard," he complained. "You're getting me all wore out."

"Me, too," Tracy gasped, her clothing and hair obviously damp from her last foray into the water.

Out of breath herself, Samantha apologized and scooped up both children to sit with her against the bank, promising them a story as soon as she'd recovered her oxygen supply. The wind had come up, frothing the waves into whitecaps, but the sun was still warm and the bank sheltered them.

She was telling them a long fictional tale about an Indian maiden who had lived long ago in the Cascade Mountains—"Yes, Brian, those mountains right there"—and trying not to let her thoughts turn to Jon, which they traitorously wanted to do, when her eye caught a flutter of movement a few feet from the shore and some distance along the beach. "What's that?" she asked, shading her eyes with her hand against the glare of sun on water.

Tracy jumped to her feet. "It's a sea gull," she said after gazing at it for a moment.

Brian stood up and looked, too. "Something's wrong with it," he exclaimed.

At once both children set off at a run along the beach, shouting to Samantha to follow. Their high voices frightened the bird so much that it struggled to fly away but couldn't seem to lift itself from the water.

"Stand still," Samantha yelled, following the twins as fast as she could. They obeyed but a little too late. Confused, frightened, the bird struggled even more frantically, flopping around in a circle, making high mewling cries.

Without breaking stride Samantha plunged into the water and scooped the bird up in both hands, falling on her knees as her own momentum carried her forward and getting soaked to her waist in the process. Not that that worried her—she was dressed in an old T-shirt and cut offs and her feet were bare. The dousing chilled her, though.

Shivering slightly, she straightened and walked carefully to dry sand, cradling the struggling bird under one arm. Something bumped hard against her leg, and she looked down to see a heavy lead fishing weight swinging from a long tangle of monofilament. Closer examination showed her that the abandoned fishing line had wrapped itself around the bird, pinioning one wing and dragging the bird down so that it couldn't fly.

"Go get some scissors or clippers or something," Samantha ordered, and both children raced for the house. They were back in record time, followed by their grandfather, who had come to see what all the fuss was about.

Talking softly to the bird in an effort to soothe him,

Samantha held him firmly while Ben clipped the line free. Immediately the gull's struggles increased, and she set him down carefully on the beach. He moved a little way away from her, wobbling slightly, obviously exhausted by his experience. "Come on, bird, fly," Tracy exhorted.

As though her piping voice had galvanized him into motion, the bird lifted his wings and flapped them furiously, falling over in the process. At once Samantha saw what was wrong. The outer half of the bird's right wing hung at an odd angle.

Soothingly she spoke to him as she checked him over for further damage. The broken wing seemed to be his only major injury, though a couple of red spots on his feathers indicated that the strong monofilament had cut into his flesh. The bird had stopped fighting her as she handled him, seeming to understand that she was trying to help. His heart was beating erratically, though.

"Do you know how to fix a broken wing?" Samantha asked Ben.

"Not me," Ben said, peering at the bird. "Maybe he should have a splint of some kind."

"Uncle Jon can fix him," Tracy said.

"Uncle Jon knows all about birds as well as fish and stuff," Brian agreed.

Crouched down, Samantha looked doubtfully at both worried faces. "You think you could carry him up to Uncle Jon?"

Brian backed away a step. "I might hurt him. I already frightened him."

Tracy put her hands behind her back. "My hands are too little," she said, shaking her head.

Samantha glanced at Ben. "Don't look at me," he said. "My rheumatism's been acting up. No way am I going to climb up that hill." He looked at Samantha sideways, his lips parting in his mirthless grin. "Looks like you're stuck with the job, lass."

Exasperated, Samantha frowned up at him. "I don't want to go up there tonight, Ben."

"Looks like fate thinks otherwise."

"Aren't you ever going to give up?"

"Not me, lass. I'm a magician, remember? I've cast a spell in your name and one other's. Looks like this bird was sent to help."

"I'm not going up there, Ben," she said firmly.

"Guess that bird's just going to have to manage by himself then."

"That bird's going to die if we don't do something," Brian said gruffly.

Samantha sighed. Ben was right, of course. It was up to her. The bird's heart was beating more steadily now, but it seemed weak. It was making no effort to escape from her grip. She had to set aside personal considerations and take it to Jon.

Fifteen minutes later she was in the Blakes' kitchen, holding the gull still on the big table while Jon carefully extended the bird's wing and taped it down. His hands moved capably, surely, his long fingers gentle. The bird seemed to know he was in the hands of an expert. He had stopped struggling entirely and was examining Jon with unblinking eyes.

Jon had taken off his suit jacket and rolled up the sleeves of his white cambric shirt, but the dark tie carefully knotted under the shirt's collar gave him a look of formality. His blond hair was newly shampooed, neatly brushed to one side. Looking at him, at the concern for the bird that showed in his face, Samantha ached with love for him. If only she could come up with words, the right words, the magic words that would ease the strain between them, she thought.

"I owe you another apology, Jon," she said stiffly.

He glanced up at her, blue eyes quizzical, then went back to his task of taping the bird's other wing. "That should keep him properly balanced," he explained as he set the bird down in a large towel-lined box he'd already prepared. The bird wobbled for a moment, rocked precariously as it attempted to flap its wings, pecked at the tape, gave up and contentedly waddled around the box, curiously examining his new quarters.

"He'll be okay," Jon said. "Mostly he needs rest and a chance to heal. Tell the twins I'll take good care of him and they can come and visit whenever they want."

"They wanted to come up with me, but I persuaded them not to. I knew you were having a party—" She broke off. Jon was looking at her questioningly.

"You said something about an apology?"

Samantha swallowed. "I—Anne Marie told me about the swamp and Dr. Birmann's contribution. I should have known—"

She broke off as Anne Marie's voice came from behind her. "How's the bird? Let me see him. Oh, isn't he beautiful? Poor thing!"

If she hadn't spoken, Samantha wouldn't have recognized her. She'd had her hair cut in a short cap style that feathered around her face, emphasizing her cheekbones and making her gray eyes look enormous. She'd experimented with the cosmetics Samantha had bought her, too, using eyeliner, mascara and shadow to excellent effect, and she was wearing a red jersey dress that flattered her petite figure to perfection. "Anne Marie, you look fantastic," Samantha exclaimed.

"Don't I though?" Anne Marie agreed, turning from her examination of the bird to smile happily at Samantha. "The hairdresser said my hair was much too long for my overall size, and the cosmetologist taught me how to apply the makeup. Quite a change, isn't it?" She pirouetted, showing off in such an ingenuous way that no one watching her could have thought her conceited.

"Absolutely fabulous," Samantha said, hugging her—a difficult operation when she was trying to keep her wet clothing away from her.

Jon, she noticed, was gazing at the girl with a smug expression, as though he'd been responsible for the transformation himself.

"What does your father think?" Samantha asked, her enthusiasm abruptly dampened.

Anne Marie giggled and flashed a glance at Jon, who smiled—rather fatuously, Samantha thought. "I think he's in shock," Anne Marie confided. "He's hardly said a word all evening." She laughed, then smiled hopefully at Samantha. "Are you going to stay for some birthday cake?"

Jon had turned away to wash his hands at the kitchen sink. As Anne Marie offered her invitation, he looked over his shoulder, frowning slightly.

"I can't, I'm afraid," Samantha said at once, conscious of her soggy cut offs, old UCLA T-shirt and her bare feet.

"You're welcome to stay, Sam," Jon said courteously, drying his hands on the towel, his blue gaze meeting hers.

"The twins would kill me," she excused herself. "They'll be dying to know what happened to the bird."

Jon nodded. After checking the gull once more, his fingers gentle on the snowy feathers, he picked up his jacket from the back of a chair and shrugged into it. "I'll see you to the door then. And you, birthday girl," he added, smiling down at Anne Marie, his hand on her shoulder, "should get back to your guests."

Anne Marie flashed him an adoring smile and flounced out of the kitchen ahead of them, her skirts flaring around her slim legs.

"I can't get over the way she looks," Samantha said. "I knew she could look prettier, but—"

"I understand from Jakob that you added your persuasions to mine." He glanced at her sideways as she preceded him into the hall. "I just hope we haven't created a monster. Anne Marie's been practicing her wiles on me all evening. I'm getting pretty hot under the collar." There was fond amusement in his voice. Was she supposed to be jealous?

She could hear voices in the drawing room. Anne Marie was reporting on the gull. She heard Deborah's gurgling chuckle, Thelma Delaney's boisterous laugh and then a male voice she hadn't heard before. Glancing in as they passed the doorway, she saw a tall nice-looking man with dark hair, neatly cropped beard and frameless glasses. He was leaning against the mantel looking down at Eileen, who was sitting on one of the sofas with a glass in her hand. *That must be Peter Darrell,* she thought.

Eileen caught sight of her and waved at her to come in, but Samantha shook her head, gestured at her disheveled appearance and kept walking.

"I telephoned you at the spa, but of course you weren't there," Jon said as he opened the front door for her. "I had a call from Mike."

She looked at him. "And?"

"Nothing." He regarded her thoughtfully. "You're looking suspicious again. You still think Mike might not be in the FBI?"

"I—" She brushed her tangled hair back from her forehead, then shook her head wearily. "Of course, Jon, if you say he's in the FBI, then he must be." She could hear the doubt in her own voice.

Jon's face stiffened. He gestured her to go outside, then followed her and closed the door behind him. When he spoke again, his voice sounded clipped. "According to Mike, a Jakob Birmann was born in Switzerland on March 14, 1927, in the town Jakob told me was his. He attended medical school where his diplomas say he did, became an American citizen, married, fathered Anne Marie and practiced medicine in the proper sequence and at the proper times. He opened the spa in San Diego in the year he told me he'd opened it. All his papers are in order, it seems."

Her humiliation was complete. "Then I suppose that's the end of it," she said in a small voice.

"Don't feel bad, Sam," Jon said in a kind voice that infuriated her. "You did the right thing. There's no harm done."

If he didn't wipe that supercilious smile off his face she was going to slap it off. "What about Tom Greene?" she asked.

"Mike didn't mention him."

"I see." She wanted to ask if Mike had even checked on Tom Greene, but she couldn't bear to make more of a fool of herself than she'd already done. She still wasn't sure if she believed Jon about Mike or not. Turning away from him, she looked toward the mountains, which were starkly clear this evening, seeming to loom closer than usual. "I'd better get back to the twins," she said after a while.

"I suppose so." She thought he was going to say something more, but instead he gave her a rather stiff smile and turned away to open the door.

"Thank Mike for me, will you?" she said carefully. And then blurted out, "I really am sorry, Jon, for everything. The swamp, I mean. I had no business asking about the money Jakob paid you—" She broke off. The supercilious smile was gone, but it had left an expression in its place that was a sort of polite expectancy, barely curbing impatience. Probably he just wanted to get back to the party and enjoy himself.

He shrugged. "As a matter of fact, the swamp was brought to my attention purely by accident—a group of developers wanted to fill it. Hell—a diverse and productive ecosystem like that! Its value to the environment is priceless...." He trailed off, smiling wryly. "Sorry. I didn't mean to lecture. I would have told you about the swamp project right away except that I was...smarting, I guess."

"Jon—"

He shook his head, cutting off whatever she'd been about to say. She didn't really know herself what she'd *wanted* to say; she just knew she didn't want to walk away and leave him like this, with everything...*dead* between them.

"I'd better get back," he said mildly. "Be sure to tell the twins the bird is in good hands."

"I will, yes, thank you. . . ."

She was talking to empty air. He'd already gone inside, leaving her to trudge along the driveway feeling like some sad child who'd behaved badly and had been turned away from the party the grown-ups were enjoying so much.

But that was ridiculous, she scolded herself, lifting her chin. She *had* been invited to the party. Twice. *She* had turned *them* down. And if Jon wouldn't accept her apologies for the way she'd suspected him, or treated him in the past, there wasn't much she could do about it except retreat with dignity intact.

This had been quite a day, she thought as she scrambled down the hillside back to the waiting twins.

THE DAY WAS NOT QUITE THROUGH with her yet. When she returned to her chalet, she found the red light on the telephone blinking, indicating there was a message for her. Adrian? She wondered. Had he called to protest after all? At least that might help to assuage her damaged pride.

The caller had been her father, the operator told her, telephoning from Paris, France. He would call back at 10:00 P.M. Pacific time. Samantha cradled the receiver, knowing instinctively that Adrian had talked to Dwight. Now Dwight would start putting pressure on her to reconsider, and she'd have a fight on her hands. Was this awful day never going to end?

But to her surprise, when her father called back he had apparently taken the news of her broken engagement rather well. He expressed regret, of course, that she wouldn't be marrying Adrian after all, but seemed resigned to the fact that her decision was final. "Adrian was awfully upset, though," he added.

"He didn't seem so to me."

"He has his pride, Samantha."

"I'm sick of hearing about pride," she said sharply.

There was a silence, then her father said mildly, "Does your decision have anything to do with Jonathan Blake?"

Samantha hesitated. "Not really. I've thought for some time that marrying Adrian would probably be a mistake."

"But you have seen Jon?"

"Yes." She couldn't resist adding, "You wouldn't know him, daddy. He inherited Ethan Blake's house, and quite a lot of money, I understand. And he's going to head up some kind of Oceanic Commission in Washington, D.C. He has a book coming out...."

"I read about it." Dwight paused. The hollow sound of long distance was uninterrupted for so long Samantha was afraid they'd been cut off. But then Dwight said, "I've been doing some thinking, kitten." He hadn't called her kitten for years! "I've never felt too proud of myself for the way I treated Jon. Not because I offered him a job or money—I still think he was crazy to turn me down. But I was pretty nasty to him at the same time." He sighed. "There's been a sadness in you for a long time, and I've always felt it was my fault." Another pause. "Jon called you last year. I didn't tell you."

"I know."

Another long hesitation. Then, "Are you seeing him again? I mean...hell, you know what I mean."

"I've seen him several times, daddy," Samantha said carefully. "But there's not much likelihood of—" She cut herself off. "It's a bit complicated."

"Hell, I hoped you'd got back together again. I'd feel a lot better if you did. I keep thinking that I was responsible. I've thought and thought since Adrian called."

It was unusual for her father to admit to introspection, or even to admit he might possibly have been wrong about something. Samantha was amazed. "It's all right, daddy," she said comfortingly. "I'm fine."

"You're enjoying your job?"

"Yes." She wasn't going to tell *him* of her reservations.

"You aren't ready to call it quits and come back to my office where you belong?"

Samantha smiled into the receiver. Her father hadn't changed *that* much after all. "Not yet. I'll let you know if I ever am."

Dwight seemed satisfied with that. He talked for a few more minutes, then passed the receiver to Claudia, who was even more concerned about Samantha's relationship with Jon and wanted to know in more detail exactly what was going on. She'd always liked Jon. Samantha answered her voluble questions as evasively as she could and was relieved when Claudia finally brought the conversation to an end.

Hanging up the phone, Samantha decided to shower and crawl into bed. She thought longingly for a moment of the hot tub at the spa but dismissed the idea at once. She hadn't felt able to return there since the incident with Jon. Once she'd got as far as the door, then turned away when his face came immediately into her mind, his eyebrows raised in that quizzical way he had, his mouth curved, eyes mischievous.

She felt an emptiness inside her that was as acute as though she'd fasted for a week. "I can never forgive," Jon had said at the hotel when he thought she'd set him up out of suspicion. If he couldn't forgive, if he wouldn't accept her apologies, there wasn't much hope for her where he was concerned. And he'd be going away soon. Quite possibly she'd never see him again.

CHAPTER SEVENTEEN

SHE WAS SWIMMING deep in the ocean. The water was very dark and empty and she was afraid. And tired. Her arms and legs were becoming leaden. Her lungs screamed for air. Any second now she would have to breathe in, and then her mouth and throat and lungs would fill with water and she would drown.

She had to surface. She had to breathe. Dear God, it was dark. What kind of ocean was this, anyway? There were no fish, no aquatic plants. *Where was the sunlight?* There must be sunlight somewhere. Had she turned upside down? Which way was the surface? Panicking, turning in rolling somersaults, her hair streaming out from her head and eyes straining, she heard the blessed sound of someone tapping on the side of a boat, tapping to guide her to the surface and the light of day.

She woke tangled in bedclothes, gasping for air, arms and legs thrashing. Only a nightmare, after all! But the tapping continued. She glanced at her bedside clock. Eight forty-five—she had overslept. And someone was tapping on her door.

Grabbing her terry robe, she yanked it on as she stumbled, still sleep laden, across the sitting room to the door.

Jon stood on the porch in blue jeans and a yellow T-shirt, sunlight gilding his hair. "Thank goodness you woke me," she exclaimed groggily, gesturing him into the chalet. "I must have forgotten to set the alarm. You wouldn't believe the dream—" Abruptly her mind cleared and she stopped in midsentence, the door half open. This was not her old friend Jon, come to take her on a fishing trip or a run on the beach. This was Jonathan Blake, famous oceanographer, success, heartbreaker.

"What do you want?" she asked rudely, then shook her head as his eyebrows registered surprise at her change of tone. "I guess I'm not awake yet." She glanced at him apologetically. "Listen, I'm sorry, but I'm going to have to rush or I'll be late for work. How's the gull?"

"Okay. He's taken over the kitchen. The cats are terrified of him and Tonto follows him around adoringly." His mind didn't seem to be on his words. There was a strange expression on his face. She couldn't make it out for a moment as he stood there in her sitting room, looking around in a hesitant way. And then she realized that his hands were stuck in the pockets of his jeans as though he wasn't sure what to do with them, and his usually direct eyes were avoiding hers. There was a distinctly sheepish look around his crooked smile. Well, well, what had happened to chasten the lordly Mr. Blake this morning?

"I've had a humbling experience," he said at last. "I had another call from Mike half an hour ago. It seems all is not as it should be with Jakob Birmann after all."

"My gosh!" The exclamation was forced from her. She sat down hard on one of the armchairs, gestured for him to take the other, then jumped to her feet again before he could sit down. "This calls for coffee," she said. "Hang on a minute."

When she returned from the bathroom, he was sitting in the chair, one ankle resting on the other knee while he fiddled with his sneaker shoelaces. She handed him a steaming mug, sat down with the other clasped between both hands. "What happened?" she demanded.

Both his feet were flat on the floor now, but he still hadn't met her eyes. He was gazing into the mug as though the liquid might give him some hint of what the future held. "The Jakob Birmann who was born on March 14, 1927, died in a skiing accident at age twenty," he said.

Samantha stared at his bent head. "I don't understand. What does that mean?"

He looked up and met her eyes at last. "The boy who died was a medical student. There was no other Jakob Birmann born on that day in that town, nor was there a Jakob Birmann born on any other day in that town. According to Mike, there is a distinct possibility that *our* Jakob Birmann stole his identity and had papers drawn up, forged, in order to gain admittance to this country."

Shocked into silence, Samantha felt no jubilation that she'd been proved not to be so stupid after all. She felt sick. She took a sip of coffee, felt it warm her, but the sickness didn't go away.

Jon sighed. "I owe you a very large and humble apology, Samantha. I treated your suspicions far too lightly. I could not believe that Jakob...." He took a swallow of coffee. "I thought he was above suspicion. But he's not. Which indicates to me that no one is ever really above suspicion, not even me. I can see now why you wondered about me. I did evade your questions. There were factors in my actions—taking money from Jacob, refusing to tell you what kind of work I was doing.... You were right to be suspicious. In my own defense I can only say that I had no idea...."

Samantha let out a long breath she hadn't realized she'd been holding. "I didn't ever really suspect you, Jon," she said softly. "I was just puzzled, and concerned that perhaps Jakob had involved you in something without your knowledge. Anyway," she added, "there might still be an explanation."

He was shaking his head, his mouth grim now. "Mike was very interested in your description of Tom Greene. He put it on the wire and came up with a match. There's a possibility he might be a man known to the FBI as Boris Rogov."

"A *Russian*?"

"Yes. A foreign-trade consultant who worked out of Los Angeles. A couple of years ago he was caught smuggling computer components out of the country. He was getting them from workers in the Bay Area, buying them or blackmailing people into stealing them. He was sent to prison in California to await deportation. After a couple of months he escaped. U.S. Marshals have him on their list of most-wanted fugitives. It was thought that he was on the East Coast."

Samantha stared at him, finding nothing to say. After a moment she got up, picked up her telephone receiver and called Deborah to tell her she'd be late. She had a migraine headache, she said. Which at least was close to the truth.

"What happens now?" she asked, sitting down again.

"Mike can't be sure Tom Greene is Rogov. He's check-ing on it, he says. I imagine someone's on the way to Victoria. In the meantime, Mike would like to meet Jakob. Casually. He's coming over to the island today and wants me to arrange to invite Jakob to dinner. I'm supposed to introduce Mike as an old college friend—which is the truth. After that, Mike will play it by ear." He frowned. "I have the feeling he told me as little as was necessary to get my cooperation. There was an undercurrent of excitement in his voice that...." His voice trailed away. "I guess it's stupid of me, but I keep hoping this will all turn out to be a mistake. I have such respect for Jakob. I just can't believe—"

"Nor can I." She leaned forward and put her hand on his knee. "We have to see this through, Jon. No mat-ter how we personally feel about Dr. Birmann, we have to *know*."

Setting down his mug, he lifted her hand between both of his, held it warmly. "I begin to see what you've been going through, suspecting some of this and then having me dismiss your worries as foolishness. I really am sorry, Sam. Why do you suppose we keep hurting each other like this? It's destructive to both of us. Are we perhaps not good for each other?"

Pain struck through her like a sudden pang of hunger, accompanied by fear. Was he saying they'd be better off apart?

Apparently he didn't expect an answer. "Will you come to dinner, too?" he asked. "Mike wants you to, as camouflage, I guess. I...it would make me feel better if you were there. I'm supposed to invite Anne Marie, also."

She hesitated. "You know, I have an idea Anne

Marie may know more than she told me. I think we'll
have to be careful not to let her suspect we have another
motive for this dinner.''

He looked at her bleakly. "I don't really want to involve her at all, but it would look odd if I left her out,
especially after last night's party. I've no idea what to
tell either of them, what reason to give for having them
over again so soon.''

"You could tell them that as I was unable to come,
you thought it would be nice to do it again.''

"That might do it." He stood up, pulling her with
him. Putting his hands on her shoulders, he attempted a
smile. "Thank you, Sam.''

"Oh Jon, it's so horrible," she blurted out. "It all
seems so devious, so underhanded. . . .''

Unexpectedly, he drew her into his arms and held her
close, resting his face against her hair. She could feel his
heart beating against her, counterpoint to her own rapid
pulse. But there was no sexual tension between them,
only a comfort in being together.

"I think perhaps we'd better put our own relationship
on hold," Jon said quietly after a while. "At least until
this thing with Jakob is sorted out.''

She felt another pang of fear but recognized at the
same time that he was right. If their bruised feelings
were ever going to heal they needed a normal climate to
heal in, not one that was clouded with suspicion and
doubt of a mutual friend.

With an effort, she forced herself to step away from
him. "I'll see you later then," she said. She shook her
head worriedly. "I'm not sure I can carry it off. I'm not
that good an actress.''

"You said you were." A glimmer of amusement had

appeared in his blue eyes, and a charge of electricity arced between them, setting her nerve endings tingling.

Abruptly she wanted to kiss him, and knew that he also wanted to kiss her. She wanted to take him by the hand and lead him into the next room to her terribly rumpled bed and forget there was such a person as Jakob Birmann in the world. But she knew there could be no forgetting. They were both sickened by the possibility of Jakob's treachery. Love couldn't flourish in such an atmosphere. In any case, acting on their undeniable physical attraction hadn't solved any of their problems so far.

Jon must have guessed what was going on in her mind. He suddenly pulled her against him hard and wrapped his arms around her tightly, holding her as though he would never let her go. But he did let her go. His hand reached again to brush against her cheek, and then he touched her shoulder lightly once, looked at her with anguish in his eyes and was gone, leaving her to wonder if his anguish was due to a half-formed decision to put her out of his life altogether when this awful business was done.

IT HELPED that Mike was a good-looking young man. Anne Marie was immediately, obviously attracted to him. And he played his part to perfection, flirting with her gallantly, making her blush with his suggestive remarks. "I had no idea the island had such great scenery or I'd have visited before." This while smiling into her eyes.

He greeted Jakob with a firm handshake and an ingenuous smile. "Jon's told me about your work here," he said solemnly. "My dad's a dermatologist. I bet he'd love to meet you."

"He lives here in Washington?" Jakob asked.

"Unfortunately, no. He and Mom moved to Florida in search of more sunshine than we get here."

Because of Mike's easy manner it turned out to be simpler than Samantha had expected to converse normally. There were even times during the evening when she forgot the purpose of this gathering. When she did remember she felt chilled, but the moments were rare.

A lot of the conversation around the large table in the formal dining room centered naturally on Jon and his book. Jakob and Anne Marie had read the same article as Samantha and were patently impressed. When they discovered Jon had received an advance copy of *Destruction*, they insisted he bring it out.

Samantha took it reverently into her hands when her turn came. The cover was dramatic—a seabird covered in oil against a background of a magnificent sunset, the word "Destruction" written in stark black letters above. On the back was the same photograph of Jon she'd seen earlier. She turned the book over, leafed through it, seeing impressive pictures of a burning offshore oil platform shooting columns of black smoke into a pale evening sky; litter floating like some misbegotten island far out at sea, discarded cans and hubcaps and bottles glinting in the sunlight; chemicals and sludgy detergents spewing into a river where children played with little boats. Industries were named, organizations and governments indicted.

She looked up and caught Jon's eyes. "You always were subtle," she said dryly.

His answering smile was wry. "It's too late for subtlety. My intention was to go Theodore Roosevelt one better—speak *loudly* and carry a big stick."

"Look at the dedication, Samantha," Eileen ordered as she started picking up plates.

"That coq au vin was delicious," Dr. Birmann murmured. "My ladies would probably kill for a taste."

The laughter was general. This was just like any normal friendly gathering, Samantha thought as she flipped the pages of the book back to the front. Then she stopped thinking. Her breath caught in her throat. The dedication was very simple, only two words on the whole page. *For Sam.*

She was having difficulty swallowing. There seemed to be an obstruction in her throat. The same obstruction was having an effect on her vision, blurring the printed words. When she finally managed to look at Jon, she could feel the tears in her eyes. "This must have been written before...."

"Before you came back, yes."

The others were still in the room. The old dog Tonto was even snoring comfortably under the table, his head resting on Samantha's foot. Yet it seemed to Samantha that they had all become very minor characters in a drama in which she and Jon were the stars. His level blue gaze seemed to hold her in an all-embracing sphere of light that lifted both of them onto another plane. It seemed an eternity that they gazed at each other. She couldn't possibly have looked away. Inside her all the pain, all the anxiety, seemed to melt away—and hope was born.

"May I see?" Anne Marie asked, breaking the spell. Samantha passed the open book across the table to her. She looked at the dedication, then at Samantha, her eyes wide with astonishment. Then she glanced quickly at the others.

Eileen had gone out to the kitchen. Mike had drawn Jon and Jakob into a conversation about an incident he'd witnessed at the ocean beach. Some time ago, he said, a local newspaper had run a story about an oil spill that was killing off seabirds. A lot of people had gone to see. One old man, standing next to Mike, drinking beer from a bottle, had commented in angry tones about the wickedness of people who allowed such a terribly destructive thing to happen. Mike had been impressed by his eloquent tirade, agreeing with him, but then the old man had taken a final swig of beer, dropped the bottle on the beach and walked away.

Dr. Birmann was listening to him gravely, watching the younger man's face in the intent way he had. Jon's attention was also on Mike. She'd noticed Jon was having difficulty looking Dr. Birmann in the eye. She'd had a problem with that herself.

"I'm so sorry, Samantha," Anne Marie whispered.

Samantha looked at the girl, who was gazing at her with mournful eyes. "I didn't know, didn't guess.... When I think of how I went on about Jon. You must really hate me. I even implied—"

Samantha reached across the table and patted her hand. "It's okay, Anne Marie. I had an idea you were just trying on feelings for size. No harm done."

Anne Marie smiled gratefully. She really was an extraordinarily attractive girl, Samantha thought. The use of makeup had brought out oddly luminous depths in her gray eyes, making them look like burnished silver. Her lashes, now darkened, looked incredibly long and silky. Samantha frowned a little, trying to think where she had seen similar eyes. They were the same color as the doctor's, of course, and his lashes were just as thick, though shorter, blunter....

The connection took place somewhere deep in her brain, and it took a moment to come forward where Samantha could recognize it. When she did, she felt as though she'd been dealt a blow to her stomach that took all her breath away. She *had* seen eyes like Anne Marie's on another person. Tom Greene had taken off his hat and glasses and mopped his forehead! Now that she'd made the connection, she could see that even the line of her mouth, the shape of her nose were the same.

Luckily Mike had chosen that moment to speak to Anne Marie, so her attention was elsewhere. Samantha had to fight the urge to blurt out her recognition, but she managed to suppress it. And also to question it. Was her imagination running away with her again? There was still no proof. Tom Greene might *not* be Boris Rogov.

She took a deep unsteady breath and made herself join in the conversation again. Eileen had brought out a wonderful-looking dessert. "Chocolate mousse," she announced.

Dr. Birmann groaned aloud. "Eileen, you are going to be the death of me," he moaned, and Jon and Samantha exchanged a quick, startled, guilty glance. Samantha's stomach churned. Jon winced. Only Mike was able to respond naturally. "Everyone's entitled to an indulgence once in a while," he said blithely, and started helping himself from the dish Eileen had placed in front of him.

Yet at the same time, Samantha became abruptly aware that his apparent boyish zest was just a pose. Underneath that ingenuous grin of his she could see his alert brown eyes flicking glances at the doctor from time to time, drawing conclusions, making up his mind.

What had he decided, she wondered. Guilty or innocent? Or had he not reached any decision at all?

She had hoped to be able to stay on after Dr. Birmann and his daughter departed, but when the time came, the doctor seemed to take for granted that she would drive back to the spa with them. Not wanting to give him any food for thought, Samantha felt it would be wise to go along with him. She tried to catch Jon's eyes as he saw them to the door, but he seemed preoccupied and didn't look directly at her. Probably he couldn't wait to be alone with Mike and ask him the questions that were burning through her own mind. She could only hope that he would call her later.

But he didn't call. Several times Samantha was on the point of telephoning him. Surely he didn't expect her not to wonder. . . .

But she couldn't bring herself to dial his number. There was still constraint between them. If she made a nuisance of herself, she might upset the delicate balance. For once she would be patient, she decided. She would wait until Mike or Jon let her know what was going on.

IN THE MORNING she regretted this decision. When she arrived at her office, she found Dr. Birmann turned sideways, sitting behind his desk. He was going through his office safe, putting papers in an attaché case. She caught a glimpse of a small blue book—a passport?

"Ah, Samantha, I'm glad you're here," he said as soon as she poked her head around the door. "I've decided to go to Seattle for a few days. There are some people I have to see. I briefed the rest of the staff at breakfast."

Samantha had skipped breakfast altogether, still too worried to want to eat. "Do you want me to come with you?" she asked.

"Not this time. I'm taking Anne Marie with me." He was smiling rather fixedly, and there were lines of strain around his eyes and mouth. "I promised her a trip, remember?"

Samantha came all the way into the office. "Can I help you with anything?" she asked. "Would you like me to call Steve Cory to pick you up?"

"No." His voice was more adamant than seemed called for and he must have realized it. He shook his head as though castigating himself for his lack of manners and looked up at her. "We will take the ferry. I wish to have the use of the car." He ran an agitated hand through his gray hair. "Would you mind checking to see if Anne Marie is ready? We must leave immediately."

Samantha hesitated. "I didn't see anything on your calendar...."

"This...meeting wasn't arranged until this morning," he interrupted. "Please, Samantha, hurry. I don't want to miss the ferry."

Samantha glanced at the clock on the office wall. Nine in the morning. The meeting had been arranged very hurriedly and at an awfully early hour. "Are you sure you don't want me to come, too?"

"Quite sure." The usually unflappable doctor was having to make an effort to hang on to his patience. His mouth had tightened, his hands were clenched above the litter of papers on his desk.

Was there any way she could delay him, Samantha wondered. At least until she could get hold of Jon, tell him.... Tell him what? Why was she so suddenly convinced that Dr. Birmann was making a run for it? This could quite easily be a coincidence. It was not unheard of for the doctor to go into Seattle—he quite often did. He hadn't taken the car since she'd been here, though. In fact, when they went to the seminar he'd made a point of leaving the car so it could be used along with the station wagon if new guests arrived.

"Please hurry, Samantha," he said again, snapping the locks closed on the attaché case and setting it on the floor. There was a suitcase there already, she noticed for the first time. Quite a large suitcase.

"Did you know anything about this?" she whispered to Deborah as she passed her desk on the way out.

Deborah shook her head. "I've no idea what's going on. As long as I've been here, he's never gone off in such a hurry. Usually he's so well organized we all know weeks ahead what he's got in mind. A family emergency, do you suppose?"

A *family* emergency. The image of Tom Greene's eyes came back into her mind as she hurried up the steps to the Birmanns' chalet. She had to call Jon, let him know....

Anne Marie was just closing her own suitcase, sitting on it so that she could fasten the locks. Her face was flushed, her new hairdo a little out of place, her mouth petulant. "Your father wants you to hurry," Samantha told her.

She pouted. "I don't see why I have to go."

"I thought you wanted to take a trip to Seattle?"

"I did, but not today. Mike Summers invited me to have lunch with him at the marina. My first real date and daddy insists I have to leave."

"Did you call to let Mike know?" Samantha asked, feeling a spurt of relief.

"I telephoned the house, but Mike and Jon had gone to the marina to do something to Jon's boat. I had to leave a message with Eileen. Probably he'll never ask me again."

"Did you tell your father you don't want to go?"

"Of course I did. He says I have no choice, I have to do what I'm told. He was angry with me for arguing. Probably he just came up with this idea to get me from away from Mike. He was annoyed with me last night. He said I was flirting with Mike. What's wrong with flirting?" Her voice had risen to a wail.

"Where are you going?" Samantha asked.

"I've no idea. Daddy says it's a surprise. Some surprise! Anyone would think we hadn't paid the rent and the landlord was coming to evict us."

So Anne Marie had also sensed something odd about this sudden departure. Samantha hesitated in the doorway as the girl lugged her suitcase out to the porch. She was waving to somebody, gesturing toward herself. One of the employees probably—she was most likely wanting help with her suitcase. Samantha decided to take a chance. Hurrying into the sitting room, she picked up the telephone receiver and dialed Jon's number. She could at least alert Eileen, ask her to drive to the marina.

The line was busy. Eileen must be talking to someone. *Dammit*. She tried again, raging inwardly when the busy signal again reverberated in her ear, then cradled the phone hurriedly when she heard Anne Marie's light footsteps coming her way. "I have to lock up, Samantha," she called.

Samantha hurried to meet her. She would have to wait until the Birmanns left for the ferry, then call the marina.

Dr. Birmann was pacing across the front of the parking lot when Samantha and Anne Marie arrived. The car was parked beside a group of birch trees, the trunk open. The doctor took the suitcase from the hand of the young man who'd carried it down and waved him away, lifting it into the trunk himself. Then he turned to Samantha, attempting a smile that didn't reach his eyes. "Thank you, Miss Austin."

She stared at him, nonplussed. He hadn't called her Miss Austin after the first couple of days she'd worked for him. "Do you know when you'll be back?" she asked hesitantly.

"Three, perhaps four days."

He was waiting for her to leave, making no attempt to close the trunk. "You'll find a list on your desk of things I want you to do," he said brusquely. "There's another list of people arriving in the next day or so, and which guests are departing. Everyone has their instructions. I'm sure there won't be any difficulties."

Samantha seized the opening. "Can I reach you if there are?"

His mouth was stern. "I'm not sure where we'll be staying. I'll call you later today."

She felt sure this promise was meant to reassure her, but it didn't. However, there didn't seem to be anything she could do. He was glancing at his wristwatch meaningfully. She could almost feel him vibrating with eagerness for her to leave.

"I. . . have a good trip," she said lamely.

"Thank you." He took her elbow and eased her toward the pathway that led up to the main building, preventing her from saying goodbye to Anne Marie, who had already climbed into the car. As soon as he was

satisfied she was on her way, he himself turned back.
From the corner of her eye she saw him hesitate, watching her, before he finally slammed the lid closed on the
trunk. Then he hurried around to the driver's door.

She kept going until the next cluster of birch trees hid
her from view, then peered around one of the slender
trunks, curious to know why he'd delayed so long when
he was obviously in a hurry. Had the trunk lid blocked
something she wasn't supposed to see?

The engine started and the long black car moved
slowly forward, heading for the curving driveway that
led up the hill. At the first curve it slowed for safety's
sake, and she saw, quite clearly, that there were *three*
heads showing above the front seat. Dr. Birmann, Anne
Marie—and who else? Could it be, could it *possibly* be
Tom Greene?

Galvanized by her thoughts, Samantha rushed into
the spa's main building and grabbed the telephone on
the receptionist's desk. A male voice answered at the
marina, and she blurted out a request for Jon in such a
breathless voice that she had to repeat his name before
the man could understand it. Then she was left to wait
for endless minutes, while her heart pounded like a trip-
hammer in her chest. At last the man returned, to tell
her Dr. Blake had taken his boat to Seattle. There was
something wrong with the engine, and they couldn't fix
it at the marina. "He'll probably be gone all day," the
man said complacently.

"Did anyone go with him?" Samantha asked. "He
had a friend with him—Mike Summers. Do you know if
they left together?"

"I dunno. Hold on."

Several more agonizing minutes passed, then the man

returned again. "Sorry, ma'am," he drawled. "Nobody here seems to know."

"I...thank you."

Samantha hung up the phone, then quickly dialed Jon's number. Still busy. She'd have to go over there to find out for sure if Mike had left the island.

She considered stopping by her office to let Deborah know she wasn't going to be around for a while, but then decided she couldn't take the time. Deborah was resourceful; if any crises came up she'd find a way to handle them.

She was halfway across the point, driving the spa's station wagon for which Matt had provided the keys, when she heard the booming blast of the ferry's whistle. Stopping the car, she got out and ran through the trees to the bluff, arriving there just as the ferry came into sight beyond the curve of the promontory, gleaming white in the sunlight, heading toward Seattle. She stared after it for a long time, feeling helpless and vaguely frightened. Ever since she'd found Dr. Birmann packing she'd been overwhelmed by a nameless feeling of dread.

Realizing that she could hardly turn the ferry around by the force of her desperate gaze, she ran back to the car and started it up again.

It took a couple of minutes for Eileen to answer the door. "Sorry, Samantha, I was talking to Peter on the phone." She hesitated, looking at Samantha's face with her direct gaze. "Is something wrong?"

"Yes, no...I need to see Mike. Did he come back here?"

"He went to the marina with Jon. The boat—"

"Yes, I know. Jon's taken the boat to Seattle for repair. Do you suppose Mike went with him?"

"I doubt it. He was planning to have lunch with Anne Marie."

"*Of course.* Then he must be coming back."

"I suppose so. He's going to be disappointed, I'm afraid. Anne Marie called to say—"

"Yes, I know about that, too."

"Samantha, honey, what on earth is wrong?"

Samantha had already started backing out of the doorway, too impatient to wait here for Mike. "I don't have time to explain," she called over her shoulder as she turned to go down the steps.

"But, Samantha...."

"I'll tell you later."

She drove all the way to the marina but didn't find Mike. Nobody had seen him leave. Jon's car wasn't in the parking lot, however, so Mike must have driven it away. Could he possibly have gone the other way around the island, Samantha wondered. The road was much rougher that way, but he might...

Conscious of precious minutes ticking away, Samantha made an abrupt decision. She'd take the old road and hope for the best.

The station wagon bounced and rattled over every pothole, but she persisted doggedly. She'd almost reached the northernmost point of the island when she came upon Jon's car. It was parked on the shoulder of the road, empty.

Samantha touched the hood. It was cold. Wherever Mike had gone off to, he'd been gone for some time. She started through the trees at the side of the road, cursing the thickness of the woods she normally loved, afraid Mike might return to the car by another path. She should have waited at the house for him. She was always too impulsive—she never stopped to think....

He was sitting in the rough grass, his back against the trunk of a tall Douglas fir. He'd taken off his jacket and folded it neatly beside him. He was smoking a cigarette, looking utterly relaxed, his gaze fixed on the distant Olympics. "Hi, Samantha," he said when she appeared beside him. "Were you looking for Jon? I'm amazed you found me. I was just enjoying life. I don't often get the chance to...."

Something in her expression must have alerted him. Stubbing the cigarette carefully, he stood up, pulling on his jacket. "What happened?"

"Dr. Birmann and Anne Marie. They're gone." Still short of breath, she stumbled over the words but managed to get the story told.

His intent gaze didn't leave her face as she described the circumstances. When she was done, he thought for a minute, then frowned. "It could be an innocent journey, of course, but it sounds ominous, especially if this Tom Greene was with him. You're sure it was him?"

Samantha shook her head. "The sun was on the car windows. But I could almost swear it was his cap I saw."

"Damn. I guess I'd better call in to the office. Trouble is, we don't have enough.... I'd hoped to get some information out of Anne Marie. Damn, I was hoping for more time...." He seemed to be speaking mainly to himself. After a moment he turned sharply on his heel and headed through the woods at a fast trot, Samantha following. "It takes the ferry about an hour to get to Seattle, right?" he asked over his shoulder as they reached the road.

"Right."

"How long did it take you to find me?"

"About an hour."

"Damn," he exclaimed again. "You know the license number of the car?"

As it happened, she did. She'd used the limousine several times to go to the airstrip. She gave the number to him, watched him write it down, and added a description of the car.

He got into Jon's car, started it up and drove away without indicating if he expected Samantha to follow him, but she wasn't about to be left out of whatever was going to happen now.

When she entered the Blakes' house, Mike was just hanging up the phone. "What do we do now?" Samantha asked him.

"We wait. Somebody's going to try to stop them at the other end."

"Will one of you clowns please tell me what the hell is going on?" Eileen demanded, standing with arms akimbo in the doorway.

Mike looked at her. "Believe me, Mrs. Blake, you'd rather not know."

She regarded him steadily for a moment, then shrugged. "Okay. I'll be in the basement if anybody wants me. I'm working on a head."

There was a brief silence after she left, then Samantha asked hesitantly. "Mike, would you mind, just to satisfy. . . would you mind showing me your ID?"

His eyes narrowed for a moment, then he grinned. "Why not? Always a good idea to check credentials, Samantha." He brought out a leather case with a gold-colored seal on it and flipped it open as he handed it to her.

She stared at the ID, aware of his enquiring gaze. It must seem odd to him that she'd asked for it now. "I was just . . . curious," she said as she handed it back.

"Uh-huh. How about some coffee?"

"I'll get it."

It was another half an hour before the phone rang. Mike grabbed for it, listened intently, then groaned. "Too late, huh? Just a sec." He thought briefly, then started talking again. When he hung up he looked at Samantha. "Don't worry, he'll be picked up sooner or later."

Cold struck through her like an icicle, stabbing her to the heart. "I thought you said you didn't have enough to go on."

"Lady, if Tom Greene *is* Boris Rogov, we can't take a chance on losing him. If it wasn't Tom Greene you saw, or he *isn't* Rogov, then we'll make an apology and let the good doctor go on his way." He hesitated. "Nothing more has come in on Dr. Birmann, by the way."

"Then he may not be involved?"

"If he's helping Rogov escape, he's involved up to his stethoscope."

There was a toughness about Mike she hadn't recognized before. She shivered suddenly. He was a dedicated professional. How else could he flirt with Anne Marie in the line of duty and then talk so cold-bloodedly about her father?

"What now?" she asked.

"Now it's out of our hands." He glanced at his wristwatch. "I guess I'm out one lunch date, so I might as well get back. When's the next ferry, do you know?"

"Eleven-thirty."

"Then I'd better scramble."

"When will I know?"

His face softened a little. "Hey, listen Samantha, don't take it so hard. We may all be making a mountain out of the proverbial molehill. You go on home and I'll give you or Jon a call later. You have nothing to worry about."

NOTHING TO WORRY ABOUT, she thought wryly as she drove back across the point. At her instigation the FBI was searching for the man she worked for and his daughter, of whom she'd grown fond. What if the other person in the car *was* Tom Greene? And what if *he* was Boris Rogov? What if he'd *forced* Dr. Birmann to take him to Seattle? If the FBI did catch up with the car, Anne Marie would be caught in the middle. She might even get hurt.

Still worrying, she went into her office, sure she wouldn't be able to concentrate on the paperwork she was supposed to do that day. She looked at the lists Dr. Birmann had left her. They'd been scribbled hurriedly, a far cry from his usual neat handwriting. Deborah wasn't in the office. Samantha peeked into the doctor's office, thinking she might have gone in there, but she hadn't.

Samantha went on in and started picking up papers the doctor had left littering his desk. Another unusual thing for him to do. Stacking them neatly, her glance fell on the telephone. She wished she could reach Jon somewhere, ask him if there was anything either of them could do. Her glance was caught and held by the note pad beside the phone. It was covered in the doctor's neat doodles—tidy little boxes all in rows, one word written over and over. Carlisle. Somebody's name? Or the hotel where she and Jon had stayed?

Grabbing for the phone, she looked up the number, dialed it and waited for an operator to respond. A minute later she had her answer. Yes, Dr. Birmann and his daughter were registered there for tonight.

That would seem to point to innocence, wouldn't it, she thought, her hand still on the receiver. Would a man who was fleeing make a reservation in a nearby hotel? He'd lied to her, though—said he didn't know where they'd be staying.

She pressed the button down and started to dial Jon's number, then changed her mind. Mike had probably left already. She might be able to catch him before he boarded the ferry, but if she did.... Anne Marie's sweet face appeared in her mind.

No. Damned if she'd let Mike know where they were, not until she'd had a chance to talk to Anne Marie herself, or at least had tried. She started to dial the hotel again. And then had a better idea.

Without stopping to think it over, she hung up the phone, scrawled a brief note to Deborah, then rushed out the door. Seconds later she was talking Matt into driving her to the airstrip so she could see if Steve Cory was there. She'd fly to Seattle, maybe get to the Carlisle before the FBI managed to track Dr. Birmann down. She'd started this mess. She wasn't going to let Anne Marie suffer because of it.

CHAPTER EIGHTEEN

SHE TELEPHONED FROM THE LOBBY, telling herself she'd hang up at once if Dr. Birmann or—heaven help her—Tom Greene answered.

"Hello," Anne Marie said in a cautious, little girl voice.

"Are you alone?" Samantha asked. "I'm in the lobby. I—"

"Oh, Samantha, please come up, please." She sounded on the verge of hysteria.

The suite was on the tenth floor. When Samantha got there, Anne Marie was peering around the doorway. Her face was blotched, her eyes tearful, the careful makeup not in evidence. She pulled Samantha into the room, glancing quickly up and down the hall in a furtive way before she closed the door.

"Is anyone else around?" Samantha asked, meaning Tom Greene but not wanting to say his name. She still wasn't sure he was the person she'd seen in the car.

Anne Marie shook her head. She was trembling, and Samantha's heart went out to her. Putting her arms around her, she hugged her, then said briskly, "I'm probably poking my nose where it shouldn't be, but I had the feeling you needed help, so—"

"I'm so glad you came. I was so frightened! I don't really know what's going on, or why daddy brought me here. He said I wasn't to leave the room or call anybody.''

"When do you expect him back?"

"That's just the trouble," the girl wailed. "I don't know. I don't even know where they've gone."

She was close to losing control, wringing her hands, pacing back and forth across the sitting room of the suite as fresh tears started.

Samantha sat down on an elegant wood-framed armchair, indicated the matching sofa beside it. "Sit down and start at the beginning," she ordered, speaking crisply in an effort to calm the girl.

The approach seemed to work. Anne Marie sank down into the soft cushion, blew her nose on a Kleenex and took a deep breath. "I haven't been altogether honest with you, Samantha," she began.

"I gathered that. Let's start with who 'they' are. You said you didn't know where 'they've' gone."

"My father and my Uncle Boris—Tom Greene."

Samantha's stomach dropped. "He is Boris Rogov then?"

"How did you—"

Samantha shook her head. "Let's not worry about that right now. I'm trying to get this in order."

"I shouldn't even be *talking* to you. I'm so afraid my father's in *real* trouble, Samantha. I *can't* talk about it."

"Yes, you can. You have to. The police are looking for him. We might be able to do something, to help...."

"The police? Oh, God!"

Samantha was afraid a new wave of hysteria was about to begin, but to her surprise, Anne Marie suddenly pulled herself together and drew in a deep breath, her breath catching in a manner that moved Samantha. About to rise from the chair to offer comfort, she changed her mind. She had no idea how much time they had. She had to try to keep Anne Marie calm. "Tell me about your Uncle Boris," she said evenly.

"I'm sorry I didn't tell you, but I couldn't. I didn't know then, anyway—I mean, when I asked you to go to Victoria. I always knew he was my uncle, but daddy said he used the name Greene for business purposes. I did once hear my father call him Boris, but he said I was mistaken. He didn't tell me he'd lied until we were on the ferry, and we went to get some coffee for Boris. I thought they were both Swiss, I really did. I only learned today that they were Russian."

"Did you ever see Boris before he visited your father in San Diego?"

"I didn't even know he existed before that."

She had balled up the paper tissue in her hand, but her eyes were dry.

"He and daddy quarreled, as I told you. What I didn't know was that my uncle was mixed up in smuggling stuff out of the country."

"Computer components."

"Among other things." Anne Marie stared at her. "How did you...never mind. My father was right, wasn't he? He guessed Mike Summers was with the FBI."

Samantha neither acknowledged nor denied. Anne Marie sighed. "Evidently Uncle Boris wanted my father to blackmail Esmée Taylor, a patient of his, so her husband would supply him with what he wanted. I think I told you about her—her husband manufactures com-

puters. Boris wanted daddy to set up a situation where
he'd have something to blackmail her with." She
glanced up at Samantha. "She, Mrs. Taylor, liked my
father—she was kind of turned on by him—but he
hadn't encouraged her. You know how he feels about
the doctor-patient relationship."

Samantha nodded.

"Daddy's real name is Pyotr Rogov." She stumbled
over the name. "I can't believe it, Samantha. All my life
and I never knew! Even my mother didn't know, he
says." She broke off. "Daddy hasn't done anything
wrong. I know he hasn't."

Her voice broke again and she shook her head. "I'm
sorry, Samantha. I'm okay, really. I'll try to...." She
blew her nose again. "They were both in university, in
Moscow. Daddy was majoring in chemistry. The secret
police approached him and his younger brother—
Boris—and tried to recruit them to spy on other
students. My father was terribly afraid. He wasn't even
a member of the Communist Party. He was only twenty
years old. His parents were dead—they'd died in the
war, which had just ended. World War II. He decided
to run away, to leave Russia. He hoped Boris would go
with him, but he wouldn't. So he left Moscow by himself. He knew some people. They helped him get papers
that said he was Swiss."

"I know about that, too," Samantha said gently.
"He came to the States as Jakob Birmann and went to
medical school."

"He thought everything was fine. He thought he was
free. But then all those years afterward Boris came.
He'd found out from the KGB that daddy lived in San
Diego. They never let go, daddy says. Boris hadn't

known before where my father was, and at first they were glad to see each other. But then Boris confessed he was working for the KGB. He was what they call a 'resident.' He lived in this country openly—he was a foreign-trade consultant. But he hired other people to steal or buy the stuff he needed. All the time he was sending stuff back to Russia. He even joked about it to daddy.''

''Dr. Birmann refused to help him?''

''Yes. They had a terrible fight, but daddy would have nothing to do with any part of it. He thought he'd convinced Boris. Boris was angry, but he went away.''

''And then he came to the island.''

Anne Marie nodded miserably. ''He was sent to prison a couple of years ago. Daddy knew he'd been caught—it was in the papers. My father didn't want his brother to go to jail, of course, but he figured he'd be sent back to Russia and that would be the end of it. Unfortunately, Boris escaped before he could be deported. He traveled all over the country doing odd jobs. But he felt time was running out for him—he had a few close escapes from law agencies of one kind or another. He came to the island because he wanted my father to get him out of the country. Daddy got him to Canada for the time being. He took him up in Jon's boat, but they were afraid if the authorities found out they'd extradite him easily.''

''Jon couldn't have known they'd used his boat,'' Samantha protested.

''Well, he knew daddy took it, but he didn't know about Boris.''

''Why didn't Tom—I mean Boris—want to go back to Russia?''

"He was afraid. He didn't know what would happen to him. He wasn't supposed to get caught—he was careless, I guess. Anyway, he decided daddy should help him get to Europe—he had some friends in Germany. He was going to ask them to help him get a new identity."

"And Dr. Birmann agreed?"

"I guess so. I don't really know. Daddy telephoned Boris in Victoria last night, but he couldn't get hold of him. The people there said he'd left a couple of days before."

Mike Summers, Samantha thought. Jon had guessed someone would be on the way to Victoria to check on Tom Greene. Somehow Greene—Rogov—must have had time to get away.

"He just turned up on the island?"

"In the middle of the night. I was asleep. I didn't even know he was there until I got in the car. I think he stole a boat. Evidently he knew the FBI was after him. I don't know how they found out he was there."

She looked up but Samantha didn't say anything.

"Anyway," she went on. "My father told Boris he had a suspicion that Mike Summers was connected with the FBI, and they decided they had to leave the island right away. So we came here and then they went off somewhere together."

"You don't know where they've gone?" Samantha hesitated. "I don't mean to doubt you, Anne Marie, but I have to be sure...."

"They wouldn't tell me. They argued a lot in the car on the ferry. I've never seen daddy so angry, so determined, but they spoke in—I guess it was Russian. I couldn't make out what they were saying, and they wouldn't tell me, even though I begged—"

"How long ago did they leave?"

"About fifteen minutes before you got here."

Samantha shuddered. They might have been leaving at the time she entered the lobby. If they had seen her....

"Do you know anything at all about something Dr. Birmann might have picked up for Tom Greene—for Boris? Maybe some film or something?"

Anne Marie started to shake her head, then hesitated, frowning. "Daddy did tell me a while ago that he had to get something for my uncle in Seattle, when he went to that seminar. It was something important, valuable—something he thought might help him bargain. I didn't understand what he meant."

"Who did he want to bargain with?"

"I don't know that, either. I didn't understand any of it before, and I don't now. I do know daddy refused to give whatever it was to Boris—that might be what they were arguing about."

Samantha fell silent, trying to sort through all the information Anne Marie had given her. What she had to do now, she told herself, was to get out of here before Dr. Birmann—she couldn't think of him by any other name—and his brother came back. She was quite sure the doctor wouldn't harm her, but his brother was evidently desperate—there was no knowing what he might do. But she couldn't abandon Anne Marie.

"I think we have to go to the FBI," she said finally.

Anne Marie jumped to her feet. "No, Samantha! I don't know what daddy plans to do, but I won't turn him in. I can't. He's my *father*. I love him. I—"

"I know," Samantha said soothingly. "I just think...."

She heard a sound in the hall outside. Footsteps. And they had paused at the door. She signaled Anne Marie to silence.

Somebody knocked on the door.

They exchanged startled glances. Probably, Samantha thought, there was as much fear in her eyes as showed in Anne Marie's.

The knock was repeated.

"Do you think we'd better..." Anne Marie whispered.

Samantha swallowed against the dryness in her throat. And then Jon's voice called through the closed door. "Are you in there, Anne Marie?" And without hesitation Samantha ran to the door and flung it open.

Jon started to speak immediately. "Have you lost your mind, Samantha? Why the hell did you come charging over here? Don't you know—"

"How did you know I was here?" she interrupted.

He made an impatient gesture with his hand, walked past her into the room to Anne Marie, who had started crying again. He put his arms around her, which had the effect of increasing her sobs. "Are you all right?" he asked gently.

She shook her head, clinging to him. "I don't know what to do," she wailed.

"Don't worry, we'll figure it out." He turned back to Samantha, who was still standing by the half-open door. "Mike called me at the boatyard. He's still on the island—evidently he missed the ferry. My mother said she'd drive him, but her hands were covered with clay, and by the time she got cleaned up they were too late. So she suggested Steve Cory. He wasn't on the island, so mom called him in Seattle. He told her he'd just flown you into town. Mike got on the line and asked where you'd gone. Steve said he'd heard you tell the taxi driver to take you to the Carlisle."

Samantha remembered that Steve had followed her from the plane to the cab. He'd been hinting without subtlety that wherever she was going he'd be delighted to accompany her. She'd had a hard time shaking him off. Now she was glad he'd persisted. No matter how angry Jon was with her, she was tremendously relieved to see him.

"Mike is going to want an explanation, Sam," Jon went on, still holding Anne Marie, comforting her.

"I was worried about Anne Marie."

"You could have told Mike where she was. He's furious with you. Obstructing justice, he called it. And I must say I agree with him. You had no business—"

Samantha closed the door. "All right, Jon," she said wearily. "I behaved too impulsively again. I know that. I was afraid Anne Marie would get hurt. I'm not too sure the FBI would have protected her."

"I'm sure your motives were the highest, however...."

"For heaven's sake, Jon, what does it matter now? We have to decide what to do before Dr. Birmann and Tom—Boris Rogov—come back. *If* they come back."

His startled eyes met hers. "He *is* Rogov? You're sure of that?"

"He's my uncle," Anne Marie sniffed.

"But I don't understand. How did he...." He set Anne Marie away from him. "Can you give a brief summary?" His voice was as deliberately crisp as Samantha's had been, and again the girl was calmed.

Haltingly, but evenly, she was able to tell him the story she'd told Samantha.

Jon's reaction was swift and determined. "Samantha's right. We go to the FBI at once. No," he said tersely as Anne Marie began to argue. "We've no choice. If your father is assisting his brother to leave the country, he's in deep trouble. And if we let it happen, we're all responsible, too."

Five minutes later they were escorting a subdued Anne Marie out of the Carlisle and into a taxi.

They rode in a silence punctuated by the sound of Anne Marie's muffled sobs. Samantha put her arm around the girl's shoulders, holding her close, feeling like bawling herself. She'd been relieved to see Jon, but in the face of his cold anger with her, she was beginning to realize she *had* acted stupidly. He must think she was a ninny. Of course she should have let the authorities know where Dr. Birmann had gone. While she was flying over they could probably have picked him up, he and his brother and.... No. She'd still do the same thing, she decided. Anne Marie was an innocent bystander. She couldn't have taken a chance on her getting hurt.

"Jon," she said tentatively, wanting to try again to explain. But the taxi stopped as she hesitated, and she looked out to see the huge concrete bulk of the Federal Building. Jon paid the driver, opened the door and helped Anne Marie out. The girl looked up at the towering institutional-looking building and shuddered. Jon put his arm around her and eased her toward the glass doors, leaving Samantha to follow alone.

The office they were shown into was drab. Jon stated his business to a young fresh-faced man, who told them tersely to wait. A minute later an older, smartly dressed man came into the room. There was an air of authority about him that set him apart from the usual businessman, even though on the street he might have passed for one. He wasted no time with preliminaries. He introduced himself as Howard Pearson and said that he wished to talk to Miss Birmann. Alone.

"But I don't *know* where my father is," she said.

"He's here," Pearson said.

Samantha and Anne Marie both gasped. "You caught him?" Samantha asked.

Rather cold gray green eyes looked at her. "He came in voluntarily, Miss Austin." He paused. "You *are* Miss Austin?"

Samantha swallowed, nodded.

"I'd like you to wait here, please. You too, Dr. Blake."

"You have Rogov, too?" Jon asked.

The gray green eyes became colder, if that was possible. "He is here." He stepped back, gestured toward the door behind him. "Miss Birmann."

With an anguished glance at Samantha, Anne Marie preceded the man thorugh the doorway. Samantha sank down on a chair. "Are we under arrest?" she asked Jon, looking up at him.

He sat beside her, took her hand. The anger was gone from his face now, she was relieved to see. "I don't think so," he said thoughtfully. "But I don't think it would be a good idea to try to leave."

"Good thinkin'," the young man behind the desk said laconically. Then the phone on his desk rang, and he picked it up and started taking notes.

"I'm sorry, Jon," Samantha whispered. "I should

have thought before acting, but even so, I'm sure I did the right thing. Anne Marie would still have been sitting there in that hotel room, wondering. And I did check first to make sure her father wasn't with her. I know you think it was stupid of me, but—"

He pressed her hand warmly. "I don't think that at all, Sam. I was angry because it scared the hell out of me when Mike told me what you'd done. I'm sure we can straighten it out, convince them you were only worried and not coming to *warn* anybody."

"Is that what Mike thinks?"

"He had a moment of doubt, until I reminded him you were the one who reported Tom Greene originally. Then he calmed down. I'm sure there won't be a problem, Sam."

"But what about Dr. Birmann?"

He shrugged. "That I don't know. Evidently he's turned himself in. That's got to help."

It seemed for a while that they would never get to know exactly what was in store for Dr. Birmann. After waiting for an hour, Jon asked the young man if he could check on Anne Marie and see if she was all right.

"She's all right," the man said without moving.

Another hour went by. Samantha felt as though she'd been sitting in that drab little room all her life and would never be able to leave. Jon sensed her despair. Ignoring the young man at the desk, he put his arms around her, held her close. "It's going to be okay, Sam," he assured her.

"But maybe they've forgotten we're here."

"They haven't forgotten, ma'am," the young man said.

Jon looked at him. "That sounds ominous."

He shrugged and picked up the phone as it rang again.

"I'm sorry about everything, Sam," Jon said abruptly.

She looked at him. He was gazing at her with affection in his eyes. She touched her hand to his cheek. "I was the stupid one," she said softly.

He shook his head. "No. I should have known right from the start that you wouldn't worry about Jakob unless there was something to worry about. I've always respected your intelligence. I guess I just didn't want to believe...."

"Nor did I."

He lifted a hand to cover hers. "I've been a damn fool all along. First thinking I wanted revenge, then getting so angry with you. I was so afraid, thinking you might be in danger. That's what finally brought me to my senses. God, if anything had happened to you... I've been such a damn stubborn idiot, and all I've ever wanted in the world was to love you."

The small flicker of hope that had started in her the previous morning began to burn with a steady flame inside her, warming her. "I love you, Jon," she said softly. "I've never stopped loving you."

"Nor I you." He glanced once at the man behind the desk, who was still talking on the phone. The man's gaze was fixed on them, but Jon deliberately turned his back on him and kissed her gently. "I loved you the first moment I saw you again," he said against her mouth. "I kept fighting it and fighting it—don't ask me why. I love you, Sam. I always will."

She kissed him in return, her mouth moving softly against his. His arms were around her again, holding her close, his eyes shining with that incredibly blue light that always amazed her. Joy filled her. The drab office didn't matter, the worry over her own situation was gone. Nothing mattered but this, that she was in his arms and he was speaking of love.

"We have to forget the past," he told her softly. "We can't keep carrying it around with us, making the same mistakes, punishing each other for past pain."

"We can't forget it, Jon," she objected tenderly. "It's inside us whether we want it there or not. And some of it was wonderful. We can't ignore it, but I was wrong to think we could just go back and start from where everything came apart. What happened happened."

"But we must still try to—"

He broke off abruptly, releasing her, as the inner door opened and Anne Marie came through... smiling radiantly.

They both stood up. Anne Marie went immediately to Samantha and hugged her. "It's all right, Samantha, it's going to be all right!"

"They're letting your father go?"

She shook her head, hesitated, then looked from Samantha to Jon apologetically. "I'm not supposed to tell you what they...."

She glanced over her shoulder to where the young man was still talking on the telephone. "Uncle Boris has defected to this country," she whispered urgently. "He has something—a roll of film, I don't know what of—something daddy picked up for him. And they want it very badly. He can tell them other things, I guess, so they are willing to make a deal. They're going to keep him in protective custody. Daddy has to answer a lot more questions, too. The FBI called in the U.S. Marshalls. They are responsible for Boris, because he was a fugitive. But they're all in agreement that my father probably won't be prosecuted, even though he did harbor a fugitive and transport him to Canada. He did talk Boris into surrendering to the FBI. He wouldn't give him the film until he agreed. They say that under the circumstances daddy will probably be allowed to go free.''

''Why did Jakob bring you to Seattle with him?'' Jon asked.

''He was afraid Mike might come to the spa. He'd already invited me to have lunch with him. Daddy didn't want to take a chance on any of us being arrested before he had a chance to come in of his own accord. He was going to have someone call me and tell me whatever happened.''

Samantha let out a long breath. ''I was so afraid he was planning to leave the country. Your father, I mean. I saw him pack his passport—at least I thought it was his passport.''

Anne Marie nodded. ''He wanted it for identification here. He brought all his papers.''

Behind her someone cleared his throat. Howard Pearson was standing in the doorway, glaring at the young man, who hurriedly hung up the phone and sat at attention.

Pearson turned his gaze on Samantha and Jon for a second, then glanced at Anne Marie, suddenly looking surprisingly avuncular. ''You may go back to your father, Miss Birmann,'' he said.

Anne Marie nodded, smiled happily at Samantha and hugged Jon. ''Thank you,'' she whispered.

"Can we wait and take her home?" Jon asked after she'd gone.

Pearson leveled his cool gray-green glance at him. "No."

"But she'll be all right?"

"Of course." He looked at Samantha. "We are going to need a statement from you, Miss Austin." He hesitated. "I understand from Special Agent Summers that you have been very co-operative in this affair. I thank you. And I am willing to overlook—"

"Mike's here?" Samantha asked.

"He's here. He has informed me that you are both merely concerned observers and that Miss Austin especially—"

"What's going to happen to Dr. Birmann and Anne Marie?" Samantha demanded.

Something flickered in the gray green eyes. For a second she thought it might be amusement, but his voice was grave and he continued as though she hadn't interrupted. "Summers tells me you might qualify as an agent yourself," he said. "I understand you staged a couple of cloak-and-dagger operations in Victoria and Seattle Center."

Samantha felt herself blush. But before she could think of a reply, Pearson continued smoothly, "I will need assurance from both of you that nothing you have heard or seen will go beyond this room."

"Of course," Jon said.

"I don't want *anyone* to know about it," Samantha said fervently. "But I do want to know what's going to happen to—

"You have no cause for concern Miss Austin."

"But I—"

"If you'll come with me?"

SAMANTHA WAS STILL FEELING FRUSTRATED when she and Jon were finally allowed to leave. She sat in the taxi, frowning, wondering if she should have refused to sign her statement until she knew the fate of her friends. She'd been a coward, she decided. She should have insisted.

"They'll be okay," Jon said, reading her mind as he always did. "I managed to see Mike for a moment, and he assured me they'll be back at the spa in a few days, none the worse for their adventure."

"And Tom Greene? Rogov?"

"I don't know. Frankly, I didn't even ask."

"But Jon, weren't you even curious?"

"I leave curiosity to you," he said with a smile. "You have enough for both of us." He hesitated. "It's possible, I suppose, that Boris might be recruited to work for our side. As for the film you saw Jakob pick up— obviously no one's going to tell us what it is, and frankly, I'd rather not know. All that's sure is that a deal is being made. We'll probably never know exactly what transpires. I'm very relieved that Jakob isn't in as bad a fix as we thought."

He glanced at her sideways. "Though I always knew he couldn't be a spy."

He laughed as she glared at him. "Come on, Sam, smile! The situation did have its humorous side. You went rushing over there like Nancy Drew, flying in with Steve Cory like an avenging angel." He put an arm around her, squeezing her shoulders. "I think Cory's

smitten with you, by the way. He wasn't about to tell
Mike where you'd gone at first. Mike had to just about
threaten him with imprisonment to get it out of him.
Mike told me he was never so frustrated in his life.''

"Good," Samantha said. "I didn't think much of the
way Mike flirted with Anne Marie. I know he had a job
to do, but he hardly needed to lead her to think—"

"But he *was* attracted to her," Jon interrupted.
"Last I saw of them, he was holding her hand and
telling her he would see to it personally that she was
okay."

"Oh." Deflated, Samantha sat back, then leaned forward as she saw to her surprise that they were drawing
up to the ferry terminal. "Aren't we going home in your
boat?"

Jon shook his head. "I can't pick up *Aegir* for a
couple of days."

The taxi stopped. Jon fumbled in his back pocket for
his billfold, and Samantha looked at him. "We could
always miss the ferry," she said softly.

His eyes met hers and she couldn't quite interpret his
expression, but it caused a shiver of apprehension to
travel up her spine. "I think not," he said.

He didn't enlarge on that while they waited in line to
board the ferry. Samantha felt strangely suspended in
time. Not knowing what kind of emotion to feel, she felt
nothing but a kind of emptiness. Surely Jon wasn't going to back away from her again. Not after what he'd
said in the FBI office. Surely. . . .

It did no good to speculate, she decided. She'd just
have to wait and see. In the meantime she looked
around her, surprised by how ordinary everything
seemed. It was about five-thirty in the evening. Com-

muters were going home from work. They were standing in little groups or singly, patiently waiting for the ferry to dock.

They looked so...so *normal*, Samantha thought. After the events of the last few days, she felt everybody should look different somehow. Yet how could anyone possibly know about the drama that had just taken place?

All the same, she felt vaguely disoriented. It was going to take some time, she judged, for *her* to feel normal again. If she ever did.

THE SUN WAS SHINING, the sky hazy all around. Once the ferry was underway the breeze was cold, but Samantha felt comfortable in her spa uniform. Jon was wearing his usual boating clothes, a blue crew-neck top and chinos. She felt the softness of the shirt fabric brush against her hand as he leaned on the rail. He never seemed to feel the cold.

She wished he would say something, anything. They'd talked only of Jakob and Anne Marie since they came on board. At last she couldn't stand his silence any longer. "Why didn't you want to stay in town?" she asked.

He turned his head, smiling crookedly. "I knew what would happen if we did. We'd have holed up in some hotel and made love until dawn."

Samantha swallowed. "Would that be so bad?"

His smile widened. Straightening, he pulled her into his arms, heedless of the other people on board. "I wanted a chance to court you properly."

"You still want to...start again?"

He nodded soberly. "I agree with you that we

shouldn't dwell on the pain we inflicted on each other years ago, or the hurt feelings of the past few weeks. But I don't think we can successfully pick up where we left off seven years ago. We're different people now.''

He hesitated, looking deeply into her eyes, his own eyes reflecting the sunlight on the water, so that she still couldn't be sure what he was thinking. His hair was blowing in the breeze, as was hers, but held in his arms she didn't feel cold. The heady excitement that she always felt when he touched her was rising in her, warming her.

''Do you remember watching my mother when she was sculpting something?'' he asked.

Puzzled, she nodded.

''Remember when it wasn't going well, she'd just pull all the clay off, strip the model right down to the armature and start again?''

She began to see the direction he was taking. ''You mean that's what we should do? The armature, the past, would still be there, but we could build on it with new materials?''

His hands pulled her closer as he smiled. ''That's why I want to court you. I think we need to take time to find out exactly what kind of people we are now.''

''You mean you don't want to commit yourself to—''

He tugged at her as though impatient. ''That's not what I mean at all. I want you to marry me, Samantha. If you'll have me.''

She closed her eyes momentarily in a brief celebration of thanksgiving, then opened them to look at him, letting all her love for him show. ''Of course I'll marry you, Jon.''

He grinned. ''You're sure you know what you're getting into? I've decided to take that job. We'll have to live in Washington, D.C. for a couple of years.''

She gave a mock shudder, remembering all Liz had told her about that other Washington. "I'm not sure I'm up to being a Washington wife," she warned him. "I want to write, you know. I won't have time for all that socializing." Her voice was light, but she felt worried suddenly. If Jon wanted a wife such as Liz Vandervort had described. . . .

"I won't have time for much socializing myself," Jon interrupted. "I'm planning another book. *Destruction* laid out the problem. The next one will offer some possible solutions." He smiled ruefully. "The reviews I've seen so far described *Destruction*'s text as 'economical.' I have a feeling they really meant I should have used more prose."

"The pictures were enough," she protested.

"Not quite, I'm afraid. And in the next book I won't be able to use so many photographs. It's a little difficult to photograph things as they should be, rather than as they are. I can use some old pictures to show the way the oceans and shorelines used to be, but I'm going to have to rely on words to suggest how we can achieve the proper results."

"I can help with words," Samantha said.

"Would you, Sam?" His eyes were filled with light, spillng love all around her, so that she wouldn't have been surprised if they were surrounded by a nimbus as bright as any sun. Excitement filled her. To work on such an important project would give her life a meaning it hadn't had before.

"I'll make sure you have time for any other writing you want to do on your own," Jon assured her. "We'll be coming back to the island from time to time. I've no idea what we'll be doing a few years from now, though.''

"It doesn't matter," she assured him. "As long as we're together, I don't care where we are.''

"Even if I become a beach bum again?''

She winced but knew he hadn't intended the words to sting. There was no mistaking the love in his voice. "I fell in love with a beach bum once," she reminded him.

He laughed, then sobered again. "I'm going to hang on to the house even after mom marries Peter," he said as though reassuring her.

She stared at him. "They're getting married?''

His eyebrows rose. "I guess in all the...the excitement, I forgot to tell you that. Yes, next month. They'll be living in Seattle.''

"Maybe we should make it a double wedding.''

He hugged her close. "No way! We've waited long enough for our wedding, and it's going to be ours alone. Besides, I'm not going to spend my honeymoon on a promotion tour, so I guess we'll have to wait a while.''

"And I have a contract at the spa to work out.''

He looked at her tenderly. "It looks as though I'll have time to court you after all.''

She hesitated, touching his mouth with her fingertips. "What exactly do you mean by courting? Are we going to go out on formal dates?''

"Of course. Crab Louie at Charlie's at least. I might even stand you another meal at the Space Needle, costly as it is.''

"And we're going to wait before becoming...intimate again?''

His eyes showed exaggerated shock. "Not on your life. What gave you that idea?''

"You. 'I think not,' you said when I suggested we stay in town."

"Oh, that." He smiled his old familiar, mischievous smile. "I didn't *want* to stay in a hotel room. Cold places, hotel rooms. Besides, I'm about to get married, and I grew up with thrifty ideals. I couldn't see paying eighty dollars for a hotel room when you have an empty chalet. I've never made love in a health spa. It's bound to be beneficial to our health, wouldn't you say?"

Samantha laughed delightedly, then sobered as she remembered how close she had come to losing this man.

"Hey," he murmured. "I won't allow shadows in your beautiful eyes. If anything's still bothering you, spit it out."

"Nothing's bothering me. I'm just so happy, it's hard to believe—"

"Believe," he said firmly.

THEY HAD DRAWN THE LIGHT DRAPES over the window in Samantha's bedroom, but the evening sunlight filtered through, creating shadows that were as erotic as dancing firelight. Jon's tanned body was dappled with shadow as he leaned over her. His mouth brushed hers, and she felt a shiver pass through her body.

It seemed delightfully decadent to be here, with this man, at this early hour of the evening. Deborah must have had a terrible day, Samantha thought suddenly. But she was efficient; she'd probably coped just fine. Tomorrow she would find out what was going to happen at the spa, if Dr. Birmann and Anne Marie would return and—

She broke off her thoughts. The spa and its problems

didn't seem at all important to her now. Joh's flesh was cool against hers and she stroked the length of his spine, reveling in the smoothness of his back, the long ridges of muscle. "I love you, Sam," he murmured against her mouth.

"I love you," she answered.

There was such a silence all around. The spa guests must be preparing to go to dinner. The breeze had dropped to a mere whisper, barely stirring the drapes at the window. Jon's arms were around her, holding her, his face so close to hers that his features were blurred, softened so that he looked very young, like the boy she had once known. But he was no longer a boy, and she was glad.

"Jon," she whispered. "Jonathan, Jon."

His mouth smiled against hers, then stilled. His breathing had quickened, and she knew that there would be no more waiting. There was an urgency in his body that was mirrored by hers. His next kiss was more passionate than any she had ever known. She clung to him, returning the kiss, wanting it to go on and on. She could not get enough of his mouth, his beautiful mouth. She could hardly bear to let his mouth move from hers, and yet when he trailed a line of kisses down her throat to her breast she stopped regretting the absence as his lips unerringly found the area of most sensation and played there. Gently, delicately, they teased the nipple erect, before shifting to the other breast to give it the same careful attention.

His hands moved over her, his breath was warm on her, his hair was coarse and clean under her fingers. She knew every part of him—his smell, his feel, his every bone and hollow.

In spite of his own urgency, he was taking the time to arouse her fully, though she needed no arousal. She was ready for him. Now. She pressed her hands against the sides of his head, lifting it. He studied her face for a moment, one hand rising to touch her parted lips. "You always were impatient, Sam," he said.

There were spaces between his words, betraying his own impatience, and she smiled knowingly, mischievously, as he raised himself over her. "Is impatience always a flaw?" she asked.

His mouth found hers hungrily. "Not always," he admitted thickly.

His head blotted out the light and he lifted her against him. Curling herself around him, Samantha though that she had never felt such happiness in her life. And then she stopped thinking and gave herself over to pure sensation, letting herself climb without effort to the highest level of arousal he had ever brought her to.

There was no doubt that he was in command, reading her physical and vocal responses, acting on them. Yet she knew that he would be just as willing to let her take command if she wanted to. But she didn't *want* to take control now. There would be other times, other moods. For now she was content to let him take the lead, which he did with a tenderness that told her more clearly than words that he loved her.

That his own response was high showed in his increasingly rapid movements, the words he muttered beneath his breath, words that had no meaning but somehow managed to convey his love, his ardor. More and more quickly they climbed together, until shadow and light exploded into a starburst of sensation that brought tears to her eyes and his. The blurred light shimmered on both of them with rainbowlike brilliance.

She didn't want to move a single muscle. She felt replete, serene. For a long time they lay peacefully, then Jon rolled with her so that they lay side by side, still holding each other.

She smiled at him. "You know Ben's going to take credit for all this," she said.

His eyebrows rose in the quizzical way she loved. "Why so?"

"He cast a spell on us. He told me so."

Jon nodded seriously. "I felt *something* in the air. I thought it was my desire for you. And all the time it was old Ben."

Samantha laughed and he smiled approvingly. "I'd almost forgotten how beautifully you laugh. I used to remember your laughter—the way it would brighten a room, like music played on a fine violin." He paused, his hands lifting to cup her face between his palms. "There was always so much light inside you, Sam. There still is. May I please have some of it for my own?"

"It all belongs to you, Jon."

There was another moment in which they looked at each other, and love was offered, received and returned. "Do you remember the day you came back to the island?" he asked.

"Of course."

"There was something I should have said to you then, but I didn't. I'd like to say it now."

She looked a question at him and his hands moved down behind her, pulling her close. "Welcome home,

Samantha,'' he said. And then he bent his head to hers, and their lips met in a kiss that brought a magic sweetness flowing through her body.

Yes, she thought, her mouth warm against his. She was home.

ABOUT THE AUTHOR

Rosalind Carson has always loved islands. She grew up on one—Great Britain—within sight of the North Sea. She feels most comfortable when she's near an ocean, she says—when she can smell salty air and hear the cries of the gulls.

Her husband, stationed in England with the American Air Force when they met, took his bride back to the States—and introduced her to the Pacific. On his various tours of duty they've lived in California and Japan, but they finally settled in Tacoma, Washington. From their home it's a simple ferry ride to the numerous islands of Puget Sound, and the two of them like nothing better than to go exploring, poking around in out-of-the-way corners.

Rosalind decided deliberately to make her hero in *Such Sweet Magic* an oceanographer. Through him she could express some of the concern she feels for our oceans, and for the sea life within them. It's not surprising that her next Superromance will be set in Cape Cod.

HARLEQUIN
PREMIERE AUTHOR EDITIONS

6 top Harlequin authors — 6 of their best books!

1. JANET DAILEY Giant of Mesabi
2. CHARLOTTE LAMB Dark Master
3. ROBERTA LEIGH Heart of the Lion
4. ANNE MATHER Legacy of the Past
5. ANNE WEALE Stowaway
6. VIOLET WINSPEAR The Burning Sands

Harlequin is proud to offer these 6 exciting romance novels by
6 of our most popular authors. In brand-new beautifully
designed covers, each Harlequin Premiere Author Edition
is a bestselling love story—a contemporary, compelling and
passionate read to remember!

Available wherever paperback books are sold, or through
Harlequin Reader Service. Simply complete and mail the coupon below.

Enter a uniquely exciting new world with

Harlequin American Romance ™

Harlequin American Romances are the first romances to explore today's love relationships. These compelling novels reach into the hearts and minds of women across America... probing the most intimate moments of romance, love and desire.

You'll follow romantic heroines and irresistible men as they boldly face confusing choices. Career first, love later? Love without marriage? Long-distance relationships? All the experiences that make love real are captured in the tender, loving pages of **Harlequin American Romances.**

What makes American women so different when it comes to love? Find out with **Harlequin American Romance!**

Send for your introductory FREE book now!

Get this book FREE!

Mail to:

Harlequin Reader Service

In the U.S.
2504 West Southern Avenue
Tempe, AZ 85282

In Canada
649 Ontario Street
Stratford, Ontario N5A 6W2

YES! I want to be one of the first to discover

Harlequin American Romance. Send me FREE and without obligation *Twice in a Lifetime.* If you do not hear from me after I have examined my FREE book, please send me the 4 new **Harlequin American Romances** each month as soon as they come off the presses. I understand that I will be billed only $2.25 for each book (total $9.00). There are no shipping or handling charges. There is no minimum number of books that I have to purchase. In fact, I may cancel this arrangement at any time. *Twice in a Lifetime* is mine to keep as a FREE gift, even if I do not buy any additional books.

Name _____ (please print)

Address _____ Apt. no.

City _____ State/Prov. _____ Zip/Postal Code

Signature (If under 18, parent or guardian must sign.)

AR-SUB-300

ROBERTA LEIGH

A specially designed collection of six exciting love stories by one of the world's favorite romance writers—Roberta Leigh, author of more than 60 bestselling novels!

1 **Love in Store**
2 **Night of Love**
3 **Flower of the Desert**

4 **The Savage Aristocrat**
5 **The Facts of Love**
6 **Too Young to Love**

Available now wherever paperback books are sold, or available through Harlequin Reader Service. Simply complete and mail the coupon below.

- -

Harlequin Reader Service

In the U.S.
P.O. Box 52040
Phoenix, AZ 85072-9988

In Canada
649 Ontario Street
Stratford, Ontario N5A 6W2

Please send me the following editions of the Harlequin Roberta Leigh Collector's Editions. I am enclosing my check or money order for $1.95 for each copy ordered, plus 75¢ to cover postage and handling.

☐ 1 ☐ 2 ☐ 3 ☐ 4 ☐ 5 ☐ 6

Number of books checked_____ @ $1.95 each = $_____

N.Y. state and Ariz. residents add appropriate sales tax $_____

Postage and handling $___.75___

                                                   TOTAL $_____

I enclose_____

(Please send check or money order. We cannot be responsible for cash sent through the mail.) Price subject to change without notice.

NAME_____
                        (Please Print)
ADDRESS_____ APT. NO._____

CITY_____

STATE/PROV._____ ZIP/POSTAL CODE_____

Offer expires June 30, 1984   31256000000